Island Man

Island Man

a novel

Joanne Skerrett

Red Hen Press | *Pasadena, CA*

Book layout by Shelby Wallace

Library of Congress Cataloging-in-Publication Data

Names: Skerrett, Joanne, author.
Title: Island man: a novel / Joanne Skerrett.
Description: First edition. | Pasadena, CA: Red Hen Press, 2023.
Identifiers: LCCN 2023019099 (print) | LCCN 2023019100 (ebook) | ISBN
   9781636281308 (paperback) | ISBN 9781636281315 (ebook)
Subjects: LCSH: Fathers and sons—Fiction. | Family secrets—Fiction. |
   LCGFT: Novels.
Classification: LCC PS3619.K53 I85 2023 (print) | LCC PS3619.K53 (ebook)
   | DDC 813/.6—dc23/eng/20230425
LC record available at https://lccn.loc.gov/2023019099
LC ebook record available at https://lccn.loc.gov/2023019100

The National Endowment for the Arts, the Los Angeles County Arts Commis-
sion, the Ahmanson Foundation, the Dwight Stuart Youth Fund, the Max Factor
Family Foundation, the Pasadena Tournament of Roses Foundation, the Pasadena
Arts & Culture Commission and the City of Pasadena Cultural Affairs Division,
the City of Los Angeles Department of Cultural Affairs, the Audrey & Sydney Ir-
mas Charitable Foundation, the Kinder Morgan Foundation, the Meta & George
Rosenberg Foundation, the Albert and Elaine Borchard Foundation, the Adams
Family Foundation, the Riordan Foundation, Amazon Literary Partnership, the
Sam Francis Foundation, and the Mara W. Breech Foundation partially support
Red Hen Press.

First Edition
Published by Red Hen Press
www.redhen.org

Acknowledgments

I will never be able to thank everyone who encouraged me to move ahead with this project. Without God, of course, nothing is possible and all things are indeed possible with Him. Much gratitude to my family in the US, Guadeloupe, Dominica (St. Joseph and Roseau), and France who never failed to answer my questions, corrected my faulty memory, and continue to keep me grounded. My sisters and Daddy, I have no words except that I will drive ten hours through a snowstorm to be with you all anytime. Marita Golden, for your brilliant and honest critiques; cannot thank you enough. And thank you also for creating a space for Black women writers to grow together. Much thanks also to my agent Sha-Shana Crichton for her determination and for being a great friend. And to my friends near and dear to my heart, you know who you are, much love.

In Memory of Curtis J. Timothy

Island Man

Hurricane

Chapter 1

Canefield, Dominica
September 2017

The wind began to pick up around 9:00 p.m., but it hardly stopped our partying. We'd started early, around 6:00 a.m., boarding up the windows and doors, or battening down the hatches, as Dad described it. Cousin Eddie's wife Missy brought us plates and plates of fried plantains, fish, rice and beans, and endless bottles of Carib and Heineken. By nightfall, we were sore and exhausted, but everyone was in high spirits. Eventually Missy and the girls went upstairs to bed, and Cousin Eddie reminded them to run into the bathroom stall if things got really bad. We all got a good laugh out of that one.

But by eleven, we couldn't ignore the wind anymore, though not for lack of trying. Cousin Eddie kept trashing the United Workers' Party, but our drinking had significantly slowed down. Dad had been holding the same beer for the last two hours. The lights flickered two, three times. "Everything okay?" Cousin Eddie shouted at the staircase.

Screw it. I called home. Leandra's face filled up on my phone screen. "Hey," I said, wanting to tell her how beautiful she looked. She was in a good mood, lucky for me. "Weather's not too bad yet," I assured her. "Where's my son?"

I shared the video of Dante grinning in his SpongeBob pajamas. Dante lit up at seeing Dad's face. "Goodnight, Grandpa!" he waved, and Dad beamed into the screen. "Don't get eaten by the hurricane, Grandpa!" Dante grinned his three-toothed smile, holding up a drawing of a monster that I supposed was his rendering of Hurricane Maria.

"I won't, little man," Dad said, poking a wrinkled finger at the screen. "You keep safe in Boston, okay?"

I waved goodbye to Dante and tried to lock eyes with Leandra, but she, consciously or unconsciously, barely looked at me before hanging up.

Dad and I had arrived in Dominica just the week before. His victory lap—or "grand tour," as I was calling it—took us the length and breadth of the island, introducing us to new family members and sites like the Boiling Lake and the Emerald Pool that earned the island its reputation as the Nature Island. Everyone said we looked like brothers, which reminded me that maybe I should shave my virtually all-gray beard and get a haircut.

Two weeks, I'd told him, then I needed to get back to Dante. True, there was really nothing waiting for me in Boston except watching the Celtics lose and the Patriots cheat their way to the Super Bowl. But I'd stalled long enough. The one-year anniversary of Mom's death was coming up, and I had to keep my promise to her. Dad and I planned to spread her ashes in the bay in Roseau. Leaving her in this place of her birth, as she wanted, would not bring me any peace. In all honesty, I would have kept her with me, even to my own grave, where she could be safe. But a promise was a promise.

Then the weather warnings began. At first, I thought it would be kind of cool to be in a hurricane. I'd survived a lifetime of blizzards and nor'easters in Boston, so why not add a little tropical disaster to the mix? Still, when the weather forecasters began to try on their grim expressions, I called up JetBlue and bought Dad a ticket home. Of course, he refused. Why should I be the one to stay? Did he not have even more of a claim to Mom's memory than I did? He had his own promises to keep, I guessed, his own guilty conscience to absolve. If I was staying, he would stay. And I'd learned over the years not to argue with the man.

So I got into it. Hurricane prep in Cousin Eddie's neighborhood seemed more like tailgating than anything else. It was bright and sunny that morning with just a few pregnant clouds high in the sky. I was still getting used to the rhythms of tropical suburban life with the constant backbeat of soca music and its younger version, bouyon, which made Dad roll his eyes. "That is nonsense music," he said, sucking his teeth. "These children are ruining our music, our traditions." Shirtless men and women in brightly colored blouses and tank tops, shorts and dresses were out on their front lawns with planks, hammers, drills, and saws; eating, drinking, and boarding up or knotting down everything that could move.

Cousin Eddie's house had large glass-paned windows on the first floor, and it took all day for Dad and me to board them up while Cousin Eddie and his friends secured the rest of the house. I had to admit, after twenty years of sitting at a desk or in an airplane seat, the physical labor was exhilarating. My atrophied muscles were springing to life again. At one point, Dad looked over at me and wiped his brow, grinning. "Boy, I haven't sweat like this in a long time!"

The neighbors ribbed me without end. "Eh, eh! How a spoiled American like you going to survive a big hurricane like that? Is not like snow, you know? We don't have no FEMA to come and rescue you, eh." I took it all in stride.

Around eleven thirty, I went upstairs to my room, leaving Dad and Cousin Eddie in the living room reminiscing about the old days. Cousin Eddie's house was large and modern, so I wasn't too concerned. Over the years, Dad had taken care of his entire extended family on the island, so all had climbed out of the poverty that had plagued his early life.

I was so beat from all the manual labor that I collapsed into bed still in my shorts and T-shirt. The rain and wind were causing a ruckus outside, but I was too exhausted to care. I wanted to savor the events of the day: working with Dad and saying goodnight to Dante's face on the screen. But in a few minutes, I was out cold.

I don't know how long I'd been asleep when a loud crash and wail jolted me upright. The wind, screaming like a banshee, had torn off the roof over my room, opening the black sky and vibrating through the walls. Suddenly I was in a wind tunnel with raindrops flying at me from every direction, into my nose, my ears, my eyes. Before I could cry out, the partition wall, liquefying before my eyes, caved in right next to my bed. I must have blacked out at that moment. When Cousin Eddie came running in to pull me out, I had a mouthful of concrete and my hearing was completely gone in one ear. Eddie's strong hands on my shoulder jolted me awake, pulled me onto my feet. "Come on!" I ignored the dizziness, my unsteady legs and stood, groping around for my backpack. "Come on, Hector!" He was by the bedroom door, which was half off its hinges when I crawled away from the debris. The heavy urn in my backpack slowed our dash to safety. As I tripped and slid down the slippery tiled staircase, I was as terrified of losing the urn as I was my own life.

Completely dazed, I stumbled to the living room. Everyone—Dad, Missy holding the kids close—was there, wide-awake. The girls were crying; Missy's eyes were wide with terror. Dad ran toward me, arms out, his eyes searching me from head to toe. "You hurt? You hurt?"

I cleaned myself off in the bathroom and tried to clear the fog in my head. Outside, the wind sounded like a 747 on takeoff, and raindrops slapped at the house from top to bottom.

Cousin Eddie, normally joking and talkative, was doing his best to keep his family's spirits up. "I went through this in '79. David was much bigger than this one," he said. "We just have to wait it out. Don't mind too much what is going on outside." He grabbed a box of playing cards and set them on the coffee table.

"Hector, we save all the excitement for you. When you go back you can tell all your friends you was in a hurricane." His smile couldn't hide his uneasiness. Missy and the girls took the cards, but their lack of enthusiasm was palpable as the wind whooshed and hollered outside. Dad leaned back in an armchair, staring off into the distance.

The bedlam grew in decibels as Maria shook the outside world like a snow globe. The girls dropped their cards and burrowed their heads into Missy's shoulder. Dad and I exchanged looks. Cousin Eddie was beginning to say something when a massive bellowing, like a pregnant cow right before it drops a calf, filled the air. Then, immediately after, another wrenching groan and a cascade of rain on our heads. We jumped up and cards scattered everywhere. "The roof! The roof!" Cousin Eddie yelled. "Come!" He pulled his wife and kids into the downstairs bathroom. Dad and I flew to the kitchen pantry. We'd planned this earlier, thinking we'd never have to seek that refuge because the roof was state of the art, only a few years old.

We hunkered down as water, flung by violent wind gusts, hit the aluminum louvers of the pantry like a million pellets. Who knew there were so many cracks in Cousin Eddie's house? The doors and windows were barred shut, but Maria would not be kept out. Rain seeped in from invisible places. The wind was not a whistle or a scream. It was a million voices screaming, wailing, crying. My eyes burned from the rain, and my throat hurt. The floor was wet, strewn with canned beans and tomatoes that had fallen off the shelves.

We'd been in the pantry an hour, since after midnight, and I'd expected a lull by this point. But the assault continued. On and on it went, the ghoulish howling wind, the crash of branches, trunks and debris hitting the earth, the house, colliding with other debris in midair. Indescribable sounds from an outside we couldn't see, so we imagined the worst.

Dad was praying. His bald head was bowed, his wrinkled hands clasped between his knees. His shoulders shook. We were surrounded by shelves of pots, pans, and groceries now soggy and spoiled by the rain. Occasionally, we could hear the girls screaming in the bathroom and Cousin Eddie trying to soothe them.

I tried to sound brave. "Dad, don't worry. Ma Relene . . . Auntie Valina . . . they're fine. That hotel has been around since the 1700s. It's solid." We'd forced Dad's relatives into safer quarters earlier that day, but he still looked worried.

"I haven't been back here in thirty years, and this is what happens? I think . . . maybe it's my turn now . . ." The wind howled so loudly I couldn't hear him as his mouth kept moving.

We thought we heard a knock on the pantry door, but it was only debris flying about. Each time Cousin Eddie came out to check on Dad and me, Missy and the girls screamed, and he'd have to run back to them. The situation would have been funny if we weren't in the middle of the biggest hurricane that had ever struck the island.

Then, around one thirty, it died down. The sound of just the rain sighing and writhing about was as welcome as a calm sunrise. I took a deep breath and tried to relax a bit. Dad was holding himself together. Water was still seeping in from everywhere. "Do you want to light the candle?"

He shook his head. "It's not over. We should save it."

I peeked outside the pantry door. Water was streaming into the living room from upstairs and the furniture was askew, all over the place, as if there'd been a bar fight in the room. Half the roof was gone, we'd find out later. My left ear was still ringing, and my mouth was still weird.

Dad could be superstitious. I wouldn't have been surprised if he'd thought this was somehow all related to him. That the cosmos was paying him back for some imagined wrong. I tried to suppress the image of Dante's face looming in my mind, his tinny voice yelling goodnight, his missing tooth. Jesus! What if tonight was the last . . .

A huge crack and boom outside froze us. My heart leapt but I tried to stay calm. "Sounds like Cousin Eddie just lost another tree."

Dad took a deep breath. "Lord, deliver us from this evil." He shook his head, worried eyes staring up. He held out his arm and touched mine, as if to make sure I was still there with him in the wet, cramped pantry.

The wind was now an eerie whoo, whoooo, whooo, and it was hard not to ascribe supernatural powers to its almost-human cries. Reflexively, I reached for my phone, as if that would do me any good. As if I were stranded in the Financial District and could just call a car to get me home. Despair sent me reeling against a shelf where something hit the back of my head. I needed to preserve the battery; who knew when the power would be back on?

"If we survive this, you are to never come back here," Dad whispered. "Never. I left this place for a good reason."

"Dad . . . we will be fine. This is a solid house."

"I never should have . . ."

"Mom wanted this. I wanted this!"

He looked down at the wet floor, at his wet Nikes, at the wet edges of his sweatpants. This was supposed to be an important trip for us. I hadn't planned for a Category 5 hurricane.

"I missed David in '79," he said, a hand half over his mouth. "But this one was waiting for me." He began tapping his foot on the soggy floor, the anxious tap that over the years I'd learned signaled worry.

"Dad . . . the hurricane was not waiting for you."

He looked at me as if I could not possibly understand. I was about to ask him why when the wind began to whip up again into a sickly keening I'd heard only in horror movies. I imagined ghosts flying about waving white sheets, sailing above the house, riding atop Flamboyant and mango trees, howling, laughing, and crying. My chest was suddenly tight as the entire house swayed and shook. I grabbed a corner wall and leaned against it. Dad remained in the chair opposite me, against the rattling door, his head bowed, his mouth moving.

How long were we there? I dozed off at times, soaked, battered by wind, fear, and helplessness. Dad never closed his eyes.

The night wore on, second by second, the minutes piling on top of each other. I thought of all the things I had ever done wrong. Big things, small things that had left a mound of ruins back in the States. One year since Mom's death. Almost a year since Leandra filed for divorce, since the scandal that cost me my career, my marriage, and my treasured mornings with Dante. I closed my eyes and told God I was sorry. If I should die here, please let my family live and let them be happy. Let Dante grow up to be a good man. Not like me. More like Dad.

I remembered Jonah on the boat to Tarshish with the pagan men. Everything was calm after they threw him overboard. Maybe if I ran outside and gave myself to the storm, everything would be okay. Dad would be okay and so would Cousin Eddie and his family. But the truth was, I didn't want to die. I wanted to live like a resurrected, new man. I prayed harder. But the wind only intensified, marching steadily like a legion of soldiers. The house shuddered, then there was a loud bang. "Lord, help us," Dad gasped. Then another bang, like a tank firing. Then another. More trees down. More debris flying about and hitting the battered house.

I heard sobbing and realized it was mine. Terror took over as the wind shouted accusations and hurled insults at us in our tiny cell. No one is coming to save you. You are doomed to die here. And you deserve it.

Chapter 2

Two weeks earlier

I used to imagine that Dad would land in Dominica and some inner flood-gate would burst open, or the tropical sun would dissolve all that repressed anger—or stoicism—in a wave of tears or emotion. But we walked off the plane onto the hot tarmac, and he just stood in customs looking around. Like a tourist. He said out loud that he couldn't believe the airport's sole terminal was smaller than his house. Smaller than his biggest Dunkin' Donuts store. "No progress," he shook his head. "All those years." He stared at passengers, customs workers, as if they were aliens. The immigration officer was annoyed by his condescension, and I was almost ashamed of him. He rolled his eyes. "These customs people are slow, eh?"

Of course, I never believed him when he said he'd never return to Dominica, that he was an American now and the past would remain in the past. No. He spent too much time reading those history books, listening to that music, and talking to Aunt Zoom and Uncle Edward about the old days. I knew he'd eventually go back. And here he was now, making this pilgrimage for Mom.

I observed him out of the corner of my eye, among his fellow Dominicans, the urn holding Mom's ashes in his carry-on. He is bald, lean, and slightly stooped, too old around the eyes for his fifty-seven years, but still managing the softish look of a middle-aged Black golfer. He fit in well with the crowd of UK and US emigrants who toil in the lands of opportunity and return home for fortification every year or two.

We flew first class from Boston to Puerto Rico, then waited in the American Airlines club for our connecting flight. Dad ate all the junk food he could get his hands on, a four-dollar bag of Cheez-Its, greasy pretzels covered in salt, a milk shake from McDonald's. He drove me nuts with ridiculous requests. "Can you go buy some more hand sanitizer before we take off?" He wore down his cell phone battery, talking nonstop with Ms. Karen, Aunt Zoom, the aunts in Dominica, telegraphing every second of the journey. He didn't fool me; he was trying to hide his nervousness. The only other times I remember Dad losing his cool and acting like a fool were back in the early days of his and Mom's reunion. On the final leg from Antigua to Dominica, he finally fell silent. There was no first class or coach on the tiny ATR-42 600, nowhere to hide. As soon as the pilot took off, Dad leaned his head back and feigned sleep.

The guy across from me wore five gold chains and three very large rings on his left hand. He couldn't have been older than thirty. I remembered myself at thirty. Leandra and I had been married nearly seven years; I already had an on office on the twentieth floor at Summit Bank. Mom, who was wildly in love with Dad yet getting sicker by the year, weighed on me more than I admitted in actual words. Leandra and I were building our lives, and despite our tragedies, we still had hope. At age thirty, I still thought of myself as a good man.

At twelve thousand feet, below the tiny plane window were miles and miles of blue sea and sandy beaches. Already, I felt my breathing evening out, a burden lifting from my shoulders. Maybe I could get myself straightened out here. Maybe I wouldn't be rejected and spit out here. Maybe I'd find a new home.

Whitecaps frothed up on the Caribbean Sea, and dolphins danced in the air as we neared Guadeloupe, which appeared green and rocky—French, even from twenty thousand feet up. Passengers—the white people, really—leaned over to marvel and snap pictures. The plane slowed, then began to descend as Dominica came into view, a mountainous landscape blanketed in deep green, surrounded by an intensely navy ocean. The pilot maneuvered a careful landing between the peaks, a slow and terrifying experience, even though I'd flown in tiny planes before. I clapped with the other passengers when we finally touched down. Dad finally opened his eyes.

"Where is Eddie?" he muttered impatiently as we cleared customs and poured out into a crowded waiting area with other passengers. The sound and color were what hit me first, reds, yellows, greens, and a loud clatter of uninhibited patois. The fervid array of colors against the emerald green surrounding the low-slung airport made me feel instantly at home. No one hurried, people smiled, laughed, waved, stopped and patted each other on the shoulder. "How you doing? Eh?" "You going back Antigua?" Young professionally dressed people waited in line, heads held high. A couple of young Black pilots strode by with their luggage. My heart immediately began to fill with a sense of belonging that I'd felt only inside my mother's house and within the boundaries of our Dorchester neighborhood.

Then there he was, Cousin Eddie, waving at us, backslapping and small-talking his way through a throng of taxi and minibus drivers. Cousin Eddie, dressed in shorts and a T-shirt, was lean with weathered brown skin and a wild head of curly hair. He and Dad embraced like brothers, and I thought I began to see a crack in Dad's stoic armor. "Boy, why you don't cut that hair?" Dad ruffled Cousin Eddie's hair, causing him to duck. He looked nothing like

Dad, who was baked-through brown with tight afro hair. Not too unexpected; Eddie's mom, my Auntie Valina, and Dad had different fathers.

They lost me with their catching-up stories filled with unrecognizable names and places. The talk turned to politics. "Man, Skerrit is doing good things. It's sad the people don't trust him," Dad said. Cousin Eddie made a scoffing sound. "No, Uncle. Trust me. You have to live here to understand why people feel that way." And off to the races they went, Dad holding firmly to his opinion built on decades of not living in Dominica.

I lost myself in the visual tropical feast before me. This quaint northern village of Marigot, peeking over the sea with its narrow, winding roads made me miss Leandra with such a force tears pricked at my eyes. She would love this place. She would have wanted to stop and walk through this village, talk to the people, throw back a beer at the roadside bar. Miles on, I turned down the window to feel the cool air and smell the lush, moist greenness of the interior forest. It was the cleanest air I'd ever breathed. My father, my mother, were born in this paradise? Had left and never wanted to return?

"Dad, is this like you remembered it?"

His gaze was locked straight ahead. "Something like that. Roseau is not like this, though," he said gruffly. I wondered how he would hold up under the weight of his silent grief over Mom. In the last year, we had circled each other like fighters in a cage; I would ask how he was doing, and he would turn the tables back on me. "Where is Leandra?" he'd accuse when I arrived solo for strained Sunday dinners with him and Ms. Karen.

Once Cousin Eddie stopped talking, Dad remained silent, far away in his thoughts. "What are you thinking, Dad?" I asked, trying to snap pictures of red, orange, coral, and blue birds darting about on trees I could reach by just holding out my hands.

"Just this road . . ." he sighed but never finished. I left him alone.

That night, we gathered for the first of many feasts at Cousin Eddie's house high on a hill in the suburb of Canefield, which I assumed was an old slave plantation from the ruins of a sugar mill resting at the bottom of the hill. I saw a hint of tears as Dad reunited with his cousin Mikey, who was uncomfortable and ill at ease the entire evening. I was under constant inspection from my Aunt Valina and Ma Relene who took care of Dad when he was a boy—old, traditional ladies, pleasant and thoroughly steeped in their Dominican ways. My wife had to work, and that's why she and my son are not here, I lied. How do you explain a messy divorce to sweet elderly ladies?

We were planning to visit the Boiling Lake (the second largest in the world, Cousin Eddie reminded me) when the hurricane warnings began. I shrugged them off. Instead, I texted scenic pictures of Dominica to Leandra and got a sick thrill out of her ooohing and aahing over the pictures, and her "jealousy" that I was there and not stuck in gray Boston. "You'd better hope that hurricane doesn't hit you guys," she joked.

Our fifth day in Dominica, I asked Dad to take me to Mom's village. He tensed up. "She doesn't have any people left there. You know that."

"I just want to see it," I insisted. "To know where she grew up."

He sighed, irritated. "Hector, your mother didn't want you dwelling on these things. We will spread her ashes, then we will go home. You have your own family to worry about."

We were already beginning to get on each other's nerves. I threatened to go find Mom's village myself and spread her ashes there. "If you do that, you can forget about me then," Dad snapped. "Foolish!" He stalked out of Cousin Eddie's kitchen, leaving me staring after him.

I wanted to follow him and yell at him—for what I didn't know. Seems I can't just move on from anything. Like I'm forever to circle around the ruins of my forty years on this planet trying to pick a fight with this man.

It's been about twenty years since that Sunday in '98 when Dad came into my life, still I hardly know what to make of him. Our relationship has idled at strained; my old resentments and grudges only calcifying with each passing year. His patient equanimity only makes me more furious.

The shrink, who my CEO forced me to see as a condition of my generous severance package, said I should write down everything I feel while I am on this trip. I wrote that night that I know Dad is keeping something, many things from me. First Mom, and now him. This is 1998 again, and it's like he and Mom have tag-teamed to make my life a living hell.

Chapter 3

Two days before the hurricane, I stood swaying on a patched-over spring bridge in desperate need of repairs. "It has seen too many hurricanes," Cousin Eddie said. Sort of like me, I thought. Cousin Eddie slapped me on the shoulder. "I'm going back to the bus. I'll wait for you." I should have been as careful. The old Bath Estate Bridge was closed to traffic now, a monument to the past. The new bridge, which ran alongside it, was busy with cars, motorbikes, passengers.

The clear waters below churned in discrete pools yet all flowed in one direction toward the sea. I wanted to leave Mom here. It seemed a fitting place to end this chapter, wash away the lies and half-truths and leave only the beauty and the good like the polished stones beneath. But Dad was already turning away. "No!" he snapped. "Not here in Bath Estate. That was my family's place, not hers." He didn't look back when I called out to him. I lingered on the bridge, thinking.

My mother told me when I was around six years old that she and my father met at a church camp when she was a teenager. She became pregnant and her parents sent her away to America to live with an aunt, ashamed she had betrayed them and their faith. Then her parents died in a fiery car crash on their way to a revival service in the village of Bagatelle. There was no time to mourn, not even a chance to attend their funeral. One day she had parents and the next day she didn't. "You'll never understand how lucky you are, Hector," she sobbed. I had no choice but to comfort her and quiet my questions, to be a good, grateful son.

When I was in eighth grade, my mother told me my father had been a smart young boy who was very poor, but she loved him very much. They were in love and she would have stayed with him had it not been for her strict parents who wanted better for her. She didn't know what became of him. Then, no. He was living in Dominica and he had a family of his own and couldn't care less about her. One day when I was older, she promised, she would tell me more about him, but for now I should concentrate on school.

When I was sixteen, Mom told me my father was probably dead and that I should just forget about him and stop screwing around with girls who would only get pregnant and ruin my future. That this was what probably happened to my father.

When I was seventeen, before I left home for college, she told me, tears streaming from her eyes, that he would have been proud of me if he were alive today.

When I graduated from high school, she told me sometimes she felt in her spirit that my father was still alive somewhere in the world. By then, I knew to keep my fantasies to myself and not rely on Mom for a shred of truth when it came to my father.

July fourth of that year, Uncle Desi got drunk at our barbecue and told me my father was killed in a raid by Dominican soldiers during the 1970s because my father belonged to a group of rebel Rastafarians. My mother flew out of her folding chair and pushed Uncle Desi so hard he fell over backwards into the cooler of beers. Uncle Desi guffawed on the grass as Mom stalked away cursing him. "Shut your stupid, ignorant mouth, Desi!" She flew into her bedroom and didn't emerge for the rest of the day.

"Want to go to the Brockton Fair and see the fireworks?" Uncle Desi asked me, grinning like nothing had happened. Mom spoke in one-word sentences for weeks afterward, almost daring me or anyone else to ask her any more questions. I buried that episode deep in my memory. I'd learned how she used anger and silence to ward off these unpleasant conversations. We all learned.

The year I would graduate from college, she woke me up in the middle of the night crying. It was a miracle, she sobbed. She had run into my father on the street in Boston. On Blue Hill Avenue. During the carnival. Did I want to meet him? I rubbed my eyes and nodded sleepily. The next morning, she was teary-eyed at the kitchen table, staring into a mug of basil tea that overpowered the lemony smell of the kitchen. She looked up at me. "I can't believe he's alive," she whispered.

She was serious, I realized, and a shiver ran through me.

Fast-forward decades and the tropical sun is blazing down on my back from a clear blue sky. I pat the urn in my backpack; it feels heavier today. It seems right to leave the messy past where it all began, to let it flow down the Roseau River and into the peaceful Caribbean Sea.

But I look up and Dad is frowning in the distance, waiting for me. And I go to him bearing the weight of the ashes because that's what Mom would have wanted.

Before Dad

Chapter 4

Boston, 1998
Five days before I meet my father

"I wanted to give you enough time to get yourself together," Mom said, her quavering voice causing the string of the tea bag to swing against the mug in her hand. Weeks had passed since she'd met him at the carnival, and she'd turned it over in her mind endlessly, she said. "But I think," she paused. "Now is a good time. Right?" She stood in the doorway of my room, frowning at my Bulls jersey, my shorts, my red-and-white Js.

On Sunday, August 16, 1998, my father would come over for dinner around five. No, I didn't have to dress up; but I shouldn't wear those shorts. Oh, and wear the shirt she bought me for Christmas. "Don't make that face, Hector. Why you have to make things harder than they need to be?" She walked away shaking her head, dreadlocks tossing side to side.

It was a humid Saturday on Hawkins Street, the kind that wilted tree branches already heavy with foliage. Uncle Desi was revving up his motorcycle in the driveway, the neighbor was blasting Naughty by Nature for the whole neighborhood to hey and ho, and big kids were chasing some little kids down the middle of the street. Uncle Desi's plan was fried clam bellies from Simco's in Mattapan then a lightning streak ride up I-93 to get fireworks in New Hampshire.

"I'll be back, Mom!"

She didn't answer but I felt her staring at me as I hopped onto the bike and put on my helmet. Before she could say another word Uncle Desi revved the engine and we were gone.

I caught Uncle Desi staring at me as the red-faced guy wearing a coffee-stained T-shirt that read "Londonderry" shoved bottle rockets and 16-shot cakes into a garish red plastic bag at the cash register. My stomach was a little sick from the ride, the fried clam bellies from Simco's, and the burger we'd stopped for at McDonald's in Manchester, but I was feeling good. Not really thinking about things because it was summer and I wanted to feel normal even though I would meet my father in a couple weeks and there was nothing normal about that. There was a long line of kids from Boston behind us, white,

Black, Hispanic, all on the same mission for fireworks. It's what we did in our hoods in the summer, from Southie to Lawrence to the 'Bury.

"Don't worry," Uncle Desi said softly, bushy eyebrows close together over his dark eyes. "Your father is a good guy. I don't really remember him though. But he come from good people."

"I'm not worried."

I didn't want to talk about it. At least she gave me two weeks. Enough time to pick stupid fights with Leandra, call out sick from my dumb security job at the Corner Mall for no reason but to hound Mom around the house, and drink myself into oblivion while she worked the overnight shift at the hospital. Every day leading up to that Sunday I had at least three questions for Mom. So, you just saw him on the street and you knew it was him? How do you know it's not some crazy person? What if he's a killer, a con man? She took to not answering her bedroom door when I knocked.

We raced back to Boston with some other dudes on bikes wearing leather jackets. Uncle Desi laughed out loud while I gritted my teeth as he flew in and out of lanes, drivers honking at us all the way to the Tobin Bridge. "Wooo!" He exhaled as the outline of the State Street buildings and the sign for the Boston Garden came into view.

We were almost back home, and I would meet my father in a few days. Just a few days, after twenty years of waiting. Two decades of questions, lies, and halfway answers. Hard to believe that in just a few days the truth would appear in the flesh. A truth I grew up struggling to piece together, to form a pattern out of pieces of unmatched lies. I reached way back into my memory to construct an edifice, an expectation of what he would look like, sound like, be like. But those memories yielded nothing, ultimately falling in on each other, just castles built with sand.

At my eighth birthday party, a man knocked at the front door and had strong words with Mom. He had to be my father because I'd never heard my mother scream and yell so angrily at a complete stranger. For years, she claimed to forget this happened, but I never did.

The doorbell rang right after Auntie Bebe spilled out of the kitchen barefoot in jeans, a Cross Colours shirt, and door-knocker earrings, singing "Happy Birthday" while struggling to keep my blue-and-white cake from slipping off the platter.

Mom groaned as she flew downstairs to answer the bell. We were living near Upham's Corner, on the corner of Columbia Road and Bird Street on the third floor of Mr. Dockser's triple-decker. I was allowed eight guests at my party: three from school, the neighbors' kids from the first floor, and my two baby cousins. I invited the three kids from my second-grade class at Mather Elementary who I knew wouldn't make fun of our West Indian food and Mom's accent.

It was 1986, and our neighborhood was frayed at the edges, never quite recovered from the wounds of the '68 riots, the busing crisis, and white flight, and now taking fire from the gang wars on Intervale, Humboldt, and Castlegate. Mom's wide dark eyes were always alert when we walked to the bus stop, her hands gripping mine. "Don't look at anybody, Hector!" Our survival strategy was to stay inside and mind our own business.

The off-key shout-singing of Stevie Wonder's birthday song almost drowned out Mom's screaming downstairs. But I could hear her: "Get away! Get out of here! Go! Go!"

Uncle Track, who'd just finished lighting the eight candles on my birthday cake, dropped the lighter and raced down the stairs. "Jemma!"

I couldn't move. My eyes watered over the flickering candles, and my heart pounded as Mom's voice grew louder, more frantic. "Get out! You piece of garbage!"

Auntie Bebe's eyes widened, and her slender fingers quivered. "Come on, kids," she smiled. "Let's finish singing 'Happy Birthday' to Hector." I blew out my candles, my ear tuned to the door, waiting for the shouting to stop.

"Man, don't come back here. You understand?" Uncle Track's voice boomed. "Them things happen so long ago! Them people long gone!" Then I couldn't hear anything else but muffled, heated talking. Mr. Dockser, our landlord, had stepped out from his second-floor apartment and ordered them to keep the noise down. "I don't want that kind of mess in my place, you hear?"

My guests were unbothered, impatiently holding out their colorful paper plates for cake. Blue rainbows, blue ocean, sailboats in the middle, with the paper cups to match. I'd picked the pattern at Bradlee's with Mom the weekend before along with balloons, party hats, and all the candy that now covered the rug.

Auntie Bebe turned up the TV volume when Stacy Lattisaw's "Nail it to the Wall" flashed on the screen. She'd promised me the night before: "Your birthday party is going to be so much fun! We're gonna have a *Soul Train* line!" After everyone had their cake and soda, she began to sing and clap, her bangs bobbing on her forehead. "Dance! Everybody, dance!" I hopped around with the other kids until I couldn't hear any more shouting from downstairs. "Auntie Bebe, can I open my presents now?"

"Yay!" my cousins shouted. And that's what we did, while Auntie Bebe kept one nervous eye on the door. We were spent from sugar and playing cars, puzzles, and Legos when Mom rushed back into the living room followed by Uncle Track. He shut the door to her room behind them, and they remained there speaking in muffled voices. She didn't even stop to see my presents, to see that even Mr. Dockser had bought me a book, and my teacher had sent me a hundred-piece puzzle. She didn't come out to say goodbye when everyone left—on time at six as Mr. Dockser had warned us.

The night before my birthday, I'd prayed: please send me my father as my birthday present, for real this year. The man who was just downstairs had to have been my father because God couldn't lie.

When Mom finally emerged red-eyed, apologetic, wrapped in a blanket from head to toe, I turned away from her. I was alone with my race cars on the living room floor. BET videos played on the screen behind me. Auntie Bebe had left for her babysitting job on Beacon Hill. Uncle Desi had disappeared, probably hanging outside the barbershop on Bird Street.

"You like the Transformers Autobot?" She kneeled in front of me. I was knee-deep in wrapping paper, gaudy paper plates with crusted blue icing, and half-full Dixie cups of Pepsi.

The Transformers Autobot was hidden underneath all of it, unwrapped.

"Yes." I looked into her sad eyes, which didn't fool me. I knew he came for me and she sent him away. She hugged me but I didn't hug her back.

Later that night, she held me close to her on the couch as we watched *Dallas*. Her long, wiry legs stretched way past mine and her long dreadlocks tickled my cheek. She smelled of rose oil and lemonade. I was terrified to ask her about the man from earlier. I wished and wished she would bring it up.

"Hector, I want to tell you something," she said during a commercial break.

My heart was racing. She was going to tell that my father had come for me.

"I am working very hard so we can move out of this place. By next year, I will have my LPN, and we can get a bigger place. In Brookline or one of those rich places, eh?"

"For all of us, Mommy?" I was shocked and couldn't imagine life without uncles Desi and Track, Auntie Bebe, and my baby cousins. I liked where we lived . Upham's Corner was always busy with people shopping on Columbia Road and Dudley Street. Some Saturday nights fancydressed people lined up outside the Strand Theater. The library was right across the street.

"Of course," Mom said, wincing. "Our family cannot ever be separate! We will always live together." She laughed. "Even when you get married and have your own children."

I snuggled up close to her, happy at this news. "So why do we have to leave Mr. Dockser's house?"

She sighed fiercely. "Too many West Indians in Dorchester now. People think they know you and they don't know nothing."

"Me, Mommy?"

"Noooo, Hector." She squeezed my shoulder. "Us. Our family. Because of things that happen long time ago, people say all kinds of lies. But it's not true. We come from good people. Good people."

She wasn't speaking to me at this point but to the TV screen. "We here since 1978. But is now people coming and knock my door asking me stupid questions about Dominica!" She sucked her teeth. "Listen to me, Hector, we will leave this nonsense ghetto place. We don't need to be living around these ignorant people." She shifted on the couch, breathing out her disgust. "Uneducated people!"

I struggled in vain to understand. Uncle Desi would say sometimes, "Your mother live in her own world. Just leave her there."

I hoped someday she'd tell me why she sent my father away. But in that moment, I was happy. We were in our rightful place—on the couch watching *Dallas* together.

Chapter 5

Three days before I meet my father

The summer of 1998 the weather lurched about like my mood, humid one day, cool the next. It was sixty-eight degrees on Thursday, August 13. Leandra and I had just finished summer classes and internships; part of her plan (which became our plan) to graduate early from Northeastern, move on to grad school and finally launch our quest to become a better version of the Huxtables.

Leandra said I needed to blow off steam. We could go clubbing on Route 1 in Saugus or chill out at Wally's—her cousin was playing trombone with his Berklee crew that night. But I was too wired for all that. "I'm dying for a slice," I told her. So we headed out into the clammy, gray afternoon toward Allston. Truth is, I was craving pizza specifically from the joint near where we lived when I was in middle school.

"I think it's cute you're so nervous about meeting your dad." Leandra carefully picked off each slice of pepperoni from her slice only to eat them one by one. I focused on her bright pink nails; her weird, obsessive habits drove me crazy. "I hope he's better than my father. Every time I see my dad, he tells me how wonderful his new wife and kids are." She laughed. "Like, gee thanks, man. Miss you too." Leandra leaned over and kissed me on the forehead, her tank top revealing the edges of her lacy bra sparkling white against her brown skin.

The pizza shop—which was smack dab on a gritty stretch of Commonwealth Avenue that featured shoe repair shops, ethnic restaurants, dark bars, and Tarot readers—buzzed with drunks, babushkas, young guys in tank tops with Eastern European accents, and college students who stayed the summer. Inside was a microcosm of the neighborhood that I'd always loved despite its reputation as the armpit of Boston. Three Asian kids played checkers at a table near the kitchen. A homeless man wearing a winter coat, gloves, and boots sat alone at a table slowly lifting a slice to his lips. On the walls were hundreds of Red Sox photos, some signed, and maps and pastoral images of the Italian countryside.

Paul Marzullo, who owned Mars Pizza with his father, waddled over to our rickety table and sank his meaty hand onto my shoulder. "This kid here," he shook me playfully. "He's a smart one. You got yourself a smart one."

"I know." Leandra grinned, putting on all of her charm.

"I've known him since he was up to here." Paul patted his hip. "His mother brought him here on his birthday and said: you can eat a whole pizza if you want. And you know what? He did it." Paul laughed. "I never seen a thirteen-year-old eat as much as this kid here."

The glass door chimed, and a crew of punk rockers swaggered in straight from The Rat wearing leather jackets, shoulder spikes, and laced-up Doc Martens. Paul immediately began to kid them and left us alone.

Leandra reached across the table and took a sip of my Coke. "They remember you from way back when? You need to tell me about all that."

"Not a lot to tell." Why was I there now? Back in those days, sitting in this pizza shop with Mom and my uncles had made me feel safe and warm, like I belonged somewhere. Sometimes kids from my middle school would come in with their parents and they'd nod at me or sit at our table for a bit. Allston was different in that way. Mom was okay with going out and getting pizza or sitting at the Dunkin' Donuts on a Sunday afternoon watching me eat donuts. When we lived in Dorchester, we were always inside. She never told me what we were hiding from.

Leandra rolled her eyes, transporting me to the present. "Come on. I told you about every miserable year I lived in the projects." Leandra pushed bangs off her forehead. She wasn't wearing makeup today, and I liked that the sun had brought out a natural red just under the surface of her smooth brown skin. Her full lips were tawny-orange with gloss and her perfectly straight teeth glinted when she bit into the pizza. She was so perfect, I thought. So perfect for me.

"Your two years in Orchard Park?" I scoffed. Leandra and I both knew she'd had it better than most of the kids living in those dank, gritty buildings off Harrison Avenue. She did spend two years in Orchard Park after her parents divorced. Then her mom dusted herself off, got on her feet and moved them to Fort Hill. "At least it gives you street cred to flex for all your pre-law friends," I teased. If there was one thing I envied, it was Leandra's ability to move and be comfortable among all kinds of people. Her friends were every single person she ever met, no matter the color or background. She was the perfect foil for my awkward, introverted self.

Her clear brown eyes were large and laughing—always searching mine. "Spill it," she nudged me. "You brought me to this pizza place for a reason."

What the hell, I thought. I already knew I'd spend the rest of my life with her. I had nothing to hide. Not at that point anyway.

∾

The four-story brick apartment building at 1202 Commonwealth Avenue was less warm, less homey, than the top floor of Mr. Dockser's triple-decker. But Mom was determined. We *needed* to move up in the world. She passed on her drive for upward mobility to me; it took long, hard years to undo the indoctrination, to realize that staying put and happy is always an option, sometimes the best option.

A framed miniature American flag hung on our living room wall above the new navy blue couch she bought from Ann & Hope in Watertown, along with pictures of me and Uncle Desi, Uncle Track, and Auntie Bebe as kids, then teenagers in Dorchester with the family members I didn't recognize—the ones who took them in when they first moved to America but who moved to the suburbs. From Mom's telephone conversations, I knew that these relatives, "those people" thought they were better than Mom because they lived in Medford, didn't want Mom to succeed, wanted her to remain backward and ignorant like she didn't have her papers, and were not worth an ounce of her time or energy.

Our new building manager lived on the first floor and brought Mom groceries when Uncle Desi and Uncle Track were doing their shifts at Mars Pizza Shop. Auntie Bebe giggled when the building manager came bringing boxes of Cheerios, milk, cheese, and Cadbury chocolate bars in a Purity Supreme bag for Mom. "Ooh, he like you, Jemma. And he have that nice American accent."

Mom would screw up her face. "I don't like that man. Why he bring me groceries? I already work in the grocery store!" The Purity Supreme was only two blocks away on Harvard Avenue. It took ten minutes to run there from the Horace Mann School off Brighton Avenue. I'd do my homework in the freezing stockroom until Mom got off at six. Then we walked hand in hand down Harvard Street, slowing to read the marquee at the movie theater before we turned into our building.

At Horace Mann, my teacher Mr. Ravid told me that since I was good with numbers, I should sit up front instead of in the back with the dumb kids who threw stuff and said curse words. But I didn't want to sit up front—mainly because of Jean Desrosiers.

Laura Fry whispered in my ear one day, "He is from Haiti. Do you know where that is?" I could feel her warm breath on my neck, her long dark hair brushing against my sweater. I did know about Haiti (Mom had tons of Haitian friends). But from the look in Laura's bright hazel eyes, I knew my answer. "No! I don't even know where that is!"

Jean Desrosiers spoke English but in a slow, thick accent that caused our entire sixth-grade class to explode in laughter every time Mr. Ravid called on him to answer a question. Jean was also the smartest kid in class.

Mr. Ravid told me I should talk to Jean, but I saw no reason to. I had finally begun to make friends with Mike Kelly, Anthony Primo, and Bobby Pavlicek, the toughest white boys in our class. They played basketball with the eighth graders and wore baggy jeans and bright-colored baggy T-shirts. The Black guys at Horace Mann who called me corny to my face respected Mike, Anthony, and Bobby, who knew all the lyrics to "Don't Sweat the Technique" and could compare rap emcees better than I could. But they still asked me what it was like to grow up in Dorchester surrounded by gangs and drug dealers. They threw intimidating stares at other groups of white kids when we walked together to the Osco Drug after school. They thought I was cool. I was American. Jean was Haitian. No way they'd talk to me if I even looked at Jean.

One day after school, I was waiting for Mom at the Purity Supreme when the double doors to the stockroom opened. A fat, dark lady with braided hair walked in, hung up her coat, and put on her blue smock. I was on the floor surrounded by crates of paper bags and toilet paper. It took a while before I noticed there was a boy with her.

She pointed to me and said something to the boy in a garbled language. That's when I recognized him. Jean Desrosiers's face lit up in a smile. "Your mother and my mother work in the same place!"

I was petrified. What would happen if the boys at school found out? And Laura Fry! I waved at him and quickly looked down at my book. Jean must have picked up on my coldness and, eventually, he carved out his own spot in the stockroom. Over the next many weeks, we did our homework together, maintaining a cordial "Hey" or "How ya doing?" Sometimes he helped me with chemistry. Sometimes I helped him with history. In school, we never acknowledged each other. I never stood up for him when the boys made fun of his accent or when the girls said he smelled bad. There was just that one time, when Bobby Kearns called him Pepé Le Pew, and I told Bobby to cut it out. Jean waved at me from the bus stop that afternoon and I waved back, not caring what any of the guys thought.

One Friday as I was leaving school, a tall, thin white man ran up to me from the line of parked cars on Brighton Ave. Next to him was Laura Fry, red-faced and looking down at the ground. "That him, honey?" The man glared at me, his gray eyes sharp and narrow. I looked around and could see no one I knew. My head felt light. What had I done? The man was breathing heavily as he placed a hand on Laura's shoulder. "Hey buddy," he leaned down. His breath smelled like sugar and coffee. "Listen to me," he said, baring two rows of straight yellowing teeth. "You stay away from my daughter. You understand?"

I opened my mouth to speak but all I could hear was the thumping of my heart. I had never been this close to a white man before in my entire life. I shook as he stood back and smirked at me. "Stick with your own kind!" Laura's eyes never left the pavement.

Paralyzed with fear, I scanned the schoolyard and the sidewalk for a familiar face but all I saw was a blur of kids and parents, teachers, bus drivers, cafeteria workers. It was Friday and everyone was going home. Then I felt a tap on my shoulder. "You want to walk to the Purity Supreme?" It was Jean Desrosiers. We walked in silence down the crowded sidewalk, past the store selling plastic flowers and cheap perfumes, another Dunkin' Donuts, a liquor store, an Italian restaurant. I had never felt so relieved to know someone as I was to know Jean that day.

Mom invited Jean's family to our Thanksgiving dinner that snowy November. Mom and Auntie Bebe had been cooking and baking for days, it seemed, and every corner of our crowded three-bedroom apartment smelled like cake batter and turkey drippings. My little cousins were toddlers, always getting into things, and I played with them while I watched cartoons.

When Uncle Desi, Uncle Track, and his latest girlfriend arrived, I couldn't hear the TV anymore. The landlord was splayed out on the couch watching TV and drinking, Heineken after Heineken lined up neatly on the side table at his elbow. Uncle Track put a cassette in the stereo and began to play calypso music. I watched Mom's face fade from a smile into a grimace. "Why you have to play that music? Play American music instead! Play new jack swing!"

"Come on, Jemma," Uncle Track said. "We can't listen to our own music on an American holiday?"

She didn't fight him as she had in years past when she would push past him and turn off the stereo herself. Maybe it's because the building manager was there, watching her every move, smiling like a fool. Snow crusted the edges of the window facing the street. The Green Line trolley rattled along the icy tracks, coming to a creaky halt at Harvard Avenue. Passengers wearing heavy coats crossed Commonwealth, heads bowed under descending snowflakes. The men who always stood sentry at the Store 24 maintained their post, shivering in the twenty-degree weather.

The clanking radiator sent warm waves of heat under my Chicago Bulls sweatshirt. I waited some more. Finally, the Number 66 bus lumbered to a stop in front of the liquor store. There they were, Jean Desrosiers and his mother Patrice. A man was with them; a short round man. "Mom! Jean is here!" I ran out to the freezing foyer to let them in.

Mom and Ms. Patrice hugged each other tightly and immediately began to talk loudly. The short round man was Ms. Patrice's husband. Jean's father. "Mr. Desrosiers, you can call me."

His pudgy hand was callused. "Yes, sir." I shook his hand, awed that Jean had a father. Mr. Desrosiers was balding, and his belly protruded over his belt, straining against his striped sweater. He had the same wide, flat nose as Jean and the thick, tightly curled hair that sat like a mat on his wide head.

Jean was beaming. "Let me see your games. My father won't let me play with digital games at home." Jean was soon on the floor with my cousins, all of us jumbled into the mess of board games, plastic toys, and Atari, cluttering every inch of Mom's new fake Persian rug. Mr. Desrosiers often called out to him to keep his voice down or to not be so rough with the baby.

Out of curiosity, I crept into the dining room where the adults had gathered. The turkey was still in the oven, and Mom was laying out dishes on the table. Ms. Patrice was showing Mom a large dish of dirty rice she'd brought along with deep-fried kingfish. Mom was speaking in Creole and English with Ms. Patrice, laughing at the Creole words she got wrong, slapping Ms. Patrice on the shoulder. "Oui, oui! C'est chaud!"

Mr. Desrosiers and the building manager were staring hungrily at the food and talking about the Charles Stuart murder. "I know for a fact that white man killed his wife," the building manager said. "From the first day, I knew it!"

Mr. Desrosiers nodded. "The police cannot conduct a fair investigation. They are too biased," he said in his French accent.

"My brother, my cousins," the building manager railed, waving his hands. "They all got stopped by the cops. All of them! A cop pushed my brother down on the sidewalk in Dudley Square!" The building manager stood shakily and shook the chair with both hands as if they were his brother being harassed by the cops. "Damn racists! And that bastard killed his own pregnant wife!" The building manager's eyes were red, his voice trembling. "Then had the nerve to jump off the Tobin Bridge after all that. Damn coward!"

Ms. Patrice, noticing my open-mouthed stare at the building manager's outburst, shouted sharply in French at Mr. Desrosiers. They suddenly dropped the subject and the building manager settled back down, caressing his beer and taking longing looks at Mom. Uncle Track and Desi were in Auntie Bebe's bedroom with their girlfriends, drinking their own kinds of drinks, playing music and watching basketball, and asking every five minutes if the food was ready.

"Young man, you know how to speak Creole," Mr. Desrosiers turned toward me.

"What?" I stood in the arched entrance to the dining room/kitchen.

Mr. Desrosiers's dark glasses almost hid his kind eyes. "You should learn how to speak Creole. Dominica is a beautiful place with a beautiful culture."

"Why?"

Then Mom was in the middle of us. "Hector! Go and play with your friend!" She grabbed my arm. "When it's time to eat I will call you," she hissed. "Go!"

I obeyed her, turning back to see Mr. Desrosiers shrugging and apologizing.

Jean was happily picking up puzzle pieces my cousins had scattered. I had never seen him so relaxed, so happy. "Can you speak Creole?" I asked him, sinking down into the carpet.

Jean looked up from the puzzle board. "I'm allowed to speak only Creole in our house. My father said English is for outside."

I was shocked. How did Mr. Desrosiers expect Jean to ever fit in at school? "Have you even been to Haiti?" From what the girls said at school, it was a dirty and frightening place with lots of ghosts and wars and starving people.

Jean shook his head. "I was three when we came here. I speak to my grand-parents every weekend on the phone though." He grinned. "They don't speak English. They have a house as big as this whole building with their own beach."

I stared at him in disbelief. That could not be true based on what I'd heard about Haiti. Jean must simply be trying to make himself and his family look good.

"I have a lot of cousins down there too. But in America, it's just me and my parents. And you."

Me? What did he mean?

Jean grinned. "You and Ms. Jemma and Mr. Desi and . . ."

"We don't speak Creole," I said defensively. I was angry that Jean knew this language, this world, that I didn't know. That he had a father to teach him these things. To tell him when to speak English and when not to. To announce that the Boston Police were biased with such calm confidence.

"Your mom, your uncles, and your auntie can speak Creole," Jean said, still fumbling around with the puzzle.

I looked at Mom happily laughing in the kitchen with Ms. Patrice. Why hadn't she told me about this? What was Creole? What other languages did people in Dominica speak?

"Don't worry," Jean said. "If you really want to learn, I can teach you."

～

On Black Friday, Mom and I rode the bus to the Arsenal Mall in Watertown for new winter coats and boots at the Ann & Hope sale. She was still excited about Thanksgiving dinner. "That was so nice. People say all kinds of mean things about Haitians but they are nice people. Nicer than some of those gossiping West Indians!" She patted her purse as it bumped up and down on her legs each time the crowded bus stopped to pick up a passenger.

"Mom, where is Dominica again?" I had looked it up in the *World Atlas*. It was a dot, a pinprick, in a chain of tiny squiggles in the ocean.

She flinched as if someone had poked her with a hot tong. "What?"

"Mr. Desrosiers was telling me about it yesterday."

She sighed and turned to me. "It's where we are from, Hector. I told you already! Me and Uncle and Auntie. Okay?"

"So it's like Haiti?"

She relaxed her shoulders. "In some ways." Then she smiled. "It's beautiful. It's mountainous and green and we have a lot of rivers and beaches. And no snow." She shook her head emphatically. "No blizzards. And no Charles Stuart."

"So that's where you were born?"

She nodded as the bell signaled the next stop at Armington Street.

"Mommy, why did you come to America?"

"Because it was better for us." She shifted in her seat. "Dominica is a very poor place, and it's hard for people to have a good life there. Same like Haiti."

"But we are poor in Boston." I didn't have the words for the questions I wanted to ask. I didn't even know what argument I was trying to make. I just wanted answers.

Her arm was around my shoulder over my hooded goose-down parka. "Don't worry. Next year by this time, Hector," she said almost fiercely, "we will be in our own house." She hugged her purse to her chest. "I'm telling you, Hector. As soon as I graduate and get a nursing job, I am buying a house. Just like Patrice and her husband."

We rode in silence from Packard's Corner to Lower Allston as people, mostly Russian, Eastern European, and Haitian immigrants, stepped on and off the bus and disappeared into triple-deckers and low-slung apartment buildings surrounded by piles of dirty snow. I thought of Laura Fry and her father. They lived in one of those brick apartment buildings.

"Mom, when someone says stick to your kind, what kind are they talking about?"

She turned to me with such force that my baseball cap fell off my head. "Who?" Her eyes narrowed. "Who said that to you?"

"No one," I said in a small voice, sinking into the rattling bus seat.

She rubbed her forehead with her gloved hands, and her entire body shook. "Somebody said that to you in school?"

I told her the story, leaving out the parts of Laura Fry passing me notes in class with hearts drawn on them, my name and hers linked together in red marker.

"This disgusting man threatened you at school?" Her voice was loud enough that other riders were turning our way. "Did you tell your teacher?" Her forehead was shiny with sweat and the pom-poms on her hat shook. Her lips, painted red, were tight and thin now, her narrowed eyes glinted. "Tell me!"

I shook my head. "Mom, it's okay. I don't care. Please don't make a big deal out of it."

But she was in school after Thanksgiving break in the principal's office. She wore a blue turtleneck sweater and black slacks with high-heeled boots, causing her to tower over the principal. She crossed her legs and tapped her toes the entire time she sat across from his desk, explaining to him this injustice that had befallen me. The next day we were all back in the principal's office: Mom, Laura Fry's dad, and me. He apologized. "I didn't mean nothing by it, kid." He wore a gray Champion sweatshirt with a hood, jeans, and work boots. His eyes were hard and cold, and he kicked the trash can near the door as he left the principal's office. But Mom was triumphant. "Thank you, Principal Hastings," she beamed. "These people have to learn to treat others with dignity and respect. This is America."

That night after dinner, she plopped down next to me in the living room. "We are going to learn about the Civil Rights Movement," she announced. "Bebe! Desi! Track!" she called out. "Come in here. We are going to learn about some important American history." And, just like that, we sat every night and watched all the episodes of *Eyes on the Prize* on WHDH.

I had heard a little bit about the Civil Rights Movement in school, enough to make me feel small and ashamed at the pity I felt emanating from my white classmates and their disbelief that these things happened in their America. But Mom's reaction to the images of lynching and lunch counter sit-ins were even more shocking. She wept, clutched her heart, clung to Aunt Bebe, and sometimes ran from the room when grainy violent scenes filled the screen. She hugged me tightly when the Emmett Till story was told, flinched each time an angry police or pro-segregation protester snarled on screen. "Oh, my Lord! Oh, my Lord," she cried out. "These are the things my father would talk about when I was small. I never knew it was that bad!"

"Your dad? My grandfather?" I asked, hoping she would tell me more. But she simply nodded, transfixed by the images on the screen.

"Hector, you must always stay far away from these racist kinds of people. They are evil. Evil! Do you understand?"

"Mom, my teacher said it's not like that anymore." But she was deaf to my voice, lost in a past of turmoil and trouble that triggered her tightly guarded memories. I had so many questions, but her face was a stone wall, completely blocking me out.

Chapter 6

When Mom finally graduated from Emmanuel College with her RN degree, she was twenty-eight but seemed so much older. From outward appearances, she could pass for a busy undergrad—wiry-limbed with smooth, orangey-brown skin and tiny dreads spilling down the middle of her back that she liked to hold back with colorful hair bands. Her face was slender, her nose strong, and her full, wide lips always painted the color of a plum. Yet she smiled little and always carried around a strong sense of purpose in her swift, straight-backed steps. Mom reigned over our family like a matriarch despite her lack of tenure. She was five years older than Uncle Track; Uncle Desi was next. Auntie Bebe was the youngest of the four and, although she was a married woman now, she still had the obedience of a child when it came to Mom. Auntie Bebe and Mr. Mohamed agreed without argument to chip in on the down payment for the triple-decker on Hawkins Street and took the third floor; Uncle Desi and his family took the second floor. Mom and I were on the first floor with a spare bedroom for when Uncle Track eventually got out of prison.

"It's better now," Mom rationalized about our new home. She painted a carved wooden sign above our mailbox: The Peterson Family. The house was a step up from Allston in that we were no longer renting, but we were definitely back in the hood. Still, I'd hear her on the phone with her work and school friends. "It's a really nice house. In the good part of Dorchester. Not too many renters on this street, and those gangbangers in Roxbury don't come over here."

By then "those people," our family members who we no longer talked to, had moved on to bigger and better things, from Medford to Littleton. From my determined eavesdropping I'd learned that Mom lived with her aunt when she first arrived in Boston in 1978, pregnant with me and her siblings trailing behind, all recently orphaned. That aunt, married to a white man (always whispered by Mom), had forgotten her roots and was now living in the lily-white west suburbs, where Mom would never visit. "How am I supposed to go all the way out there? She always say she want to see you but when last she come and visit us?" Mom was a nurse now, with her own car and her name on a house deed. She didn't give a lick what *those people* said about her, and she didn't want to waste time going to their stupid dinner party when she could be making money. Her own words.

I missed Allston though. I missed watching the howling, puking BU and BC students from my bedroom window on a Friday night. I missed the clank and clamor of the Green Line, the punk rockers standing outside The Rat, the candy row at the Store 24, and Mars Pizza Shop. Our new neighborhood was quiet; a long street with triple-decker and single-family homes close together with small yards in front and back. Some kids up the street had stared at me with a question in their eyes but I was too shy to go over and say hello as Mom urged me to. I'd begged Mom to keep me at Horace Mann, and she grumbled every morning we woke up at 5:30 so she could drive me there before her 7:00 a.m. shift at the hospital. "You're lucky you only have a year left else I would put you in one of the schools over here." I could think of nothing worse. My Horace Mann friends stared at me with a kind of respect and fear. "Your Mom made you move back to Dorchester? You guys are gonna get killed!" Uncle Desi said the next kid who said that to me should get a fist in his nose.

Auntie Bebe, still girlish and fun-loving, was a married woman now. Her husband, Mr. Olu Mohamed, worked seven days a week. I stood in for him on Sundays, wearing an uncomfortable tie and dress shoes, in the stilted pews of St. Cyprians with the Haitians, Bajans, Jamaicans, and other immigrants who were too dignified for the storefront churches that dotted Blue Hill and too foreign for the stalwart, historic Black churches along Warren Street.

Auntie Bebe and Uncle Desi had decent, middle-class jobs, took nice vacations to Florida and California and went to the Caribbean carnival in the Bronx every August. Indeed, the Petersons were all ascending in America, except one.

Mom used Uncle Track as a cautionary tale, to warn me about what could happen when people strayed too far away from family ways. "He thought he was an American," she'd say bitterly. "Running about with those drug dealers. See how fast they throw him in prison? He better hope they don't put him on a plane and send him back home." It was all his fault, according to Mom. At Jeremiah Burke High School, Uncle Track was ashamed of his foreigner sister, pregnant in the tenth grade. She was the big sister, but he was the main man at the Burke. Even in ninth grade, he was big and tall, man-sized even, and the B-Boys needed him for muscle. Uncle Track dropped out in eleventh grade and embarked on his life of crime, sporadically surfacing on weekends, holidays, summer cookouts with a new girl, a new car, a fancy chain and a leather jacket. He gave me my first pair of Air Jordans. Mom had no idea what they were else I'm sure she would have thrown them out as she did the gold chain he gave me for my fourteenth birthday.

Uncle Track's last court trial was in the Metro section of both the *Boston Globe* and *Herald*. He was one of three men sent to prison for robbing a liquor store, shooting and crippling the owner. Around the time of his sentencing, Mom took two weeks off from work and shut the door to her room, emerging once or twice a day for a few minutes.

"What's with her?" I asked Uncle Desi as we stood at her door for five minutes, knocking, knocking, knocking.

"Today is the anniversary of our parents' death," he shook his head. "And that thing with Track going on at the same time." We gave up. "Come upstairs."

I played video games with my cousins in Uncle Desi's apartment, starving and angry that Mom was right downstairs refusing to talk to me. Uncle Desi's wife was making ackee and saltfish and my empty stomach growled menacingly.

I wouldn't have been mad at her if she'd just told me. I wouldn't have banged on her door so hard when she refused to answer me. I wouldn't have called Uncle Desi to come downstairs to check on her to make sure she was alive. Crying and snotting like a little kid.

"Uncle Desi," I asked, almost begged him, "is she going to get better soon?" I couldn't bear the thought of her continuing to walk around like a zombie, overhearing her sobs in the night. He nodded without hesitating. "Yes. Give her a couple days." A year later she fell into the same funk.

Uncle Desi made me swear I'd never tell Mom as he drove down Route 1 to the men's prison at Walpole. My heart pounded as the landscape of Route 1 changed from car dealerships, furniture warehouses, and strip malls to desolate shrubbery the closer we got to the prison. I was terrified by the muscular guards, the drabness of the rural facility, the lost look in Uncle Track's unfocused eyes when they finally brought him out into the miserably freezing waiting area. For days afterward I'd remember the series of metal gates we passed through to reach his unit, each one taking us deeper and deeper into the belly of a beast, it seemed.

Uncle Track tried to smile as the burly, tight-faced guard ushered him out from the depths. Blue denim shirt, blue baggy jeans, and stark white no-brand sneakers. His eyes briefly lit up at the sight of Uncle Desi, but when he saw me, his shoulders drooped. I waved excitedly. The last time I saw him was before the trial. He sat down heavily, avoiding me and questioning Uncle Desi with his eyes. "Why you bring him here? He shouldn't be here. He just a kid."

"I'm not a little kid!" I shot back at Uncle Track, who glanced at me, startled.

"Little man," he sighed, "I ain't never want you to see me like this." He shook his head. "Desi, y'all go on back home." He stood; the baggy jeans were cheap, nothing close to the Girbaud or Guess he normally wore. "Take me back," he gestured evenly at the guard, no emotion in his voice.

Uncle Desi was silent as the guards led us out into the gray, clammy freedom outside. I was more disappointed than sad about Uncle Track. I believed what Mom said: that he could have made all the right choices just like Uncle Desi who had gone to college, gotten an office job, and still kept his barbershop business on the side. Naively, I believed that it was always simple to just make the right choice, like deciding to shut the door or to leave it open.

I asked Uncle Desi, "You think Mom would feel better if she went back to Dominica?"

He shook his head. "I don't know. I myself don't really want to go back. Life has to move on. I don't really have nothing back there except memories."

"What about my father?" I asked him. "He's back there still, right?"

He shrugged. "I don't know, Hector." He sighed. "I really don't know."

I was in my last year of middle school and had already grown tired of my own questions about my father.

Chapter 7

One day before I meet my father

I was baking in the grass at Fort Adams State Park that blazing hot Saturday. Middle-aged bankers, lawyers, and doctors in tank tops and baggy shorts danced, drank, flirted, and wilted under the cloudless sky as pleasure boats of all sizes bobbed in shimmery blue Newport Harbor. Jean removed his glasses and emptied a Poland Springs bottle over his head, panting. "This tradition really needs to come to an end. Let's just shoot it and put it out of its misery once and for all this year."

Coach Dan was twirling Ms. Mary around, not self-conscious at all, near the stage where Arturo Sandoval's trumpet warbled and wailed over the tipsy, sweaty rainbow crowd. "The sexiest sixty-year-olds alive," Jean snorted.

We'd been coming to the festival since high school when Coach Dan introduced us to his passion for jazz. For four years we'd lived in the man's house, we had no choice but to board the bebop train with him.

"So, your father is coming to your house for dinner? Why does this sound like a made-for-TV drama?"

I'd told Jean the same night Mom told me a couple weeks ago. Since middle school, Jean and I had never succeeded at making any other real friends. Those afternoons spent waiting for our mothers in the stockroom at the Allston Purity Supreme had created a bond that, despite my initial resistance, only grew stronger over the years. Even when Jean went off to Western Mass for college, we talked almost every day. Mr. Desrosiers and Ms. Patrice remained fixtures of every holiday dinner or summer cookout, bringing Haitian black rice and fried fish each time. It was to the point where people asked if we were related.

"Yep," I tried to joke my way out of getting too deep. "That means I got two major events in one year. You're getting hitched and I'm finally getting a father."

Jean shrugged. "Overrated."

"What? Getting hitched?" Jean and Mayowa met in tenth grade. I was there the first day she ordered him to join the Students of Color Network in our very white suburban high school.

"No," Jean shook his head. "Fathers. They can be vastly overrated." Mr. Desrosiers had carefully engineered and charted Jean's every path in life, including the fact that Jean was surely headed to Tufts Medical School next fall whether he liked it or not.

"Mr. D still ain't coming to your wedding?"

Mr. Desrosiers was angry that Jean and Mayowa were getting married before Jean had his MD in hand. But unplanned babies had a way of disrupting grand career plans.

"Don't care." Jean frowned. "Whatever you do, don't ever let your father think he has complete control over your life. Assert your independence early and often."

I chuckled at Jean's squinty-eyed, bespectacled face, seasoned a deep brown in the summer sun. He had grown more bookish and nebbish over the years, but he would hurt me in the paint if I even tried him—and wouldn't apologize. In high school, our running joke was that he was Isiah Thomas and I was MJ.

"Here they come," he said as Coach Dan and Ms. Mary walked toward us holding hands and laughing.

"You boys should get something to drink," Coach Dan said. He hadn't coached in maybe twenty years but was still in good shape, tanned, tall and lanky, with gray hairs sprouting from each side of his baseball hat.

"I'll go!" Jean leapt up.

Ms. Mary glanced at Coach Dan. "Why don't I go with you, Jean?"

Jean wiped his sweaty forehead off with a towel, his baggy shorts and T-shirt sticking to him. Ms. Mary rubbed Jean's shoulder, causing her bracelets to fall down her arm. Her peasant dress and waist-length brown hair gave her the trademark hippie look that was so opposite of Coach Dan's retired athlete persona. As soon as they were a few yards away, he cleared his throat, and I steeled myself for a "Coach Dan talk."

"You holding up okay, Hec?" Coach eased into one of the lawn chairs we'd lugged from the van that morning. I shrugged. Whatever I said would be scrutinized, analyzed, and therapy would be recommended. Story of my life since high school.

"Listen, Hector. As you know, your mother and I don't talk much these days."

Understatement of the year! I shifted in the grass; the last thing I wanted to hear about was the saga between Coach Dan and Mom. I still felt a sense of guilt and betrayal every time Ms. Mary winced at just the mention of Mom.

He adjusted his baseball hat. His face was reddening from the sun. "But I'm glad . . . so glad she found your father. I just worry." He cleared his throat again. "I don't want you to get your hopes up too high. You've lived nineteen, twenty years of your life without him."

"I know," I said. "I'm kinda blasé about the whole thing, actually," I lied. Blasé, yeah. Everyone around us was blasé, I thought, as a couple giggled and groped each other as they sunk to a towel on the grass. That's what jazz, booze, and ocean breeze did to people, right? Blasé all the way. The truth was, until I saw my father with my own two eyes, I would have to be prepared that this still could be one of Mom's stunts. That this could be her biggest, cruelest lie. And the closer the day drew, the more I began to mentally plan for the disappointment and how I would deal. Would I leave her, never speak to her again, never return to Boston?

"No. No. Don't say that." He grabbed a sandwich out of the cooler; his spotted, wrinkled hands quickly pulled away layers of cellophane. "It's a big deal, Hector. And you have to be prepared for your life to change in a big way. Emotionally, for sure."

A slight breeze ruffled my shirt, bringing little relief from the heat. I don't know what was making me sweat more, the sun or this conversation.

"If you want, I highly recommend you talk to someone. It would help you process the . . . transition. You know? Accept things, however they turn out."

"Thanks, Coach," I smiled at him. "I'll think about it."

His eyes were sad, slowing my cavalier reaction. Did he think my meeting Dad would affect our relationship? I hadn't even considered that. What he said next caused me to bite my lip hard.

"You're a fine young man, Hector. You're going to be a great success. And you did it all by yourself. Don't ever forget that."

I pawed the green grass, which was still cool despite the unrelenting sun, trying hard to distract from the knot forming in my throat.

"From the day we took you and Jean in, I knew you were special. Yeah, I was hoping you'd bring Southbury High to the state championships," he chuckled. He gripped my shoulder firmly. "No matter what happens with your Dad, don't forget the distance you've already come on your own."

We sat watching the stage, listening to Arturo Sandoval for several long minutes.

The distance I came? I can hardly measure it.

One Saturday when we were still living in Allston, I must have been in sixth or seventh grade, Mr. Desrosiers came over with a shopping bag full of papers and brochures and sat Mom down at the dining table. For two hours,

I strained to eavesdrop as my toddler cousins screamed and fought in our shared bedroom. I peeked out and saw Mr. D showing Mom how to apply for METCO and the tests for the Boston exam schools. I had no say in the matter. I thought I'd end up at Brighton High like most of my working class Horace Mann classmates, who saw school as a sentence to be served until their fathers or uncles got them onto the Boston Fire or Police Department or in construction or into some low-level City Hall job. At Horace Mann Middle, I vaguely knew I wanted to be a businessman, like the smooth characters in the movies I watched with Auntie Bebe—Eddie Murphy in *Boomerang*, Will Smith in *Bad Boys*. I knew from Uncle Track's legal problems that a glorified ghetto lifestyle was not for me. But I had no plan or vision to achieve those aspirations beyond the empty advice and vague encouragement from middle-school teachers to just keep working hard. I had wrongly assumed that life would simply fall into place if I just kept showing up to school every day. That's how America worked, Mom said, work hard and you will succeed. Thank God for Mr. Desrosiers, who held a more realistic view of the American Dream.

Mom celebrated like she'd won the lottery when I gained a spot in METCO, a high-school integration program which was supposed to be a kinder, gentler version of busing after the horrors of the late seventies. The following September, Jean and I began at Southbury High School, among a handful of Black kids, in the quietly wealthy, rural school system worlds away from Boston.

In some ways, Southbury felt like a prison sentence. In my freshman year, I came home every weekend fighting tears and full of rage. But Mom would hear none of it. "You have to be out there and mingle, Hector. Make friends. Go and see movies with them and things like that. Laugh at their jokes," she lectured me daily. There were only two choices for me in America: education or prison, if I was lucky. Her eyes darkened intensely and her hands shook when she delivered those speeches to me. "If you knew how I grew up," she would pause, take a deep breath and collect herself. "It's not just about getting a good job and getting rich, Hector. I don't care about that. I don't want you to become a target, lying dead on the street or in prison like your uncle."

But she could never understand the misery of being one of five Black inner-city kids in a rich white school, unceremoniously dumped there by a system relieving itself of decades of bad policy and centuries of injustice. How was that not being a target?

I roamed the streets of Boston on weekends with vague acquaintances from the neighborhood who were making realer, cooler friends at Madison Park and Jeremiah Burke where their identity and sense of belonging was as sure as the sidewalk beneath our feet. I stood outside with them at the Chez Vous skating rink on Saturday nights and called out to girls wearing tight Guess jeans and large hoop earrings. Those girls' eyes glazed over when I told them where I went to high school, and they turned to my neighborhood friends, who looked right through me, chanting Wu-Tang rhymes at my problems.

Monday to Friday after school and basketball, I moped around in Coach Dan and Ms. Mary's large rambling house surrounded by woods, bugs, and persistent deer. I spent my days in class bewildered and annoyed by the inordinate amount of friendliness and kindness showered on me, like I was an alien invader who couldn't possibly grasp my host school's complex ways. Dumb kids offered to tutor me, even after I repeatedly got all the answers correct when called on. I complained to Mom about it. "Hector, you will always look for something wrong. They are just being nice. Why you cannot just accept that? You want them to be mean to you?"

Life became a Lego structure with every piece needing to fit perfectly in its correct place. Coach Dan had made it his life's work to board inner-city kids from the METCO program. Ms. Mary had been a high-school teacher and still substituted now that they were empty nesters. Jean and I, not wanting to admit our homesickness, shared a very large bedroom in the cavernous house with its built-in speakers that piped saxophone jazz all day long.

Every night we ate dinner under a crystal chandelier at 7:30 p.m. After Coach Dan or Ms. Mary said grace, we ate with napkins on our laps and talked about what happened at school and what was in the *Boston Globe* or the evening news. If there was a gap in the conversation, Coach Dan talked about Pharaoh Sanders, Sun Ra, or some other jazz artist he was rediscovering or obsessed with at the moment.

The shrieking bugs did nothing to quell the screaming silence of those suburban nights. I missed the streets, the sirens, the booming sound systems, the neighbors calling out to each other from windows. I called Mom every night despite her brushing off my every gripe and complaint. "Maybe you would have gotten into Boston Latin if I was more like Coach Dan. The change is good for you."

I kept up the complaining for two years straight. Southbury was too white, too quiet. The crickets and frogs were creepy and kept me up all night. The Southbury kids were too different from the Polish, Irish, and Italian kids at Horace Mann. They asked dumb questions or said dumb things about my clothes, my hair, about the city, about what I was listening to on my Walkman. They got cars for their birthdays. Their parents actually gave them condoms and let them have sex at home. They thought everything in the world belonged to them. "You have to get used to it," Mom said. "When you go to college how you think it's going to be? That's how the real world works, Hector!"

Jean and I never felt 100 percent comfortable in Southbury. In fact, I only completely let my guard down when we were goofing off in our room or shooting hoops in the backyard with Coach. I would say that hip-hop saved me in those years. Mom bought me a Walkman for my sixteenth birthday and every extra penny I scraped up went to tapes and CDs. On weekends, I spent hours at Skippy White's and Tower Music browsing through rap and R&B titles. I listened to EPMD's *Strictly Business* so many times the tape broke. "You're bobbing your head like a madman," Jean said, elbowing me in the hall between classes. I closed my ears to the sounds, blinded my eyes to the life at Southbury High School, and became completely immersed in a world peopled by Eric B. & Rakim, Big Daddy Kane, and the Audio Two. That world at least felt familiar. Our street in Dorchester was not Brooklyn, but it was close enough for me to see and hear myself in those staccato rhymes and beats that dug deep, creating a protective, comforting moat around my soul.

Back at Horace Mann, I'd eventually retreated from wanting to be in the in-crowd and found my home among other nerdy or immigrant kids. At Southbury, I only wanted to survive and get out. Grades became mission No. 1. Basketball fell to a distant third or lower, even though it was one of the few activities that made me feel myself. But I needed to shatter and silence the condescending stares and comments, real or imagined, that shouted I was out of my league.

Still, by junior year I began to find my way. The high school was a well-equipped, well-funded structure paid for by tax brackets I couldn't have imagined at the time. Most of the teachers hovered over us like protective hens, and I stopped resisting their coddling when I realized their priorities lined up with mine—high SAT score and a good college. My favorite teacher, a Dorchester native, checked in on me daily. Ms. Denzil, red-haired and round, would say, "Us Dot natives gotta stick togethah, Hectwah." She baked brownies for our algebra class and sneaked me extra plates of chocolate chip cookies.

Jean and I walked the halls, took classes, and did everything together until he fell hard for Mayowa. She was Nigerian, and her parents were medical students at Tufts, new immigrants just like us. Jean and I were heading to class when he saw her braids, dark skin, and heard her accented voice loudly proclaiming that it was too damned cold in this school. That's what he said anyway; I don't really remember. "She doesn't give a damn what people think. She doesn't want to be like them at all." "Them" being the kids atop the power and social structure at Southbury.

Mayowa, who had grown up in Lagos and either didn't accept or understand the social order of our school, began to invite herself and us to parties. She became the president of the Students of Color Network and began to host parties at her parents' rented colonial in the least fancy section of the town. I reluctantly joined the SCN—by then seven or eight of us—but I still went home some weekends.

Mom and I would drive to the Braintree mall on Saturday afternoons and I'd gaze at girls for hours while she rifled the racks at Macy's and Lord & Taylor. She would open up her shopping bags as we ate pizza at the food court or got clam chowder at the Legal Sea Foods. "What you think about this dress? I'm wearing it tonight." She never told me who she was dating, and I didn't ask. I was too preoccupied with the bunches of girls—Black, white, Puerto Rican, Vietnamese—roaming the mall. Hordes of them, so many types. It was dizzying. I began to look forward to these torturous mall trips, dreaming of these girls during class and as Coach drove me home on Friday afternoons.

Then Danielle Foster came along.

Nerd that I was, I lost my virginity in a classroom, thanks to her. Danielle had been flirting with me all year, or so I suspected from the crazed screeching and giggling when she and her friends walked by Jean and me. She had her own car and lived in one of those houses way, way back from the road, their opulence hidden and protected by a forest of trees and an interminable driveway.

The annual Fall Formal was held in the school gym, decorated in harvest colors meant to resemble the town which exploded in rust, orange, red, and gold for a good six weeks. "Aren't the leaves just glorious?" Ms. Mary would ask every morning as she ate breakfast on the back patio overlooking the woods. "I guess," I would shrug. Later in life, I would take my wife on three-hour drives just to gaze at fall foliage.

Danielle and I circled around each other, pretending and ignoring. She was with her group of friends at the dance and I with mine from the SCN. The chasm between us was oh so fraught, so wide. Danielle, biracial, had chosen not to join the Students of Color Network, which made her name mud to our more militant members. But she was always sweet and friendly to me—more than I could say for the girls in our group. I didn't quite get that; I was taller than most of them and I dressed okay. Yeah, I was shy and could clam up sometimes but that gave them no right to act like I didn't even exist.

Danielle didn't wait for me to ask, but walked right over to our group, grinning all the way while parting a curtain of wavy brown hair away from her face. She asked me to dance "later on, when something danceable comes on."

Hundreds of pairs of eyes burned into us as Danielle shimmied and shook and gyrated against me to Sheryl Crow's "All I Wanna Do." Vindication surged powerfully. A tidal wave of courage took over, and I pulled her to me, causing her to stumble and giggle. Danielle was pretty and slim, full of freckles and a wide smile, popular enough to make other boys jealous. The girls, too, who wouldn't give me the time of day. So I pulled out every dance move I picked up from my cousins, summer cookouts, and BET videos. I actually was enjoying myself, maybe for the first time since I came to Southbury. Danielle was direct and demanding, leading me by the hand into an empty classroom and grinding her hips against me. I fell hard in love with her that night, I suppose, and began spending less weekends at home.

Just like that, I had a girlfriend. It was a weird, comforting feeling that relieved most of my fears about "those other girls." They didn't matter as much anymore—their approval or lack thereof. Danielle was chatty, bossy, trivial, and strange, but it didn't matter. I simply went along with her MTV and *Beverly Hills 90210* obsessions while envying Jean and Mayowa's arguments about whether Haitian Kompa music originated in Nigeria or Benin.

Danielle's parents let me call them by their first names. Her mother—a confident, fit, blonde investment banker—worked in New York and came home some weekends. Her father, a dark-skinned nerd just like me, worked in software sales and traveled most of the time. He offered me a case of beer one Friday night before they went away for the weekend, leaving Danielle and me alone in their four-bedroom colonial. He seemed exhausted most of the time and spoke very little. "Don't go driving with Danielle around here after dark," he warned me. "The cops know me, but they don't know you."

Danielle stepped between us, raising her voice above his. "Really, Dad? I mean, really?" He shrugged, grabbed his keys and left. He was like no other Black man I had ever or would ever meet.

Mom was skeptical. "You using protection?" she flat-out asked me one Friday when I drunkenly told her I'd be staying in Southbury for the weekend. "Don't let those little hussies ruin your life, Hector. I worked too hard! You know how many hours I broke my back at those nursing homes? Don't end up broke on my couch or in prison like your uncle because of some fast little girl!" When Danielle asked if she could meet my mother, I said no.

The stress of college applications and longing for senior year loomed and eventually I came up for air from my carnal adventures with Danielle. It was then I realized that Coach Dan had never stopped driving to Boston on Friday evenings, even though I hardly went home on weekends anymore. Ms. Mary had also begun to act strange. She would seek me out, away from Coach Dan or Jean, always asking about Mom and our family.

One Saturday after Danielle had left my room where we'd supposedly been doing homework all afternoon, Ms. Mary cornered me in the kitchen. "So, Hector, I've been doing some research on your island."

"Ma'am?" I had no idea what she was getting at, and I did have a lot of studying to do. Unlike Jean and Mayowa, who pushed each other to work hard and succeed, Danielle and I brought out the slacker in each other except when it came to sex.

"Dominica?" Her eyebrows arched.

"Um . . . I've never been there."

"I know," Ms. Mary laughed. "But you really ought to get more into it. It could really help your college essays."

"Yeah? You think so?"

"Of course! Did you know that your island elected its first female prime minister in 1980?" And on and on she went with the trivia.

"Your mom," she paused. "Such a strong, determined woman."

I nodded.

"And beautiful, too. So beautiful." Ms. Mary smiled at me with only her mouth. "Your father must have been an idiot to leave her."

I shrugged. "I've never met him."

She stared at me, not saying anything for several long moments.

"But wouldn't you like to know more about him?" Her eyes were large and gray. Ms. Mary was always well put together in a sort of flower-child way, loved by everyone in the town and the school community. Her hurt and confused expression made me want to flee the room.

"Mom doesn't like to talk about it," I said, putting away the orange juice, which I suddenly no longer wanted. "She doesn't like to talk about the past."

Ms. Mary nodded. "But she talks about everything to Dan, doesn't she?"

"She does?" The conversation was a big ocean and I was flailing about trying to stay afloat. Mom and Coach Dan did talk a lot on the phone, I guessed. But I always assumed they were talking about me.

Ms. Mary nodded. "He told me she grew up in a commune? Did you know that?"

I shook my head. A commune? Was that like the places hippies went to during the 1960s? Ms. Mary had to be confused. I made up an excuse about having to study and went to my room.

Danielle broke up with me on the cusp of senior year and began to parade around the halls with a new METCO boy. He was from Roxbury, Howland Street, just a few blocks away from our house. He played football, spoke in street slang, bragged about seeing gangbangers selling crack in broad daylight, and the girls began to compete over him. He was a nice guy, and I liked him, even though I knew for sure that Howland Street wasn't as bad as he made it sound. He joined the SCN with no fuss although he never attended any meetings. Soon, the football team and the rich kids snapped him up, and he was lost to our tiny misfit group of Black and brown students. And Danielle was lost to me.

I began to go back home every weekend again, guilty that I was more heartbroken by the rejection letters from Columbia and NYU than Danielle dumping me. The fact is, I didn't miss the countless hours of meaningless conversation; her cavalier assumption that I was lucky to be with her; her lack of interest in my life outside Southbury. Years later, I would struggle to remember her exact dimensions, the shape of her nose and mouth, her likes, dislikes, and even the color of her eyes. Without really trying, she got into Wellesley College where her mom attended. I had a full ride from Fordham and most of my safeties in New England. Both Coach Dan and Mom said I should go to Williams and we'd find a way to pay for it. By that time, it was clear to me that Coach Dan and Mom were more than just friends.

One August Saturday at 3:00 a.m. I watched from the window as Mom stumbled out of Coach Dan's car and into the house. I stood in the middle of the living room waiting, shaking with fear. I meant to confront her and ask her what was going on. My heart raced faster and faster as I heard her key turn in the lock.

She froze when our eyes met. My mouth opened but no words came as she leaned on the door handle. I stared at her: the low-cut black dress, the high-heeled shoes, the smudged makeup. She dropped her purse on the floor and strode to where I stood in front of the fireplace, clenched her teeth and jabbed at my chest with her index finger. "Mind your damned business! Okay?" She stalked off to her room and slammed the door.

I stayed awake, staring blindly at ESPN for hours and hours of replays and meaningless commentary. I'd mistakenly thought that the city, the hood, was my sanctuary, my refuge. But Southbury had invaded, trespassed into my real life. How could she do it? How could he? The hours ticked on and my anger took shape, like a ball rolling down a hill, picking up speed and kinetic energy. I wanted to pound on her door and demand the truth about my father, demand that she stop telling lies and ruining things for Coach Dan and Ms. Mary who'd been so nice to us. My room grew stifling and I threw off my damp T-shirt. I hated Southbury at that moment—every stately colonial, farmhouse, emerald-green pastoral meadow, horse farm, and ice cream stand of it.

∾

Ms. Mary held a graduation party for Jean and me. "Guys, invite anyone you want. Yes, your entire family!" And, boy, did we.

Red-faced and evasive, Coach Dan took up his post near the grill with one eye on Mom as she nervously greeted my classmates. The boys gawked at her tight capri jeans and yellow halter top that revealed her muscled arms and cleavage. She'd only shrugged when I told her it could get chilly and she should wear a sweater. Uncle Desi gave out business cards for his barbershop without a hint of embarrassment. Auntie Bebe tried in vain to corral my cousins from running into everything and everyone in the yard. It was chaos but I didn't care. "We did it!" I high-fived Jean as he scooped a burger from a table laden with grub.

"No offense, Coach," Jean said. "But I'm never coming back to this countrified town again."

Mr. Desrosiers, Coach Dan, and Uncle Desi chatted near the grill over burgers and hot dogs, handing out platters. Pillowy clouds floated in a guileless blue sky above; the breeziness made June feel like early spring, the kind of day New Englanders described as "good sleeping weather."

I had never heard so much laughter from Coach's neighbors and my classmates' folks. They knocked back beers, tossed Frisbees, and threw footballs with us kids. It had taken four whole years for me to see that they were normal people who could actually let loose and have a good time. Maybe I'd been wrong about them all along. Maybe my time at Southbury could have been different if I had taken Mom's advice earlier on. She really was enjoying herself, shaking hands, tapping shoulders, laughing, laughing, never glancing at Coach even once.

Uncle Desi asked Coach Dan if he could play one of the CDs he'd brought, and we turned the pleasant quiet-storm-jazz garden party into a scene from *House Party*. Even Mom got in on the action and danced with me and a couple of the boys from class, who wanted their pictures taken with her. "Your mom is a fox," one of them slurred.

I'd just slid into a makeshift base, getting damp grass all over my shorts, when I saw Mom and Ms. Mary huddling in the kitchen, wine glasses in their hands. I leapt up from the grass. "I'll be right back." The guys cursed as I fled the game.

They stood across from each other at the counter wrapped in deep conversation. I could only stare at the picture framed by the glass doors: Ms. Mary, tall and ethereal peering down at Mom, who stood erect, balancing her athletic frame on platform sandals, dreads grazing the center of her back. My heart pounded as I debated whether to barge in and stop whatever storm was brewing. Before I could do anything, Jean came up from behind and dragged me into a Super Soaker shootout. Later I asked Mom what they talked about and she shrugged. "Nothing. Typical nosy white woman."

We didn't get back to Hawkins Street till around eleven that night. I was exhausted, relieved the party came and went without a scene from Mom.

Uncle Desi knocked on our door. "Old man," he said, poking his head in, "take a shower and get dressed. We going to a real party now."

Uncle Desi was known from Seaver Street to Four Corners and all the way into Codman Square because he'd cut folks' hair or their kids' hair. Tall and wiry like Mom, Uncle Desi could be stylish when he set his mind to it. Tonight, he was dressed to the nines in a gray suit, satin gray tie, and white shirt. I felt shabby in my black slacks and boring maroon shirt. At least he'd let me wear one of his simple gold watches. We drove down Columbia Road and turned down Mass. Avenue, the stereo in his pearly Beemer thumping the bass line from Pete Rock & CL Smooth's "They Reminisce Over You."

"My man!" Uncle Desi held out the keys to his BMW to a young guy who called him "boss." My nerves were a mess as we entered an industrial build-ing in one of the darkest, shadiest sections of Mass. Avenue. R&B music was pounding, and I couldn't distinguish the thudding between my heartbeat and the bass. The doorman pulled Uncle Desi into a hug and let the two of us into the club without asking for ID or a cover charge.

Girls poured into tiny dresses teetered past us up a dark flight of stairs. Purple, green, and red strobe lights streaked across the dance floor, where a tightly packed crowd swayed and popped to Keith Sweat and Guy. Uncle Desi was hand-shaking, hugging, and fist-bumping guys, some dressed in suits, some more casual, most surrounded by beautiful Black and brown girls. It felt like I was in a movie, as if I'd entered a dream world. Where had this place been the last four years of my life?

All of my high-school years, I'd struggled with a double existence. When I came home on the weekends, I spent most Saturdays sleeping or at SAT tutoring, sometimes I went to St. Cyprians on Sunday with Auntie Bebe. I never fully submitted myself to the rhythms of the city; I lived solely within my family. Neighborhood boys I'd known faded out of my sightline the longer I stayed at Southbury. My "friends" were Southbury boys from the basketball team whose lives were too different for me to try to find any common ground. I'd visited their homes on occasion, but none had come to Boston to visit mine. I didn't care to try skiing or camping more than two or three times, and eventually they stopped asking. I wasn't even as connected as Jean, who was part of a close-knit and powerful Haitian community.

Entering this dark nightclub was like stepping into the light. I felt known, accounted for, recognized. A feeling beyond words. Guys who looked like me—dark, medium brown, tall, short—nodded or just held out a fist in greeting. No one's eyes seemed to question why I was there. All I knew was I felt completely and utterly okay in this place full of Black and brown strangers. The guardrails I'd placed around my emotions during four years of integrated high school began to shudder and fall as Rob Base rocked the house.

One hour into my first night at the Gallery, I was fidgeting on the sidelines holding a beer and staring at a petite girl with an Anita Baker haircut dancing like a pro with two other girls. She was maple-syrup colored and athletic looking, like she'd done gymnastics as a kid. She was barely over 5'2", so teeny from where I stood.

"You having a good time?" Uncle Desi was behind me. "Your mother's not here to spy on you. Loosen up."

I couldn't take my eyes off that one girl. Soon, another girl, as tall as me and wearing a tight, short shiny skirt, bumped against me. "Wanna dance?" I would have said no but she dragged me onto the dance floor. She barely noticed my wooden movements as she shimmied and twirled and did all sorts of moves I'd only seen in music videos. Before I knew it, I was next to the teeny girl with the short hair. Without thinking, I elbowed her, not enough to hurt I hoped. She whirled around, a spark in her eye. "Watch it, man!"

"I'm sorry. Really sorry."

She shifted away, rolling her eyes.

"Can I buy you a drink to make up for it?" I yelled over the music.

She looked me over skeptically. "I can't drink." She held out her bare wrist.

I laughed. "Neither can I. My uncle gave me his wristband."

"You want to dance then? That's my jam!" Her smile was wide, and her perfect teeth bit the corner of her lip. Relief washed over me as her friend disappeared into the tight crowd.

Hopefully, my terrible dancing wouldn't ruin my good luck.

So there we were. Leandra Martin, recent graduate of Boston Latin School, and I dancing the night away. Well, she danced, and I shuffled around bobbing my head to an SWV song. Five songs later, my underarms were soaked, and she was fanning her glistening face. I followed her off the dance floor and asked her name as Total and Biggie made the dance floor rumble.

Years later, Leandra would say that I never made any sacrifices for her, but she was so wrong. Until that Saturday night, I was 100 percent sure I was headed to Williams College. On Monday morning I called Northeastern

University, where Leandra was to start as a freshman that fall, and asked the admissions office if it was too late to apply. Mom almost had a heart attack when I told her, but she got over it.

Being with Leandra was like floating in a warm pool compared to the freezing, roiling waters of Southbury. The summer before college, she taught me how to be comfortable in my Black skin. I didn't have to apologize, explain, or pretend with Leandra. We spent hours talking at the McDonald's on Warren Street, sharing one medium shake and fries. We rode the bus downtown or walked to the Corner Mall to her summer job at Tello's. Southbury began to evaporate in the summer heat. I followed her everywhere, to the Middle East in Central Square, to taquerias in West Cambridge. Some Saturdays we sat in the grass outside the Abbotsford in Roxbury, staring at sculpture, talking and dreaming about building an indestructible place for ourselves in the world. Ironically, I was certainly wildly out of my league when it came to Leandra. She knew it, I knew it, and we spent the entire summer dancing and laughing about it.

Mom rolled her eyes when I told her about Leandra. "She's an American girl? Hmmph."

I had to come clean. "She can be kinda moody," I warned Leandra one Friday night on our way to Club Avalon.

Leandra was undeterred. "It's okay. So am I." I shrugged off my fear of Mom, absorbing and feeding off Leandra's confidence.

Eventually, Leandra swept into our house on Hawkins Street with a gift bag of scented oils from a little shop in Jamaica Plain. Mom's suspicious glare softened into a smile. "That lady in the store? She's my good friend. Yes, I've known her for years! Wow. These smell so good."

My sigh of relief could have rippled through the ceiling paint. Mom took Leandra's hand. "Come, come! Sit down. Hector, go get your friend something to drink."

"No, Ms. Peterson. Let me help you in the kitchen. I've been cooking for my family since I was eleven," Leandra said, following Mom into the kitchen and winking at me.

I swallowed the lump in my throat as the two of them cackled in laughter. This was Leandra—she got things done. And I fully signed on for the ride, determined never to look back.

We volunteered with the Urban League, joined MLK community cleanup drives, served in student government in our freshman year. We applied for and got every internship possible. She knew she wanted to be a lawyer; I was less sure of what I wanted to be. One thing I did know was that I wanted to be a man who commanded respect, with my beautiful wife at my side, and a big house and a yard like Coach Dan's, and lots of children. I wanted Leandra and I to be like the couples on TV, the Huxtables. She was the one who suggested I go to business school.

Our last year of college, Mom was still grieving the end of her affair with Coach Dan. I had gotten into Northeastern business school and Leandra into BU law school. We were planning a trip to Europe over Labor Day, and I planned to propose to her in Paris. Then Mom told me about my father.

Chapter 8

I woke up sick to my stomach the day I was to meet my father. The economics paper stalling and sputtering on page two was already five days overdue. Empty bottles of Heineken hidden under my bed mocked me as I bent over the side, hugging my middle. I'd sunk to my lowest low and called Leandra.

She immediately let me know what was up. "I told you last night to let me help you but you said no." Obviously, she was down to her last nerve. "You need to get hold of yourself. This is the last paper, then we're done with the stupid class. Come on, Hector."

She asked again if I wanted her to come over there. No, I insisted. Mom being there will make things hard enough. The hours crept on, slowly even for a summer Sunday. Mom looked into my room every hour. "You okay?" Her eyes were darting, her breaths shallow. She was as nervous as I was. How many more times could I check the time? I showered at three. Showered again at four thirty because I'd sweated through my shirt. Geez. Couldn't Mom just get central AC like a civilized human being?

At exactly 5:00 p.m. the doorbell rang and, like a spooked four-year-old, I turned straight back for my bedroom, almost sprinting, my heart pounding out of my shirt. Mom reached out and grabbed my arm, pulling me back into the living room. "Come on, Hector," she sighed.

I shook her off and fled to the kitchen where I gulped down a glass of water over the sink.

"Hector! Come back here!"

My heart galloped as if I'd been chased up and down the basketball court. I leaned on the counter, my breath fogging up the face of the microwave. The heavy front door groaned, creaked, and whined, and heavy footsteps sounded. She invited him in more than once. "Come in. Come in, Winston." Then I heard a man's low voice greeting her, saying, how are you, Jemma.

I wiped my sweaty hands on my jeans, swallowed a roomful of air and walked out into the living room as she called out my name.

He stood at the entry of the living room in the middle of the doorframe, the large canvas watercolor of daises on the wall behind him and the bucket of umbrellas at his side. My eyes burned, then watered. In those few seconds—before my reflexes or my pride told me to look away, don't stare like an idiot, I realized that he was me: the walnut skin and roundish dark brown eyes; wide, flat yet dignified nose. Me but older. Slightly taller. Balding and kind of bent at the shoulders. I must have smiled or something because he said, "Hello, Hector."

Our eyes met and I saw the long eyelashes—like mine, which I'd never noticed until Leandra pronounced them one of my finer features. He had thick eyebrows and a wide mouth that slightly turned down at the corners. His face was long but sort of full. A serious looking face. Not handsome, not ugly. Yes. He was my father.

My entire body was itchy with blooms of perspiration.

"Nice to meet you, Hector." He grabbed my hand and shook it formally. "I am Winston. Winston Telemacque." He raised his eyebrows when he spoke, as if asking a question.

"Telemacque?" His voice was deeper than Mr. Desrosiers's and his accent even thicker.

He reminded me of the actor Delroy Lindo.

"That was my mother's last name," he said, showing a row of straight white teeth. "It's how we do it in the islands when the parents don't marry."

"Same thing here," Mom said way too brightly. "Come, Hector! Winston! Sit down! I made a pelau. But sit here for now." She patted the sofa. "Do you want something to drink? I still don't eat meat, but I cook meat all the time for everybody." She grinned at him. "They wore me down a long time ago. I have fish, too, if you want!"

"Who is they?" he asked, placing wide hands with long fingers into his pockets. His dark brown slacks were baggy; his brown shoes looked expensive. He was wearing a blue collared shirt, like I was. He remained standing, looking around the room awkwardly, until Mom sat in the armchair across from us. We eventually sat, a full cushion between us, on the living room couch.

"Desi, Track, and Bebe. You remember my brothers and sister?" Mom had painted her nails pink, matching her lips and cheeks. She wore her dreads down, parted on the right, making her look much younger than her thirty-seven years. She hadn't looked this beautiful since the Coach Dan days, I thought.

"They live here with you?" He looked confused but the smile remained.

She fingered the edge of the armrest, crossing and uncrossing her legs, her dress falling away from her legs each time. I leaned back heavily, wanting her to settle down, to stop squirming around so nervously.

"So, where are they? Your brothers and sisters." He asked this in a hushed voice, as if he could hurt her with his words.

"Desi lives on the second floor with his family and Bebe lives upstairs. She has three kids. Two in high school now. Her husband is an African, a nice man."

He squinted. "What about the other one?"

"Track?" She glanced at me and then back at him. "He's away. We're not that close anymore."

He nodded. "That's good the rest of you all live so close together."

Mom lifted her gaze, her expression pensive. Slowly, her eyes focused on the wall with the framed photos of our family, the ones she put out—not the ones she kept under her bed that I found only last week. The ones with her, Uncle Desi, Uncle Track, and Auntie Bebe when they were very small. The ones taken in a field or a village with two adults, all of them wearing loose, long clothes and dreadlocks down to their backs. Even Auntie Bebe who couldn't have been more than five years old. I assumed the adults were her parents, my grandparents. The people we did not talk about. Was that where her mind had gone now? Did seeing my father take her back there? I was used to these faraway spells of hers so I looked to see how he was taking it in. He cast his eyes down after several moments. I cleared my throat and she snapped out of it. I piped up awkwardly, "Mom, you brought out all the nice plates you normally keep in the cabinet."

"Okay. What you want to drink, Winston? I don't have alcohol. Hector keeps beer and those things in his room even though he's not supposed to."

"Mom!"

She disappeared into the kitchen and we were left alone.

He laughed and clasped his hands together. "I still cannot believe it," he said slowly, his eyes trained on me. "You look just like I used to look when I was really young."

His curious stare was unnerving, like he was assessing my every trait and feature. Maybe he had doubts; maybe he was looking for the lie or the proof.

"You can call me whatever you want." He straightened up. "Most people call me Mr. Winston or Mr. W."

"Okay," I said. "Who calls you Mr. W?"

"Mostly the employees." He paused and looked at the doorway where Mom disappeared. "I run a couple of donut shops. Did she tell you?"

She'd told me he was a businessman but I didn't follow up, not wanting to rely on another of Mom's half-truths. I wanted to forget every image of him I'd based on her half-truths: evil villain, drug kingpin, petty criminal, Casanova. He was here in the flesh and he was simply a man like the thousands I'd seen driving down Blue Hill Avenue or stopped at the light on Warren Street in Grove Hall impatiently checking their watches.

"So, you are at Northeastern. Graduating next year?"

"We're on the quarter system," I corrected him. "I graduate in December."

"Your mother said you live with your girlfriend sometimes?"

"Yeah, Leandra has her own apartment. But I hang out with mom all the time."

"It must be serious then."

"What?"

"Your girlfriend."

I shrugged. I didn't want to talk about Leandra with him. I wanted to know how he met Mom and why he left her to raise me on her own. Why he never tried to find us all these years. Wasn't he curious about what happened to her? Even though he hadn't known about me, he couldn't have just forgotten about Mom. Could he have? Just then Mom signaled from the dining room, holding a wooden bowl with the steaming rice, lentils, and chicken. "Time to eee-eatt!"

Dinner lasted hours and was completely on Mom's terms. He kept glancing from her to me with a sort of bewildered smile as Mom peppered the air with her observations about life in Boston, the latest news, weather, and politics. Either he felt lost or he couldn't believe he was here with us, buttering the warm rolls on Mom's prized Wedgewood dinner set. He ate with his fork only and took large swallows of Sprite.

She performed for him the role of the perfect sacrificing mother who not only raised me to be a perfect son but did so while caring for Uncle Desi, Auntie Bebe, and Uncle Track. "When we came up, we lived with my aunt and her husband on Quincy Street. They sent us to high school, right after that busing nonsense. Track got beat up in Charlestown so much, he quit after a while. We all ended up going to Jeremiah Burke," She turned to me. "That's why I wanted better for Hector. They don't really care about the schools in Boston as much as they care in the rich neighborhoods."

He swallowed and nodded. "I have heard that."

Mom went on, barely touching her food. "Track didn't graduate but Desi and I did okay. Desi went to junior college. I was too busy working and taking care of everybody but I ended up getting my nursing degree part-time." He was entranced, fully under her spell.

By the time we moved back to the living room, it was time to talk about me. She brought out tea and pineapple upside-down cake on dishware I'd never seen before. Mom smiled, patting my shoulder. "Don't worry. Hector and I will clean up later."

She sat in the armchair, beaming at me, her prized possession, as she dramatized my entire life story, flourishing every little detail with her pink-tipped fingers. My love for basketball, the Celtics games I faithfully attended with Coach, my remarkable career on the Southbury team all while getting stellar grades, the wonderful notes my middle-school teachers wrote about me. He listened, rapt, his eyes glued to her sparkling face. Every now and then he would turn to me and nod in approval, as if I had done exactly what he'd asked. Eventually, Mom's show began to lose steam. She hardly ever stayed up past ten and the clock was ticking past eleven.

"I should go home," he said, after finishing a second gigantic slice of cake. Mom had a small bowl of grapes in front of her that she hadn't touched.

"Oh! Let me get you some more of that cake to take with you." Mom shot up from the armchair, grinning.

He stood as she flitted across the living room, his eyes lingering on her for a long time. I recognized the look; Coach Dan had given Mom the same longing stare. He, too, was wearing a wedding ring.

I followed him to the front door.

"Hector," he said, shaking my hand again. "I hope we can meet for a lunch or something. I feel like you might have questions for me, and I would like to answer them."

"Yeah, sure." What else could I say?

"And I want you to meet the rest of the family. My sister is here in Boston. And," he paused, "my wife, of course."

It was an awkward goodbye, with Mom bringing cake wrapped in foil as we shook hands for the third or fourth time. He told me to call him if I needed anything, that Mom had his phone number.

I stood at the door long after the sound of the engine faded away, shivering even though the house was plenty warm. What was I supposed to be feeling now? The world had changed, but my feet hadn't moved. I was still standing at the door.

Mom was washing dishes when I finally entered the kitchen. "You okay?" she asked over her shoulder.

I leaned on the counter, scratching my chin. "He looks just like me."

"But you feeling okay?"

"Yes, Mom. Thanks."

She narrowed her eyes. "For what?"

"For giving me the chance. You know? Not keeping him away from me. I mean, I don't know if I'll ever—"

"You will see him again," she said emphatically. "And you will have a good relationship with him." She rinsed a dinner plate and shook the water off.

I should have just gone to my room at that point, but I had to ask her. "So he knew Uncle Desi and Auntie Bebe when they were little?"

She carefully put down the china. "We were all living in the same village. I was around sixteen."

I bit my lip. "Then what happened? What really happened to your parents?"

She closed her eyes tightly, the sponge in her right hand seeping water into the sink. "Don't ask me about that now. Hector, these are hard things for me to think about." She shook her head. "I already dealt with enough tonight."

I stepped back when the tears began to roll down her cheek. "Mom . . . Mommy, I'm so sorry. I won't bring it up again."

She gathered a large breath, her face grief-stricken, her eyes tightly shut.

"All right. Good night. Sorry, Mom."

I sat on my bed staring past Michael Jordan suspended in midair. Textbooks and paper littered the floor. Leandra had called my cell phone six times. But I simply wanted to be in my room alone, to sit with what I'd seen, touched, and heard, to fully consider the man who was responsible for me being in this world.

Meeting him only added to my long list of questions. Where exactly had he come from? What were his secrets? And would he reveal them to me?

I gave up on sleep as the hours curdled into one other, questions building and multiplying as Mom sobbed softly in her room next door. I wondered why. Maybe because his story was no longer in her hands? Because she could no longer throw me scraps of truth, leaving me wanting more yet too afraid to ask?

I sighed loudly so she could know that I heard her, that I was no longer afraid to know or to ask.

Chapter 9

I walked the fifteen minutes from our house—across Columbia Road, to Washington Street, up Cheney Street, down Howland. All these years, and he was only two thousand footsteps away. I desperately wanted someone to blame, but who?

The house loomed large on the edge of the block of grand single-family homes in a still, almost pastoral section of Roxbury. An ice cream truck jingle broke the silence, comforting me that I was still near home. Neighbors waved to me from their porches as I walked up to the front door. He answered instantly, wearing a navy polo shirt, khaki shorts, and sandals that revealed cracked, browning toenails. He held my hand tightly, barely shaking it, just holding it and grinning. His wife appeared and broke the spell. "Come in, Hector," she smiled. "It is so nice to meet you."

My father's house was a big drafty mansion with old-style dark wood furniture, lots of fireplaces, shiny wood floors, and Persian carpets everywhere. Ms. Karen, who was small and pretty and radiated a quiet kindness, seemed dwarf-like in the massive foyer.

Her sharp accent reminded me of Mom's nursing home friends who sounded like they'd never left the islands. "Your father told me you liked barbecue chicken so that's what I made." I followed her to the dining room, which was overpowered by a massive shiny mahogany table. She was nervous and busied herself repeatedly running from the dining room to the kitchen, her blue flowered dress swishing about her calves, her flat shoes tapping the wood floor. She could be a nun, I thought.

The doorbell rang and Dad went to answer it. I pawed my cell phone in the pocket of my shorts. Why hadn't Mom come? What if these people were weird, hated me, or worse?

Soon, the dining room seemed much smaller. An older woman who vaguely resembled Dad entered with her husband, a tall dark man who shook my hand very formally. "I'm Rose Clair, but you can call me Zoom." She laughed shyly, showing the same measured reserve as Dad. She was lighter

than he, round and maternal. "Auntie Zoom to you," she beamed, eyes lighting up through her glasses.

Twin college-aged girls wearing long braids were behind them, smiling
wildly and hugging my father. "Uncle Winston! You have a son! That's so
crazy!" They turned to me and hugged me in turn. Their names were Denise
and Destiny. They were cute, very cute. I reminded myself we were related.
"You look just like Uncle! Wow!"

Dad was smiling as he told them where I went to middle and high school,
my college major, that I was applying for internships at all the big banks in
the area and in New York, that I had a girlfriend, and did they know Leandra's
mom because she was a famous teacher at Boston Latin, and so on and on. Mr.
Edward and Ms. Rose Clair (I couldn't call her Aunt Zoom; not yet) replied:
"Oh!" "Is that so?" "That is so inTRESTing" They asked polite questions about
Mom, where she worked and where we lived. "I know Hawkins Street," Ms.
Rose Clair exclaimed. "I know your neighbors the Williams! They go to
our church. Right, honey?" And Mr. Edward nodded. "All these years!" she
said over and over again. "God's ways are just not ours," she shook her head
ruefully. "It's all a mystery. But He is good."

The twins were less reserved as they stared me down, giggled, and asked
me questions directly. "So, do you go out? Where do you go?"

"I mostly hang out with my girl. Sometimes we go to Wally's."

"Jazz? You like jazz? Oooh, sophisticated." They collapsed in laughter again.

"No," I said, embarrassed. "I got into jazz in high school because of my
coach."

"She was just kidding," said Denise, the gigglier of the two. "We should
have drinks some time."

"We used to go dancing at Narcissus in Kenmore Square back in the day,"
Denise said, pushing a bushel of braids away from her narrow mahogany face,
and they broke down laughing again. "Those were some good days. Remember the Paradise on Friday nights?"

My father cocked his head to the side. "He is not twenty-one yet, Denise."

"Oh," she raised an eyebrow. "So-rry."

Ms. Rose Clair, whom Dad called Zoom, stared and stared at me. She
wore her hair in a short curly 'fro and was a nurse, just like mom and it
seemed every other immigrant lady in the neighborhood. Like Mom, she had
an efficient, businesslike manner, though hers was more seasoned by years
and experience.

I was in a fishbowl. A circus animal in a cage. Why wasn't Mom here to
take away the spotlight? They were nice enough people but seemed completely
foreign. They *were* foreign. Everyone in the room, except the twins, spoke

with an accent. Everything about them—their mannerisms, the way they sat and ate—made me doubt we were family.

My father worked overtime throughout the meal, trying to make light conversation. "Karen, you wanted to study accounting, too, right?"

But Ms. Karen only nodded. "Yes, sure, Winston." She said very little all evening, instead making sure everyone's plates and glasses were full. Mercifully, the dinner ended in less than an hour.

The twins took my phone number. "We should definitely hang out when we're in Boston," the perkier of the two said. "You're a little bit younger than us but I still think we can chill." They were away in graduate school but were always visiting, they said cheerfully. I suspected their parents told them to be extra nice to me so I'd feel welcome.

Mr. Edward and Ms. Zoom lingered at the door. "You don't know what a gift you are to your father," she said very seriously, searching my eyes. "I hope you will understand why someday."

My walk home was slower. It was eight thirty, still not completely dark yet. My mind raced. Had I made a good impression? I vacillated between wanting their approval and indifference. Who were they to me anyway?

The homies were out on the corner, a few recognized me and waved. Blue Hill Avenue at Warren was busy with loud traffic, car stereos pounding the latest KRS-One banger, pedestrians making their way into and out of the Flames takeout, Brother's corner store, Suds laundromat. A police car streaked by, blue lights flashing. My eyes landed on a young girl waiting at the bus stop holding hands with a little boy. A strange sadness wore my shoulders down as a warm drizzle began right as I reached Jeremiah Burke High School. I imagined a pregnant Mom climbing those steps every day, books in hand, going to class with me in her belly. And now, here I was, a college graduate with a bright future. And a father. She had to be younger than me. Our eyes met and she glared, pulling the little boy close to her leg. I wanted to apologize to him, to tell him that happy endings can be complicated.

Aftermath

Chapter 10

One week after Hurricane Maria, Dad and I stood in a fearful awe near the banks of the Roseau River where it flows into the bay. It was a staggering sight, barely recognizable from the first week we arrived. The peaceful wading pools scattered across the river's rocky bed were replaced by a raging, beast-like torrent thrashing toward the ocean. "Jeez, can you believe this, Dad?" Roseau itself was a sandy, debris-clogged, stinky mess, and the river raged by, making a terrible rushing sound, not quite a roar but more like a million rah, rah, rahs, careening into the Caribbean Sea. Silvery drops of rain trickled into turbulent gray boil and down the back of my T-shirt.

Death tolls were being adjusted and readjusted daily from what we knew. Was it twenty, one hundred, thirty-five? For an island of seventy thousand people, any loss of life was too much. People cried on the streets, sharing horror stories of that terrible night, and I wished I could unhear them, especially at night, under the leaky roof of Cousin Eddie's house when sleep was a struggle.

My stomach rumbled as the river churned below. It took two agonizing days after Maria blew out before my cell phone picked up a signal. Then Leandra was frantic on the other end. She was crying, then I was crying. "Are you okay? Oh my God! I'm so sorry. I'm so sorry, Hector." The reports on CNN, the BBC, the horrible aerial shots of denuded forests, flattened villages, and water, water everywhere had thrown everyone back home into a panic.

Dominica was cut off from communications to the outside world for over twenty-four hours after Maria. The two days of silence had all but broken our spirits. In those unbearable hours, I distracted myself by helping with the cleanup, going house to house with Cousin Eddie checking on neighbors, and trying not to think about what Leandra and Dante were thinking. I would have swum to America just to show them that I was fine. I don't recall how many tree branches, soggy couches, mattresses, and debris we moved and piled up across the neighborhood. Compared to the rest of the island, we were lucky. Cousin Eddie's house was still standing with only part of the roof blown off and a few broken windows.

It was hard to calm Leandra at first. "The news, the pictures were so bad!

We didn't know what to think when we couldn't get through." Leandra said I should just come home now, that the hurricane was a sign. "Dante's dealing with enough as it is with this . . . divorce. Just come home, Hector."

Oh, how I wished it could have been that simple. Dante, not understanding why I was so emotional, was his normal cheerful self. He was laughing when he came to the phone. "Daddy, I drew a picture of you riding on the hurricane." She'd lied, told him everything was fine; that Daddy and Grandpa were having adventures together.

"Leandra . . . I love you. I . . . love my family. I want us back together." I blurted without thinking or planning, and I almost regretted saying it. It was a wasted moment; we were both too raw for it to mean anything. I should have waited.

She was silent for a long minute. "Okay. Okay. Hector, I'm just glad you're okay. Get out of that place as soon as you can. Okay?"

And I planned to, sincerely intended to at that moment.

I would have scattered Mom's ashes in the Roseau River right there and then if not for Dad. He also had promised Ms. Karen that he would get back to Boston as soon as possible. But there we were on the bridge, ready to perform the final act, and he was pacing, clearing his throat, stonewalling. I was about to ask him to say some words, a prayer. But he shook his head sullenly. "No. No." He began to walk away from the bridge. "This is not . . . It's not right."

"Dad! Come back!" He kept walking away. "What do you mean, Dad?" I groaned in frustration.

He threw up both hands in a kind of surrender. "No! Not like that. Not when the river is like that." He didn't even look back, leaving me standing on the bridge holding the urn.

Dad's sloping figure blended in with groups of people milling about the mountains of debris on sidewalks near the Roseau Market. I'd just placed the urn back in my backpack when the bridge began to sway. I grabbed the railing as the bridge seesawed beneath me. This frigging place! A few people cried out and raced toward the market. It took a few more seconds of my heart pounding out of my chest to realize that it was the debris-clearing machines. This rickety bridge and seawall already survived Hurricane David in 1979. Hell, why wouldn't they fling my body into the Caribbean Sea?

On the street, I fell in with scores of other shell-shocked Dominicans and wide-eyed aid workers who came in on the boats that ferried the fortunate on and off the island. Dad's receding tracksuit-clad figure ambled toward the bus stop where Cousin Eddie was chatting with other drivers. The busy area was anchored by a large grocery and a KFC, all decimated and barely recognizable. A car inexplicably was perched high atop a building-sized hill of garbage, causing onlookers to stop and stare in utter disbelief. People queued up with empty buckets and jerry cans for the water truck and covered their noses with headscarves while telling muffled hurricane stories. "Boy! I never hear wind like that in my life!"

It was every recovery-search-and-rescue scene I'd seen in disaster movies and on the weather channel. An earth-moving machine built a mountain of corrugated iron, bald tree limbs, clothing, half-eaten chicken dinners, a refrigerator, a bicycle, and tons and tons of sand in the corner of the grocery parking lot. Trinidadian soldiers stood guard nearby with guns even though the looters were beaten back days ago. The bok-bok-bok of circling helicopters added an apocalyptic soundtrack.

Raindrops trickled over my backpack and into my sneakers as I kept one eye on the bus stop so I wouldn't lose Dad. Under the awning of the grocery store, fear clouded the people's eyes. Each strong wind gust or heavy rain only multiplied the terror. The news trickling in from Barbuda and Puerto Rico was devastating and only fed the fear. "I hear the hurricane can turn around and come back here," one lady said, hugging herself tightly. I turned to her and said, "That is not true, ma'am." I know nothing about hurricanes, but I wanted her to not be afraid. "A hurricane can't do that. Everything will be okay." Dad was in the distance climbing into Cousin Eddie's minibus. He was right. This was not the right time nor place. Everyone was so jittery and afraid. That agitated river was not a place of rest; Mom deserved better. A calm blue sea or gently rolling river with swaying rushes and reeds on each side was what I'd imagined. That boisterous, debris-filled river was no resting place.

Chapter 11

Even in its battered state, Cousin Eddie's house was still an impressive, rambling two-level structure—all white with a wraparound verandah on each level. His wife Missy, an artist in the garden, had ringed the property with hydrangeas, hibiscus, roses, and crocuses and other flowers I couldn't name, the first thing I noticed when we drove in that day from the airport. That was all gone now. The red roof was blown off, leaving a skeleton of timber and tarpaulin to face the daily showers. Cousin Eddie wept on Dad's shoulder the morning after Maria as we surveyed the damage around the house.

We'd walked around the house, stepping over broken dishes in the bathroom, bars of soap in the backyard, photo albums in the neighbor's driveway. We swept, mopped, and tossed out everything we could. We heaped up all of Maria's ruins in a monstrous pile on Cousin Eddie's treasured front lawn and made a bonfire.

I was in a daze, completely done in by the tears and wails coming from the neighbors' houses. What would I have done if all my possessions had been pulverized and flung around like worthless trash? Dad took on the role of comforter, wrapping his arms around Cousin Eddie's daughters when they broke down crying. "It will be okay," Dad said to them. "You will have your house and you will be back on Facebook in no time." He told them lame jokes. He cooked oatmeal over an open fire in the front yard as they waited on the verandah. He spread brown sugar atop the oatmeal and brought it to them. "Careful. It is very hot." In a couple days they began to call him Grandpa. I tried not to cry.

As the days went on, recovery and cleanup signs began to sprout. Foreign crews drove by our neighborhood offering help, water, medical attention. The crew hammering away on Cousin Eddie's roof sang and told jokes as they worked. "Don't run down my generator playing music all day!" Cousin Eddie shouted at them.

Deprivation became my new way of life. I washed my shirts and shorts with my own hands on the front lawn. Just like camping in the rough. Missy slapped her thighs, laughing from the verandah, as I plunged a pair of jeans into soapy water in a bucket. "Boy, you don't know how to wash?" Missy was about my age but seemed so much older and wiser, almost motherly to me. "I'll get the hang of it," I insisted.

Every morning began with internal pep talks. I forced myself to forget the cleaning lady who came once a week to our house in Jamaica Plain, the view of the Jamaica Pond from my study, the Central Persian rug I loved feeling under my bare feet, and the Montecristo cigar collection Dad bought me for my thirty-fifth birthday. No use in thinking about these comforts. Leandra may never let me in the house again anyway. Instead, I tried to imagine myself a different person: single, able to adapt to any and everything. Yet, every night as I slept in a corner of the room I shared with Dad, water leaking into a bucket near my head, I considered getting on the next boat out. Beside me, Dad would be deep in sleep, snoring peacefully.

A couple weeks after the hurricane, after our scant breakfast of stale bread, soggy cheese, and lime juice with sugar, an SUV groaned up the driveway and an efficient-looking man climbed out. He was carrying a leather work-bag—like the government men around here. "Are you Mr. Hector Peterson?" he asked, and I invited him in.

He shook hands with Dad and sat on the couch, crunchy-dry after a few days in the sun. The man was deferential and low-voiced; he refused the beer we offered him. It's too early, he said. That never stopped the guys working on the roof, I thought. We heard him out and, eventually, he dipped his head and clomped over to his truck.

The rain was steady through midmorning, leaving a cool, breathy mist hovering above the lawn and its several piles of broken-off branches and twigs. Up here away from the dystopia of Roseau, the neighborhood seemed peaceful even with the downed trees, the mauled homes, and tangles of debris everywhere. It was easy even to forget that the little stream a mile away took an entire house to the sea; we helped the family set up house in Uncle Eddie's garage.

The government man walked down the muddy road to his muddy truck. Cousin Eddie had listened to the conversation on the edge of the verandah. "So, you not going home with the rest of the Americans?"

"Not ready yet." Dad watched the government man drive away, stroking the gray hairs sprouting from his chin. The white beard made him look even older. I, too, must've looked like hell.

I begged Dad to take the offer, leave with the students from Ross Medical School. "They will take you to Antigua and you can fly direct from there. Come on, Dad! You can come back in a couple months when things are better." I reminded him that his high blood pressure medication could run out, that he might have trouble adjusting to the heat without air conditioning.

He snorted. "Boy, this is my home! What nonsense you talking about air conditioner?" His anger left me to think: what was I even doing here? Maybe I should get on the boat and get out of here. Take Mom's ashes back to the States and leave Dad here to sort himself out.

Chapter 12

The construction crew arrived around 7:00 a.m. each day and seemed to want me out of their way, though they enjoyed talking to Dad. When I told him this, he laughed. "I speak their language, that's why." But weren't we all speaking English? I didn't like that they lowered their eyes and called me "boss" while they hailed Dad in the mornings: "Mr. W! Mr. W!" Dad would grin and kid them: "What de hell you bothering me about so early in the morning, bwoy?"

Dad disappeared early to have breakfast at the hotel with Aunt Valina and Ma Relene. I volunteered to go with Cousin Eddie transporting people to their villages so they could check on their families. "My partner tell me which roads I can pass," Cousin Eddie explained. There was still flooding everywhere, and most bridges had been washed away, and tree trunks as big as houses took up entire country roads. "If I can't get through, I'll take them as close as I can. Dominicans used to struggling. They will hack through to get to their people."

We loaded up the bus at the bottom of Canefield close to the Old Mill, an eighteenth-century structure standing strong as if Maria never happened. Seven somber-faced people boarded. "Good morning," was all it took to launch into their Maria stories. The older folks compared Maria to Hurricane David in 1979. "At least in '79 people weren't charging their own neighbors $50 to charge their phones!" one lady piped up, causing the others to nod and cluck in remorse. The price gouging and fraud was already problematic enough for the police to get involved. Cousin Eddie refused to get into the business of charging for use of his generator, instead telling the neighbors that he himself was limiting the use to nighttime only, although he did relent a few times.

"Boy!" a round lady in a colorful dress exclaimed from the back row. "You see how all those foreign soldiers come so quick? Eh beh, weh. God didn't turn his back on us yet, nuh."

It was true. British soldiers and crews from nearby islands were breaking through the blocked roads, rebuilding bridges, and clearing away massive boulders and tree trunks with heavy equipment. The DOMLEC workers and their imported help hoisted high on cherry pickers were working around the clock. I was impressed. For all of Cousin Eddie's pessimism, things were actually moving along. The first international aid ships had come in, and people were queued up for water, canned goods, and toiletries. International news reporters were filming from atop piles of twisted rubble and interviewing teary-eyed Dominicans for the entire world to see. *We need help. Dominicans need help. Please help us. Don't close your eyes to this suffering. Please. Help.*

"Ay, ay, ay. People suffering," Cousin Eddie shook his head as we dropped off a couple of people to join a throng of grim-faced locals walking purposely, most likely to check on their loved ones.

Devastation quieted us the further we drove out from Canefield. It shocked our bus riders into a numb silence. Piles of rubble where houses once stood. Sand, water, dirt, tree branches scraped clean everywhere. Brightly colored houses still standing but roofless, crumbled walls leaving an unobstructed view of domestic wreckage inside. Weary residents hauling out trash, piling up the effects of their lives on the roadsides to be burned. They moved slowly, lacking the natural cheeriness and liveliness I'd envied the day I landed here.

The lady behind me covered her mouth as she glanced out the window. "They tell me it was bad . . . but not this bad . . . Magwe sah."

Another passenger gasped as Uncle Eddie slowly steered around a massive boulder in the middle of the highway. "*Papa, Bon Dieu!*" She got out in the town of Mahaut, which was still mostly underwater.

I wracked my brain for the little Creole that I'd tried to pick up. *Magwe sah. Magwe Ca?* Look at that awful sight? What a tragedy? What wickedness?

Dominica had been stripped bare of all her natural beauty. Grayish, skeletal tree limbs bracketed the road and peered eerily over the vast blue sea or stood scarecrow-like in the dilapidated forest. The landscape appeared worse than the dreariest of New England winter days, with the trees shivering like withered octogenarians, shorn bare of leaves and branches rudely snapped off, leaving them armless, headless. It took an hour to travel just two towns over to Mero, where two other people jumped out.

"I don't know if we'll make it to St. Joe," Uncle Eddie warned. The four men in the back sighed. "I cannot believe what I seeing there, partner. I don't think Dominica can ever come back from this kind of thing, monsieur."

Another man shook his head, looking around. "All de trees gone . . . All de trees?"

Cousin Eddie pulled off to the side to let a big truck full of debris-clearing equipment by. Then another truck with soldiers. "Trinidadian army." The soldiers, young boys with bored eyes, stared at us. Uncle Eddie sucked his teeth. "I don't like these soldiers here. This is not a war."

"They still looting in some places," a passenger said.

At Layou, a small group congregated at a bus stop near a massive pile of debris, A fire burned in the distance. All was exposed: colorful underwear on a clothesline, green bananas boiling in a pot, bottled water baking under the sun.

Another group, twenty or so, were sitting in chairs further up the roadside. "What are they—?" I strained my head forward. A man was standing in front of them, waving his hands and moving his lips.

"They are having church," Cousin Eddie said, and I realized it was Sunday. I rolled down the windows to listen.

I've seen it in the lightning, heard it in the thunder,
And felt it in the rain;
My Lord is near me all the time,
My Lord is near me all the time.

Once we were on the road again the talking stopped because the nakedness of the rainforest was almost vulgar. Maria decimated the entire interior forest, the 150-mile-per-hour winds lashing the trees and flying debris de-robing branches, leaving just sharp, jagged stumps behind. It was as if someone had blowtorched the entire landscape, what had been the crown jewel, the impenetrably green emerald rainforest. I wondered where the exotic birds, the parrots had gone. Had they escaped? Had anything survived?

"What does 'magwe sah' mean?" I asked Cousin Eddie.

He shrugged. "Look around you."

Days later Cousin Eddie was raising a beer to us as the sun began to seep into the horizon. We were on the verandah after another day of work, and I was exhausted. We transported tons of water and food to people who couldn't get out on their own. Ms. Karen and Aunt Zoom had allied their friends in Boston and were sending a shipment of goods for Cousin Eddie's entire neighborhood.

I felt good, being a part of something that would achieve a good result. At night, when I was too exhausted to sleep, I looked up and could see the starry sky through the damaged roof. It was utterly still; no frogs or lizards grunting, no owls hooting. The stillness began to ease my anxieties, the lingering dread and terror from that awful night Maria swept through. Every morning I awoke eager to work, to help, to do something. I wanted to be hopeful, to defy every indication that the wreckage around us was the end of the story. These trees, these houses, these ruins would come to life again.

Cousin Eddie at these nighttime gatherings would begin to roast Dad, allowing me glimpses into the father I never knew. "One other thing I can tell you about your father. He could play cricket . . . yes, man. He was an all-star bowler." Cousin Eddie was grinning, lying back on his elbows on the grass, a beer next to him.

"Boy, why you talking that nonsense?" Dad sucked his teeth, but he seemed to be basking in the memory, correcting Cousin Eddie when he got the facts wrong. There was so much I was learning about him now. Like I'd been given a whole new father.

I lingered on the porch long after they'd all gone inside. Those recovery days of sorrow and joy in Dominica would last a while, and I had a choice. Stay here or go home to face a different kind of disaster. The Caribbean Sea was dark and mysterious in the distance. I thought of the first natives from South America braving these waters in canoes way before Columbus and his three lost ships discovered their way here in 1493, leading to more ships, and more ships that eventually led to my father, and to me. I pulled up Dante's picture on my phone. I heard him asking me when I'm coming home. I heard him say that he wants to go to J.P. Licks for ice cream. I said to the dark tropical night: I'll go home soon but I'm not ready to leave this place. The guilt weighed heavy on me—Mom's ashes, Dante's grinning face. And, I think, this was for him as much as it was for me.

Mom

Chapter 13

That fall after Dad came into our lives, Mom began to take early morning walks even through the dreadful winter months. She was breathless and bubbly when we spoke, going on about calorie counts and workout gear while carefully avoiding the topic of her relationship with Dad.

I was home the summer before my second year of business school while Leandra was in New York City doing a legal internship at the Southern District of New York. I was an intern in the wealth management unit at Summit Bank in the Back Bay, and it felt like a real job—with real money I was saving up for our wedding.

Mom's healthy lifestyle did not prevent her constant respiratory distress; every winter she came down with bronchitis that some years sent her to the hospital. She'd blamed it on her parents. "Your parents smoked that much?" I asked incredulously.

She shrugged. "For them, smoking was a spiritual thing."

The morning walks in Franklin Park, she said, were good for her lungs. She was loving and affectionate with me now, constantly hugging me and telling me she loved me. I thought she was just happy to have me at home all to herself now that Leandra was away.

Home was a nice anchor as my life changed quickly from college student to working professional. My workplace, like high school and college, was competitive in all the expected ways. My fellow interns used their every advantage—mansion on the Cape, family membership in the Somerset Club— to impress our VP bosses who were busy trying to impress their Director bosses who were trying to impress their C-suite bosses. Our triple-decker on Hawkins Street grounded me in reality, a refuge from these starched-white-shirt corporate masquerade games. In our hood, I was just Hector who'd done well for himself and even got himself a fine girl. My cousins and the other kids on the street asked my advice on college or high-school drama or wanted to just shoot hoops or set off firecrackers in the driveway.

Inexplicably, Uncle Desi and I had grown closer since my father entered my life. He was the one to whom I ranted and raved every Friday night about my week in the Back Bay while Leandra put in late nights at her legal internship in New York. We'd drink beer after beer on the front steps while the kids lit firecrackers and played tag in the middle of the street, dodging the dudes driving by with the booming systems. "If you don't want to be in that white world, come and work for me. I'll show you how to cut hair. You can take over the shop when I retire," Uncle Desi would joke. Most times he'd just encourage me. "Do your work on the low. You gotta work harder than them but don't let them think you're a threat. Let them think they're better and smarter than you. Otherwise they'll just try to get rid of you." Uncle Desi did five years in corporate advertising before he left those skyscraper days behind. "I wanted to be myself all day every day." He warned me, "Don't try to be too much like those guys in the big corner offices. You have to sell your soul to get there. They'll never come right out and tell you, but that's what it takes."

My talks with my father, on the other hand, were stilted and formal. His employees—from cashiers to bakers—were adoring of him. "Mr. W! He looks just like you!" He proudly put his arm around my shoulder when he introduced me. His business partner, Mr. Sheehan, was more easygoing. "You should have seen your father's face when he saw your mother that day," he told me as my father took a phone call. "It was like he was waiting his whole life to find her again. And when he told me had a son." Mr. Sheehan shook his head. "Tears. Hector, your father cried when he told me about you."

We would sit in his coffee shop drinking coffee and eating crullers talking about the Celtics, the Pacers, the Bulls, the possibilities of threepeats. Safe topics. He was struggling and so was I. Mom would ask: "How did it go? What did you all talk about?" The whole world, it seemed, was waiting with bated breath for us to finally connect in one singular, emotional moment. Well, I was waiting too.

A couple times the three of us, Uncle Desi, my father, and I, went fishing at Houghton's Pond. We said very little though we always had a good time. He and Uncle Desi sometimes cracked a joke about Dominica or Dominicans, leaving me begging for an explanation.

This late July Saturday, the weekend before the carnival, Uncle Desi and I sat on the steps. I showed him the wedding ring I'd just bought for Leandra. His eyebrows shot up. "Boy, you have all that money?" I grinned proudly.

"You talk to your father about the wedding?" Uncle Desi asked. Dad had offered to pay for our wedding, but I'd told him no. He'd also offered to pay off my college loans and my grad school tuition. I'd also said no to that. Uncle Desi thought I was insane. "You have to let him do something for you. Even though it's just one thing."

"Why? Why does it matter? I'm gonna be making a lot of money—"

"Hector, he's your father. And that's what fathers do."

I shrugged. "He and Mom are out somewhere again." She'd dressed up earlier in a formfitting dress and high heels and gave me a quick goodbye kiss. I'd looked out the window to see her slipping into my father's Mercedes.

Uncle Desi chuckled. "You know they go walking every morning in Franklin Park at four o'clock when it's still dark?"

It bothered me—mainly because Mom had been sick since the winter. I heard her coughing her lungs out every night. This fresh air she was getting on these morning walks wasn't making a lick of difference.

"Wonder what his wife think about all that," Uncle Desi said.

I thought about Ms. Karen and her quiet, churchy ways. "She probably doesn't know. She's not the type to question Dad about anything." Ms. Karen, like Dad's employees, worshiped him, as if he possessed godlike qualities. I never saw him enjoying Ms. Karen's adulation; instead, he seemed to tolerate her like one would an adoring five-year-old.

Uncle Desi shook his head. "I hope Jemma know what she doing. After that thing with your coach . . ."

"She seems really happy." Mom sang even more passionately now to her Shirley Murdock and Brian McKnight CDs while she cooked and cleaned on her days off. "Maybe he will leave his wife."

Uncle Desi scoffed. "Pfft! An island man not gonna leave his wife. Let me tell you!"

"Come on, Uncle Desi. This is America. He's an American citizen now."

"You want to bet on that?"

I let the topic slide. Coach Dan stopped coming to visit Mom in my freshman year of college. I came home one weekend to find her a mess on the couch, almost catatonic. "Hector, Dan and I are not friends anymore. Okay?" She was taking short breaths; her eyes were red and crusty with mascara. She had not changed out of her scrubs. Four empty mugs with drained tea bags were lined up on the floor. I knelt near her feet and began to gather up the mugs. I put her nursing clogs in the closet. She shook her head when I asked if she was okay, should I call a doctor, Auntie Bebe, somebody? "No. Hector, No. Just . . . stay with me this week. You can use my car to drive to school every day." It was months before she got over it. Coach Dan never called our house phone anymore. When he called me, I learned not to bring up Mom. It took another year before she went out on another date—with a man she met on Match.com. She came home angry. "Never again!" she raged. "Men are useless!" An hour later she texted me: "Not you, Hector. I didn't mean you. I raised you right. Any woman would be lucky to have you."

∾

Later that summer, I sat with Dad and Mom at our dinner table. Ms. Karen was away on a two-week missionary trip with her church. "They go to work in an orphanage in Haiti every year," he said. Mom pulled out the Scrabble after dinner and half-heartedly asked me if I wanted to play. I told her I needed to call Leandra.

I pretended not to notice hearing him in Mom's room after midnight. I pretended not to notice that he'd parked his Mercedes a block away from our house so the neighbors wouldn't see that he was spending the night. He appeared around dinnertime almost every night during those two weeks Ms. Karen was away.

"So, you're planning the wedding for next Labor Day?" Mom grinned at me. She was wearing a flowered red dress with thin straps. The summer heat and the long walks had made her toned and leaner. He had set up a card table in the backyard and she'd brought out salad and lobster. She'd begun coloring her dreads again, and they were chocolate brown with buttery highlights. Dad gazed at her lovingly and then back at me. "Your mother is going to look so beautiful at your wedding. I cannot wait to see her."

"Not more beautiful than Leandra!" Mom smacked my father on his shoulder playfully. "Leandra already looks like a princess. She looks like Halle Berry. Doesn't she, Winston?"

I allowed myself to fall under the spell of their make-believe world as they played old calypso records, drank wine, and reminisced about a past unfamiliar to me. I went to my room slightly giddy, envisioning a future with the family I'd always wanted: Leandra and me with our children, Mom and Dad doting over their grandkids. It was one of the best dreams I'd ever had. A perfect family, with generations of rich history and an even grander legacy on the horizon.

Chapter 14

Graduations, weddings, moving trucks, long hours at the office and on golf courses, power lunches, and happy hour spots dominated the next few years as I filled out my new corporate identity. Leandra and I, spit-polished in our Brooks Brothers suits and proper Black professional affiliations, moved into to our dream house in Jamaica Plain near the Pond. We were into the first phase of our carefully laid plans: work like maniacs for the first three years, save a ton, then she would leave the law firm for something less stressful so we could start a family.

The first part of the plan worked like a dream. My mentor Paul Maniscalco who worked on the top floor of headquarters brought me to the executive offices and introduced me to everyone during my first week at Summit Bank. It was implied to me that the keys to the kingdom were mine for the taking if I did what was expected of me. And I had no plans to disappoint once I saw the expansive views from that top-floor office stretching from the Southeast Expressway to the steeples on the Harvard campus.

So Thanksgiving 2005 was a special one. I'd just been promoted to a VP at age twenty-seven and was on the cover of the bank's brochure and a small write-up in the *Boston Business Journal*. It hadn't come easy. Leandra and I put in our time hosting and attending dinners and dining with the bank's CEO once a month in his sprawling waterfront home in Scituate, cringing through BSO openings when we both hated classical music, always balancing our citified, blue-collar Black selves with our blue-blooded work selves, fearing we would lose our true selves somewhere in the middle. But I was flying high and working hard and everyone was proud of me. So proud that Mom agreed to having Thanksgiving dinner at Dad's and Ms. Karen's. It would be the first time that we would all be together since the wedding, and Leandra and I had big news.

The fireplaces radiated warmth across Dad's house, which was buzzing with conversation and laughter. The twins were both married now with toddlers, and Aunt Zoom and Mr. Edward treated their three grandchildren with all the care and abandon of besotted grandparents. "Mom, don't give him any more cake!" Denise frowned as she chased after her little girl. Ms. Karen, Mom, Aunt Zoom, and Destiny were in the kitchen, their clanking baking pans, crockery, chatter, and laughter filling the hallway.

Leandra, dressed in knee-high boots, white sweater, and tight black jeans, sat in the den animatedly chatting with Denise's husband, who was also a corporate lawyer. The tug of jealousy at seeing her with another man was instant and visceral and I quickly put it away. I had done worse than talk with an attractive woman, and the guilt was always nagging at the edges of these family gatherings when I felt our marriage was on display for everyone to grade and evaluate. But I was glad she found someone to commiserate with about genteel law-firm racism; I certainly heard no end of it at home. Dad and I were working on an old record player that neither of us knew how to fix while Uncle Desi gave us useless advice. "No. You need to put that wire over the blue one. Yes. No."

Ms. Karen swept into the den, wearing a high-necked velvet dress, her permed hair swept up into a bun. She wore glasses now, making her look even more like a kindly librarian. "Everybody, we have two tables set up this year." She beamed around the room. "But, kids, don't feel you have to sit down in one place. The whole house is yours, so run around all you want!"

A latent anger simmered as I watched Ms. Karen perform her ruler-of-the-roost role. She was matriarchal, confident in her role as Dad's wife, while Mom was relegated to visitor status, idling with a wine glass at Uncle Desi's elbow. Mom observed the room with a placid smile, occasionally meeting my eyes with a look that seemed to say: "Can you believe this crap?" Anyone with functioning eyes could see that Dad could not possibly love Ms. Karen. Yet she refused to leave him. Or he refused to leave her. I left it alone after Mom told me to mind my own business more than once. But the anger flared up at random moments. What was he holding on to with Ms. Karen? It defied explanation, this stubborn loyalty of his.

"Everybody," Ms. Karen announced once the adults were all seated, "you have to share at least one thing you are thankful for this year."

Leandra squeezed my hand under the table as the others spoke. Aunt Zoom waxed on about having the twins and the grandkids. Mr. Edward, always nostalgic for Dominica, was thankful for "the two weeks Zoom and I spent in Dominica this year. Always the best two weeks of the year for me." That led to a conversation about why they didn't move back.

"But I'd never see my grandchildren!" Aunt Zoom exclaimed.

Then it was our turn. Leandra leaned forward, my hand over hers. She'd let her hair grow in the last few years and her skin glowed under the chandelier lights. Leandra had always been pretty, but she'd developed a more put-together look that made her positively stunning, like she'd just walked off the page of a magazine. Every morning I stared at her as she put on her makeup and dressed for work in complete awe; I've never regretted marrying her.

The table erupted in cheers before Leandra could finish. Dad almost ran around to my chair and clapped me on the back. "My son! Finally! Yes!" Uncle Desi raised a beer to me. And so on. Everyone clapped and cheered. While Mom applauded along with the rest of the family, there was a deep sadness in her eyes, and I made sure to stay close to her throughout the dinner. "I'm so glad you came with us tonight," I whispered in her ear as we ate.

Later that night, Mom sat in my living room while Leandra slept upstairs. I'd forbidden her from going home to the Hawkins Street apartment; I couldn't bear the thought of her being alone in that house on Thanksgiving night.

"Mom, I hate to say it, but I don't think Dad being in your life is a good thing. You should at least start dating other guys. Or something."

"Oh, Hector. Not again," she brushed me away, changing the channel to CNN. "We just had a nice day with everybody together. Come on!"

"Mom! You had to sit there all afternoon and watch them play happy husband and wife!" And it was all my fault. I'd begged her to come so Leandra and I could do our big reveal. Now I felt terrible.

But she rolled her eyes and sighed. "Hector, you'll never understand."

"I do understand! You deserve better! He's getting away with murder . . ."

She turned to me fiercely. "Shut up! Shut up!" I flinched at the fire in her eyes.

"Just shut up about this, okay?"

Before I knew it, she grabbed her purse and swept out of the house before I could stop her. I stood at the window watching her speed off toward the Jamaicaway.

"Where's your mom?" Leandra asked sleepily from the staircase.

I shook my head. We sat in front of the large crackling fireplace, not saying much. My heart hurt for Mom. After all these years, I thought. Why couldn't she be happy? Why was there no happy ending for her? My heart burned with resentment at the thought of Dad and Ms. Karen in their grand old house with each other while Mom slept alone.

Leandra leaned in close to me. "Everything will be okay, Hector. Your mother and father knew each other before you were born. They know what's best for them better than you."

I held her close, hoping she was right. Mom could handle herself. Maybe I was just butting in where I didn't belong. I could focus on the here and now, on the family I was about to have, my son or my daughter and the life Leandra and I would give to them. He or she would never have a sleepless night wondering and worrying like I did. I would learn from my parents' mistakes. The cycle of lies and dishonesty would stop with me.

Chapter 15

Mom spent the following January at the Mass. Eye and Ear Infirmary tethered to a ventilator. The snow and cruelly cold temperatures had begun soon after Thanksgiving and never let up. It was the kind of winter when flights were cancelled and kids stayed home from school at least one or two days every single week. The city was short-tempered and stir-crazy as mounds of snow piled up on curbs, in yards, in the middle of the street sometimes.

"I'm going to start looking at houses in Florida," Mom tried to laugh and fell into a fit of coughing as I drove her home from the hospital. I had no words left except a deep, iron-hot anger deep inside of me. I blamed him. Sure, she'd been sick before but never this sick. His half-in, half-out presence completely dominated her life. Everything she did was for him even though he would not move an inch for her. He remained in his big drafty house with his cold little wife, while Mom accepted his scraps of affection, wasting and wasting away.

"So, Leandra and I think you should just stay with us for good after you're all recovered." I should have told her and not asked.

"What?" She shook her head. "No way. I can stay in my house. Did the doctor say that?"

"No, but Mom—"

"But nothing! Hector, I can take care of myself. I'm not an old woman. I'm not even fifty yet." She sucked her teeth. "Once it gets warmer outside, I'll be back in my sneakers again. You'll see."

"Mom, I wasn't trying to say—"

And so it goes. She stayed with us for two weeks, refusing to stay in bed and rest. She helped Leandra paint and decorate the nursery. We ate her fried plantains, rice and beans, and stewed chicken while we watched the Patriots beat the Rams in the Super Bowl. Dad asked if he could come and see her and I told him no. I begged her to stay but eventually she moved back to Hawkins Street, back to him, or the half of him he gave to her.

The cold of that winter never quite left us that year. By the time spring rolled around, Leandra began to feel ill. She called me from work one afternoon, crying, hyperventilating. I met her at the OB-GYN's office, my shirt soaked and stuck to me, my heart racing. Leandra was admitted to Mass General that same night. The next morning our baby girl, my first daughter, slipped away from the world, wrapped head to toe in a white hospital sheet, her eyes unopened.

∽

The two of us, unable and unprepared for the onslaught of grief, burrowed deep in our house, bundled up under the covers crying together for days. We did not answer the phone, nor did we talk to anyone. At some point, spring began to turn into summer and Mom used her key to come in and clean up and leave us food that we did not eat. Over those weeks, I may have heard Dad's voice several times outside our bedroom door. "Hector? Hector? I just want to see how you are doing." I may have looked out the window one day to see him mowing my front yard while Mom watered Leandra's flower bed.

I went back to work that summer, and my twentieth-floor Financial District office, expense account, secretary, and hefty travel schedule were waiting just as I'd left them. But I was not the same. Before our tenth wedding anniversary Leandra and I would have three more miscarriages. This first one, however, caused a volcano of grief to erupt in me, sending scalding lava everywhere, kindling little fires all over my life.

By the third loss in 2008, Leandra was laid completely low. She turned away from the tiny bundle the nurse handed to her and begged them to take him away. But I held him, looked into his tiny purple face, his coily black hair, willing a blink, a shiver, a breath.

"Get it out of here," Leandra moaned, pulling the pillow over her head. I gave our baby to the nurse, who wouldn't meet my eyes. Leandra pushed me away forcefully when I tried to comfort her. "Leave, Hector. Just leave. Please."

She couldn't surface. My strong, beautiful Leandra couldn't be raised from the depths. The psychiatrist said it wasn't just the miscarriages; this breakdown sprung up from a lifetime of Leandra being Leandra, her mother's daughter, her sister's sister, everybody's best friend. I hid my devastation by being there, willingly absorbing every angry, grief-stricken blow she lobbed at me. I didn't know what to do. My beautiful, capable, rock of a wife was crumbling, coming apart in my hands. At the same time, I was running a division of forty ambitious, competitive bankers and had less and less capacity for my own emotional baggage. I threw myself into work, taking on every project, traveling to every unnecessary meeting, heading every affinity committee that kept me out of the house. I had to leave my pain at home, in the car, in illicit hotel room encounters; it didn't matter as long as I could keep us going.

At some point in her grieving, I had become Leandra's enemy or the source of her pain. She lashed out constantly and I took it quietly. "You're late again! Who works till 10:00 p.m. on a Friday?"

I stood at our bedroom door helplessly, not explaining myself, knowing it could be years until she fully healed from the loss. She might never go back to work, and that thought terrified me. That I would be solely responsible for all of our hopes and dreams. That's what the doctor said anyway. That I should not expect much from her. That I shouldn't even complain that we no longer shared the same bed.

What about me? How was I doing? Only Mom asked and I blew her off. I simply tried to forget. That they had been people, little versions of me, that had died before they'd had a chance to live. I'd never been given a chance to be their dad, to be the dad I'd wanted to be. I learned to simply not think about them. And I trusted Leandra to do the same, to not think about them, to not talk about them, to not remind me of them in any way.

Our house grew more and more silent. The few weekends I sat still long enough, a cavernous void echoed through the hallways and the rooms, even between us at the dining table. We watched movies together silently. Went to family dinners and quickly separated. She flocked to the men's circle, terri-fied of joining Auntie Bebe and the other moms with their talk of children's clothes, the best schools, pediatricians and after-school activities. She lost herself in the safety of professional sports, jazz, politics, and irrelevant gossip. How we had attended a fundraiser for Obama and how impressive he was; absolutely guaranteed to win the nomination. How Uncle Desi had managed to open his second barbershop with a big investment from Dad. How Aunt Zoom was about to turn fifty and was looking so good. How Ms. Karen really did finish her bachelor's degree. In all of this chatting, she seldom smiled, and one eye remained on the kids playing and racing across the house.

A year later, she was back at work part-time, inspired by Obama and his promise of a new day of hope and change. We'd flown to Washington for an inauguration party and she'd cried in our hotel room. "Hector, I can't believe I'm alive to see this day." I'd cried too, and it was more than just the polit-ical moment. We remembered our freshman year dreams, our graduation dreams, our first mortgage dreams. We had come far. We could go further. When we considered our beginnings, our parents and their beginnings, we could look past our murky present. We were starting to believe in us again.

She found a job with a nonprofit that helped lower-income city resi-dents. We were going to be fine, she promised me. That spring we painted the house inside and out. We redid the kitchen and finished the basement. She bought a treadmill and exercise bike and arranged them in the empty, repainted nursery.

Aftermath

Chapter 16

Our neighborhood glowed like Vegas when the lights finally came on. Whoops and cheers spilled out from windows and onto front lawns. It really felt miraculous after four weeks of steamy, dark nights. I plugged in my laptop slowly and almost wept with joy when it buzzed to life. I could finally forget to turn the bathroom light off without worrying about straining the generator.

Still, life was nowhere back to normal for most of the island. Maria's aftermath remained terrible for most, and small mercies like a few hours of electricity felt like winning the lottery. Thousands of children were shuttled overseas to attend school, and most people had not returned to work. Hordes of international aid workers still roamed the streets of Roseau like an army of Patagonia and Apple-branded aliens. Food was plentiful but terrible. Fresh fruits and vegetables had been replaced with sardines, luncheon meat, and boxed donations needing only boiling water and a sense of humor. Spirits were lifting slowly, even though many people remained listless and grim-faced. Even though many elderly were passing away.

We were having breakfast at the Fort Young Hotel with Auntie Valina and Ma Relene. They were petulant, itching to get back to their homes, and Dad's impatience was showing. "It's hard to get people to work fast when there is so much construction work to do everywhere," Dad bristled. "Everybody who want to work is working." The house will be finished by the end of November, he promised, tapping his foot on the wooden floor of the airy hotel restaurant.

I highly doubted that, and Ma Relene was skeptical too. She pouted, raising her wrinkled brown face to the sky, gold loops dangling from her ear. "I live through Hurricane David. I had tarpaulin on my roof for six months and I survived," she said defiantly. I couldn't get a bead on the strained, yet close relationship between Dad and Ma Relene. I'd never understand how he cared so much for her, like he'd simply forced her into the void his mother left when she died.

"I'm sure you were younger and healthier then," I interjected and immediately regretted it when her dark eyes darted over me.

"Boy, what kind of nonsense you talking about younger? I still take care of my three grandchildren. I carry my water every day!"

"I didn't mean anything . . ." She dismissed me with a glare.

"Winston, you sure that is your son?" She was dead serious when she asked this question. Dad laughed uneasily, and I glimpsed an ancient pain behind his eyes. I decided then to stay out of Ma Relene's way as much as possible. It was clear to me that she nursed deep resentments over her losses in life and that Dad would forever be working off that self-imposed guilt for as long as she was alive. I'd seen this in him before—his loyalty to his platonic marriage even when he could finally be with the woman he loved. Watching him trying to sooth a recalcitrant Ma Relene made me feel pity and a tenderness toward him.

The Balas bar smelled like bamboo, tomatoes, and spicy peppers. It was wide open with a breeze pouring in from the ocean and swarming with international aid workers. They stared over at our table as Ma Relene raised her voice. She was eighty-two, bent over but still vibrant in her colorful dress and thick, braided gray hair. A potted palm tree leaned over her intently as she complained about the food. "It's always cold. These people can't cook. If I was in my own house . . ."

"Ma Relene . . ." Dad held up his hand.

Auntie Valina, always cheerful, laughed at the dustup brewing between Dad and Ma Relene. Her scattered memory left her to fade into and out of conversations. "So, Hector. You go and ride with Eddie every day?" She was proud that her son and I were bonding. She thought he should go back to America with us and bring his entire family. Cousin Eddie said he'd rather live through Maria once every year than leave Dominica. "Who would take care of you, Mammy?" he asked Aunt Valina.

It was a lazy tropical morning with sunrays seeping into the wooden slats dividing the restaurant from the main hotel. In the distance were the aid ships, a few sailboats, and a couple of fishing boats. As I relayed what Cousin Eddie and I saw on the bus trips across the island, Auntie Valina muttered prayers to the Virgin Mary. "We take so much pride in our island. It's God's wrath on us for that to be happening." She shook her head.

We could have spent all morning rehashing hurricane woes, but I was anxious to get on the road again. Cousin Eddie had agreed to take a couple of aid workers south to Grand Bay near where Mom grew up, and Dad reluctantly agreed to come along. "Well, you will finally get your wish," he said woodenly.

～

Outside the hotel was the two-hundred-year-old Anglican church, its gray stone still impressive despite the carnage Maria wrought on the structure. It was a similar scene at the stately Governor's residence, its pristine white facade and elegant gardens veiled by construction equipment and fallen tree branches. Dad sighed. "*Oui, Papa.*" More traces of dialect and Creole crept into his speech with each passing day. "I used to be so proud of that place."

Cousin Eddie was unmoved. "Skerrit send his wife and his children overseas when the hurricane warnings start. Imagine that?"

"But he himself was there for the whole thing," Dad countered. "The man was on CNN telling the world about our pain with the wind blowing outside. Crying real tears! What more you want from the man, Eddie?"

"Uncle, Uncle, Uncle." Cousin Eddie groaned. "You will never understand."

Our passengers, aid workers in their twenties, pecked away at phones, ignoring us completely. The drive south grew more and more treacherous beyond Loubiere, past the Anchorage Hotel which was still under repair. Dad grimaced. "I will tell you one day about how I come to hate that place." The bus's gears groaned and strained as we climbed the murderously pitted roads to the damp green villages of Giraudel and Eggleston. Residents waved at us as they corralled children to safety away from the narrow two-lane road. The aroma of roasting meat filled the cool village air; it seemed everyone was cooking outside these days.

The earth movers had pushed boulders as big as houses off to the side, but they left gawping craters in the road. I closed my eyes several times as we narrowly missed several of these holes. We climbed higher along the rocky mountainside with unstable soil, pebbles, and rocks still rolling down precipices at will. The true terror was on my right: a several-hundred-foot drop into mangled, devastated forest. Stretching out beyond that forest were miles and miles of obscenely beautiful ocean. The paradoxes of Dominica, I thought, were hard to look at and hard to look away from. Cousin Eddie's jaw tightened as he maneuvered in silence, perspiring in concentration. A packed bus full of steely-faced passengers headed to Roseau crawled by us, and the driver honked.

In the village of Soufriere, a familiar tableau of people putting their lives back together came into view. Crews rebuilding houses, replacing roofs. Weeping mourners at a memorial site for an entire family washed away that night. As we went further south, the side-by-side scenes of outrageous beauty and unfathomable destruction grew more and more wrenching. I turned to Dad to tell him this, but he was looking down into his hands and the corners of his eyes were wet. I left him alone.

A gorgeous stone cathedral just steps from the blue Atlantic caught my eye as we finally eased into Grand Bay. "Dad, look!" He nodded but seemed lost in another world or time. We came to a stop and the aid workers jumped out first. The soft earth under my feet after that harrowing ride felt like heaven. "If this was the US, the government would close those mountain roads. There's no way they'd allow people to be on those roads," I said.

Dad shrugged. "People here know how to take care of themselves."

Cousin Eddie grinned. "They gave me a tip. Can you imagine those Americans?" He counted out twenty US dollars in five-dollar bills. "You all want to look around?"

I had the urn in my backpack, ready for Dad to say: yes, this is the place.

A peaceful bay along the village couldn't hide the truth of the mounds and mounds of debris, broken houses, downed trees, and abandoned cars. I'd read of Grand Bay being a proud place known for its insurrections during slavery and colonial times. I started to say, "Yes. Let's hang out for a while." Maybe we could ask around, find someone who knew Mom's family. Maybe have an impromptu laying to rest. But Dad shook his head firmly. "No. Let's go back to Roseau. I don't want to be on those roads when it gets dark."

"Dad . . . don't you think we should . . ."

He raised his hand. "I want to go back now."

Cousin Eddie threw me a wary glance. Without waiting for us, Dad stepped into the minibus and shut the passenger door. Cousin Eddie shrugged. "He is right. I don't want to be on those roads after dark and I'm not sleeping here tonight."

We said nothing on the ride back to town. What was this encounter with the past doing to Dad? Now that the frenzy of Maria was quieting down, was reality setting in for him? I still didn't know the entire story of what happened between him and Mom back then. I'd taken for granted that one day Dad and I would sit and have "the talk" and all would be revealed. Well, I was at the scene of the crime, I thought, as we rolled back into Roseau. No time like the present.

Chapter 17

The sun blazed down in liquefying heat, and the smell of rotting fish and animal flesh still hovered as Cousin Eddie and I crossed West Bridge into Roseau. The stench was not as thick as that first week when it hung like a blanket until they took away the dead bodies. But it still lingered in my nostrils. At Hillsborough Street in the shadow of the Government Ministry Building, Cousin Eddie parked half on the sidewalk near a cluster of small houses. These cottages survived Maria with the equivalent of scrapes and bruises. The French built these things—sloped roofs, wood shutters—in the 1700s precisely with weather like Maria in mind, Cousin Eddie pointed out. A lot of the more modern homes with the newer roofs didn't live to tell their side of the story.

Dad was always evasive when I asked to see his old neighborhood. "Oh, we didn't live there long. Remember, my mother die when I was five." Now I could see why. The neighborhood, which the older people called a yard, was overcrowded and tight. Cousin Eddie and I walked single-file through a narrow alleyway with houses on each side. Curtains blew into my face, the smell of fried eggs wafted on the air, and conversations sounded as if I were in the room itself. For some reason, my anger toward Dad surged as I walked through the yard. His shame about this drove me nuts. What did he think he was protecting me from? Mom and I were poor, too! So many times I've wanted to scream at his calm, rational words of advice: *You try being the poorest Black kid in class bused in from the hood to the suburbs in 1980s Boston!* But he knew. He must have known, coming from here, this house, this yard.

Ma Relene's house, which had been rebuilt and modernized over the years thanks to Dad's generosity, was cozy-sized and humble. A crew of workers hammered at shingles on the roof. "Mikey, you here?" Cousin Eddie called out. Most of the furniture and fixtures were gone, probably destroyed by Maria.

Dad's cousin emerged from a back room. I hadn't seen him since we first arrived in Dominica. "Yes?" I'm not sure what to call Mikey. He was around Dad's age, skin a lighter brown and his hair was all white under his baseball cap. He was wearing grungy jeans, a checkered shirt, and smelled like sweat and stale beer.

"You remember me?"

He nodded. "I remember you." He turned to Cousin Eddie and laughed. "You can see that's Winston son in his face."

"So, you're . . . uh . . . rebuilding Ma Relene's house?" My bright idea was to come here and drill him for information about Dad just to satisfy my curiosity. Maybe Dad would find out, get pissed, and open up himself. Either way, I felt like an idiot when I saw his quizzical, almost mocking expression. "I mean, I could help you sometimes." I have no idea why these words came from my mouth. But I wanted to know him and what he knew about Dad growing up. He certainly didn't seem the type to sit down and chat just for the hell of it.

Mikey cast a bewildered stare at us then gestured to the bare insides of the roofless house. "We used to stay here," he said softly. As if oblivious to the workers pounding away on the roof, the loud soca music blaring from their radio, Mikey walked to the next room. He turned to me. "This used to be . . . where your father slept." He pointed to a corner, a half-smile on his face. "He used to keep a grip, a suitcase, there with all his things in it." Mikey laughed. "He used to be afraid me and my brother would take his things. You know?"

He kept talking, and I was amazed this man was so close to my father, yet Dad never mentioned him to me. "The bathroom, that kitchen?" He pointed. "All that is new. We didn't have inside toilet when we was growing up." He was half-smiling as he touched the walls, looking up to rafters that framed a blue sky. "I board up the windows for Mama before Hurricane David and before Maria. Both times, the roof gone. But the house still there. Waiting for your father to come back." He caressed the wall. "It hold up all these years waiting for Winston."

I didn't want to interrupt him, but his soft, apologetic voice carried years of regret and yearning. "Your father, Thomas, used to live in this house, too?" I asked.

"All of us." He looked me over. "Sometimes Winston would go by his sister's. But he always come back here. He love Ma Relene like his mother." He shook his head. "We had some hard times back in those days."

He pointed to the other side of the room. "My father die right there," Mikey began to say as a worker broke into our conversation to ask about ordering more nails. Cousin Eddie looked at his watch. We left, promising to bring Dad back next time. But my plan was to come back alone.

Much later that night, after I'd said goodnight to Dante, I sat on the verandah and lit up a kerosene lamp I'd found in the house. Just like the old days, Cousin Eddie said when he passed by. I tried to imagine my father as a boy in Dominica, living a life that couldn't possibly have foretold my existence. Eventually, I would get back on a plane. Not this week though, or even next week. I was anchored now, sifting through Maria's ruins for my father. The next morning, bright and early, I made my way to the tiny house on Hillsborough Street and left Mom's ashes behind.

Dad

Chapter 18

Roseau, 1971

At half past six a yolky sun crept over the emerald Roseau Valley. There was hardly any stirring in the dark of the small room, musty from three sets of breaths. Winston fixed his eyes upward, counting each coil of the bed springs in rhythm to the trumpet-like snores above him. The concrete floor poked his hipbones through bedding made up of torn dresses, sheets, pillowcases, and bath towels. Soon the roosters would crow louder, the yellow light would peek through the blue curtains, and the springs would sigh and sag, then Mikey's cracked brown feet would land on the floor, giving him clearance to slide out from underneath the bed. He'd learned the hard way to never wake Mikey or Augustus.

He waited silently, mouthing the list of mountains for the geography test: *Morne Diablotins, Morne Anglais, Morne Trois Pitons.*

The dusky, sweet smell of coffee and cocoa tea and the pans clanking on the stovetop woke his salivary glands. Ma Relene was frying bakes for breakfast. He placed his hands over his stomach, coaxing it to be quiet.

It felt like forever—like waiting for Mass to end. Finally, hunger drove Mikey and Augustus from the room and into the kitchen. Winston moved fast, quickly folding and placing each piece of bedding into a large pillowcase that he shoved under the bed.

In his tiny corner of the bedroom he kept a bureau Cousin Eustace made for him and a grip that held his good long pants, two short pants, two shirt jacks, and his holey home clothes. In a smaller wood box was the watch Uncle Thomas had left him, the credit union book evidencing the money his father threw at him that day, and pictures of Mama, Uncle Thomas, Zoom, Mona, and Valina that the missionary took with his instant camera. His things did not take up even a quarter of the room, yet Mikey and Augustus were always complaining, pushing him back into the window.

He gathered his composition book and pencils for school, talking to himself. "Boy, I late again."

"Good morning, Ma Relene." He whipped past her in the kitchen, running with a plastic bag that held his toothbrush, towel, and clean underpants.

"You going school today?" she called out in the always quavering voice.

"Yes, ma'am. I going river and bathe."

He sprinted past Mikey and Augustus who were kicking a Carnation tin back and forth in the yard while eating bakes with their dirty hands, still wearing the raggedy shorts they slept in. "I going and bathe," he announced just so they would know he planned to go to school today. They did not look up.

Pebbles pricked his soles as his skinny legs bounded through the yard, the smell of breakfast wafting from every kitchen window in the circular little neighborhood. He slowed at the sight of Ma Worth waddling over to the public latrine. Shucks! No time to wait. He turned left at Hillsborough Street, ran past Windsor Park, then jumped over the wall, river reeds brushing his knees.

The riverbank was deserted but he looked up and down for old ladies anyway. The cool air was clean with morning dew, and the smell of hibiscus hung over the calm flowing water. The Roseau River in this spot was shallow enough at times that even he could cross it to take the shortcut to Goodwill. But it had rained last night, and the water was deeper today, clear and cold as the silver Ma Relene displayed in the drawing room.

When he was smaller, about six or seven years old, Ma Relene told him to go far, far on the other side of the river if he saw a lady bathing or even washing her clothes nearby. It wasn't good for a young boy to see a lady in her personal state like that. Well, he didn't want any lady seeing him in his personal state either! The coast clear, he squatted over a couple of big rocks and did his business away from where people washed and bathed.

He hugged his skinny brown chest tightly and gingerly stepped into the icy water. "Chhhhh!!!" Goosebumps bloomed on his skin. He closed his eyes and let the water course through his afro as he sunk down, then he sliced up to the surface, making a big splash. The bridge, the bay, the contours of the Roseau Market were beginning to stir with life as he soaped himself with a bar of Lifebuoy soap, still shuddering from cold.

He dried himself quickly, pulled on his shorts and booked it back to Ma Relene's yard, a five-minute sprint. He would wash up again at the water pipe and brush his teeth there.

Mikey and Augustus were outside on the concrete steps eating their third helping of breakfast. "Mama was looking for you," Mikey sneered. "Why you stay so long at the river? You watching the girls again?"

"Is you that was watching girls, not me!" He tried to pass but they blocked him.

"You don't belong in my mother house. Go and stay with your sister!" Augustus glared down at him. His lips were coated in oil and Winston could smell the creamy cocoa on his breath. Augustus heard his stomach growling and his face loosened into a smile. "No more food for you. Greedy." Winston used the slightness of his frame to slip past as they laughed.

Ma Relene, a sturdy yet appealing woman, was at the kitchen table, her brows thick with worry and a hand on her forehead. Her sewing money and the pittance she made as a maid was barely keeping them afloat since Uncle died. He scanned the stovetop. There was about an inch of lukewarm cocoa in the saucepan. "No more bakes?"

She shrugged and pointed to three mangoes on the table. Her round, babyish eyes fluttered to the window where Mikey and Augustus were loudly arguing with another group of boys. Winston's heart thudded down to his angry belly. He walked slowly to the bedroom, and she followed him.

"Go and help Ms. Ford today. My back is hurting."

"But I going to school!"

"You can go school tomorrow. If you don't go by Ms. Ford, we will not have money. They will cut the lights again." She gave him a warning look. "I can't be expected to put food in your mouth and all you do is just eat and sleep."

He faced her defiantly and clenched his fists. "Uncle told me I have to go to school every day."

Ma Relene folded her arms and leaned against the doorframe, her chest overlapping her deep brown arms. "Well, he is dead. Your uncle is dead. And I cannot do everything for everybody!"

His mouth opened to argue, but she had already turned her back on him.

The morning sun, fully awake, shot arrows of stingrays on his forearms as he walked past the Roseau Boys School. He could have been throwing the ball plunking against a cricket bat, his feet among the rough scramble of cheap shoes on concrete, chasing a football. Desmond the accra man leaned against his wooden food cart at the school gate, a question in his eyes as Winston slunk by, too ashamed to say hello and too hungry to explain. Desmond's bull jaw sandwich was his favorite—spicy stewed saltfish surrounded by the thickest, whitest, warmest bread. The aroma from the cart was dizzying. *If I had all the money in the world, I would eat and eat and eat.*

At the bbbrrring, bbbrrring, brrrring of the bell, two hundred pairs of boys' feet clattered and shuffled, lining up for morning assembly under the stern glare of Headmaster Prince. A trumpet pierced the air and sprang over the school walls snorting the Dominican national anthem.

The sound reverberated in his heart, reminding him of his utter helplessness in the world. He was outside; they were inside. He would have laughed at

Charleston's terrible trumpet playing with the other boys and thrown a paper kite at his big head. In school everyone knew him, from the little boys who still cried for their mothers to the big boys who came once a month or left midmorning to go pick guavas. They called him Boogers because he picked at his nose, but he didn't mind. No one at home had ever called him a nickname, not Mama, not Zoom. Since Uncle Thomas died Ma Relene only called his name when she needed plates washed and water fetched. Maybe Mrs. Elwyn would come by the house to ask Ma Relene why he hadn't been to school, and maybe Ma Relene wouldn't make up a lie this time.

He kicked an empty cigarette box into an open gutter, which was beginning to roast under the morning sun, sending the thick stink into the air.

He almost ran past the hospital, not wanting to dwell too long near those painful memories of pitying nurses, Dettol-scented hallways, and a groaning Mama wasting away. He walked purposefully, head down, rubber slippers slapping at his heels and the dusty sidewalk, sweat dampening his blue T-shirt. He ignored the deep green grass, the purple, yellow, and red wildflowers and the gaily painted cottages and two-story homes along Goodwill Road.

The road widened as he entered the realm of mansions—traditional, Georgian, plantation style. He picked up three rocks, each the size of a mature guava, ready to aim at the German Shepherds that sometimes jumped the low fences.

Ms. Ford lived by herself in a bright house with green wrought-iron fencing and pink and red rose bushes, hibiscus and crocus plants all around it. The house was two stories, painted bright yellow, blue, and orange with a wrap verandah on both levels. Ma Relene's house could fit into it seven times.

Around Ms. Ford's house were similar houses with verandahs in the front and back, painted stark white or in tropical colors, all with neat trimmed hedges and wide lawns with flower gardens. In comparison, his world consisted of a *coubouyon* of crumbling Loyalist cottages and slapped-together cabins, which made Roseau seem like Neptune when he was up here.

Up here, the percussive shatter of dominoes was nonexistent. There were no rum shops for the drunks to stumble out of nor were there farmers squatting on the sidewalks offering a hand of plantains or a watermelon for fifty cents. Instead, solemn uniformed Black ladies drifted in and out from heavy front doors or peered at him from large-paned windows. The ones Ma Relene considered good friends waved to him.

This place was too quiet. Like the cemetery. He hated it.

He had barely rung the bell when a weak voice called out: "Relene's Boy? Relene's Boy?"

"Yes. Ma'am. Is Relene's nephew." He hated saying those words. Ma Relene was quick to remind him in her bad moods that she was nothing to him. Nothing. If she hadn't married his uncle . . .

Ms. Ford leaned on the door handle taking tortuous breaths. She was short, pink, and round, and a blue housedress billowed about her. Her swollen ankles spilled like porridge onto thick white leather sandals. He followed her inside and told her Ma Relene could not manage to come today. The smell of camphor balls made him dizzy.

"The whole house is flooded," she threw up a fleshy arm. "I need you to mop the floor and move some things outside so they can dry in the sun." She looked him up and down and shook her head. The last time he'd come here to help Julius the gardener weed the garden, she'd asked him if he ever ate.

"You are so small. How old are you?"

"I have ten years, ma'am." The same question year in year out.

Red and white lace curtains were drawn over the eight windows of the heavily decorated living room. The dark velvet sofas and glass center table did not get much sun and the windows were hardly ever opened.

He could hear Ma Relene's voice scolding him: "Don't let your eyes boil your peas and make that lady think I want to steal her things!" But there were so many things his eyes seized on. One wall was covered with framed photos of Ms. Ford's family—they ranged from tan to very white-skinned to somewhat white like Ms. Ford—doing various things, like playing on the beach with a big red ball, standing in front of a plane, wearing a Royal Navy uniform, wearing a graduation robe, posing in front of skyscrapers on American-looking streets. He felt her eyes on him and fixed his glance on a picture of the Virgin Mary.

"Come, come." He followed her through the dining room, which was large enough to seat a dozen people. The table was set with white fancy plates of the kind Ma Relene kept in a box under her bed, shiny silver forks, knives and spoons and white napkins. The table looked exactly the way it had the last time he came here, and he knew that Ms. Ford hardly ever saw visitors of any kind.

The wetness seeped into his plastic slippers when they reached the kitchen. He hadn't really believed the entire house was flooded; that was just how Ms. Ford talked. Ma Relene said she made up stories because she wanted someone to talk to more than anything else.

"You don't have anybody else to help you?" He asked this out of frustration, which she mistook for sympathy. Her children were abroad with their own families, she said, and she was nearly blind. "Who wants to fly two thousand miles to visit an old blind woman?"

There was a smaller table with chairs in the kitchen, a breakfast nook that looked out onto the bougainvillea and jacarandas in the backyard. He would have to take these chairs outside, she said, the legs were all wet.

"Everybody is busy with their own problems," Ms. Ford sighed. "Besides, I don't like to get too caught up with other people these days. This is not the Dominica of the forties and the fifties. These people today," she shook her head. "All thieves and rapists, you know? No schooling. You should hear them on the radio! And they want to run the country!" She caught herself and pursed her lips. "But Relene is a good girl. Loyal and honest."

Most of the house was shut away with the artifacts of a past that meant nothing to Winston. But he knew his way around from dozens of visits with Ma Relene. When she was busy puttering around, he would slip into the dusty library off the drawing room and open the big books with pictures, the encyclopedias, and the magazines with the naked Africans on the cover.

"Come," Ms. Ford now said without bothering to look back at him. The kitchen sink had flooded, and the real mess was the cupboards under the sink. He would have to take everything outside then clean it all up. "The mop and the pail are outside in the shed," she said.

The back door creaked and groaned and she said that needed fixing too, but he ignored her. He squinted in the sunlight after the gray dankness of the house. Her flower garden was whipped sideways by the last storm and not well kept up. He wondered if the gardener was sick.

"What is your name again?"

She was like a scratched-up record, always asking the same old thing.

"You are Thomas's nephew then?" She looked him over, assessing again. "Where is the rest of your family? Your mother?"

The mop and bucket were in a shed stuffed with other garden tools thrown this way and that.

"She died." Winston fumbled around with a shovel, a rake, trying to disentangle the mop. Ms. Ford's eyes opened wide. "Ooh! This was Thomas's sister who died of the cancer too?"

He yanked the mop away, leaving gray woolen strands on the rake.

She sighed and leaned her head to the side. "How old were you?"

"Five," he said. "Six." He refused to look at her. She had asked him before and she had asked Ma Relene, too. Was she the stupidest lady in the whole world?

"Why did she have you when she was so old, then?" Ms. Ford peered at him through her beady, grayish eyes, the left one clouded with cataracts.

He focused on the beetle crawling on his big toe and tried not to remember Mama's reddish hands holding his, taking him to all the shops on shopping day, then hanging paper Christmas decorations in the drawing room, as she brewed sorrel drink and ginger beer in the kitchen. She was not old. Mama was laughing and singing and drinking shandy. *"Chante, chante, chante Noel. Sing-a-ling Alleluia, Sing-a-ling Alleuia."* She was not old.

"Sometimes I think my life is hard." Ms. Ford shook her head and gave him a look of pity. "Why does God cause the innocent to suffer?" She sighed. "I will never understand."

He left her standing in the garden muttering and went to work in the kitchen. Those mangoes he had eaten had done nothing to fill the widening hole in his raging belly. He brought out the chairs and the small table then all the cleaning junk under the sink.

Lightheaded and hot, he leaned against the refrigerator and listened carefully. She was still out in the garden plunking around in the dirty shed. It would take her at least two minutes to make her way back into the kitchen.

He opened the refrigerator door. There were glass bottles of milk, Laughing Cow cheese triangles, half a cake, and some other food. He looked back toward the door and still she wasn't coming. He grabbed two triangles of cheese and put them in the pocket of his shorts. Then he quickly opened the thick glass milk bottle and drank straight from it, just two or three swallows. It felt cold and soothing all the way down to his stomach. He shut the refrigerator door quietly and waited to hear her come in. Still nothing. He began to mop up the wet floor. He carried things out to the garden that were not even wet. She was sitting, half asleep, holding on to a cane in a rocking chair. He carried the ten dining chairs out, two by two. She finally opened her eyes.

"Are you finished?" He shook his head.

"Take anything you want out of the fridge," she yawned. "The neighbors bring food every day and I can't eat it all. I always tell Relene to take it home with her. But Relene is so proud."

He went straight back to the refrigerator and finished the bottle of milk in a single gulp, then put it down breathlessly. A momentary hatred flashed through his body for Ma Relene and all the food she could never eat.

He began to mop again, slowly, stopping at times to cut slices from the buttery cold cake. Something told him he should not eat this lady's food, but he decided to ignore that voice. This was the most food he had eaten in one sitting since Christmas when Zoom cooked a feast that lasted for days.

The floors were drying and the windows still open when he ventured out again into the backyard. He cleared his throat, trying to wake her. Ma Relene said he should not leave without money. Ms. Ford did not stir so he cleared his throat loudly almost in her ear until she started.

"Oh, dearie," she repeated as he followed her into the house.

His heart pounded as she walked to the refrigerator. He felt the urge to run but it was too late. She opened the refrigerator and turned to him, the light showing the beads of sweat on her forehead. "You . . . you ate almost everything!" Her thin lips were pink slits of rage, her gray eyes accusing, burning into him. He looked for an escape like a cornered rat.

"Voracious. Greedy boy!" She glared at him waiting, daring him to explain himself.

"B-b-but . . ." He froze, not knowing what to say.

She took in a fuming breath and pulled a small red purse from the kitchen drawer. "You tell Relene how much you ate here today! You hear me, boy? I'm sure it's more food than you've ever eaten in your life. Don't you know your manners, young boy?"

He stared at her, not comprehending. She thrust five bills into his hands.

"But Ma Relene said it was ten . . ." He looked down at the money, dread creeping over him.

"You ate all my food!" she cried out, her eyes flashing in anger, her lips quivering.

"I . . . I . . . Sorry. I was . . . h-h-h-hungry . . ." The shame was like a pail of ice water dumped on his head, icy drops seeping deep under his skin.

She huffed and leaned toward him. "*Vowas*! Thief! Go!" She pointed to the back door.

He almost ran from the house, his every pore smarting with humiliation and anger. The fullness in his belly now felt sour. The five dollars burned in his pocket. How would he explain this to Ma Relene?

Chapter 19

He walked slowly down Goodwill Road, head down, sweaty hands in his pocket around the two triangles of cheese. He could think of a few things to tell her: he was running from a dog and dropped one of the bills. He crossed the river instead of walking over the bridge and dropped half the money in the river. But Ms. Ford would tell her. There was no way out of this. He had to tell her the truth. Maybe he could delay the inevitable for a while at least.

Town was busy for this time on a Monday afternoon. Even before he neared the bridge, he heard a bubbling commotion and glimpsed the contours of a colorful wave of people flooding into Roseau. He stopped, noticing that crowds of onlookers were forming on the sidewalk. Some were running into the street toward Roseau, ignoring the squawking horns and cursing drivers. He felt he had no choice but to follow.

They moved together, thrusting ahead and waving cardboard and plywood signs high in the air as they chanted, sang, and danced like a carnival band. A man wearing only his underpants and a red flapping robe beat on a *lapo-kabwit*. "Labour! Labour!" they cried, adding something in patois about "*Twavay*."

Were those the political troublemakers the announcers talked about on the radio?

The group of about a hundred took over the street, provoking a wail of car horns, curses, and even some stone-throwing. A lady ran out of the Christian gift shop and said, "Eh, eh! But look at those country bookie! Where dey think they going like that?"

He couldn't help himself. "How you know they country bookie?"

Hands on her hip, the lady scoffed. "Eh! Boy! Who else would wear raggedy clothes with all kinds of mix-up colors and have their feet so dirty in de street?"

He moved away from that lady and continued to push his way toward Hillsborough Street. If he could just get home and get inside. Yes, he would have to deal with Ma Relene, but this crowd was too loud, and their anger made his heart race.

Uncle Thomas would know what was happening. He knew everything about politics, and he was big in the Labour Party, the Roseau Town Council, and the Trade Union. Uncle Thomas could answer every question about Dominica. He'd talked on the radio about what was going to happen with the Banana Growers Association, the grapefruit packing shed workers and the lime juice factory and all of that. Winston sighed at his ignorance, the ignorance of Ma Relene and Mikey and Augustus, who hardly went to school. They would never know anything important. Ma Relene listened only to love songs and turned off the radio when the news came on. Uncle Thomas had warned him: if he never went to school, he would end up like the men playing dominoes in the yard every day, drinking rum and talking nonsense at the ladies walking to the shops.

He pushed forward through one protesting body at a time. Hardly anyone acknowledged him. He was a little boy who barely came up to their knees, ignorant of their need to be recognized as owners of their own destiny, no longer subservient to an indifferent Crown or the priggish bourgeois class. The people in red danced around, ducking stones and insults with their signs and cursing at their opponents on the sidewalks. Was this the thing Uncle Thomas had talked about before? The real end of colonialism? "No more British. No more bourgeois!" Uncle Thomas used to say. "The Black man, the Carib man, the poor man will rule Dominica one day." A radio blared from a shop window, adding to the noise. The announcer shouted the words rebellion and outlaws.

"Police protection!" a shop owner shouted from his doorway.

The noise was deafening now, traffic was completely blocked, and crowds surrounded the people in red who continued to shout: "Labour! Labour!" amid cursing and jeering from the onlookers. The people in red hooted louder and pumped their signs higher in the air.

Winston leapt out of the way as a man pushed forward to yell at the people in red. "Patrick John is a crook! All you stupid? What a poor man Black like butt can do for you?"

Oh! Uncle Thomas spoke about Patrick John all the time, about how he cared about the poor people and wanted to take Dominica back from the bourgeois and give it to the sons of slaves and give the Caribs the respect they deserved. Winston relaxed a little bit. Those country people were not making trouble then. Their supporters were now shouting. "Make them pass! Make them pass!"

"Pass where?" he asked a short lady waving a red kerchief next to him.

"Government building, boy," the lady said proudly. "Is history you seeing there! History, boy!"

How could he ever understand these things? When he was in small school Teacher Ellen showed them a map of the world and then had them take turns spinning a globe on its axis. The dot representing Dominica was smaller than the tip of his six-year-old pinky finger. Trinidad, Haiti, Dominican Republic all had black shapes next to their names. But Dominica was simply a dot, like one drop on the louvers after an afternoon shower. But his world felt enormous—the mountains above Roseau he could never climb, the towering cross at Morne Bruce that comforted him for reasons he could not explain, the wide Flamboyant trees and towering hibiscus hedges in the Botanical Gardens, even the hill leading up to St. Martin's School—it all seemed bigger than he could ever see himself. How could all of that be simply a dot on the world map?

He stopped at Sonny's bakery on River Street. The police had set up a blockade; no one was getting through. He was covered in sweat now, and his feet hurt from being stepped on a hundred times by adult feet. "Where you trying to go, boy?" A stern policeman holding a baton leaned down toward him.

"H-h-home." Winston pointed in the direction of his yard.

The policeman shook his head. "You cannot go there. You have people somewhere else? Then go there."

It was long past lunchtime, and people were pouring out of the shops, the government buildings, and all the schoolchildren had been let go. Roseau was teeming with people; no one was where they were supposed to be. Sirens were sounding. The air above the city crackled with tension and fear. He ran in the opposite direction of home.

When Mona finally came to the door, she was holding the left side of her face, which was swollen, and her eyes, big and brown like his, were red and raw. Winston was about to ask her what happened when Junior whooshed past, almost knocking him over.

"Junior! Stay inside!" Mona cried out. But Junior had already escaped, laughing. Mona sighed. "What you want, Winston?"

He hesitated and looked back to see his cousin gunning for the street. Junior was only a year younger than he, but Winston always felt like a baby next to him. Junior sneaked out to the street late at night to play marbles with the big boys no matter how many times his father dealt him blows like old clothes. Junior wasn't afraid of Mona or his bad father Mr. Clark.

"I couldn't go home. They have demonstration . . ." He was calmer now, even resigned in the telling. She stood with one hand on the doorknob as he told her the events of the morning, shaking her head at times.

From the wreckage behind her, he could see that Mona and Mr. Clark had been fighting again and he didn't want to add to her troubles. "I cannot go home until they open . . ."

"Just come inside," she said wearily. Her hair was half-braided, half-loose, scattered about her head like a dried-up bouquet of flowers. Her housedress was wet from the waist down, from what he didn't know. Mona should have been one of the giggling high-school girls spilling into Roseau's streets about now, but here she was in the broken down house she lived in with Mr. Clark and Junior, rubbing mercurochrome into a fresh set of cuts.

Broken glass littered the floor and a chair leg lay in the middle of the drawing room. Winston tiptoed around the mess, hoping no glass would pierce his plastic sandals. Gladly, Mr. Clark was nowhere in sight. He poured water from a half-full jug on the tiled counter into a plastic cup that said 7-Up. "Thank you." She drank the water slowly, standing in the middle of the room.

He began to pick up the pieces of the broken chair then cleared away the broken glass. She sized him up with the same big eyes like his and Mama's, but darker and more mysterious. She looked more like him than Zoom or Valina or even Mama. Some people said they had the same father because of the wide forehead and prominent, fleshy nose. But Mona had loose curly hair, like she was half-Carib. Mama never talked about any of their fathers so he would never know for sure if she was his only full sister—same father, same mother. Mona was the youngest of the three sisters and the most mysterious to him since she'd left the house without being forced out. Just the mention of her name made Zoom sigh and shake her head with sadness. Mama rarely talked about or even asked about Mona. He didn't know why; he simply accepted these rips and tears in his family as the normal fabric of his life.

Mona followed his cue and began to put the house in order. He piled the dirty dishes in a basin and took them out into the yard for washing. He then swept the yard with the *kokoye* broom.

"Winston," she looked down at him from the doorway, smiling, her arms full of clothes and sheets, "you want to go river with me and wash?"

"Now?" Mr. Clark's house had electricity and water running through the pipes, even an inside toilet. She could wash right there in the yard. Washing was for Saturday morning anyway.

And the streets were full of crazy people. She shrugged. "I will buy a Coke for you."

"And a bread and cheese?"

She sucked her teeth. "Boy, you too troublesome."

They headed out of the yard and into the streets, which were clearing. The shouting still echoed in the distance, near the government building. Mona sucked her teeth. "Dominicans too like trouble!"

She tried to balance the bucket of dirty laundry on her head, then gave up, laughing. They carried the bucket together between them, stepping over all kinds of litter, red T-shirts, abandoned shoes. Egbom's was the only shop open, and she bought him a Coke and a bread with sliced salami, which he finished in three to four bites.

The banks of the Roseau River were mostly deserted. Some ladies picking up sheets and rugs drying on the big rocks stared at them curiously. The women shook their heads and whispered at first. "Mona, what happen to your face?" an older lady asked, standing a few yards away atop a rock the size of the premier's Renault.

Mona looked down into the clear water rustling past her ankles and continued to sink the laundry into the water piece by piece.

"Mona, you need to leave that Clark alone. How much time people have to tell you that? Leave that Black devil man alone. Eh? Tonneh!" The lady sucked her teeth, muttering and gathering up her sheets. She kept up the mumbling and grumbling as her bare feet swiftly navigated the rocks to the sandy bank. "Your mother must be turning in her grave when she hear Clark bursting your tail every night!"

"Shut your mouth, dry-up old lady!" Mona yelled at the top of her voice with a rage burning hotter than any kerosene fire. The lady jumped, taken aback. Then with a look of undiluted hostility she gathered herself and turned away, hurling curses back at them. Mona cackled loudly in response.

Winston winced as Mona laughed. He himself couldn't explain his burning hatred for that old lady for speaking that way to Mona. "She so ugly," he hissed.

"Yes," Mona nodded. "Ugly old woman!"

He wriggled his toes in the sediment and rocks as three little gray fish swum over his feet. The water was clear and cool from the rain yesterday. He could see even the scar on his little toe. His stomach was full, and he could for a while forget about the bad news he had to deliver to Ma Relene.

"Remember, when you used to live with Mama, and you used to tell me stories in the night to frighten me?"

She laughed. "You remember that? You was too easy to frighten."

Washing in the river was a girl's job and the boys would remind him of this the next time he went to school, but he didn't care right now. He sank a bath towel into the river and then rubbed the blue Bomber soap into the cloth, forming a thick lather. Then he pounded the towel onto a rock a good two dozen times or so. Mona was more methodical and elegant. She rubbed the dresses, slips, and pants between both hands, then squeezed, spilling out a luxurious, white lather. Her process was rhythmic and delicate, like a hand dance, and her hands would be raw and red when they were finished. She disappeared into another world as she washed. And he, too, enjoyed the quietness of the late afternoon, the gentle gurgle of the river, a light breeze bending the reeds at the riverbank. A Rastaman sat on a rock off in the distance simply looking past the Roseau Valley into the hills of Trafalgar and Laudat.

"I will tell you another story. Not to frighten you though," Mona washed one of Mr. Clark's shirts carefully.

"About what this time?" Winston smiled eagerly.

"About *Compere Lapere*."

"A new *Compere Lapere* story?" This was one of his favorite characters, a proud but unfortunate trickster who couldn't seem to get his life together.

Darkness soon crept at the edges of the day as they gathered up the laundry, some dry, most damp. "Those clothes not going to dry before the sun go down," he said. But Mona was far away in thought.

"Mona, what Mama used to do before she get sick?" The horizon was adorned in a gauzy carnival costume of pinks, purples, and red, and the air swished cool against his chest. He pulled his now crispy-clean blue T-shirt over his head. In the distance, crowds were walking slowly over the bridge, laughing and singing groups of people. Maybe they got what they wanted from the government, he thought.

"You don't know?" Mona asked. He assumed Mama had cleaned houses, like Ma Relene and other ladies in the neighborhood, before she fell sick.

"She was a banana lady. Mama used to carry bananas. Quick, quick, quick to the Geest boat on the harbor." Mona snapped her fingers three times. "She used to get three shillings a week for that."

"Three shillings a day?" He tried to figure out how many bunches of bananas he could carry in a day.

"No. A week. That's a dollar for a whole week." Mona shook her head. "Those ladies used to work fast, man. Back and forth, back and forth all day. They carry a bunch of bananas on their head and run to the boat, come back and pick up another bunch and run to the boat. For a whole day when the Geest boat come."

"They wouldn't fall?"

"Sometimes they would fall. But Mama was fast and strong."

"So how she get sick then?"

Mona shrugged and looked off into the horizon. They sat in silence for several minutes listening to the sighing river, watching the parade of colors salute the setting sun. He couldn't reconcile the memories of a sickly, weak, shrunken Mama balancing a bunch of bananas on her head and running for hours under the Roseau sun. The few times he had seen her well, she'd had just enough strength to cut his hair or cook a *balao*, cabbage and dumpling broth.

They walked back quietly to Mona's yard, the bucket of clean clothes swinging between them. It was dark now and the closer they drew to Mr. Clark's house, the slower Mona walked. She fished something out of her pocket and handed it to him.

He looked down and saw it was a five-dollar bill.

"Take it," she said.

His eyes opened wide. "But that's Mr. Clark's money?"

Mona did not work; there were no jobs for most people in Roseau, least of all for a sixteen-year-old mother with no education. She shook her head intensely. "Take it and tell Relene to stick it where the sun don't shine."

He tried to stifle a laugh as he put the five-dollar bill in his pocket next to the other one from Ms. Ford.

Roseau's streets were mainly deserted, but lights glowed in the windows of the houses. The very few houses of the bourgeois that owned televisions emitted a blue glare that filled Winston with a deep longing and curiosity. He longed for the day when one of his sisters, maybe Valina, would finally own a television. Then he'd never have to steal his way into the Arawak cinema again or peek into a stranger's window from outside.

Junior was in the yard playing when they arrived, and a light was on in the main room of the house. "You want to play marbles?" Junior looked up at Winston wistfully.

"I have to go home," Winston replied, setting down his end of the bucket.

"Mona!" The voice from inside the house was raspy.

Mona's back straightened and she turned to Winston, taking three quick breaths. "Remember," Mona said, walking into the house, a hand on her chest, "tell Relene to stick that money where the sun don't shine."

Mikey and Augustus were on the front steps eating supper—twenty-five-cent bread and ginger tea—when he finally dragged himself to the house. "My mother was looking for you all day," Augustus said through a mouthful. "She say you cannot stay here and you have to go and live with Zoom because you causing her too much headache." The two brothers laughed.

Winston's heart sank. Did Ma Relene know? Had Ms. Ford told her what happened? He entered the house with the ten dollars in his shaky hand.

Ma Relene's feet bobbed up and down on the sewing machine's pedal, keeping step with the hum-dee-hum of the needle sinking down into the colorful cloth. He greeted her as respectfully as he could. "You making another dress?" Ma Relene was a pretty but sad woman who thought everyone was her enemy because of Mikey and Augustus's bad reputation.

"You see all that trouble in town today?" she asked, glancing up from her sewing.

He nodded. "Yes, but I go river with Mona. I didn't get in trouble with those demonstration people."

"She give you food?"

He didn't answer. He placed the ten dollars on the sewing machine table where she kept bobbins of thread and extra needles. "I hide some pelau for you in the cupboard," she said, taking the money with one swipe and swiftly placing it into her bra.

He ate his pelau in peace in the kitchen at the small table with only two chairs where he and Uncle Thomas would listen to so many cricket and football games. He was ten years old and already longing for the good, older, simpler days when they all lived with Mama in the crowded little house. Before Mr. Clark came and took Mona to live with him and gave her a baby. Before Valina began to run off on the cargo boats with the big men. Before Zoom stopped going to school and lost her wide-open-mouth laugh. Before Mama got sick and their house turned into a sick place full of Mama's groans and Zoom's tight-lipped grumbling.

Chapter 20

Roseau, 1966

On Saturday mornings, Winston belonged to Zoom. Zoom, birth name Rose Clair Telemacque, was of average height, and like Mama, had reddish skin and frizzy black hair that she wore in two thick plaits parted in the middle and pulled back in a bun at the base of her neck. This Saturday, as always, she strode quickly through town, her flowery skirt swishing, her slippers flapping, her eyes straight ahead; uttering an efficient "good morning" here and there.

Winston skipped and stumbled close behind as she chided him. "Keep up with me. No. Stay right by me. You want a car to bounce you?"

Winston would say Zoom was the most serious of his three big sisters. Uncle Thomas said she took after her father, who was in the Mason Lodge— all those men were real serious people. Still, Zoom was the best cook, and Mama trusted her the most with everything in the house. She was the one who stayed with him in school that first day when he couldn't stop crying and carried him to Doctor McFarlane when he had mumps. But he knew never to get on her bad side because she would twist up her lips, put her hands on her round hips, and threaten to put a *calotte* in his ears.

Saturday was Roseau's busiest and loudest day with car horns and music blaring, people malingering and talking in the middle of the street like they hadn't seen each other in a hundred years. Music was pounding from the groaning Bedford trucks bringing the country folks from the villages to sell their fruits, flowers and ground provisions in the market. Eyes squinted against an almost pernicious sun. Men, stooped with heavy sacks of vegetables on their backs, were soaked in sweat. Ladies wearing nice Creole dresses and fancy shoes fanned themselves and wiped away balls of talcum powder collecting in their chest cleavage.

Winston eagerly snaked his way through the market stalls ablaze with oranges, yellow peppers, radishes, green bananas, and limes plucked from small village farms and large estates owned by the bourgeois. The earthy sweet cane and custard apple smells intoxicated him, and he was spoiled by the vendors squatting over heaps of produce who would toss him a plum, a mango, a guava without expecting a single coin.

Zoom flinched when vendors asked if that was her handsome little son. "No. That's my little brother. Eh!" One time she was so vexed, she grumbled, "Is not my fault Mama decide to go and have child in her old age."

As they barreled through the vendors, a nun dressed in full habit stepped fully into their path forcing Zoom to stop. Winston froze as the towering pink woman in the flowing black robe clutched Zoom's arm with all the authority of the police. "Rose Clair Telemacque! Why haven't we seen you at school?"

Zoom shrugged her arm away and frowned at the pink-faced woman with the *beke* Irish accent. "Sorry, Sister. My mother is sick. In an out of the hospital and I have to take care of her."

"What about your older sister? Can't she help?" The nun looked down at him and smiled. Winston fused himself into Zoom's left leg, hiding his face behind her full thighs.

"She back and forth in Martinique, St. Martin. I don't know." Zoom sighed and held his shoulder, trying to cajole him front and center, but he was frozen in awe of the nun's confident way with Zoom. Only Mama could command this respectful tone, these lowered eyes, these tight shoulders from Zoom.

The nun's face, roughened and freckled from decades under an unforgiving tropical sun, reflected all her frustration with these inevitabilities of poverty. She was a pillar in an order fervently committed to a heavenly calling that began long before the British and the French finally quit their battling over this little green patch in the Caribbean Sea. She'd seen and heard it all before. "Young lady, you will lose your scholarship this term if you don't return soon." The harsh tone was betrayed by a softness in her silvery eyes. Such a tragedy to lose yet another one to the indolence and apathy wrought by hopelessness and sin. This one was smart, a feeling girl with a bright imagination who inspired the other girls to follow the right ways.

Zoom reclaimed her arm and began to edge away. "Sorry, Sister."

Winston clung to her heel, skipping over a puddle, a half-eaten mango, a banana peel. Zoom was almost running away now, looking back over her shoulder at the nun who stood watching, shaking her head.

"Zoom, you don't want to go to school?" Winston looked back at the nun.

"Of course I want to go to school! You stupid or you mad?"

"So go to school then."

"And who going to fix your food and wash your clothes and take care of Mama?" She blew a torrent of air through her mouth and shifted the basket of provisions from one elbow crook to the other.

Winston considered this then arrived at the solution. "When Mama get better you will go then."

Zoom grumbled as she raced through the stalls, bargaining for root vegetables, plantains, potatoes. "Fifty cents for a hand of fig! Ah wah! You wicked, man! Take twenty-five cents and be happy I even give you that!"

They filed out of the market as fishermen, just in from the bay with heavy boats, blew their conch horns calling out: "Buttttt! Tuna! Flying Fish!"

On the way back to their yard they stopped in the grocery for meat and cheese. There was no reason Zoom couldn't go to school, Winston thought. Mama had money saved in a box under her bed. They were not *poor malaway*; they ate chicken-backs-and-neck on Saturday and Sunday—not fish like the really poor people in Lagoon. Zoom was just making excuses.

His attention was soon swallowed up by the grocery shelves of things he could only dream of eating. Grapes and apples, large hunks of beef and chicken nicely cut and packaged in clear plastic, beautiful cheeses, peanut butter, and orange, red, and purple jams. He took in these sights open-mouthed. What would it be like to eat these things every day? He recalled a picture book with a little white boy eating a slice of white bread with orange marmalade spread on top. What did marmalade taste like? Was it nicer than the oranges he'd picked off a tree in Laudat?

Zoom filled a shopping basket with rice, flour, powdered milk, sugar, and salt, Breeze, Clorox, and Blue. By the time they were finished, they each held four plastic bags. His bony shoulders drooped with each step, but he refused to complain. It was barely a ten-minute walk, and his legs felt more like lead with each step. When they finally reached home, he dropped the bags in the drawing room, sweat pouring from his forehead, his shoulders screaming. Zoom shooed him out to the public bath to get cleaned up.

"You wash your hair?" She had a tall glass of sweet passion fruit juice, a thick chunk of bread with a slice of precious cheese waiting for him. His hair was still dripping onto his T-shirt, and she told him as much as he sat at the small table in the tiny kitchen.

Their house was a four-room assemblage of thin wood covered in leaky corrugated iron they rented for ten dollars a month from a family that owned many such houses in Roseau. These colonial-era artifacts, despite their weak appearance, survived hurricanes, tropical storms, flooding, and decades of physical neglect by landlords down to the last few dollars of their shame-ridden inheritances. He was born in this house in 1961 and so were Zoom, Mona, and Valina. Mama and Uncle Thomas were from Veille Case, a cool green village up north where you ate all your food straight from the ground, Zoom told him once. But they, the family, were town people now, not country bookies. And even though life was hard and sometimes cruel in Roseau, it was better than breaking one's back in the soil for 365 days with nothing but more dirt and sweat to pass down to your children.

Zoom watched him eat, smiling, as she spooned flour porridge from a metal bowl into her mouth. She always did this; rewarding him with his favorite foods. Their work was not finished though: there was still a week's worth of laundry to carry to the river. The river was the best part of Saturday chores because for him it meant splashing around and hunting for crayfish with the neighborhood boys over the three hours it would take Zoom to wash and dry.

Amid all of this activity, Mama slept, closed off from him and the world in her dark room, waking only to groan for water and her medicine. Every morning, he poked his head in to say, "Good morning, Mama. You sleep well?" Most times she answered with a groan or to ask for Zoom. He had stopped crawling into the bed with her when Zoom scolded him that he was too rough and made Mama's pain even worse. Sometimes, when Zoom left the house, he stood by Mama's bed and they talked. He told her about Teacher Rose and the catechism class, about Junior's escapades from Mona and Mr. Clark's house, and how Valina was filling her little house with more and more gifts from overseas. Mama, on her good days, laughed or rolled her eyes at these news updates. On most days, though, she simply held out her hand so she could grasp his while he talked and talked about his six-year-old world.

Under Zoom's orders, he was allowed to go into Mama's room only on Sundays after Mass. On the days or nights when Mama was screaming from the pain, Uncle Thomas would appear, scoop him from bed and carry him to his house on Hillsborough Street. On the quiet nights, he slept fitfully, clutching Zoom tightly, feeling her tense up each time Mama groaned or coughed.

With the washing paper-dry, Winston would slip away from Zoom and sprint to Uncle Thomas's house. It was the summer of 1966 when the West Indies cricket team bowled and batted through their tour of England, and all through Roseau men huddled around radios, clenching their fists and furrowing their brows through the ups and downs of that series.

With their knees touching under the kitchen table, Winston and Uncle Thomas bowed their heads as if in prayer over the Phillips radio, always shifting to pick up the clearest signal. Uncle Thomas cursed the umpire's mother and father as the games wore on through lazy afternoon showers and long past kaleidoscopic sunsets. Winston laughed as Uncle Thomas ripped at his eye patch or kicked his chair across the kitchen floor. "*Dem Mudda Arse!*" At least once Ma Relene threatened to throw the radio into the sea. Then, late at night Uncle Thomas sat outside with the other men replaying every minute of the games, cursing, smoking, and drinking until four o'clock in the morning. The West Indies won three of those five games that year, spreading a pride and excitement Dominicans had never felt before.

He looked forward to those Saturday afternoons, despite the chores, despite the teasing from Mikey and Augustus. He imagined himself someday a spin-bowler or a batsman as he played with the cousins and boys from the yard. Windsor Park—the same Windsor Park where the Shillingford Brothers put the Windies Dominica on the world stage—only a few steps away was their field of dreams. They snuck in over and under fences during the big cricket and soccer matches because they lived here and why should they pay an entry fee to their own playing field? Uncle Thomas came out some Saturday afternoons, keeping the wicket or just cheering on the boys, smoking cigarette upon cigarette.

On these afternoons, Roseau belonged to them as they threw themselves into whatever mischief the lanes and yards offered, swiping guava from a vendor in the market, harassing the *womyels*, street vagrants, who cursed at them as they ran away, jumping into the Roseau River for a quick dip, running all the way to Donkey Beach for a swim. There were no cares or worries beyond each tropical, golden day.

Chapter 21

"Uncle, you think you will go England one day?" Winston was batting the balls Uncle Thomas lobbed at him in a corner of the field, a bit away from where the professional cricket team were practicing. Big men like Uncle Thomas knew the famous cricket and football players and even practiced with them right here on this grass. The players were loud and boisterous, and a crowd from the neighborhood watched from the stands.

"If I want to go England? Yes, boy. I want to see snow before I die. That's one thing I want to see." Uncle Thomas touched his eye patch. "That would be something, eh. And to see all those tall buildings."

"I want to go England too, then."

"You can go anywhere in the world," Uncle Thomas said. "But you have to do your work in school and get high marks."

"When you go, I want to go with you."

Uncle Thomas only laughed because, at that point, he was very sick.

Winston had just switched positions to bowl when, like a ghost floating through a cloud of dust, Zoom's figure raced toward them. Barefoot, with her hands flapping at her sides, she cried, "Come! Come! Mama!"

Winston dropped the ball and pointed at Zoom, his mouth open. Uncle Thomas turned his full body around so he could see. Zoom was upon them now, breathless and wiping sweat from her brow. "Mama sick again. She throwing up blood this time."

Uncle Thomas grabbed Zoom by the arm so he could keep up without falling. "Since this morning she coughing, coughing like that but I thought it would pass after I give her the medicine." Zoom's breath was out of control, and she was moving too fast for Uncle Thomas, who kept patting his eyepatch every few seconds as he stumbled alongside.

Winston trotted after them, his heart pounding. Zoom had never come to Windsor Park to disturb them like this. In the past, when Mama got really sick, they just took her to the hospital; sometimes she was back in her bed same day. A dark, heavy feeling like the clouds over the cross in Morne Bruce began to press down on his shoulders.

Ma Celia and Ma Joan stood at the entrance to their yard, hands on hips, mournfully shaking heads wrapped in colorful kerchiefs. "Zoom," they called out. "Roy coming with the car. Just put something on her and bring her by the street."

"Alas. Poor Pity. That's a lot on Zoom, eh."

They wouldn't let Winston inside the house, though later he would see the bloody cloths.

He stood alone as Uncle Thomas, Mr. Roy and Ma Celia's sons carried Mama to the green Peugeot. Her tiny body indented the middle of a make-shift stretcher—a sheet with each of the four men holding an edge. Zoom's face tightened as she spoke to the men. "Don't drop her too hard." Voice quivering, Zoom seemed smaller to Winston now. He tried to swallow a rising terror and squeezed his eyes to corral the tears.

Uncle Thomas shook his shoulder. "We will finish the game when I come back, eh?"

"Winston, go back and play!" Zoom, leaning into the back seat of the car, pointed toward the stadium. But her red, puffy eyes were distant, and her pudgy hands shook. Then she squeezed her eyes. "No. No. Go to Pound and tell Valina what happened. And if you see Mona, tell her we go hospital with Mama."

He straightened up at the command, desperate to erase the too-bright image of the men struggling to settle Mama into the Peugeot. Without waiting to hear more, he raced over to Pound where his oldest sister lived.

The flimsy wooden door with glass louvers in the top half was wide open, sending Mighty Sparrow's baritone wafting into the yard. Mr. Squires's record player, which Zoom grudgingly talked about nonstop, was turned up full volume, serenading the neighborhood of tiny wooden houses.

Winston walked in on Valina, who was dancing trancelike in the drawing room near a rose-pink velvet settee and drinking D Special rum straight from the bottle. Her gold loop earrings dangled against her powdered-ruby cheekbones; her gloriously high afro shifted with her every undulation. "What happen?" She sensed his presence and halted, hands and bottle midair, as she read Winston's expression.

Panic began to rise in his chest. "Zoom and Uncle go hospital with Mama." He took in several gulps of air. "She throw up blood." He moved closer to her long, bare legs. "And all her bed is blood." He took another few gulps of air that exploded into a wail that he tried to suck back in but instead turned into a cough followed by hot, heavy, uncontrollable waves of water from his eyes, nose, mouth.

Valina flinched as if the music had stopped in her head, but quickly collected herself. The artificial lashes that framed her big brown eyes fluttered. She smoothed one hand on the tiny shorts that strained at her thighs. "Boy, what you crying like that for?" She leaned down and put a hand on his head, her fingers soothing his thick, uncombed hair.

He choked and sputtered. "M-M-M-Mama was . . . she . . . was . . ." The words were held hostage in his throat; tears and snot ran down his face, onto Valina's legs, her platform sandals and red-painted toenails.

Mr. Squires's frame suddenly darkened the room. "What happen? What going on?" He was a big man, with a gold front tooth and a big, mesmerizing watch on his left wrist. He and Valina had been off and on for years, and she eventually won out over the other girls who vied for his attention and the benefits of his big job on the port. Mr. Squires's presence immediately sent a chill through Valina's sympathy for Winston, and she straightened herself, taking her hand away from his head. Winston looked up into Mr. Squires's anger and confusion.

"I will go and see her tomorrow." Valina smoothed herself over, her Cutex-red nails glinting in the sunlight. The finality in her voice signaled it was time for him to leave. The music seemed louder now, and Mr. Squires turned back to the kitchen singing Mighty Sparrow's "Winer Girl."

Valina was moving her hips again, staring off into the distance, past the curtain and the open door, into the crowded yard of shanty houses. Winston stared at his sister as she took another sip of the rum, her eyes drifting off someplace else altogether. He was standing in the room all alone, and Mr. Squires was in the kitchen tap, tap, tapping to the music.

"Go!" Valina pointed to the open door. He hopped to, almost entangling himself in the beaded curtain from St. Martin that Zoom also talked about nonstop. Those stupid beads caught him up every time. Then he was out in the yard, not looking back but feeling her wet eyes on him nonetheless.

He blinked and kicked a rock between the houses of Pound, alive with conversations, radios playing, babies crying. Out on the street, he looked north toward Windsor Park and south toward the rest of town and the bay-front. He was too afraid to go home to the dark, lonely, sick house.

It was nearing 5:00 p.m. and a nicely dressed crowd had lined up outside the Arawak cinema. The Lone Ranger scowled at him from a black-and-white poster as big as a house. Desperate as he was for a diversion, he could not muster the desire to sneak in through the cinema's back window.

Instead, he lingered outside Mona's kitchen, hoping she would look out the back door by accident. Just as he was about to give up and go home, Junior tapped his shoulder, causing him to cry out in fright. "Boy! What you doing?"

Junior laughed, throwing himself onto the ground and kicking up his four-year-old legs. "I frighten you! I frighten you!" The boy howled in laughter.

Mona soon came out through the back door, exasperatedly calling out to Junior, "Who out there with you?"

"It's me," Winston called out.

She sucked her teeth. "What you hiding outside for?"

Mr. Clark was nowhere to be found, and the house was clean and peaceful, not nearly as pretty as Valina's, but at least it was neat today. Winston sat on a rickety plastic chair in the drawing room as Junior crawled on all fours, pushing a race car around.

"You want to go to hospital and see Mama?" Mona lit a cigarette and crossed her legs. She was sitting on the new sofa Mr. Clark had just bought from Cort's to replace the one he had broken in their last fight. Winston shook his head. "I can stay with you tonight?"

She stared long at him, taking several drags on the cigarette. "Clark don't want my family in his house. You know."

"Maybe he will stay in the rum shop tonight again," Junior said loudly, causing Mona to swat at him. "Shut up, Junior!"

She sighed and took another drag on the cigarette. "Okay. You can stay tonight, but if he come back you have to go by Valina. Or go by Relene. Okay?"

"Okay," Winston said softly. He didn't want to risk Mr. Clark finding him here in the middle of the night but the prospect of sharing a room with Augustus and Mikey seemed unbearable.

Staying at Valina's was an option, but from her reaction earlier, he knew better than to even ask. It was only last year that Mama finally threw Valina out. She'd returned from a big shopping trip with Mr. Squires in St. Martin and brought him a set of bright-colored plastic racing cars. He hadn't been prepared for the knock-down drag-out fight in the yard, which started when Mama asked Valina about a glass elephant she'd placed on the buffet in the drawing room. Valina said it was a gift from Mr. Squires. "How many times I have to tell you don't run around with other people's husbands old enough to be your father!" Mama cried out loud enough for the neighbors to hear. Then the quarreling began. Zoom grabbed his arm and ordered him to go play outside. But he turned back when he heard Valina screaming. Mama was swinging the broomstick, sick as she was, repeatedly hitting a crouching, screaming Valina in the head. He fled and sat in the stands of Windsor Park, shaking, mind completely blank. He remained there till dark when Zoom came looking for him. Valina had already left by the time he sat down for a supper of bread and cheese for him; flour porridge for Zoom. They never talked about that day again. Valina's house, with all the nice things from Mr. Squires and her other overseas friends, signaled to Winston that she would never again live in their dark, sick little house. Mama, confirming this change, even let Zoom sleep in Valina's bed. "You have one sister left," Mama said to him weakly, anger flashing in her helpless eyes, when he went into her room to say goodnight. "One sister."

Now Junior was at his feet, jamming the race car at his big toe. "Junior, stop that!" Mona hissed.

"Let us build a shack and sleep outside like brothers," Junior said to Winston. "You will be big brother and I will be little brother."

Winston shook his head. "No. Not tonight."

"Okay. We will sleep inside then," Junior said.

But there was no sleep for Winston. He kept waking from dreams of Mama, pale and sickly in a hospital ward full of white-uniformed nurses, calling his name. It was comforting to hear Junior's peaceful, untroubled breaths next to him.

Chapter 22

Christmas lights, like an army of fireflies, illuminated Roseau, creating a magical world of twinkling greens, reds, and yellows in the shop windows. Giddy with anticipation, Winston conjured up the fanciest toys he could wish for: a G.I. Joe, a firetruck, a set of racing cars with their own track. He could spend hours staring into the store windows, and shopkeepers swept up in the season would not shoo him away. He sang along with the radio in the drawing room. *"Dominique pas ni niege. Dominique pas connete sleigh bell . . ."*

Zoom was making her famous brown stew with chicken-backs-and-neck and chayote; red bean soup with salted *jel cochon* and dumplings. He hovered in the yard all day, taking orders to bring her salt and seasoning, to fan the coals on the coal pot, and to watch the cats and the dogs loitering around for scraps. Mama was under the covers inside; the packing for her trip had made her tired.

"Zoom, you not coming to the airport with me and uncle?"

Zoom stirred the pot of soup and shook her head. "Boy, why you asking me stupid questions like that for?" She sucked her teeth. "You think I have time to go airport when I have things to do?"

"But tomorrow Sunday, Zoom. All you have to do is go Mass."

She stopped stirring. "Why you so rude? I don't have to be your mother for you to respect me! You hear?" She stalked into the house. He took her place and began to stir.

Ma Joan was in the always-open doorway of her blue house; he could feel her eyes on him. "Winston, you sad your Mama going away?"

Ma Joan, with her colorful kerchief over her gray hair, was always minding somebody else's business. "No, Ma Joan. I going to the airport with them tomorrow."

Ma Joan shook her head sadly. "Zoom will take good care of you. Your mother teach her really good." She emerged to empty a watering can over the ferns and roses growing in rubber tires outside her house.

"Zoom and Mama will take good care of me," Winston corrected her. "And Uncle Thomas."

Ma Joan shook her head, muttering, "Jesus, Mary, mother of God. That is some sadness, eh."

Zoom emerged wiping her eyes. Her hair was in pink and yellow rollers, framing her round face. She handed him five dollars and a list. "Don't walk too fast with my eggs, eh?"

On the way to the shop, he bumped into Uncle Thomas, who was carrying a plastic bag full of flying fish, red fish, and tittiwee that he'd been seasoning since he bought them from the fisherman. "You ready for de party, boy?" Uncle Thomas grinned. His khaki pants were even looser on him these days, and his neck was like a pencil sticking out of his collared blue shirt. Yet he was a cheery, tall version of Mama with big curly hair, reddish-yellow skin, and a deep brown eye.

"Yes, sir!" Winston rushed to the shop so he wouldn't miss anything, especially Uncle Thomas's fried fish.

Later, he hurried through his shower at the bathhouse, ignoring the freezing water that made him shiver like a leaf in the wind. He covered his torso in sweet-smelling baby powder, then donned his good shirt with the buttons and blue short pants.

Zoom was soon after him again with more chores as he tried not to trip her up in the tiny kitchen. His hands moved like a band conductor's as he beat eggs for a pound cake, singing in rhythm to the whisker's strokes. *Christmas is coming; the goose is getting fat.* He grazed his fingertips a hundred times as he grated a coconut.

Suddenly, a voice, weak and shaky like a warbler's song, startled him. The sight caused him to stop short, grater in midair. "But Zoom, why you not saying nothing? You just working, working and not saying nothing." It was Mama, in a yellow-and-black duster, leaning in the doorway. The duster dwarfed her frame, and her translucent yellow hands quivered with every word she spoke. There was a time, Winston thought, when she took up most of the doorframe. Now she was so small he could see the dark drawing room behind her: the settee, the center table, the buffet with the radio on top. She touched her hair, which was still in the orange curlers Zoom put in last night.

Zoom jumped to attention. "Mama! Everybody coming just now. I have to get all the food ready." She rushed to Mama's side, ready to hold her up, but Mama shrunk back from her.

"Where Valina and Mona?"

"Mama, you know Valina not coming till food ready and Mona have to do for Clark."

Mama sighed. "Zoom, the whole world don't always have to be on your shoulder." Zoom muttered under her breath, and Mama turned slowly back to her bedroom.

"*She* put the whole world on my shoulder," Zoom hissed and looked down at Winston. "You hear me? Is *she* that do it!"

Winston, not understanding, yet certain that he was on Zoom's side, sidled up close and hugged her spongy legs. "Ma Joan say you will take good care of me, Zoom."

Zoom tensed, and her hands quit their furious battle with the cake batter. "I don't mind taking good care of you," she said and patted his head. "You're a good boy."

She sniffed and was still for several moments. "Okay," she finally said, sniffing again and restarting the rattle with the batter. "Go and get a bucket of water to wash these bowls, okay?"

He ran off, eager to please her, eager for everyone to be happy, to eat, drink, and be merry.

That night the moon was a bright disc of fine china, lavishing its beams over the yard, over Pound, over Lagoon, and all of Roseau. The neighbors flocked to the middle of the yard with a plate or for a plate, with a drink or for a drink. Mona arrived with Junior running ahead, and Valina came with Mr. Squires, who brought a record player, speakers, and a tangle of electrical wires to connect to the street post. Cousin Eustace came from Fond Cole to help set everything up. Then Uncle Thomas came with Ma Relene, Mikey, and Augustus. Soon loud cadence and soca music blared beyond the yard, drawing more neighbors from all the way up by the fire station. Even Ma Joan was shaking her tail like it was *Jouvert*.

Winston and the cousins, full of rich food, ran off into the streets playing cowboys, then tag, then hide-and-seek, then football with anything worth kicking.

The aroma of Uncle Thomas's frying fish drew him back breathlessly to where Uncle and Zoom sat around the coal pot. Winston eavesdropped as Uncle Thomas dipped each flying fish into a floury mix before sinking it into the cast-iron skillet bubbling with hot oil.

"Thomas, I doh have nothing to say."

"Is better for your mother to go Barbados and get the surgery. Look at how your own face look so nice now. You go there, and they fixed you up."

Zoom shook her head. "I not saying is not good for her to go. Is just a lot of money."

"Ah," he waved a hand. "I will pay back the credit union."

"So, okay. She will go and leave me with . . ."

"Winston will come and live with me. You can come and live with us too."

She said nothing.

"Mama wanted you to go to school. If she didn't get sick you would go to school, Zoom."

She cast her head defiantly. "I don't care about no school."

He stooped next to her. "If Valina help out then you can go to school. If Mama can get better, then you can go," Uncle Thomas paused. "Mama really appreciate how you take care of the house and everybody."

"If she appreciate it, then why she treat me so bad then?" Zoom threw a fish into the pot, causing sparks and oil to sizzle in the night air.

Uncle Thomas glanced at the scar on Zoom's face, then shook his head sorrowfully. "I don't know."

Winston followed him into the house where Mama was laying in the bed, looking out the window at everyone having a nice time. A light bulb hanging from the wood rafter illuminated a picture of the Virgin Mary on the wall. Black rosary beads lay on the pillow.

"Louise, you sleeping?"

"Tommy?" she croaked.

"Is me and Winston."

Mama's bedroom smelled like Vicks and Breeze. Zoom was always soaking, washing, and Bluing the sheets, the curtains, all of Mama's things.

Mama put her hand on Winston's head. "You see they having a big party for me tonight?"

"Yes, Mama. I wish you could come outside and see." His heart was pounding and he was having trouble keeping his breath steady. He wanted to cry out in fear or in sadness; he couldn't decide which. He reached his hand onto her bed and left it on her warm, thin arm.

"Everybody in the yard come, Lou," Uncle Thomas said, his hands in his pockets. "Even Cylma and her children from Kings Hill."

"Valina and Mona still there?"

Uncle Thomas looked out the window. "They outside dancing."

"Zoom cook so much food and people bring smoke meat, cake . . ." she smiled. "Boy, I wish I could eat that." A longing came over Mama's gray face.

"Mama, when you come back home and the doctors cure you, you will eat everything you want," Winston said, the words bursting from his mouth like a passionate vow. He made up his mind; Zoom would have another party just like this one when Mama came back from Barbados strong and healthy. But Mama closed her eyes and turned to the wall. A hand went up to her left breast and she grimaced in pain.

"Go and help them outside!" Uncle Thomas said sharply, pointing to the door. Winston ran out of the room just as he heard Mama's anguished cry of pain.

Chapter 23

"Look!" Mama pointed out the passenger window to a pair of Jaco parrots. But the birds fled the branch in a fluttering streak of green, yellow, and red feathers faster than Winston's eyes could follow.

"That's a good sign, Mama?" She rubbed the top of his head the way he liked, and he leaned into her good side carefully as the car bumped along the road to Melville Hall airport, a treacherous, one-lane highway pitted from falling rocks and the weight of too many overburdened trucks. Depending on the weather, entire sections could be washed away by rain or the ravenous rivers. The road was a money pit, one of the many battles the government continually lost to nature.

A cluster of clouds shaded the miles ahead, behind them more gray, thick clouds marched forward. "Something coming," Mama said softly. She'd complained about having to travel during the rainy season. "Those small, little planes." She crossed herself.

This would be the last surgery, Zoom said, and then Mama would finally be cured. This was the strongest medicine the doctors had; it was so strong they didn't have this medicine in Dominica. Only big rich countries like Barbados and Trinidad had such good, strong medicines. And when he'd cried, she told him he could ride in the big car with Uncle Thomas and Mama and see the plane fly away in the sky.

When he was four, Mama had gone away to St. Martin and brought him back a plastic plane, race cars, and six packets of Shirley biscuits. So he had high hopes for this trip. Barbados. Bar-ba-dos. Days of practicing, and still he couldn't say it right, with his stuttering that grew worse and worse the closer it got to Mama's departure. He leaned his head on her shoulder and she winced a little. "Sorry, Mama."

"You are big and too strong for your age."

"Is because I eat my arrowroot like you tell me."

"Yes. And make sure you eat whatever Zoom make for you, okay? And don't give Ma Relene trouble. Okay?"

Winston squinted through the drizzle on the car windows. He'd told

Mikey that the plane taking Mama to Barbados was not small. LIAT had big, big planes that could hold twenty people. He'd overheard Uncle Thomas and Cousin Eustace talking about this at the party. Winston savored Mikey and Augustus's envy as he schooled them in his knowledge about planes.

Uncle Thomas had borrowed the car from his boss to drive Mama to the airport, but he was driving it like it was his own. "It's just a little rain, Lou," He looked back from the front seat. "Only a little more to go."

"I see so much in life already," Mama said suddenly. She sucked her teeth, turning to the strand of cedars and sandalwood fronting the impenetrable green of the interior forest. "I so tired."

"Lou, what you talking like that for?"

"Remember when Queen Elizabeth come, and I was right in front of all those people? I had Winston with me, you know? He was so small, but he see everything. The queen see him."

Winston looked up in shock. He had never heard this story before.

"Yes," Mama said. "March 1964. Boy, it was hot, hot, hot. Everybody was there, pushing and fighting just to see the Queen. But I come early, and I see her up close." She squeezed his shoulder. "She look at you with her blue eyes, and she smile and say, that's a nice little boy."

"Mama! Is true?" Winston's mouth hung open.

"Yes, is true. Zoom was there. Zoom was right behind me and she see everything."

"And the Queen say I'm a nice little boy?"

Mama was smiling, juggling items in her memory. "When I was young and I see the big Geest banana boat, I think, that's the biggest, best thing I will ever see in my life. But seeing the Queen was better than that. Much better."

Winston inhaled. He could not believe that the Queen of England had seen him with her own two eyes and had voiced an opinion about him!

"Yes, boy. I never see Roseau look so clean and beautiful. All the school-children so neat and nicely behaved that week. You remember, Thomas?"

Uncle Thomas sucked his teeth. "Don't ask me about those wicked kind of people." He began to grumble about British imperialism and the broke United Kingdom that was abandoning the colonies after robbing them for hundreds of years. But Mama kept smiling, lost in her memories. By the time they bumped and winded through Marigot village, sheets of rain poured from the gray sky. "We are almost there," Uncle Thomas said to reassure Mama.

At the airport, Winston almost forgot Mama at his side as he gawked at the travelers, the tourists, hucksters dragging large grips, and the taxi drivers waiting for the plane to come in. He held Mama's hand but barely paid attention as she took careful steps through customs and immigration.

Uncle Thomas spoke to the man at the desk, who stamped Mama's passport. Another man wearing a green uniform took Mama's heavy grip. The plane would not arrive for another hour, the man behind the desk said, but they could sit in the waiting area.

"Alas, Ma Louise!" a lady in a bright orange dress exclaimed, flying to them, her wide face stricken. "You going for operation again?"

Mama shrugged weakly. "The doctor said they can't do nothing for me here."

"Eh! But what happening in de world, nuh? Ma Louise, you shouldn't have to be sick like that. A young woman like you."

Mama laughed. "Young? Child, I live my whole life already. I have three almost grown girls. Don't let that little one here fool you." She rubbed Winston's head.

But he was too distracted. The plane was landing, and its slow descent onto the small runway absorbed every ounce of his attention. It was nothing like the paper planes he sent flying through the air at Teacher Rose's school, or even the real planes that buzzed high above Roseau so far away he could barely make them out. This was the real thing, with an engine, wings, and a propeller that spun faster than the big fan in Astaphan's grocery store.

He was not the only one gawking as the Cessna swayed through the air, side to side, up and down, then slowly kissed the tarmac. Mama covered her ears as the engine bellowed. Winston's heart was nearly bursting. Wait till he told Mikey and Augustus!

The anticipation in the waiting room was thick, and everyone stood, waiting for the white plane door to open. Then the passengers emerged, gingerly stepping down the plane's steps—big people, men wearing shirt-jacs and real leather shoes, ladies with red lips and rosy cheeks wearing high heels who looked like what Mama called the bourgeois, and the *bekes* from the UK and America.

The waiting room began to churn as uniformed airport workers shouted announcements. "Dominican residents to the left-hand side! Visitors to the right-hand side!"

Soon another announcement was made; it was time to board the plane. Uncle Thomas straightened his back and faced Mama. "I will see you in three weeks then, Lou?" Before she could answer, he turned away, his shoulders heaving up and down. Winston was perplexed and looked up at Mama for an explanation. She bit her lips, which she'd painted red this morning while Zoom held up a hand mirror. She was wearing her best Sunday Mass dress, a white hat with red flowers and a Creole-style bag that held her cosmetics, talcum powder, and perfumes. To Winston, she looked beautiful, although entirely too small in the loose-fitting dress. "What Uncle crying for, Mama?" His heart began to race. Should he be afraid?

"Is nothing." She stooped slowly to kiss both his cheeks. "I will see you when I come back, and I will bring the G.I. Joe, okay? Do what your uncle and sisters say. Okay?"

"Yes, Mama."

"Act like a big boy, eh?" She was smiling when she patted his head and walked slowly to the plane. A man helped her up the steps. Uncle Thomas wiped his eyes and hugged Winston tight to his pant leg.

Winston did not stop waving even after she disappeared into the plane. He pulled away from Uncle Thomas and ran to the glass partition as the plane rose into the air, above the tarmac then straight out over the Caribbean Sea, pointing up into the gray sky, growing smaller and smaller until all he could see were turbulent nimbostratus clouds.

Uncle Thomas was silent for the bumpy two-hour drive back to Roseau. Winston's thoughts were a jumble—elation at the exciting events of the day mixed with trepidation over Uncle Thomas's tears.

The weight only grew heavier when he was not allowed to go home that night. Zoom was sullen and red-eyed when she brought him a bowl of red bean soup the next afternoon at Uncle Thomas's house. She stooped to his eye level when he asked if he could come home. "Stay and keep your uncle company."

But Uncle Thomas shut the door to his room and did not come out for the rest of the day, not even when Ma Relene asked him if he wanted supper.

Over the next few days, Winston played soccer with the neighborhood boys till after midnight because no one asked them to come inside. No one took him to school or asked if he wanted to go. Each night, he slept underneath Mikcy's bed, listening to Uncle Thomas sobbing in the room next door as Ma Relene murmured softly to him. He couldn't understand. Wouldn't Mama be back in just three weeks?

Chapter 24

In the year Uncle Thomas died, Winston saw Mr. Timothy, his father, for the first time.

He bounded breathlessly into the house that afternoon, chased by two boys all the way from Teacher Rose's schoolhouse. At the threshold of Uncle Thomas's house, he turned around triumphantly, dropped his school shorts and wiggled his bottom as they howled in protest. "In ya fadda head!" one shouted. "I will cuff you so hard in your Black tail tomorrow! You will see!" Winston stuck his tongue out and slammed the door laughing.

Ah, freedom! Ma Relene was at Ms. Ford's and Mikey and Augustus were either in Big School or up to trouble in the streets. He threw his books into his corner of the room and changed into his worn-out blue T-shirt and khaki shorts. If he was living with Zoom this week, he would have to wash his uniform and hang it out to dry before he could even eat a bakes and saltfish. But at Uncle Thomas's, he could be as dirty as he wanted to be. Sometimes he would see Zoom on his way to school and she would inspect his collar in the middle of the street. "I don't know how Relene can let you go to school looking like that!" she would say, wrinkling her nose.

Zoom worked for some *beke* people, watching their two babies. She'd become a Christian because the couple, missionaries from Ohio, made her go to church with them. But Zoom still crossed herself when she looked at Mama's picture on Saturdays, when they would sit quietly together in the little house, doing the chores at a less frenzied pace. Zoom would be tender with him, sometimes forgetting what she was doing, sitting on Mama's bed and staring off into the darkness. He'd sit next to her and it would be that way for as long as it took her to sigh. "Okay. Let's go and wash." He'd follow her to the river, where she washed, slower now even without the load of Mama's endless sheets, nighties, and things.

Her face brightened, however, on Sunday, Wednesday, and Friday as she dressed up for the Christian Union Church in Newtown, where they sang songs, clapped their hands, and listened to a sweaty pastor shout about sins for an hour. Winston liked the lively music better than the singing at the

Cathedral, but he fell asleep during the fiery preaching. Zoom's boyfriend, Mr. Edward, a wharf ranger on the port, went to church, too. Winston imagined he made a lot of money because Mr. Edward told Uncle Thomas he was going to ask Zoom to marry him. Only men with good money married—men like Mr. Squires and Uncle Thomas.

A shuffling in the next room stopped him in his tracks, threatening his plan to play cricket before he did homework. He remained still, hoping Uncle Thomas would stay in bed. "Winston?" Uncle's voice was weak and scratchy; he hardly went outside these days. Winston had come to accept Uncle Thomas's sickness. In his mind, he imagined this sickness, the cancer which the grown-ups whispered when he was in the room, was what eventually happened to all the big people in his family.

"Yes, Uncle?" He reluctantly walked into the bedroom. On the wall were framed photos of him and Ma Relene on their wedding day outside the Roseau Cathedral, a picture of Mikey and Augustus as babies, and a large photo of Mama standing under a Flamboyant tree in the Botanical Gardens. Newspapers were stacked high on the floor next to Uncle Thomas's side of the bed. The windows were open wide so Uncle could talk to the men playing dominoes in the yard as if he were right out there with them.

"Uncle, I get ninety-nine on my spelling test today." Winston produced a yellow-lined sheet of paper that showed the hundred words he had spelled.

"'Knight'? You couldn't spell 'knight'?" Uncle Thomas pulled the paper close to his face and adjusted his eye patch.

"It was a trick," Winston defended himself. "She said the clue was King Arthur's Court. But I couldn't remember that . . ."

"But we read that book about King Arthur's knights . . ."

"I forget, Uncle. Sorry." He sighed and sat at the foot of the bed. "You want me to make tea for you?" Maybe he could redeem himself by being helpful.

"No. Zoom bring food for me a little while ago."

"Okay. I going and play cricket before I do my homework. Okay?"

Uncle Thomas shifted himself up in the bed. "No. I need you to help me to get ready. We have to go somewhere. Put on your good pants and shoes."

Winston opened his mouth to grumble but he sensed a seriousness in Uncle Thomas. Zoom must have something to do with this since there were good pants and shoes involved. It was probably church. Or worse, another trip to the cemetery to stand over Mama's grave in silence for an hour. Zoom was always meddling, especially now that she worked for these white missionaries who talked about God, God, God all the time.

Uncle Thomas gripped his hand as they slowly navigated the path out of the yard, past the men playing dominoes who stared and nodded at them.

Winston looked around nervously. If those boys from school saw him walking hand in hand with Uncle, they would call him *Mako, Zaman*, and all kinds of bad names.

Out on the street, a crowd massed under the government building holding up signs. "Uncle, what they doing again?"

"People want to be independent from Britain. Dominica can stand on its own two feet." Uncle Thomas turned his body toward the protesters.

"Uncle, my teacher said Labour is for poor people and Freedom Party is for rich people. Is true?"

Uncle Thomas laughed. "They have corruption in both parties. But one thing I telling you: I will put all my money on Patrick John every day. You hear me? That man look me in my one good eye and tell me go and see Dr. Roche and don't worry about having to pay no kind of money."

Winston had heard this story before. If he had to make a choice between the two political parties, it would be the Labour Party then. "But my teacher said Ms. Charles is a good leader."

Uncle Thomas's fingers tightened around his. "Boy, if this country ever have woman prime minister then pigs will fly. A cold day in hell. Over my dead body, like those Americans say." He laughed but there was no happiness in his laughter. Winston would remember that sardonic laughter on a shiny, bright night in a bar in St. Thomas the day of Eugenia Charles's victory, and later again when she stood before the world with Ronald Reagan.

Uncle Thomas walked slow, sometimes stopping to rest and cough. Winston made sure to guide him away from the drains and over the ups and downs of the uneven sidewalks. They finally stopped at the dry goods store in the middle of town where Winston had walked so many times; Teacher Rose was right up the street, the man who cut his hair was three doors down. The week before, Uncle Thomas had taken Winston to the registry to get his birth certificate. He put the birth certificate in a box with a lock and key and showed Winston where he kept it. Winston had nodded, thinking these activities had to do with him eventually going to the Roseau Boys School with the bigger boys.

In front of the busy store strong men in sleeveless shirts and dungarees hoisted bags of seed, flour, and pails of paint onto pallets for Bedford trucks headed to the villages. At the Shillingford's across the street, ladies emerged with bags of groceries. The aroma of evening bread wafted from Suki's depot as sidewalks buzzed with loitering schoolchildren and government workers slow to turn toward home in the mellow, late afternoon sun.

Uncle Thomas, still holding Winston's hand, led him into the store. "Where de boss man?" he asked the lady at the cash register, who sent another clerk running to the back of the store. They waited for a good while as the lady rang up customers' purchases. Winston searched the store shelves in vain for sweets, toys, books or anything he was vaguely interested in. All he could see were nails, screwdrivers, and other boring items. Various men greeted Uncle Thomas by name. "That's my sister's last child," was how he explained Winston to them.

"Eh! Yes! He look just like Louise, eh!" The ladies inspected Winston and smiled at the reflection of his mother in his face. He squirmed under their attentiveness, annoyed at the closeness of their faces to his.

"I have eight years," he repeated for the hundredth time.

The boss man came down, a tall, dark narrow-eyed man with a cross sneer and a cigarette dangling from the corner of his mouth. "What you want?" He looked down at Winston and stepped back as if someone just threw hot tea on him.

"That your son, Timothy!" Uncle Thomas, like a lawyer presenting evidence, thrust Winston forward. "You know you have a son with Louise. Don't act shocked!"

The man looked down without saying a word, the cigarette smoldering, ashes threatening to drop any second. Winston looked up and saw where his wide nose, brown eyes, and thick eyebrows came from. Shaken, he looked down just as quickly. His heart was pounding in his ear, like the waves hitting the bayfront during a storm. He moved until he could feel Uncle Thomas's leather belt against his ear.

"Louise die over two years now, and you never even come and say two words to me and ask about your child!" Uncle Thomas was breathing heavy in anger and exhaustion from his overworked lungs.

The man inspected his cigarette, then stubbed it into an ashtray near the cash register. The lady cashier looked off into the distance, blind and deaf to evil for the moment.

"That is your son," Uncle Thomas repeated.

The man reached into his pocket and retrieved several wrinkled bills. He counted out three or four and thrust them at Uncle Thomas, who caught them before they fell to the ground. The man did not look down at Winston again. He turned away from them, disappearing into the busy store and fading into the customers and the sacks of flour, sugar, rice, and salt.

Uncle Thomas touched his eye patch, then coughed for a good spell. The cashier shook her head. "You want some water, Mister?" But Uncle Thomas pulled Winston out into the sunshine, into crowded Kings Lane. "We are going to the credit union and I will put this money on a book for you. Don't tell nobody. Okay?"

Winston followed Uncle Thomas's brisk pace. "Come, come! The credit union closing."

The credit union's floor was shiny, and neat women smiled behind glass partitions. It was the first time he had ever experienced air conditioning, and his loud, sharp intake of breath drew stares. "Uncle, why it so cold!" But Uncle Thomas shushed him and took a place in the queue.

Winston recognized a shopkeeper ahead of them in the line, a teacher, a fancy lady who looked like Ms. Ford's kind of people. Then, finally, it was their turn. The lady behind the glass counter smiled and said, "How can I help you today, Mister?" There was a lot of writing and stamping of papers and incomprehensible questions being asked and answered. At the end of it, the smiling lady behind the counter handed him a lollipop, the kind with the chewing gum inside. It was the best thing to happen to him that day.

"You have your own savings account now," Uncle Thomas said as they stepped into the sultry crowded streets. "And you know where to go and look for your father," he said with a heavy resignation.

As he lay in bed that night, listening to Uncle Thomas cough, he wondered what a father was supposed to mean to him. Was he to go and live with the man? Should he go to him in the future and get some money as Uncle Thomas did today? He remembered the man's face and the streak of pain he felt seeing those familiar features. In some ways it felt like he was looking in a mirror. But there was nothing about the man that *felt* familiar. He hadn't even liked the man—at least what he saw of him. He decided he had no use for such a person in his life. A part of him was angry with Uncle Thomas for bringing him to see that man. He looked up at the springs under Mikey's bed for hours as the image of the narrowed eyes and the dangling cigarette loomed over him. He would have preferred to go to the river to catch crayfish instead of having to see that man count out some money to throw at Uncle Thomas while hardly looking at him.

Two weeks later, Uncle Thomas died in Princess Margaret Hospital on a Saturday. The radio in the kitchen played the football match between Dominica and Grenada while Winston sat alone, listening, hoping, and wishing for a million different outcomes.

Aftermath

Chapter 25

Six weeks after Maria, and I was losing my ability to reconcile the two men I saw in Dad. The one who easily cracked jokes in patois with Mikey and the construction workers who hammered away at Ma Relene's house and the father who had seemed so reserved, so formal to me when I met him twenty years ago. The more history Mikey fed me, the hungrier I got. I spent days and nights skulking around Roseau, buying Aunt Valina cocktails with umbrellas from the Balas bar to clear her memories. I couldn't hear enough. If Dad knew about my fact-finding missions, he didn't let on. He acted the same way as we worked all day. At nights when I tried to initiate conversations, he would yawn. "I'm too tired for all that talk, Hector." He'd be snoring in no time. I'd listen to him across the room, thinking, remembering. Sometimes laughing when I compared this salt-of-the-earth millionaire Bostonian with his peasant boy beginnings. Who knew we had so much in common?

Missy and Cousin Eddie woke that late October morning and wished everyone a happy Creole Day. "I wish I had some breadfruit," Missy complained. "I'd make some breadfruit and codfish for you."

Creole Day kicked off the annual independence celebrations, with parties, pageants, food and music festivals, and lots of overseas visitors. This year would be different, Cousin Eddie tutted and shook his head. "Man, if this was a normal year you would never want to leave Dominica. It's the best time to be here."

Missy decorated the house in red, green, and yellow streamers. She set the dining room table with colorful table linens. The neighbors, too, had dressed up in colorful clothing. Even Steve, the most buttoned-up of Cousin Eddie's neighbors, wore a Creole-print tie with his starched white shirt to his job at the Inland Revenue service.

Cousin Eddie turned it all the way up as we drove into town, spruced up in his colorful madras shirt, orange, green, blue, red, and yellow with his customary cargo shorts. It was a strange dissonance, him wearing his traditional shirt while blasting KRS-One's "Step into a World" on the stereo. He bobbed his head to the beat as he drove. "I don't know what kind of food they gonna have this year. All the trees down. It will take a whole year before we can have good dasheen, bananas, and breadfruit again." The music took me back to the late nineties, when Leandra and I were young and beautiful, hitting the clubs every weekend after long hours in the library. I'd felt so liberated in those days. The beat and the lyrics transported me back decades as we streaked by the steely ocean. Cousin Eddie began to rap and, before I knew it, we were both into it, like we were a couple of teenagers battling on the block. I glanced at him, feigning shock that he knew all the lyrics, and we went for the entire song.

At the end we were whooping, laughing.

We rolled into Roseau feeling like a couple of bad dudes on a mission, gray hair and all. The streets were festive, loud with soca music and fragrant with the aromas of fried fish, fried dough, and roasted corn. Little kids wearing traditional dress sent pangs through my heart. I desperately wished Dante were here to experience this with me. We picked up passengers and Cousin Eddie changed the music to soca, which wasn't that bad to my ear either. Passengers were singing and swaying to the beats of "Rock and Come In" as Cousin Eddie pointed the bus north. But hip-hop and Leandra remained on my mind all day, leaving me melancholy, not just contemplating Dad's difficult life here as a boy but my own difficulties awaiting me in the States. In an impulsive fit I texted her a link to Wu-Tang's "Can It Be All So Simple." "Remember you used to call me 1993 exoticness?" She responded within seconds. "That was a long, long time ago." Yeah, I thought. I hadn't messed up yet.

On a bright blue Tuesday Dad and I loitered around the port, waiting for building materials we'd ordered from Trinidad. Dad and Cousin Eddie had gotten into some construction projects, helping neighbors repair their houses. Typical of Dad, I thought, to dip his toes into business while he was here. But I didn't mind because we kept busy. Many days we spent painting, installing cabinets at Ma Relene's house, and he talked nonstop about his young days in Roseau as Mikey filled in the memory gaps. I'd never heard Dad laugh as loud as he did when we were all together working on that house.

The port at Fond Cole was busy and crowded. Sweaty, uniformed workers drove forklifts with massive containers shipped in from all around the world. Harried residents wandered around, bills of lading flapping in sunscorched hands, searching for barrels and packages sent by overseas family. Intense-looking government officials surveyed the scene, alert for the slightest flicker of conflict. Already, the aid distribution had been politicized. A news reporter walked around asking people if they had received aid, if the rumors were true that only the Freedom Party supporters were receiving aid. Dad shook his head. "Nothing change in this country. Same old nonsense politics." His accent had fully returned, and I wondered how he would assimilate back into the US. A man came to help us retrieve the massive container and to show us to a truck that would deliver it to town.

"Winston! Man, I remember you from back in the day," he grinned at Dad.

"Yes?" Dad squinted at the older man.

"You used to sail with Edward for WIT?" The man was wrinkled, Snickers-bar brown with white speckled through his hair, mustache, and beard. He wore a shirt-jac, slacks, and dress shoes. He reminded me of the type of man Dad's Uncle Thomas would have been had he lived. The type of man Dad would have been if he had stayed in Dominica.

"Yes, man," Dad said enthusiastically. Their joking around made me desperate for a long missing part of myself. I hadn't seen Jean in over a year. He was busy with his medical practice; his marriage was thriving; his wife was pregnant with their third; the last I saw him was at one fundraising dinner that brought all of Black Boston together.

I would be too ashamed to call Jean now. To tell him that I'd received an email from my lawyer saying that Leandra was pushing things forward. That she wanted me to think about how I wanted to arrange custody. I hadn't told Dad. I hadn't told anyone.

As I watched the cranes and machinery, the bustling workers, the water slapping against the edges of the harbor, I realized that I wanted to stay here. There was nothing for me in Boston.

I looked over and saw Dad laughing so hard he was bent over at the waist.

Jean picked up on the first ring. "Hector! You all right, man?" I would have been shocked too if he'd called me out of the blue.

"Guess where I'm at, man." And I tried to catch him up on the last year of my life.

"When you get back, you gotta come over, man. The kids want to see Dante." That was how we ended that conversation. I felt stupid as I slipped the phone into my pocket. Dad was still laughing and talking with his old friend, had barely turned around to see if I was still there.

My phone rang, and I hesitated to answer. Leandra wanted to remind me that it was almost Thanksgiving and I'd been gone almost three months. My shoulders began to tighten and my heart raced: a familiar rage at being interrogated by her. Her voice was brittle and businesslike on the other end. Did my lawyer contact me?

"I haven't had a chance to talk to him," I lied, "but I can't agree to anything that would hurt Dante."

She sighed. "It's really hard to," she paused, probably racking her lawyer-trained mind for the appropriate words, "believe that when you stay away this long. I mean, Dante would probably like to have his dad home for the holidays."

"I know," I said quickly. "I plan to be home by Christmas. I just—" And I couldn't finish the sentence. I couldn't tell her that I'm afraid to come home to the end of us, that I'd rather stay here forever and hope for a different ending.

Her voice was low and calm, what she would describe as her client-voice. "Hector, I think the sooner we can get on with our lives, the better it will be. Especially for Dante. We have to tell him at some point."

I told her another lie. "I'll be home soon. As soon we're done fixing up Ma Relene's house."

She ignored me. "You really should call your lawyer, Hector. It will impact things going forward."

I swallow the bile rising in my throat. "What's the rush? Are you dating someone else or something? I hope you're not bringing random dudes into my house." And off we went, she reminding me of my lying, cheating ways and every mistake I'd ever made in our marriage.

"You're ridiculous!" I spat. I clicked off the call and almost tossed the phone into a forklift operator's lap. How did we get to this point? I took several deep, heaving breaths to slow my heart rate. I remembered my doctor's warnings, the threat of blood pressure medicine. Jeez! I walked in circles around a large puddle of water. Dad was still catching up with his buddy.

A desperate rage came over me and squeezed my eyes shut as I stood in the middle of the teeming harbor. Redirect your thoughts. Think back to better times.

Leandra cut her hair right after she filed for divorce—the same haircut she wore the night we met at the Gallery in 1996. That look is the picture of her that lingered in my mind: smooth brown skin, slender shoulders, and short hair above her ears, deep brown eyes sparkling like the diamond earrings I bought on her thirty-fifth birthday. I kept hoping the haircut meant she was mourning over me, over our marriage. Not that she's ever given me any hope that we could reconcile. But the fact that we're still so angry . . . maybe there's still something there.

I couldn't have forced her to stay. I had nothing to stand on. How could I explain my absolute weakness, foolishness, hubris? I did every horrible thing I was accused of doing. But I still loved her, and I still wanted us to be a family.

Dad came up to me, grinning, then noticed my expression. "What happened? Dante all right?" He could tell when I'd just had a blowup with Leandra. I don't know how.

I shrugged, and a flood of tears bumrushed my eyes and spilled down my cheeks. I swore and turned away from him. Dad, at first, was shocked, but instantly reached out. His suffocating hug felt warm, all-encompassing. My insides quivered and shook; I was gasping for breath and he never once loosened his grip on me. "It's okay, son. It's okay. Let it out."

I don't know how long this went on, but when it ended, he placed both hands on my shoulders and looked me squarely in the eyes. "You will save your marriage. Okay? You will do it if you want to. Okay?"

I sniffed and wiped my eyes with my forearm. "I don't know." My voice was tremulous, like I was five again, crying to Mom. "Everything is just so messed up."

He shook his head decisively. "No, son. You can still fix it. You can still fix it."

Chapter 26

When the announcement hit the *Boston Business Journal* that I'd been named chief operating officer at Summit Bank, Dad hung the framed page in his home office. He took me out for a fancy steak dinner at some oak-paneled place in the Back Bay, the type of place where people like Dad and me worked hard to ignore the stares of the very white staff and clientele. Nothing could spoil Dad's effusive mood though. I was proud but struggling with impostor syndrome—this promotion felt like I'd skated by on luck and luck alone. I'd had just the right mentors rooting for me since day one, and I had done my fair share of boot-licking.

"I don't understand you," Dad said as the waiters brought him a massive porterhouse. "How you think all these white men got their positions? You worked hard to get where you are. You should be proud. As proud as I am!"

He grinned and took a big swallow of red wine. He closed his eyes, savoring. "Did I do that right?" He laughed. "Do I look like I know a lot about wine now?"

"I'm glad you're in a good mood," I chuckled as I dug into my salmon. Dad's steak was salivating but my personal trainer would kill me if I indulged that way.

"What's with the healthy eating?" he asked.

I shrugged and checked my buzzing cell phone. His expression changed. "How's Leandra?"

"Well," I said, answering a text message. Things were hopping busy at work. We were on a growth spurt and our goal was to be the biggest local bank in New England; only two or three smart acquisitions to go and we'd be there. And it was going to happen. It was 2012 and the great recession of 2008–09 was almost ancient history. This was the make-or-break time of my career.

"Just well?"

I looked up from my phone. Oh, he was asking about Leandra. "She's still working part-time." I felt his skepticism. "We're fine."

He raised his eyebrows and continued to eat, looking around the restaurant. This was a tactic he used to get me to talk more—wearing me down with silence.

"I'm fine, Dad." I repeated patiently. "It took two years for this merger to settle down and for me to get this role. And work is even more, more, non-stop now."

"I know, son. I just hope you're dealing with things at home."

"I am. I am." He'd enlisted Mom in this campaign to fix my marriage. I'd come home to find her sitting with Leandra in the den in deep conversation, which would end as soon as I entered the room. The thing was, I didn't need fixing, neither did Leandra or our marriage. She was busy saving the world with her nonprofit job and I was busy trying to keep my division running. It was maybe the first time in a long time Leandra and I weren't completely focused on what we'd lost and what we'd never have, which was completely okay with me.

Dad drained his wine glass and looked around for the waiter. "I took your mother to her appointment this morning. The doctor had good things to say this time."

I stared hard at him. Why bring up Mom now? Tonight? The rage was sudden and intense. "Thanks." I almost threw my napkin across the table, the food losing its appeal.

"She told me you and Leandra are having some problems."

"Mom told you that?" I clenched my teeth, willing my voice to remain low.

Dad put down his knife and fork and leaned in. "Hector, don't hurt your wife after everything you all went through."

"What are you talking about?" Heat rose to my forehead, and my hands shook in anger.

"The women," Dad said in a low but firm voice. He leaned closer, within a breath of my face. "The women," he repeated, making sure I caught the intensity in his tone. "You need to stop that!" His dark eyes bore into mine, not threatening or angry; it was something I hadn't seen before. Like I was a nine-year-old who'd been caught stealing. "Did you hear me?" He raised his eyebrows.

I felt like a caged animal and tried to calm the fury inside. "You're lecturing me about being faithful to my wife?" I laughed bitterly. "Well, that's rich." I swore and leaned back in my chair, taking in a couple of breaths and loosening my tie. I waved off the approaching waiter.

He didn't move or react to my swearing. "You don't have to make all my bad choices, you know," he said. "You've never had my circumstances or my reasons."

"Your reasons? What reasons? You're an absentee dad who dropped in when I'm all grown up, took advantage of my mother, and now you're filled with advice on how I should live my life?"

It was then he straightened up in his chair, and for the first time, I caught the dangerous edges of anger in the tightness of his mouth. "Let us finish our food."

"I'm done," I said, putting my napkin on the table. I wanted to storm out, throw my drink across the room, rip the table apart. But there were people in that restaurant who knew me as Hector Peterson, chief operating officer of Summit Bank. That's who I was—not some little boy crying for his daddy. I'd become who I was not because of him but in spite of him. How dare he lecture me?

But I couldn't go home just yet. I sat in the car outside the house on Hawkins Street, trying to pull myself together. I texted Leandra to let her know I would be home soon.

Mom was on the couch surrounded by pillows, her breathing tank on the floor, watching CNN. She remained beautiful, though thinner and less taut in the limbs; her dreads were silvery gray now. I would always blame him for her quick deterioration. She'd taken my advice and demanded that he leave Ms. Karen, and his answer was no. He would not leave his wife. So, here she was, on her own. He still visited occasionally, took her to appointments, brought her groceries. He'd even bought her the new SUV that she couldn't drive and which mocked me in the driveway every time I visited.

Mom extended her arms to hug me. "Shouldn't you be home? It's late."

"I wanted to see you," I said, tossing some of the pillows so I could sit next to her, feel her warmth. Her shoulders felt bony and delicate under my arm.

She rested her head on my arm. "Hector, you're still a mama's boy. I did a really bad job with you."

"No, you didn't. What are you talking about, lady?" Tears pricked at the back of my eyes. The only light in the room was the flashing light from the television; the only sounds the anchor's droning voice and the hiss of the oxygen tank.

"I did. I really did. I'm so glad your father came along to balance out all the nonsense I did when you were growing up."

"Mom, please." I shook my head, recalling dinner. "Sometimes I wish he'd never come back."

She shook as the words left my mouth. "No, no. Don't say that, Hector." She shifted on the couch. "What happened? Did you argue with him?"

I barely knew the man, I fumed. He showed up in our lives and disrupted everything, even my relationship with Mom. Sometimes I wondered if it was too late to turn the clock back and pretend that he'd never come back.

She lifted her head from my arm. "I'm sorry you feel that way," she said softly. The oxygen tank hissed, and she sniffed.

"Hector," she said after a deep sigh, "your father coming back was the best thing to happen in my life. The second-best thing. After you."

She took another wheezy breath. "That man loves me, Hector. You will never know the whole story with us. But he did right by me. Okay?" She squeezed my leg. "Okay? Always know that he did right by me."

The lump in my throat kept me from protesting. What right could he possibly have done besides showing up? My eyes watered over as we sat in silence, not watching the TV. Eventually, I'd go home to Leandra and our home brimming with silence. But for now, I wanted to sit with Mom and watch TV like old times.

Dad

Chapter 27

Roseau, 1973

Tangerine-colored days opened wide like the sky since he'd aged out of Roseau Boys School. He still liked to stand in the middle of Windsor Park to gaze at the infinite blue, then at the horseshoe of mountains that hemmed him in, grounded him in Roseau's stifling heat and bustle. Sometimes, it was almost too much to bear—the gnawing pain of loss and loneliness, the suffocating anxiety threatening to blow the cover of his teenage bravado.

Winston ran his fingers over the fast-growing woolly spikes of hair, working through a mixture of water and mashed *rachette* that a Rasta taught him how to make. Augustus found a girlfriend once he began to grow dreads—that's what Junior said anyway. Winston's were still only grazing the top of his nape, but he relished the strong ropiness of his hair on his fingertips. He assessed himself in the mirror in Valina's tiny washroom. Wide shoulders were still a bit bony, but muscles and sinew crisscrossed his upper chest and biceps. He was taller and bigger than a lot of the boys in Pound and Lagoon, and these days there was less and less need to use fists. He smoothed a barely-there mustache with his index finger.

He reached into his back pocket and retrieved the results of the entrance exam. Two days earlier when he'd received them, he went straight to the Catholic cemetery and stood over Uncle Thomas's grave listening to the quiet absence of life. What else could he do? Who else could he tell first? He held up the paper that qualified him to go to St. Mary's Academy. A breeze fluttered then whipped, causing the paper to bend. Uncle Thomas had denounced the "bourgeois school" with so much fire and brimstone. Winston never thought the priests would let in anyone like him. But he had the subjects and the marks—1's in everything. He walked four graves over to Mama's. There were fresh roses, ferns, and lilies, identical to the ones Zoom grew in her yard. He opened his mouth to say something to the grave, to the silence. But his chest tightened, his throat closed, and his eyes burned. He almost ran from the cemetery, clutching the paper in his hand all the way to Pound and the music-filled-don't-care of Valina's house.

～

He put the paper under his pillow and wrote a letter to Mona. She would have had a party for him for sure if she were here. Even now he could hardly believe she was gone, although he was glad she'd escaped Mr. Clark.

One Saturday early in the morning when Winston was the only one awake and about, he heard a knock on the louvers in Valina's drawing room. A voice whispered, "Winston, come outside." A rooster was crowing and scratching in the yard, and farmers were pushing carts full of cane, cabbage, carrots, and bananas down to the market.

"What happen?" he asked when he saw her face.

Mona was peering into the window at Junior as he slept on the floor. "I going Guadeloupe," she whispered. She pulled her eyes away from the louvers and turned to him, her brown face fully made up, her long eyelashes fluttering.

"When?" Winston's eyes widened. "Now?"

"Tell Junior I will send for him after I get a job." Her eyes were puffy and red, but she was dressed in her best clothes: a sky-blue blouse with a bow at her long neck and a long cream skirt that reached her ankles. Her slim brown face was smooth in the dawn light, hair brushed back tightly into a bun. Gold three-leaf clover earrings dangled from her ears and bangles on her wrists ran down to her elbows when she lifted her arms. "Tell Val not to worry. I will send money."

"When you going?"

"Today. I taking the boat this morning." There was a courageous smile forming on her lips and an excitement in her eye he had never seen before. "Winston," she whispered, "I going and do something for myself. You hear me?"

Two years later, Mona returned to Dominica in full makeup, real gold jewelry, and a new French husband. Like magic, she had transformed into a fancy lady. Winston, Junior, little Eddie, and Zoom's twins crowded around the bag of plastic toys, candies, and other treats Mona brought them as the adults looked on suspiciously.

Mona whirled through Roseau with the Frenchman, delivering gifts like an international charity. At night they drank with the *bekes* at the bar of the Fort Young and Anchorage Hotel. She eventually made a trade of her good fortune, staking a place among the huckster stalls near Kings Lane. She sold clothes, bras and panties and plastic slippers with the Francs tags still on them. All Winston ever asked her was to bring him peanut butter and O'Henry bars. Mona brought maybe four jars of peanut butter with each trip home, and he began to fill out from a scrawny mess of skin and bones into an athletic teenager with a massive appetite.

Someday, he thought, watching Mona count all the money she'd made selling goods on the street, he and Junior could be hucksters too. Someday, they would leave Dominica and become rich men. It didn't seem that hard, he thought, as Mona called out to passersby: "High fashion. Good price! *Haut qualité*! French!"

ᘰ

A steady rhythm-guitar strum of "Shanty Town" greeted him as he entered the yard on Hillsborough Street. "Aye ups." Mikey blew out a plume of ganja smoke toward Winston. Augustus's dreads were at his shoulders now and he stood swaying to the music, a spliff in his hand. Mikey and Augustus had begun to call each other "Ras" and "Rude Bwoy" even though they never refused a big plate when Ma Relene cooked pig snout and pig ears. Winston was being very quiet about it, but he was slowly beginning to eat only *ital*. It was easier anyway, because Mr. Squires was so devoted to little Eddie, he would make mashed plantains and arrowroot every day if it's what Eddie wanted. No more *sancoach* or fried redfish with onions—little Eddie hated fish. But Winston could always find a hand of green bananas or some dasheen or potatoes to cook for himself that would fill his belly for the rest of the day. He always could look forward to the times when Mona sent him a parcel of treats from Guadeloupe every now and then. But she had her own husband to take care of and another child on the way.

"Ma Relene there?"

Mikey nodded toward the front door, a fat lock of hair smacking his gnarly sideburns. Winston heard that Mikey had gotten a girl pregnant last year, but he'd never seen Mikey with a baby. Inside, Ma Relene was in her default position—at the kitchen table, worry clouding her face. He bent to kiss her cheek, and she stroked his shoulder absently. "Boy, you getting so tall. What Valina giving you to eat over there?"

He sat opposite her on the chair that now squeaked and swayed under his weight. "I pass my exams."

She held the paper up to the window. "You passed all your subjects?"

He nodded, smiling, fearing she didn't understand that this was the thing he wanted most. Now that he'd had a few days to put the paper under his pillow at night, it began to take on a life of its own, possessing a power to take him to places: Guadeloupe, St. Thomas, Trinidad, America, England.

She put the paper down and clapped her hands. "That's what Thomas wanted, you know?" She leaned forward and her teeth were white and straight and perfect. Winston saw then why Uncle Thomas had loved her. Her smile lifted him, and he wanted to hug her for it. She sat up proudly. "Your uncle say it all the time—Winston could be a educated man, a business owner, a politics man. I so happy I make you go to school every day, eh."

"Yes, Ma Relene." Winston's heart swelled as she rubbed his hand. Her approval washed away the years of resentment and each grudging "Yes, ma'am" he'd uttered when she'd forbidden him to go to school. The paper in his hand vindicated those years; he no longer had to do what she said.

"You make your whole family proud, eh." She looked out the window and her shoulders slumped. "But Thomas heart would break if he see his own boys today, eh? All they do is smoke and talk nonsense about Rastafari and Black power. Not a piece of work they will find to do for themselves. Don't even talk about school."

"Yes, Ma Relene." Either out of guilt or habit, he stuck around for another hour fetching water from the standpipe and working on the rickety chair. As he walked past Mikey and Augustus, he said nothing and they said nothing. He thought—mistakenly and way too soon—that he had escaped their fate and had no more need for them.

Mr. Squires and Valina were sitting outside in the yard when he arrived home. He had gone to Zoom's house to deliver the news and she had praised the Lord Jesus so much it felt like a choir of angels had invaded the house. Valina's expression spelled irritation, and his news did not change that. Settling into marriage with Mr. Squires had smoothed her edges and dulled her youthful spark. Valina no longer wore the large gold hoop earrings, bright red lipstick, tight low-cut blouses, and little shorts. She had permed her hair and wore it in pink rollers most days, except Sundays when she, little Eddie, and Mr. Squires walked slowly to Mass like a nice family. She and Mr. Squires watched little Eddie from sunup to sundown as if he were a precious, breakable toy. Eddie was the most spoiled little boy in Roseau, Winston thought resentfully. He couldn't understand why Eddie had inexplicably been given something he had always wanted: the doting, smothering love of two parents.

"Winston, where Junior?" she asked before he could even say *bon soir*.

He shrugged. He hadn't seen Junior since early that morning.

"I pass all my subjects," he announced, brandishing the paper. "I can go to St. Mary's Academy." Valina raised an eyebrow.

"Boy, you must be smart then," Mr. Squires stood and shook Winston's hand vigorously. He poured rum into a glass on the ground next to his foot and handed it to Winston. "You will be a big man, then!" Winston took a sip.

The heat shocked him, but he knew better than to show his disgust. He moved the brown drink around in the glass.

Valina squared her shoulders and took in a deep breath. "Winston, when you change your clothes, go in the shop and get some oil and flour for me, eh?" She was not impressed by his news, but Winston shrugged it off. Nothing could spoil the sense of freedom that was building inside of him. Magical powers were brewing inside him. Powers higher than those mountains, stronger and wider than the sea that surrounded him.

At the river, he struggled to read Hamlet, a dusty book he had checked out of the Roseau Public Library. A sweet-looking Grammar School girl worked behind the desk, and he thought another Hardy Boys mystery would send the wrong message. He was a man, not a little boy reading little-boy books. A stamp on the book's inside cover read DES MOINES PUBLIC LIBRARY. The story itself kept him turning the page—a prince with some *beke* problems that made him shake his head and even feel sorry for the boy. He'd been at it for a day and was almost finished. Something about the way the prince saw life spoke to him, and the language reminded him of the words in Zoom's big red King James Bible. A splash of water made him leap up from the rock, almost dropping the book in the water.

"*Zaman*, you reading book all de time now, nuh?"

"Man, what de hell!"

Junior skimmed up the rock like a crab, grinning like a fool. His curly hair stood in some parts and wilted in others like a holey sponge; the rest of him was soaking wet.

"Man, where you was yesterday? Valina looking all over for you."

Junior grinned, his brown eyes crinkling at the corners, his cat-like face lighting up. "I know. I give Eddie his breakfast and I tell her I going school. But I just stay around."

"Why you doh go school?"

Junior shrugged and sucked his teeth.

"I pass de Common Entrance." Winston wished he could show Junior the paper, but he'd already hidden it at the bottom of his grip. Junior nodded as some other kids played loudly in the clear water, their school uniforms in a pile on the riverbank, dangerously close to the water.

"Man! My mother send money for me every month, but Valina take that money to buy cigarette and rum for her husband."

At least once a week Junior would complain about this as if he even knew how to take care of himself. "What you think you can do with money if your mother send it for you?"

"Buy food for me to eat!" Junior scowled. "Valina cannot cook and Mr. Squires don't want me coming in the house in the day."

"Stop playing with the man records and he will stop giving you problems."

"I going back by my father to live." Junior stretched out his bony red legs on the rock and folded his arms. "Or I going Guadeloupe. Is one or the other."

"Your father have another woman big pregnant in his house. How you going back and live there?"

Junior threw a small stone into the water, causing the schoolchildren to yell curses at him.

"I not you, man. I not passing no kind of exam. So maybe I will go overseas."

Winston snorted. "And do what? You going to learn French and go to school there? Just go school here, then. Go back and finish Boys School."

Junior sucked his teeth. Winston had seen all of his stops and starts— more stops since Mona left for Guadeloupe. The heart of the matter was no one could keep Junior from his true loves: going to the river and getting into mischief.

"But why you want to go Guadeloupe? You going and live in your mother husband house?" Winston tried to make his voice sound less desperate. If Junior left, who would he have? To Valina and Mr. Squires, he was another mouth to feed; to Zoom he was a lost soul needing salvation. Junior was the only person who understood him and who he understood, the closest he had ever come to having a brother.

"No, man! A fella tell me I can get a job."

"Boy, what kind of job you can do? You have fourteen years!"

But on Mona's next visit home, Junior followed her back to Guadeloupe, leaving Winston standing on the port at Fond Cole staring in disbelief as the ferry inched out further and further to sea.

Chapter 28

Junior's red grinning face was stamped in Winston's memory as he walked into the gate at St. Mary's Academy that September day, feeling like a dolphin flailing around on the beach. Who would he tell about the long morning assembly, about the priests who rapped his knuckles with a ruler when he slipped up on speaking proper English, about the rich boys talking back to the priests, about having to cut off his hair in order to be let into the schoolyard, about the boys demanding to be taught about Black liberation. He simply kept these things to himself.

At least there were fewer distractions now that Junior was gone. He could stay up late every night doing his agriculture science homework by kerosene lamp so Valina wouldn't talk his ear off about her light bill. He woke before the sun to fetch water and make porridge for himself and little Eddie as roosters crowed in the yard. And as the school year went on, he grew used to the hard work, the studying, the feeling out of place. He even made friends.

But his nights were seldom peaceful, seldom free of dreams of Mama, Uncle Thomas, and now Junior waving goodbye from the port at Fond Cole. Even during class, his thoughts drifted to warm Saturdays in Windsor Park with Uncle Thomas at the wicket. His heart felt like the holey shirts and bedclothes that made his bed on Valina's drawing room floor—as if there were parts of his heart, parts of him gone missing. It seemed that happiness was not something to be captured and held forever in one place; it came and went and left big black holes in its wake.

Chapter 29

A boy named Franklin invited him to his house one sweaty Friday afternoon after basketball. Franklin was not among the typical bourgeois boys Winston avoided in school—except to outrun, out-bowl, or out-shoot whenever he could. They knew he was a poor boy from town—they alternated between asking him if he lived in Pound or Lagoon—and they treated him as such. He couldn't beat them in the classroom; the work was too hard, and the priests were brutal and demanding. But he hadn't failed anything yet, and that kept him putting on the white shirt-jac and stiff black pants every day.

He still wondered what would have happened if he'd followed Junior to Guadeloupe. Maybe freedom and making money would be better than grinding away at becoming a respectable, educated Dominican man.

This Friday, Winston had no desire to go to St. Aroment, but what else was there to do but homework? They walked up the Goodwill Road, joking around and teasing Convent High School girls. Winston had his eyes on a couple girls from the Grammar School and Wesley High School who tormented his dreams and built a frustration in him that defied explanation.

"She's too fat. She's too ugly," Franklin said of every other girl they passed on the street. Winston laughed. Franklin's type of girl looked exactly like Franklin: mid-range chocolate skin, mid-height, mid-weight. His parents were teachers and he was the only boy in the school who went asking Mr. Davis for extra calculus problems after class.

"All girls look pretty to me," Winston said.

"All of them? That's impossible!" Franklin said. "You just like those Roseau girls with their big earrings and big chests. That's all you like."

Winston felt his face grow hot. "Man! You don't know what I like." He pushed Franklin, who pushed him back, and they chased each other half a mile up the road.

"Wait . . ." Franklin said breathlessly. They'd reached the hushed, flower-lined streets of St. Aroment. "A lady die over there last week, you know."

"What? Where?" Winston looked to where Franklin was pointing.

"In that big yellow house."

Winston's breath caught, and he stopped mid-stride as Franklin spoke. "She was dead in the house for days. Then her servant come in the week and find her dead. They say the whole neighborhood was starting to stink."

His stomach turned as if he had drank milk left out in the sun. Why hadn't Ma Relene told him? Then he realized he hadn't seen Ma Relene in, what, weeks? A month? School had so taken over his life the last two years, it was all he ever thought about. Waves of guilt washed away the lightness of the afternoon.

"It's sad," Franklin eyed him with some confusion. "But she was old. Old, old."

He wanted to run, turn back and go home, but he didn't want to explain why, so he kept up the pretense that all was normal.

Franklin's house held wild echoes of Ms. Ford's house. Winston walked gingerly around the fancy furniture, asking if he should remove his shoes at the door. Franklin scoffed. "Boy, behave yourself and relax!" But his shoulders remained tensed, his buttocks clenched. Even when Franklin offered him a snack, he refused, pleading stomach pains. The afternoon couldn't go by quickly enough.

On the way home he crossed the river to Hillsborough Street, balancing his bag of books on his head, instead of taking the longer route through Goodwill and Pottersville. He lingered in the river, coolness coursing between his knees. People said the river was drying up, that soon Dominica would no longer have 365 rivers, one for each day of the year. He couldn't imagine there not being a Roseau River.

Ma Relene was sitting barefoot on the steps of the neighbor's house, drinking coffee, wearing a long colorful dress, her head tied in a blue-and-red headkerchief. He kissed her right cheek and she held his head between rough but gentle hands. "*Oh! Mon cheri!* I so glad you cut off those nasty dreadlocks and you in a nice school now. You know they arresting boys with those dreadlocks now?"

He squatted on the ground as she bragged to the neighbor about his being a student at St. Mary's Academy. He waited for a break in the conversation, then asked her, "Why you didn't tell me Ms. Ford died?"

Ma Relene threw back her head as if searching for a memory. "It just happen." She paused. "I didn't know you remember her. She was really sick; it was her time to go."

He felt tears forming, and he turned his face so the ladies wouldn't see. "Okay. Well, I glad to see you doing all right."

"Her son say she leave me a hundred dollars in her will," Ma Relene said, laughing. The neighbor laughed too. Winston wasn't sure if their laughing was for good or bad. They went back to their neighborhood gossip, ignoring him, as he sat half-listening. Ma Relene seemed happy and not in the least bothered by the fact that Ms. Ford was no longer in the world. He couldn't understand why he cared. He remembered hating Ms. Ford so many times, but she'd been a part of the world he'd known. Another part of his world slipping, slipping away. He said goodbye, promising to return soon. "Cheerio!" Ma Relene called out.

It was almost 9:00 p.m. according to the Timex Mona had sent him for his birthday and dark as a country night. Yet he followed the whispers of the Roseau River from Valina's house, across Hillsborough Street, and past a dark Windsor Park. His eyes adjusted enough that he could feel his way down his usual path to the water. Rootsman the Rasta was in his usual spot, smoking ganja and looking up at the moon. Winston nodded and walked past him, leaping over a couple of rocks to claim the biggest one in the middle of the river.

The water, black like onyx, flowed beneath, murmuring conversations of people coming and going, coming and going. He drew up his knees and dropped his head between them, listening to the murmurs: Mona telling stories, Zoom singing her God songs, Valina swishing her hips, complaining and stupesing, Mama groaning in pain, Uncle Thomas cursing at the cricket announcer, Junior telling another lie, Mr. Squires singing along with Charlie Pride. The murmuring river lulled him to sleep and he awoke under the bright sun, surrounded by water.

Chapter 30

This time, when Junior stepped off the boat at Fond Cole, he sported a leather jacket and shiny leather cowboy boots that caused him to sweat constantly. He rode into town on a motorcycle you could hear roaring from Pottersville to the Bath Estate Bridge. He came with a pocketful of money and said he left behind a real, French-speaking girlfriend back in Pointe-à-Pitre.

Like Prince Hal and Falstaff, they cased Hillsborough Street, King George V Street, Kennedy Avenue, and River Street together, dazzling the old gang with Junior's gold chains, ProKeds, and Adidas warm-up suits. He brought Winston all he asked for—jars of peanut butter, records and music tapes and magazines. They moved about Roseau like Junior was a celebrity and Winston his valet. Junior had been traveling back and forth every six months or so, sometimes with Mona or by himself, becoming a legendary huckster in Roseau. The neighbors in Pound and Lagoon began to save their money to buy radios, cloth, tinned foods, records, medicines that Junior and Mona brought from St. Martin, Guadeloupe, and Martinique.

Junior sometimes roared up to the towering gates of St. Mary's Academy on his bike, causing even the bourgeois boys to stare in envy. "What dat, boy?" one asked as Winston shrugged and hopped on behind Junior.

Zoom was not impressed. "Mona will have to account to God what she's doing to her son. That boy need to be in school, not running back and forth on a boat with criminal people, scraping for money."

Winston walked into this conversation between Zoom and Valina after watching a Harlem and Kensbro match at Windsor Park from the best seats in the stadium. Junior had disappeared with a girl he met at the disco the night before.

"So you staying up all night partying now?" Zoom accosted Winston, fire in her deep brown eyes, her curled hair wild about her round, pink face.

He dropped his head. "No. I just come from watching football."

"Valina tell me you didn't come inside until four o'clock in the morning!"

He had no answer for that; it was true. And he'd had a really good time dancing with girls and drinking beer after beer.

"Don't think I won't box you in the ears like I used to!" Zoom cried out. "You have a chance in life. Don't waste it!"

He sidestepped her and walked out onto the street before she could finish. Damn woman! Who asked for her opinion? He was old enough to take care of his own life!

That night he and Junior rode slowly through Roseau, making sure they were seen by all the boys playing ball or dominoes on the street and all the girls congregating near the boys. They sped down to Newtown then to Loubiere. Junior weaved through the uneven streets, barely missing other cars and pedestrians out drinking, digging music, or just liming on the warm Friday night.

At the Anchorage Hotel bar, Junior ordered a few Carib beers. "Man, what those people watching me like that for?" A family of four was sitting in the restaurant, staring hard at Winston and Junior. They could have been British expatriates, tourists, or rich Dominicans. Didn't matter.

Winston sucked his teeth and cursed. "Let's go, man." The bar man grinned at the bills they left behind. They brought their beers to a small beach fronted by fishermen houses in Loubiere. Lights were twinkling south at Scotts Head. On a clear day, one could see clear across the ocean to Martinique, and Winston strained his eyes across the dark horizon. "I think I going back Guadeloupe with you," Winston said, woozy from the beer. "I not going back to that stupid school." His mind wouldn't shut off the haughty expression of that family in the hotel restaurant—a look of hatred reserved just for people like him. He wanted to go back there and shout at them, "I have a right to be here! I paying my money!" But the owners would kick him out on his arse just to make the *bekes* feel comfortable.

Junior threw his head back and laughed. "Boy, you stupid? You know what I doing over there?"

"I know how to work hard," he said defensively. He could work with Mona and Junior. He would have his own money and go to bars in Pointe-à-Pitre and no one would dare look at him in any kind of way because he would be a big man with his own money. Life in Guadeloupe sounded beautiful from what Junior said. Mona and her new husband lived in Morne Marigot, a cool place with Genip trees, rivers and hills, and nice beaches.

Junior laughed again. "Is not the kind of work you think, man." For several minutes only the waves pierced the quietness of the night. "I wish I had a good head on my shoulder like you," Junior said wistfully.

Winston turned to look at him, his good head compromised by alcohol. "Good head don't do me no kind of good in Dominica, man. Nothing here for somebody like me." The daily humiliations of school were nearly unbearable. He was hating the priests more and more each day. It took all of his willpower not to fight back with his fists or his words at the priests or the worst of the boys.

Junior cracked open another beer. "No man, stay in your country. Dominica have all kind of politics movement now. Civil rights, workers' rights. Eh? For the poor man, not just the bourgeois. Trade Union. Allied Workers Union. That's what my mother tell me: go home and get a good job on the port and be a respectable man. Be like Winston and put your head inside a book."

"Your mother tell you that?"

Junior nodded. "But I like my money big and fast too much."

"What she mean by that? You have a good job now."

But Junior only laughed. They drank beer until they fell asleep, sinking into the cool sand. In the morning, Winston eased himself up on his elbows. He looked south down to Scotts Head where the fishermen were launching out in their tiny boats and north to where the Fort Young Hotel jetty marked the beginning of town. Somewhere in the middle loomed St. Mary's Academy.

The morning before Junior returned to Guadeloupe they claimed their spot on the big rock in the Roseau River and watched the crayfish scramble around below, just like old times.

"Man, I make a lot of money this time," Junior said quietly. "A lot of money." He handed Winston a handful of pounds sterling. "Hide that, eh?"

Winston began to give it back, but Junior thrust it into his hand.

"Make sure Valina don't take it."

"When you coming back?"

Junior shrugged. "Six months? Christmas? I tell you I have a girl in Pointe-à-Pitre? A real French girl," he chortled slyly. "She cannot even speak English."

"What she look like?"

Junior made a shape like a Coke bottle and took in a sharp breath. "Boy! That girl nice, man!"

Winston rolled his eyes. "Nicer than that girl from the disco?"

Junior ignored him.

"I coming back with you next time. Okay?" Winston tried to make eye contact, almost begging Junior. He'd made up his mind. He would leave St. Mary's Academy and become a huckster. He didn't want to become a respectable, educated Dominican man, whatever that meant. Junior was happy and carefree, and that's what he wanted. He was tired of the lectures, the drive and ambition talk, the respectable, educated man talk.

Junior patted him on the back. "When you finish with that school thing you can come and try it."

Then they rode on Junior's bike to the port, where a man was waiting to buy the bike off him. Winston waved as Junior hopped onto the ferry, wearing his leather jacket and cowboy boots. His huckster friends, fast-living men who were older than Junior by decades, slapped him on the back, bottles of rum in their hands as the boat slowly floated off into an untroubled Caribbean Sea.

Chapter 31

Roseau crackled with political intrigue in the mid-1970s. The colors of each dawn and every twilight were darkened by protests, rallies. The airwaves crackled with voices angry at the island's stagnation, the status quo, the Vietnam War, the world's woes. Something bigger was at stake now. Defense Force trucks were a constant presence. Neighbors were arrested, accused, suspected. Amid all of this, Winston struggled in school, and the priests never went any easier on him. Every day he had to show them with his high marks and industriousness that he was not stupid, not illiterate, not a *vieux negre*. It was too, too hard. Yet he stayed because he still had his scholarship and the stipend money gave him some independence. Only one more year, he told himself, then he would graduate. He could become a math teacher at Grammar School or try to find a job in the Labour Party with one of Uncle Thomas's friends. So he grinded out the required several hours a day of study while every other boy he knew in Pound and Lagoon ran the streets, slapping girls on the bottom, winning money at dominoes, dancing carnival days and nights away.

Then one slow, steamy afternoon Valina's new telephone trilled loudly over Hank Williams's "Hey Good Lookin'." Winston looked up from his book as Valina dropped the receiver, her mouth open. He ran to grab the dangling receiver and put it to his ear. On the other end, Mona sobbed ragged, unintelligible words while her husband shouted in the most incomprehensible English. Valina, shutting down as she did in times of crisis, called out for Mr. Squire to come take the phone.

From what Winston picked up, Junior had gone to St. Martin for a quick trip but hadn't returned. Mona had waited the whole day at the port in Pointe-à-Pitre, but he hadn't come off the ferry. No one had seen Junior, or so they said. Other hucksters had seen him get on board, but no one saw him get off. The gendarmes had given up looking after two hours.

"I cannot understand what happen," Mona sobbed. "If he wanted to stay in St. Martin, he would tell me. I think somebody do something to him!"

But there was no proof and there was no answer. No nothing. Just Mona screaming and crying and carrying on as if . . . as if she knew.

～

Once Mr. Squires lifted the needle from the Hank Williams record, Winston's world came to a complete halt.

He still rose with the roosters to make Eddie's breakfast. He learned to avert his eyes from the uniformed boys walking to school; instead, he walked in the other direction to Fond Cole. He wandered through the port, sat on the beach for hours, wishing that Junior's fourteen-year-old yellow self would materialize out of the water without the gold chains, without the leather jacket and the stupid cowboy boots. He didn't want to believe Cousin Eustace who said some hucksters threw Junior off the side of the boat because he owed them money. He sat and watched the water for hours each day, the sun beating his back. Maybe Junior had stayed in St. Martin. Met another nicely shaped French girl and just stayed with her. Or maybe he ran away to the Saints or Marie Galante where nobody would ever look for him.

Less than a year later, the gendarmes raided Mona's house. They took her husband to prison for accepting stolen goods. Mona refused to return to Dominica and remained in Guadeloupe, finding refuge in the church thanks to Zoom's fervent evangelistic letters. Winston would not see her again until they were much older, tried and tested even more by life's unfair and twisted turns. For them, Junior remained forever young, forever laughing at a too-serious world, his big, droopy afro framing his defiant, yellow, cat-like face.

Chapter 32

The world was contracting, tightening its grip on him from all sides. Junior's mocking laughter, his tricks, his breath, hovered over the plastic cups, the bedding, the settee, the red rickety chair in Valina's cloistered house. Some nights Winston stared up at the ceiling, Shakespeare on his chest and a candle melting on a plate beside his head. What did I do to you? Why am I living this kind of life? I could have been a white man from Stratford-upon-Avon, a bourgeois with an upstairs-downstairs house in St. Aroment or a big estate owner in Castle Bruce. Why did you make me like this?

One morning, when he'd had enough of the despair of Roseau, he lingered outside Zoom's house in Bath Estate. The front yard bloomed over with purple and orange crocuses, roses, lilies, and hydrangeas. The papaya trees were heavy with fruit, the aroma of pineapple filled the air. Mr. Edward had repainted the front porch green, like the Dominican flag, with black-and-white pillars. The neighborhood was bright and peaceful, still—except for the family of chickens crossing the lane and a neighbor hanging clothes on a line.

A neighbor's radio was playing Jimmy Cliff's "Many Rivers to Cross." He slowly let his fingers release the handle of his heavy grip. It made a scratching sound as it touched the concrete. He planted his feet at the bottom of the five green steps leading up to Zoom's gate, listening to the lift and whine of Cliff's voice seasoned in tropical heat and salt air. Involuntarily, his shoulders began shaking and salt tears seeped into the corners of his mouth. He covered his face with his hands, praying no one would see him in this state. Junior had sung this song so many times as they stood side by side barefoot in the river luring crayfish, as they jumped off the big rock into the deepest part of the river, as they walked to Windsor Park swinging cricket bats, as they stood on King George V Street watching steel bands during carnival.

But he pulled himself together, biting his cheek and pressing his nails into his palms. Then he took the steps. Zoom was at the door before he finished knocking, casting a narrow glance at his grip and his red eyes.

Before he could explain anything, she sat him down at the dining table and placed a heaping plate of pelau before him. A vase with roses, birds of paradise, and white ferns perfumed the kitchen. He wondered how Zoom had slid into this storybook life after those grim, gray years in the small, sick house with Mama.

She watched him intently at first, then launched into the questioning. "So, I hear you still don't go to school? It's months that thing happen with Junior." She sighed and shook her head. "What kind of life you think you going to have? Thomas had a big job in the Trade Union. He was smart. He went to school. Even Eustace have a trade. Look, he build my living room set." She gestured to the varnished Morris chairs with the cushions she'd sewn herself. "Winston, you have to go back school and get a paper to your name. Valina have her problems, but if you don't go school and you don't have no scholarship money, then how you expect her to feed you?"

The radio played softly in the background. A hymn sung by a male choir. "How Firm a Foundation." He ate slowly as she lectured. Maybe this idea wouldn't work; he couldn't live with Zoom. No way. He would sweep the yard, wash the dishes, do whatever she needed before the girls came home from school, then he would go back to Valina's. "Okay," he lied. "I will go back to school next Monday."

He moved through the chores like lightning, gritting his teeth at her off-key singing with the Chuck Wagon Gang.

He tossed the coconut branch broom aside and went back inside. He filled a glass from the kitchen faucet. "Zoom, what kind of song is that?" It made no sense to him; it was a nonsense, *beke* song full of fairy-tale words.

"Winston, is heaven they talking about. Heaven! Eyes have not seen, and ears have not heard!"

"But what dat mean?"

"It mean—they are happy to be going to a place where the streets are made out of gold and the walls are jasper."

"I don't know what that mean. What is jasper?"

"If you come to church you would know what that mean." And she kept on singing about going home at sundown.

He tried not to feel sorry for his sister, with her perfect family, her pretty drawing room with so many ornaments, flowers, pictures, glass figurines, yet still wishing for a fairy tale in a future life.

Suddenly, a memory surfaced like a flying fish leaping out of a fisherman's net. A rainy morning when he was very small. Mama was not sick yet; she was angry, strong, and wild, screaming at Zoom. "You think you are smart? You are not too smart for me!" Mama grabbing the cast-iron frying pan hanging on the kitchen partition and slamming it into the left side of Zoom's face, making a loud, metallic clunk. "You go and leave your own brother in the street because you want to act like bourgeois and go school?" Mama lunging at Zoom again. Ma Joan running into the house, her strong arms gathering him up and pulling Zoom away from

Mama at the same time. A while later four men in white uniforms carrying Zoom out of the yard on a stretcher. She wasn't screaming, just shaking all over like a jellyfish and whimpering like a hurt dog. Uncle Thomas running into the house, a look of terror on his face. "What happen to Zoom? Who hit Zoom like that?"

Then it was just Winston and Mama in the house for days. Or was it weeks? She baked him a cake and made him play outside by himself at the standpipe. A day? A week? A month later Uncle Thomas carried Zoom back into the house in his arms and gently lowered her into her bed. Winston couldn't see Zoom's eyes or her face because a big, white bandage covered most of her head for a long, long time. Since that day Zoom was never far from home; she never went back to Convent High School.

How old had he been? Three? Four? How could he not remember important things like this? Like Mama's funeral? Uncle Thomas's funeral? These events were slipping away from his memory, and it was terrifying. Even now his mind struggled to recreate an image of Junior's face. He shivered and the glass of water shook in his hand.

"What you looking at me like that for?" Zoom looked up from the white, lacy doily she was embroidering. There was the scar, flat and shiny, about the size of a man's palm on the left side of her face. Feeling the weight of his stare, she whipped her face away from him. "Get me some more ice water!" Her eyes hardened, her fingers worked the needles furiously.

He brought her the water, still shaking. "Let me tell you something," she said in a harsh, low voice. "When I accept Jesus into my heart, I say no turning back! You hear me? What happen in the past already happen?" Their eyes met. Hers were big, brown, and shiny with resolve. "Forgive and forget." She sniffed as tears brimmed over. "Forget! Just forget! You have to ask God to take all those old, bad things from your mind? You understand me, Winston?" Her voice was insistent, almost threatening. He could not take his eyes off her scar.

Not wanting her to see him cry, he fled to the yard to the garden where Mr. Edward had planted banana and plantain trees. Zoom's girls would be home from school soon and they would chase each other in the garden and shake the trees until the fruit fell to the ground. He tried to quell the envy he felt for their sweet, normal lives of wanting nothing. Maybe their only sadness being that Mr. Edward was away a lot of the time working for one of the shipping companies that moved water, gravel, and dry goods among the small islands.

Zoom was at the kitchen sink when he went back inside. He took a deep breath. "Zoom, I want to ask Mr. Edward if I can go and work with him on the boat."

She whirled around, causing a spray of soapy water to sprinkle his T-shirt. "What?"

He dropped his head, already feeling her disapproval. "Winston, no. That's not what God have for you. Go back to school!"

"I cannot go back there!" He heard his voice rising. "Everybody there . . . they are smarter than me. They have money and big name. And even if I go? What I going to do after?" He wiped his burning eyes. What he wanted . . . what he wanted was for her to tell him he didn't have to go. That he didn't need to go anymore. That he didn't need to feel stupid and worthless anymore.

Zoom sighed and put her hands on his shoulders.

"Winston, you must go to school," she said firmly but softly. "That's how Thomas make it. That's the only way people like us can make it. You don't have no rich father or mother but you have a good head. Those men on the boat don't have a mind like yours. God give you a chance . . ."

He couldn't stand to listen to her anymore. "God don't have nothing for me," he spat. "God didn't give me nothing! All he do is take, take, take!"

She gasped, her hands falling from his shoulders to her hips. He turned his back before he could absorb the full shock and hurt of her reaction. He was so tired of everything. He grabbed his heavy grip and walked down Bath Road toward Roseau, the familiar, merciless sun beating down on his head.

Aftermath

Chapter 33

The morning of Dad's birthday the sun flexed its muscles on the exposed landscape, waking me in a dripping sweat. The trees were slowly leafing up again, but the lack of vegetation gave the sun so much unshielded power it was almost unbearable. I woke Dad around six, to his irritation. "What you waking me up so early for?" he growled.

I literally dragged him into the kitchen, where Missy and the girls waited with his favorite breakfast, the dining room decorated with streamers and balloons, and the TV screen linked to my laptop. Before he could say anything, the screen began to populate: Aunt Zoom in Boston, Ms. Karen, Aunt Mona in Guadeloupe, Mr. Sheehan in his suburban mansion. Everyone he knew was there. Even Uncle Desi, Auntie Bebe, and Uncle Track logged in. We all began to sing "Happy Birthday" and his shocked face began to crumble. He stood there in his wrinkled, yellow T-shirt and shorts, sleep-crusted eyes, twisting his mouth each way as tears slid down his cheeks. I grabbed his shoulder as we finished singing. "Happy fifty-ninth, old man!"

Ms. Karen beamed through the screen. "Hector, I am so glad your father is with you on his birthday. I have never seen him so happy to be surprised."

My heart was full, but desperately sick about Leandra's made-up excuse about why she couldn't join us. Dante would have loved to wish Dad a happy birthday. But I was trying. I wouldn't focus on that. I was still going home in a couple weeks. I was still hoping against hope.

After we all had a chance to recover from the massive breakfast, Cousin Eddie entered the living room, where I was reading Dad's favorite book on the history of Dominica. "Your father want to go and take sea bath."

"That's what he wants to do?" I was hoping he would want to go to the old village, but I'd accept that. It was his birthday, after all.

Cousin Eddie dropped us at the beach at Fond Cole and went off on his morning rounds. I'd been by here many times but never with Dad. I'd taken some pictures for memory's sake, imagining Dad's mother balancing bunches of bananas on her head to be loaded onto Geest exporting ships in the 1940s. "Dad, you used to swim here when you were little?"

He shook his head as we stood on the warm black sand. Scads of young boys waffled about, turning somersaults on the beach, running into and swimming way out into the clear blue water. I couldn't stop staring at them, their joy, their freedom, their absolute lack of care. They ranged between age five and mid-teens and laughed with such loud abandon it made my heart ache. There may have been times as a kid when I experienced this kind of freedom, but I can't recall any now. It seemed that in America there was always a shadow looming, something curtailing the absolute abandon I was now seeing in those boys. God, I so wanted that for Dante!

"Hector," Dad brought me back to the present. "This port is where I used to come when I would think nothing good come out of my life," he said, a half-smile on his face. "But today, my son is with me. Can you imagine that?" I began to speak but the five boys ran up to us, asking if we were aid workers, Americans, Britons. "I'm a Dominican man," Dad said proudly. "Me and my cousin used to come to this beach long before you were born."

"Where your cousin?" one of the boys asked.

Dad smiled. "In a better place. It's hard to believe there is a better place than this. But he is in a better place."

Dad then ripped off his shirt and bounded into the water, churning sand and splashing water behind him. He dove in and began to put out to the ocean. Off he went, strongly and smoothly, like an Olympic swimmer. I worried that he was going out too far, too fast. "Dad! Dad!" But he was too far away to hear me. One of the boys laughed and mimicked my accent. "Ded! Ded!"

Dad's head was the size of a plum in the vast ocean, and my heart began to race. Maybe sensing my apprehension, he turned around and waved at me. He yelled something. Then he motioned, "Come." I stood still, fully clothed. I'd never really learned how to swim.

Still, I eased into the water slowly until I was up to my waist, then my chest. I stooped and let the water cover my head. Slowly, I began to remember how to be in water. The young boys were close by and they were screaming, laughing, caterwauling, splashing. I was in the middle of the most insane gang of Black kids and I was loving it, tears were spilling from my eyes, and I was weeping. Again. Jeez! I thought about Dante having to grow up with me at a distance. I thought about Leandra. I thought about all our ghosts, our little girl, our three boys that never lived to speak, to laugh, to swim. I stooped under the water so the kids won't see the tears splashing down my face. I held my breath and stayed down as long as I could. I saw their black, skinny legs kicking about under the clear surface. And I wanted to shout and cry out. For my kids, my losses that cannot be recovered. I was dizzy and out of breath when I finally came up for air.

Dad was at my back, exhilarated and breathing heavily. "Why you didn't come out?"

I shrugged. "I don't really swim . . . I never learned how to."

"Jemma never teach you to swim?"

"I never really wanted to . . ." I wiped my eyes and took in a breath to clear the lump in my throat. We were chest-deep in the water, facing each other. The boys were still splashing and carrying on a few feet from us. "You need to learn how to swim," he said seriously. "And I want Dante to know how to swim. Okay?"

I was taken aback by his seriousness. "Okay, Dad."

He was firm and resolute. "Next year, we will come back. And we will bring Dante with us."

I was at a loss for words. "I . . . sure, Dad. Of course . . ."

"I want my grandson to swim in this water. You hear me?"

"Yeah. Me too, Dad."

His mood shifted, and with a grin he dove under and surfaced in a huge splash. He laughed. "You think I'm getting old and mad?" Then he backstroked away from me, way out into the deep blue. We were there for over an hour, and he never left the water once.

The black sand stung my feet and the air quickly dried my skin as I sank onto the beach, tired all over yet soothed by the waves. I snapped pictures of Dad, of the kids on the beach. I even got into a conversation with a few of them. I asked them about Maria.

"I was sleeping and my Mama wake me up and bring me by the neighbor. I was really frighten," one boy around eight said. "We still living by the neighbor house." They said the best thing about the hurricane was not having to go to school. But they were going back on Monday, so they were enjoying their last day of freedom. I tried to be an adult and told them it was for their own good. They laughed and ran back into the water, mocking my accent all the way. Dad was floating, oblivious to the rest of the world. Next year, he repeated as we left an hour later, we would come back and bring Dante with us.

Cousin Eddie hardly ever needed a reason for a party, so Dad's birthday gave him all the license he needed. The entire neighborhood showed up that night. A DJ played reggae, soca, and calypso from the sixties and seventies, with some hip-hop sprinkled in. Ms. Karen had weeks before shipped all the food, decorations, and booze, including Dad's favorite whiskey—and a signed birthday card from all his employees at the donut shops.

Dad sat in his favorite chair on the verandah with Mikey and his old friend Marcus next to him with beers. I dipped into and out of their conversations, asking questions, as they relived the old days and reframed legendary cricket and football matches. Auntie Valina was up all night, dancing by herself or with Missy on the lawn.

The scene conjured scenes of Fourth of July cookouts in Boston with Uncle Desi playing DJ, Uncle Track on the grill, Aunt Bebe dancing, and Mom making sure everyone had enough food. I told myself that she is here in spirit. That she would want me to be dancing with Aunt Valina, talking sports with Dad and his buddies, not being a spectator on the sidelines. This was what she'd wanted: for me to know Dad and his family. So, here I was. Finally, feeling right at home away from home.

I looked up from my stool to catch Dad staring at me from the verandah. When our eyes met, I couldn't help but grin at him. I realized, maybe for the first time, that I loved my father. That I hadn't really known him before. He'd been a placeholder—just a man who showed up in my life to fill a void. It was different now. I knew him.

A coral sunset wrapped itself around the celebration and Auntie Valina was tipsily chatty. She came to life when I asked her about Junior, holding my hand as if I were a little boy. "Tell me the truth, Hector. Why you want to know about all those old stories?"

It was a strange question. "I just want to know. And I want to know what you think happened to him."

Auntie Valina shrugged. "Those men on the boat killed him. Somebody owed somebody money and they killed him."

I sat back in the wicker chair next to hers. "You don't think he just walked away. That he got off the boat in St. Martin and just said to hell with everything? Started a new life?"

She laughed. "Dominicans don't do that kind of thing, Hector. Especially back in those old days. Somebody would see him, and they would tell us." She shook her head. "We never hear anything from him again. And that really change your father. You know? It really change your father. He leave school and everything." She shook her head again.

"What about Aunt Mona?" Dad had invited her to come to Dominica for his birthday. He had even sent her a plane ticket for the short flight from Guadeloupe but she'd refused.

"Mona have a lot of guilt," Aunt Valina sighed. "It's not good to think too much about those old things. See the nice time we having now. Eh? Enjoy yourself!" She shooed me away and began to dance by herself. I had to laugh as Dad danced with one of Cousin Eddie's girls to a Mighty Sparrow classic.

He was singing, arms up high in the air, and moving his hips side to side, slightly off the beat, his eyes wide and laughing.

Early the next morning, I was back on the beach at Fond Cole watching the fishermen set out and come in with sparse catches. I'd been too afraid to ask him about it, afraid to see him break down, afraid to spoil the lightness surrounding him. This was the beach where Dad said goodbye to Junior, where he swam happily out into the ocean yesterday. Thinking only of the good times, I imagined. If Junior hadn't disappeared would Dad's life have gone in a completely different direction? Would I even be alive today? I can still see Dad, like those young kids, splashing out in the ocean, swimming out as far as his arms would take him, choosing to forget what needs to be forgotten. And I'm grateful for Junior and his willingness to take a risk on life, laughing all the way.

Chapter 34

As Independence Day approached, I eased into the spirit of things. Against Cousin Eddie's wishes, Dad and I attended a celebration at the prime minister's residence. The official residence was completely repaired, for the most part; the expansive front lawn almost back to its majestic, emerald-green, and flagrant rows of red, purple, and yellow flowers bloomed bounteously. The stark white of the mansion was the perfect backdrop for the dizzying colors of the Creole outfits worn by the hundred or so people in attendance: long dresses, head wraps, colorful ties, and cumberbunds. We were immersed in the brightest shades of the rainbow, music, aromas, and flavorful food. The prime minister, tall and affable, navigated the room, taking on the role of shrink, parent, homie, and pastor. A troupe of singers and musicians performed a traditional French Quadrille, a mesmerizing dance I had never seen before. The traditional music, with an accordion and goatskin drum, was melodious and haunting. Dad was so won over, we were among the last to leave the celebration. He exchanged phone numbers with the prime minister. "Next time I am in Boston I'm coming to your house for dinner, okay, Mr. W?" Dad was grinning like a smitten schoolboy. "You hear that, Hector? You hear that?"

Later, at home, I drilled Dad for as much Dominican history I could gather until he walked away in frustration.

No one wanted to talk about The Prohibited and Unlawful Societies and Associations Act, also known as the Dread Act, a 1974 Dominican law meant to root out Rastafarianism and the alleged crimes associated with them. Cousin Eddie shrugged when I asked about it. "I was too small to know much about that. But," he sighed, "that thing come from overseas. It was those boys that go America and wanted to come back here and start revolution."

"So you don't think it was wrong of the government to target them?"

"Yeah, it was wrong. But that's how it was back then."

I began to think about Mom growing up as a girl in Dominica—a Rapunzel type, swept up in her father's zeal and madness, unable to think for herself. Years later, I asked Dad, "Did you two really think you were going to be married?"

And he nodded yes. "In my mind at that time, Jemma was my life. I didn't plan to ever leave Zion. If that thing didn't happen, I would have stayed up there up till now."

People in Roseau shrugged when I asked them about the Dread Act. "Bad times, man. Bad times." In a way, I'm angry that Mom's life has been so written off, so disregarded. Undervalued. She was an imperfect person, a product of her environment, so to speak.

"Maybe the government could make an apology, at least some sort of commemoration of what happened to those Rastas," I told Cousin Eddie. "You know, like a national statement."

He shook his head. "You Americans."

I let it go. The truth was too painful even for me to think about.

Dad

Chapter 35

"Why you reading that devil philosophy, rude bwoy?"

Winston squinted up from the dog-eared V.S. Naipaul into Augustus's face. Dreads flowed down to Augustus's back, held together in a thick band colored red, yellow, black, and green. Augustus was Rasta now, a real rebel, always under harassment from police and the Defense Force. Winston hardly ever saw Mikey or Augustus anymore, not even when he crossed the street from Valina's house to help Ma Relene with chores. It's not that he was looking for them. He had a little job now at the Roseau Public Library, keeping the stacks neat, sweeping the verandah, and tending the grass under the Galba trees.

"You still going in that Babylon school to learn that devil philosophy?" Augustus lowered himself on the step next to Winston, offloading his ganja and sweat smell. His clothes were clean though; Winston wondered if Augustus had a woman taking care of those kinds of things. Ma Relene hardly ever talked about her sons now except to pray for them and Uncle Thomas while she rolled her fingers over rosary beads.

"I leave that school since last year," Winston replied. No one except Zoom asked him about school anymore. He'd begun to scrub from memory those school days and their accomplice hopes and dreams. He was learning that for most things in the past, it was simply better to forget and move on. Not once did he long to go back to those classrooms at St. Mary's Academy. It was so foreign to him now, all that structure and talk of discipline, male leadership and greatness. His life had fewer boundaries now. He wasn't happier but he felt freer. He still wondered about boys like Franklin, so sure of their rightness and the fullness of the future, that the only way to go in life was up, up, up. Well, that whole storybook thing wasn't for him.

"You want to go Bagatelle with me?" Augustus opened a cloth sack and began to tug at a ripe banana.

Winston considered the offer. His afternoon was free, so he found himself walking to the village of Bagatelle with Augustus talking, talking the whole way. All the history and politics Augustus did not understand spilled out in incomprehensible parables, tortured metaphors, and wild allegories that only showed how badly Augustus had destroyed his mind with ganja and cutting school. Winston tuned him out as they passed grazing bull cows and milk cows, dewy flower gardens in Giraudel and Eggleston, and skipped over crabs clambering up the wet road in Bordeaux.

They stopped at a shop for food in Grand Bay, and Augustus gave Winston a couple of bananas and a handful of tamarind balls. Augustus stocked red beans, salt and sugar and soap in his bags. "Who all that for?"

"You will see." Augustus nodded to the men sitting outside the shop. A stray dog barely acknowledged a hen and her chickens across the main road of the sleepy village. Winston marveled at the quietness, the slowness of life, the listlessness of the people sitting on wayside rocks passing the afternoon.

Further and further inland, the beauty and quiet made Winston occasionally forget his hunger and the fact that he likely would not make it back home that night. Augustus reassured him there would be good, hot food and a place to sleep when they arrived.

Three hours after they left Roseau, Augustus announced, "We almost reach, man."

Winston's calves seized up and it felt like only a banana leaf separated his sore feet and the unpaved road. But the pain went away when he looked back and saw the wide indigo bay with bobbing, colorful fishing boats roped to a rocky shore. The blueness of the tranquil waters, the cleanness of the entire scene were worlds away from dusty, crowded Roseau. He didn't know what Augustus had in mind, but maybe he could stay in this village for a while. He could become a fisherman like that American writer, even grow his beard long.

"Everything here is pure and clean. The way Jah mean for it to be," Augustus explained as the hill leveled off into a narrow path. Guava bushes brushed against his arms and grabbed at his hair on either side.

He followed Augustus to a clearing, where the ruins of a plantation house stood, overgrown with brush yet still eerily dominant. Augustus explained that the British and the French had built large sugarcane and lime estates over a hundred years ago on this part of the island. "Don't be afraid. Rastaman in charge now. All the ghosts and the *soucouyant* run and hide."

Why would I be afraid, Winston thought. He didn't believe in ghosts despite the many stories Mona told him when he was small. He'd wished for ghosts after Mama and Uncle Thomas died. At night, he'd lie awake wishing they would appear and talk to him or just watch over him. Once he'd wished Uncle Thomas's ghost would kill that man, his father, and return to life in the man's body. But those were stupid, little boy dreams. He could be worse—like Zoom—and believe there was some afterlife, some heaven, where he would see all of them again. Even Junior. But he wasn't stupid enough to believe in those *beke* stories.

A comforting aroma of bananas cooking filled the air as the path broadened into a grassy green and a compound of seven or eight concrete cottages with one large building in the middle. Genip, orange, mango, banana trees were all about, with dasheen, tania, and potato plants growing in the understory. Gardens with peppers, carrots, tomatoes formed the yards of the smaller wood and cement block cottages. The air was cool and fragrant, and the pastoral scene sent a warmth coursing through Winston's body.

About a dozen Rastas sat in a circle in the middle of the compound. One held a drum between his legs, long matted dreads flowing into the grass. The Rastas glanced at them curiously but seemed to relax when Augustus signaled with his right hand.

"We don't have no lights, no modern ting here. Every ting is *ital*," Augustus said. He dropped the bag of supplies at the door of the main house and a middle-aged lady dressed in a long white robe, dreads wrapped high atop her head, immediately took the sack of food.

"Come," he said. "I will bring you by everybody. You my little brother, okay?"

That night after a delicious meal of bananas, cabbage, and carrots, Winston joined the Rastas smoking ganja, the smoke dulling his mind and making him oblivious to their conversation and the entire world for that matter. He'd always imagined a perfect night as one where he could listen to Toots & the Maytals in peace with no one asking him to do anything, no growling in his belly, no anxiety about being a burden to whoever's roof he was sleeping under. On this night, the music was a chorus of voices shouting up praises to Jah the Most High accompanied by a lone goatskin drum, the soprano of the crickets, bass of the frogs, and the percussive crackle of a fire.

Far away from the dust, squeeze, and lights of Roseau, Winston truly inhaled deeply for the first time. He held the smoke and closed his eyes. When he exhaled, sixteen years of darkness dissipated into the cool night air. Finally, he thought, I've found a home.

Chapter 36

He had his own bed. "Nobody here have nothing for their self, okay?" Augustus replied after he'd asked which side of the room was his. "Every ting is *ital*. Share every ting with everybody. We sleep here tonight. Tomorrow we could sleep somewhere else. Every ting for everybody."

The thin mountain air crept into the window and made him pull the blanket closer. The quiet, the cool, the sweet smell of burning wood and the complete and enveloping darkness cocooned him. He never had to go back to those sweaty nights under the bunk beds at Ma Relene's house. Or wake up to Zoom's pre-dawn prayers. Or Mr. Squires's off-key singing to Nat King Cole. He opened his eyes to the darkness as Augustus began to snore softly. Junior's face hovered over his. If only they had known about this place. To think that such a clean, beautiful place could be his, theirs. If only they had known. Warm tears tickled his ears. This was the end of all his losses, he vowed. He would never go back to town.

The ganja smell rose with the sun as he turned over in bed. There was stirring next door, and a man and woman's voices penetrated the thin wall. Those were the neighbors, whose bleeding, lifeless bodies he would run past during his escape. But for now, he smiled at the loving and gentle way the man spoke to the woman.

He peeked outside, and the leader—the man with the longest locks—was in the middle of the gathering spot with his wife and a multitude of children. Bongo, Augustus said, was to be respected and obeyed as a prophet of Jah. Bongo taught both the children and adults—religion, agriculture, politics, history. "About Marcus Garvey and dem tings," said Augustus, who didn't seem too excited about this part of life in the village.

"You have to go in the big house to get your breakfast," Augustus said, stretching in his bed. "But you have to do a little work first: get water, pull some weeds, or work in the garden. Man don't eat if man don't work."

Out on a shaky concrete block step, the big blue sky with wide patches of puffy clouds was a security blanket. The air fresh and clean. No car horns, no radios blaring, no hammers pounding, no dominoes slapping. A gray-haired woman emerged and greeted him before taking up a bamboo broom and sweeping the dirt around her house. He had no idea what time it was, but most of the village seemed to be awake. He recalled an outhouse near the dirt path last night when they arrived. Dew seeped into his sandals as he tread the grass. A couple of Rastamen nodded at him on the path, wearing farmers' rubber boots and carrying a cutlass and an empty flour sack. He was about to ask for direction when he felt a presence behind him.

"Good morning." The voice was light and friendly.

He nodded at her, a girl, about his age, walking alongside him. "You come last night?" She stood almost eye to eye with him, one gangly arm on her hip.

His mouth opened and closed. She'd wrapped her dreads in a pile on her head, but a few fell past her small breasts and grazed her slim waist. Her loose T-shirt was thin, and she wasn't wearing a bra. A long skirt covered everything but her toes. Her skin was dark brown and smooth, her eyebrows a graceful line over clear, wide eyes. Like Bongo's. One of his daughters, Winston thought, his heartbeat marching across his chest.

"You staying here now or you going back town?" She smiled as if she already knew his answer.

"I think I staying," Winston said. "Where is the WC?"

She pointed and he almost ran off, embarrassed at himself. He relieved himself quickly and walked back slowly to the village center. Where had she gone already? There was no one on the dirt path; not a sound coming from the bushes on either side. Why hadn't he even asked her name?

"We are a family. That is why we eat together and learn together." Bongo read from Exodus and delivered an exposition comparing the Israelites' slavery and the Red Sea crossing to the Slave Trade and a coming movement back to Africa. He quoted Marcus Garvey often, and Hector thought he recognized the name. He was proud of Bongo for being a member of the United Negro Improvement Association even though he hardly knew what that meant. But it sounded good to him and how he felt about his own life needing improvement without the help of any *bekes* or bourgeois.

The girl was sitting across from him amid a pile of brown children crawling over her and pulling at her hair. She smiled, laughed, and tried to quiet them as the women shot her warning looks. Then Bongo called on her to read from the book of Psalms. She hastily pulled a white scarf over her torrent of dreads and straightened up over crossed ankles that displayed slender feet. The children, sensing the importance of the moment, fell away into each other.

Her voice, a dripping mix of honey and butter, gripped Winston in ways he couldn't explain. "The heavens declare the glory of Jah." She paused and her eyes met his. "The stars and everything in it." He was so aroused, he covered himself protectively with both hands.

Augustus elbowed his ribs. "You see why I tell you sometimes up here does feel just like church," Augustus whispered.

In fact, Winston looked forward to these morning lessons with Bongo. He'd never heard the Bible talked about in such a way. Not once had he heard from Zoom about God's judgment for the oppressors and for the rich who kept their foot on the neck of the poor man. To him, that was the best part. Jah would not leave the guilty unpunished. Jah would heap burning coals on their heads. Though he couldn't fully know what Babylon, its *bekes* and bourgeois were guilty of, the very facts of his life proved they had done wrong to the universe and deserved the day of wrath. Bongo, arm raised waving the Bible, proclaimed that day of wrath would surely come for the wicked and rest would be given to the innocent, the Rastaman.

And there was Jemma, Bongo's oldest daughter, reciting Scripture every morning to their little village. From her lips those verses inspired belief that Jah was on the side of all the peace-loving peoples of the earth who rejected Babylon and its wicked ways.

She made it easy to believe. Early every morning after the lesson, she supervised the older children's baths in the stream, then helped the women with the washing. In just two weeks, he'd gotten her routine down and made sure they crossed paths every day, that she knew who he was and where he had come from.

On this particular morning the people of Zion were beginning to peel away from the gathering to tend their gardens or to be with their own families. Augustus stretched and yawned next to him, his elbows deep into the grass. "You coming to help us cut cane?"

"I will meet you there." Augustus shrugged and joined the men changing into work boots. Winston lingered behind, listening to Bongo talk with the gray-haired Rastas, the elders of Zion. He pulled blades of grass from the dewy earth, taking in their conversation. Their talk sounded familiar, the politicians' names, the names of the police chief in Roseau, the Defense Force. It could have been a conversation with Uncle Thomas and his friends in the yard on Hillsborough Street. The elders of Zion wanted to carve out a place for themselves and their families outside of the government's control, but the government said a rich British family owned their land and the Rastas had no right to it. "These thieving baldheads say this land belong to them when they stole it in the first place!" Bongo thundered.

Jemma suddenly was at his side, her face framed by the rising sun. She was handing him a bamboo cup of steaming cocoa tea with coconut milk. One of the children who called her auntie gave him a plate with cassava bread and guava jam. He opened his mouth to say thank you, but no words came. She sat next to him on the grass, smoothing her skirt over her long legs. He ate, mainly to hide his nervousness. As Bongo began to explain to the other men why the Black man was also an Israelite, Jemma crawled closer, brushing her knee against his. "You like the jam? I make it myself. No sugar." He turned to her.

"Young man!" Bongo's booming voice startled him. "Who's your father?"

There was no time to think. What could he say? "Mr. T-t-t-t-imothy is my f-f-f-f-ather. From the d-d-d-dry goods shop."

Bongo narrowed his eyes. "Your father is a scamp." He spat on the ground. "Taking money from the poor. His whole family; all dem thieves!"

"I never live with him," Winston blurted as his hands shook like twigs in the wind. "My mother died and then my uncle died. I stay with my big sisters." There, he'd said all of it. This was who he was, the sum of his origins. Bongo's deep-set, dark eyes peered into his for momentous seconds. He was sure Jemma could hear his heart beating like the *lapo-kabwit*.

"You can stay in Zion for as long as you want. Don't be idle and learn your history. Give praises to the Most High."

"Jah!" A chorus rang out among the men. One placed a hand on Winston's shoulder. "Be free, brother. Be free." And he passed him a joint. That same brother would explain to him that Bongo was an educated man. He went to college in America during the 1950s and saw the wicked ways of Babylon and he came back to Dominica to create this Garden of Eden where the Rastaman could reign as a king over his own land. The choruses of praises to Jah and drumming drowned out the birds, frogs, and lizards which made the daily background music of Zion.

Jemma crawled away, the children following her like chickens after a mother hen. He looked around him, the smoke curling upwards from the blunt between his fingers. The men's clothes were ragged, mismatched, but all wore leather sandals handmade right here in the village. Some wore green Defense Force T-shirts and military-looking pants. The women walking by on the way to the stream were serene, always with many babies about them. Anyone could break out into drumming and chanting at a moment's prompting. No one seemed rushed or angry or hungry or thirsty. He closed his eyes as the smoke swirled through his brain. Was he dreaming? Was this place heaven?

In the midmorning, he lashed at cane stalks with a cutlass longer than his arm as sweat poured into his eyes. Augustus told him that the British, a hundred years ago, had abandoned the sugarcane estate, conceding to years of hurricanes, red rot, and red ink. Winston would learn from Bongo and the other Rastas that there was much land like this around the island—all for the taking. Neither the *beke* nor the bourgeois had claim to those lands. The decimated native Caribs did not want any of it. The Black man was free to take any land he wanted.

As the hazy, high mountain weeks passed, guilt began to cloud his otherwise sunny, peaceful disposition. What would his sisters be thinking? Ma Relene. Were they worried? Did they even notice he was missing?

But he would not, could not, go back. He went to bed with a full stomach every night, a candle, a Bible or some other book just to keep up with Bongo's vast knowledge. His muscles grew strong from cutting cane, digging the ground for provisions, slashing the bushes to clear paths to the river. He liked the work, the planting, the weeding, the feeling of cool dirt on his callused hands.

At night he sat next to Jemma and ate the provisions his hand helped to cultivate, sang Psalms and drummed with the rest of the village. He began to sleep without seeing Junior's face or coffins being lowered into the ground. Still, guilt nipped around the edges of his consciousness. He shook Augustus awake one night. "When next you going town?"

Augustus rubbed his eyes. "I don't know. When I need to go and buy something."

"I want Ma Relene and my sisters to know I am not dead."

The more he thought about it the more worried he grew. Who was helping Ma Relene fetch water and getting her things from the shop? And Zoom. She must be having a heart attack. "You have to tell them for me."

Augustus sucked his teeth. "Then go home and tell them. Nobody forcing you to stay here." Augustus hugged his pillow and was snoring again in no time.

Chapter 37

Every afternoon, when he finished working sweaty and covered in dirt, she would be waiting for him by the little stream. They talked about her days in charge of all the little children and his days in the soil, trying to keep up with the strength of the older, bigger men. It was these talks that slowly revealed Zion, their village, to him—its hierarchy, history, and Bongo's vision of a utopia filled with happy families praising Jah every day until death.

Jemma believed in her father's vision. "I never want to live in Babylon," she said when he told her about his life in Roseau. "I will always live in Zion."

"But you don't want to go to school and have a job?" He loved Zion, too, but he dreamed of taking her to watch cricket in Windsor Park, to dance behind Swinging Stars during carnival.

She shook her head, her tiny locks slapping at her cheeks. "Jah create us to live in freedom and peace. Capitalism is slavery," she said, staring deep into his eyes. "I don't have to live in Babylon to know that. I can see it in how your heart is so cold."

He shrank back at the accusation.

"That's what my father said," she smiled, touching his arm and causing him to shiver. His shirt was drying on a rock and he was wearing only the long, baggy pants he'd borrowed from a neighbor's clothesline.

"Your father said my heart was cold?" What did Bongo know about his heart?

"Yes," she smiled. "He said you have a heart frozen by unforgiveness because of the sins Babylon committed on your family. But Jah will heal you here." Her voice was certain, sure, as if she were reading from the Bible.

Her fingers brushed his forearm and he held her waist and pulled her toward him. He didn't know how he knew to do these things. He maybe had seen it in a movie or in one of the magazines Augustus and Mikey hid under their beds. But he liked that she let him touch her body and that she touched his. It was over so soon that they laughed at their inexperience.

They dressed quickly at the sound of approaching footsteps on the undergrowth. "I'll go and hide," he whispered.

But she shook her head as she pulled her T-shirt down over her head. "Why? We didn't do anything wrong."

"But . . ."

"My father said you will be my husband." She caressed his face. Her touch sent his heart soaring. Still, he froze as the footsteps drew nearer and nearer. Jemma's ease and lack of fear only made him more anxious. A voice called out her name. She rolled her eyes.

"Yes, Queen. I am here."

Queen Annette, Bongo's wife, appeared out of the clearing with two of the children. The three seemed unperturbed at the sight of Winston and Jemma sitting on the rocks.

"Bathe the children."

Queen Annette bowed slightly to Winston and turned back on the path, leaving the two children running into the water.

He watched as Jemma played with the children in the river where the two of them had just been so joined together, completely alone with each other. In his heart was a mixture of apprehension and excitement. Maybe she was right. He could be healed here if he stayed. If he could forget about home.

From that day, he lived and breathed Jemma, drinking in her every word and deed. Her affection drew him out of himself and into the heart of Zion. Even Augustus treated him with a new respect. At morning prayers, he sat up front in Bongo's circle and read from the Bible to the community, like an elder. Now he knew for certain he would never go back to Roseau.

One early morning, Augustus shook him awake. "I going town to buy some things. You still want to send those letters?"

Winston sat up in his bed. Those letters were written months before he had fallen in love and had become a member of Bongo's family. "No. Just tell them I am here, and I am doing all right." Augustus was away for an entire week, and Jemma sneaked into his room at every opportunity. Winston wished Augustus would stay away forever.

As she sneaked out of his room early one morning, she whispered, "I really like your beard." He realized that he hadn't seen his face in months since there were no mirrors in Zion. But he could feel his widening biceps, the thickness of his dreads, and the beard and mustache that covered almost half his face. "You look like a big man now. Not like a little boy." His chest swelled with pride. That morning he went to work in the fields with a sense of strength and power he'd never felt before.

Queen Annette, Bongo's wife, welcomed his presence and his willingness to fetch water and to do small jobs around the main house. The tasks all came easily to him, even in addition to mornings slashing at cane, digging in the ground, and running water back and forth. But he didn't mind the exhaustion since it gained him favor with Bongo and gave him access to the main house and, by extension, Jemma. He never went upstairs where Bongo lived but stayed downstairs near the kitchen and the library that was open to everyone in Zion.

He had fallen into a pleasant rhythm since settling into Zion, reading, working, and now allowing Jemma to fill every cracked place in his heart. Besides the Bible, he read *Things Fall Apart* and *The Life of Olaudah Equiano*. He devoured those two, three times. He was returning *The Tragedy of White Injustice* to the library when Queen Annette appeared in the doorway, a worried look on her face.

"Old Queen." He put the book down. "I can help you with anything?"

She shook her head. "Jemma go in the river?"

"Yes, Queen. Just now," he replied.

She sighed with relief. "You like to read dem books, eh?"

He nodded respectfully. She was a hardworking woman and the other ladies followed her example much like Zoom's choir women did. Her dreadlocks were piled high on her head and wrapped in a dazzling white scarf. Her skin was dark and smooth, and her body was strong and healthy despite giving birth to eight children.

"You can stay here for the rest of your life and read books and be happy because you are a man," she said softly, her expression the identical placid demeanor of the wives in the village.

"But you are happy, Queen," Winston said. "And Jemma is happy." He was surprised they were having a real conversation, a rare thing for a young man and an older woman of her stature.

"Looks can be deceiving." She took a children's picture book from the shelf. "Keep reading though."

When Augustus came back from town, he brought tins of condensed milk and sardines, salt, flour, and sugar. "This food is not *ital*," Winston hissed. But Augustus shrugged and hid the contraband under his bed.

Winston waited until after the evening devotion and he and Augustus were in the room, a haze of ganja over their beds. "You see Ma Relene and Zoom?"

Augustus was slow in answering. "Yes, Ras. But . . . things not good right now."

Winston would have leapt up from the bed, had his senses not been so dulled. "What you mean?"

"Boy, Roseau have all kinda ting going on with de politics." Augustus took a long pull on his spliff. "They have Defense Force everywhere, demonstration in the street. Zoom say she can't sleep because she so 'fraid for you. Ma Relene too."

"But . . . but you tell them everything is quiet and nice up here?" He could not see Augustus's expression in the dark, but he felt the fear in Augustus's voice.

"Everything all right, man," Augustus's voice cracked. "Things will get better."

"Better?"

"In Roseau. They want to blame Rastaman for their problems. Dem politricksters. But is lies, you know? Baldhead lies."

Winston closed his eyes and lay back, afraid to ask the many questions struggling to take shape in his altered mind. What did Augustus mean there were things going on? And why was Zoom afraid for his life? In truth, he didn't ask because a part of him didn't want to know. He turned his body against the wall, away from Augustus, away from the world. He willed himself to feel nothing and think nothing as his eyes closed and sleep pleasantly took him away.

Augustus's news from Roseau caused a big meeting of the elder Rastas and Bongo's inner circle. Winston was not invited. There was nervous whispering in Zion for a couple of days afterward, but a few weeks later everything returned to normal. Even Winston was beginning to forget the whole thing had ever happened.

One morning after he'd carried several buckets of water from the stream, he took his spot in the circle to listen to Bongo's sermon over a breakfast of plantains and avocado with ginger tea. At the end of the sermon, Bongo made an announcement.

"I will be sending Jemma and the children to the doctor in Roseau. They will bring back some medicine for the rest of the children. For the ringworm."

Winston's eyes widened as shocked gasps and whispers reverberated through the small gathering. As far as he knew, Jemma had never left the village on her own. Why was Bongo sending her on this mission? Why not Augustus or one of the older ladies? Bongo's eyes met his. "Rootsman John will bring them to Grand Bay. If anybody have messages for people, they can send it with her."

The village of Zion seemed to swallow its collective shock quickly. After

Bongo was finished with the sermon, they clamored around Jemma to arrange messages to be sent to their families. Winston hung back, stealing glances at Bongo, who was talking to his inner circle of Rastas in a low voice. When the meeting broke up, he followed Jemma to the river. "When your father first tell you that?"

She shrugged. "This morning when I wake up. He tell me to take the children to go and see the doctor. Two of them have ringworm."

He looked deep into her eyes, but could not read beyond the earnest surface. The whole thing made him suspicious and afraid. "But you have never been to town . . ."

"I went to town before," she interrupted him.

"What? You never . . ."

"I said I never lived in town. But I have been to Roseau a lot of times to buy things with my father when I was smaller." She leveled him with her eyes. "I don't like it there."

He ignored his rising confusion. "I don't really want you to go by yourself."

She dipped her toe into the river. "It's only to take the children to the doctor. Two days and I will be back." She turned her back to him.

"But . . . but I will miss you." The storm brewing in him was a distant, yet familiar churning of winds that threatened to overpower him, throw him flat on his face into the stream idling its way down the mountain, to the sea.

She turned around and put a hand on his thudding heart. "You are going to be my husband, remember?"

He took a deep breath, inhaling the words, her confidence, the hope of things unseen, the seemingly impossible.

The next day arrived quickly after his breathless, sleepless night. The morning devotions dragged on, and she arrived late dressed in a long tunic, loose pants, and leather sandals with a leather satchel on her back. He walked her all the way out of the village. The children ran ahead with Rootsman John leading them like the pied piper.

"So, you going town?" he asked stupidly when they reached the plantation ruins just before the big hill leading down into the world he had left behind.

She nodded. "You want me to give your family a message for you?"

He hesitated. Did he? Did he really want to give her those sappy letters he'd written to Zoom and Ma Relene? He shook his head. He looked down, afraid to challenge her, to even tell her that he would miss her desperately every second she was gone, that he was terrified that something bad would happen to her. She placed her hand on his heart and smiled. "I am going to the doctor. Bongo is not like some of the other Rastas that don't believe in doctors. You should be happy about that. I will come back soon."

Winston looked down at his muddy work boots. "You will walk all the way to Roseau by yourself with the children?"

Her hand was still on his heart. "To Grand Bay. Then I will take a bus." She pulled his sleeve. "I will see you when I come back, husband."

He watched her walk away, tall and slight, her dreads brushing against her back. He felt like a stupid little boy who didn't know anything about the world. She would come back. He would see her again. Soon, he thought. Soon.

Chapter 38

Two days, then a week, and another week went by and Jemma did not return. He no longer waited for her at the entrance to Zion holding a stupid bird-of-paradise in his shaking hands, ready to hear her say, "Hello, husband." He avoided lingering at the river, whose gurgling was a chorus of mocking laughter. There were no more tears. He had finished the Bible and restarted it, reading for hours and hours. The mornings began as usual, him seated in the inner circle as Bongo rained down admonitions to the village. She was not there to bring him cocoa tea with coconut milk, to smile and say, "Hot enough?' He pulled on his heavy boots, slung his machete over his back, and followed the men to the patch of cane field that was his to hack away for the rest of the day.

Queen Annette grew cold, suddenly erecting a wall of silence between them. "I don't need any help," she'd said the day Jemma left for Roseau. By the end of the second week, rumors were going around that Jemma had abandoned the village and was a traitor to their cause. He'd overheard the conversation through the thin walls of the cabin next door. "Somebody see her in town. They say she go by the police and tell them she want to surrender. She say she want to go to school and things like that."

He could have punched a hole through the wall. That wasn't the Jemma he knew. Not the Jemma who told him that there was nothing in Babylon for her, that life outside Zion was death. Would she really leave? With her three sisters and brothers? Why? Maybe someone had hurt her? But why was no one going to look for her? Not even her own mother, Queen Annette? Nothing made sense, and the questions stole hours of sleep every night.

Bongo had been angrier lately, preaching from Isaiah, Jeremiah, and Ezekiel, pronouncing judgment on the entire outside world. "We need to build mental siege works, like King Hezekiah!" he thundered to nods and grunts of agreement. "Prepare for the destroyer, the invader!" Someone had brought him a newspaper and he shook it out like a sheet over semicircle of Rastas. "They are telling lies about Rastaman! Nobody up here shed blood of the innocent! Nobody!" He paced around his strongmen then widened his circle to where the women and children had gathered. "This is a stronghold for the African family. The way Jah meant for it to be from the beginning. Zion is peace and tranquility for the Rastaman. Freedom for body, soul, and mind." Bongo's voice softened as he rolled a spliff between his fingers. "We on a higher plane of wisdom. Of spiritual freedom."

One week later, Winston stumbled through the dark walking to the latrine, hoping he wouldn't step on an iguana or something worse. He almost bumped into a klatch of four Rastas standing alert at the edge of the village holding cutlasses. In his terror, he almost ran back to the room. Instead, he greeted the men. "What going on, Ras?" he fought to still the quaver in his voice.

The men glared at him with hard eyes he could barely make out in the darkness. "Keep your eyes and questions to yourself!" one spat at him.

His urge to pee unbearable, he jogged the rest of the way to the toilet. Augustus shook his head when Winston asked him if there was anything to be worried about. "Boy, keep your eyes to yourself and your mouth shut," Augustus said.

"But what going on? Why they have guards now?"

Augustus shrugged. "Babylonian always want to kill Rastaman. Is nothing new."

Into the second month since Jemma had left, a gloom had begun to settle on Zion like algae on still water. No one left the village. The men's faces were tight and hard as they worked in the fields, and everyone looked at their neighbors with suspicion, eavesdropping on conversations and holding hushed, surreptitious gatherings at the river. Bongo's sermons were from the Psalms now, cursing the evildoers who hated Jah's people. He paced around the circle of villagers, waving his arms as he cried out for Jah to break the teeth of the Babylonians.

Winston swallowed his fear as Augustus grew mute and jumpy. Besides the little children, there was no one for him to talk to, not even the men he farmed with daily. Zion traded its tranquility for a silent wariness as each Rasta leaned away from the wider community, afraid to trust the very ones they'd called brothers and sisters. Bongo's paranoia and Jemma's absence caused a slow-building panic in the village. Everyone felt an impending doom but no one knew when or from where it would arrive.

Augustus seldom made sense now; he smoked all day until he fell asleep at night, chanting nonsense he mimicked from Bongo. He did not try to build up his mind and he hardly helped with the chores. Sometimes Winston was ashamed that Bongo thought of them as blood relatives.

One day at the river, he felt so overwhelmed by loneliness he longed for the days at Ma Relene's house, for warm bread and peanut butter in Zoom's kitchen on a Saturday afternoon, for Valina rolling her eyes as Mr. Squires serenaded her with a love song. He was beginning to think the unthinkable. Maybe he would just walk away without telling anyone. Maybe just for one day. Maybe he would find Jemma in Roseau and bring her back and everything would return to normal.

ᕰ

He was dreaming of Jemma one night when he was awakened by a sound so foreign to the midnight melodies of crickets and frogs it pierced the night like an incoming missile. He and Augustus jolted from their beds. "You hear that?"

"A car? A truck?" Augustus pulled on a T-shirt and ran outside with Winston stumbling in the dark after him. Seven or eight people had gathered in the center of the village; the women pulled children close to them.

"Where Robert and them?" a man shouted. "Who have de gun?"

"Go back inside!" a man ordered the women. "Bring those children inside and stay inside!"

Bongo emerged from the big house slowly. He was shirtless and wearing green military pants and heavy boots. He was carrying a long gun, a rifle, like the ones Winston had seen in Western movies. Two other men behind him also held rifles.

A shiver went up his spine and Winston's heart began to pound. Where was Augustus? He was nowhere to be found in the dark room. The sound of the engines was louder now, and the drivers were honking their horns to signal they were coming.

"Everybody that doh have gun, go and hide," Bongo announced calmly in his booming voice. "Dem baldhead come for trouble. We give them trouble."

The little crowd scattered hesitatingly at first, then quicker as the sound of engines and honking grew louder and louder, deafening in the normally quiet village.

With rubbery, resistant legs, Winston made it back to the room where Augustus sat on the bed, shaking from head to toe, his head in his hands.

"What happening?" Winston asked, taking off his sweat-soaked T-shirt.

Augustus shook his head, taking deep breath after deep breath.

His instincts took over and, without knowing what he was dressing for, Winston put on a clean shirt, leather sandals, and long pants. Before he could finish buttoning up, three loud bangs, like claps of thunder, exploded? Burst? into the night. Screams and shouts followed. He dropped to the floor and rolled under the bed. But Augustus ran to the window.

"Stay down!" Winston yelled, recalling every shootout scene he had seen at the Arawak movie theater.

A volley of bangs followed with more shouts, screams, and curses. On the ground in the dark, his fists clenched, and his eyes squeezed shut.

Suddenly, he heard more bangs and then a dull thud like a tree falling next to him. He closed and then opened his eyes. To his left, Augustus had fallen backwards from the window and was quivering and shaking on the floor. Winston almost cried out in terror. Outside, scattered shots and screams still pierced the night. "Augustus!" he whispered. "Augustus!" He crept over to him and stared into a large, bloody hole where Augustus's eye should have been. His cousin was completely still. It could have been one of those primary school days when they shared the same room in Ma Relene's house and Augustus would refuse to wake up for school. But this stillness tore at Winston's soul. Blood pooled around Augustus's head as his other eye, empty and dark, stared heavenward. "Augustus!" Something took over him and he shook Augustus's shoulder violently, calling out his name over and over. But Augustus never moved as he lay on the cool concrete floor, lifeless, half his face a gory, pulpy mess.

Winston turned away, leaning on his elbow, and vomited everything he had eaten that day. The cacophony of shouts, cries, and bullets continued outside. His heart was pounding and breaking at the sight of Augustus, at the sound of children crying and their mothers screaming. He crawled back under the bed and lay, still crying silently and praying to God for help as hell continued to rage outside for what felt like days.

Then there was quiet. A man's voice, booming and authoritative called out, "If there is anybody else here, come out with your hands up!"

Winston held his breath as heavy boots crunched against the dirt and stones outside.

"Come out with your hands up! We have an order to shoot to kill all dread on sight. But we will let you go if you surrender."

He squeezed his eyes shut as his bladder gave way, pulsing hot liquid down his legs. Who were these men? Should he believe them? He could hear them talking among themselves. They were maybe right outside the door.

"Man, let's go. They will come back tomorrow and clean up this shit."

"I not staying up in these hills all night. This place evil."

"You think all dem dead?"

"Bongo and his brothers dead. That was the job."

There was a long silence and more footsteps walking about. "Okay. Let's go then."

"Make sure you take Bongo. You can leave the others there."

◡

Winston did not move until long after he heard the last truck drive away, then he slid slowly from under the bed. He heard crying and whimpering outside. He moved woodenly, his legs cramped and sticky from pee, to the window. A few women walked about, crying over bodies splayed over the ground, some still alive and groaning. The air smelled of dirt, iron, and smoke.

Then something seized him, an urge so overpowering he didn't debate with himself what he should do. He ran back into his room, took one last look at Augustus, looked up at the ceiling and crossed himself. He changed his clothes again, then walked calmly out of the shack, not stopping to acknowledge the carnage in the middle of the village, his neighbors' corpses on the ground. Under the light of the half-moon, he followed the footpath to the edge of the village. As he neared the latrine, he heard a woman crying. He followed the sound and found Leesa, one of the elder's wives. "Leesa?" She was crumpled in the grass, leaning on the latrine, clutching a bundle to her chest. He remembered she'd just had a baby. "Leesa!" he repeated, but she refused to even look at him. She wept quietly, clutching the unmoving bundle to her chest.

He stepped back from her slowly and resolutely silenced every story, memory or thought about jumbees, snakes, and mabouyas, picked up his feet, and just ran.

His mind worked like a machine. There was only one way in and out of the village and he would simply follow it until his mind told him to stop. The trucks had left tread marks on the soft dirt path and he ran in their wake, his sandals landing in the tire indents. A half hour later, heart thumping and soaked in sweat, he was at the paved road that lead down the hill to Bagatelle.

A wild exhilaration took over as the cool mountain air energized him. The downhill run reminded him of school days, chasing a football, running through the streets of Roseau with Junior, barefoot on the grass in Windsor Park with Uncle Thomas. The fear began to lift as freedom and adrenaline powered him forward and forward, past Grand Bay, Point Michel, Soufriere. His legs were not even close to tired.

The first streetlamp he saw at Eggleston village seemed blindingly bright, like the sun. He slowed his pace but did not stop running. In Newtown, the traffic picked up and men playing dominoes outside a rum shop briefly glanced up as he ran by. He ran all through town, like an invisible man, his dreadlocks flying behind him like a shredded flag, past his father's dry goods store, past Roseau Boys School, past Pound, Lagoon, Hillsborough Street, Kennedy Avenue, and the Ministry Building.

It was nearly 2:00 a.m. when he crept around the back door and called out her name under the bedroom window.

Aftermath

Chapter 39

Mom had planned out her own memorial service months beforehand. She and Leandra sat for hours plotting what she would wear in her casket, perusing through pages and pages of urns for her ashes, and choosing a caterer for the memorial repast at St. Cyprians. I fled the room whenever these topics came up, hiding in my room with the pillows over my head. Mom would admonish me like I was twelve again, melting down over some middle-school crisis. "Hector, listen to me. Everything is going to be all right. Okay? Okay. Do you hear me?" Her firm hand felt cool and spindly on my shaky one.

I should have been ready; still I crumbled, then dissolved, like a tractor trailer had repeatedly run over me.

I was with her when it happened. She'd been struggling to breathe all week and, in some ways, so was I. Things had blown up at work and I was being summoned to meetings with each member of the bank's board, humiliating interrogations that left me raw, exposed, and homicidal. Dad would call and text and I wouldn't respond. "Hector, don't let this break you down. Everybody makes mistakes. You are a good man who made a mistake." I couldn't face him. It was hard enough facing those hard-faced white men, some of whom had been waiting years for my downfall, some of whom I knew for a fact continued to get away with worse than I had ever done. I stared them down as they lectured about the importance of treating women as equals and how the bank could not tolerate behavior like mine. I wondered if they would laugh about this with their mistresses later. They took my cell phone and my laptop so they could identify each incriminating text and email. But I couldn't even wallow in my shame or my grief for too long.

As usual, Mom was more worried about me. I told her it was better for me to be with her in the hospital than pacing the floor of my miserable short-term stay suite in Quincy. I'd arrive at the hospital and Dad would say, "Hello. Son. You're here. I was just leaving." We barely spoke to each other.

Mom was at the Brigham for one full week of that cold February. I was at her bedside each morning waiting for her to open her eyes, smile at me and say, "Boy, go home." I drew pictures with Dante of the Tuskegee airmen for his daycare's Black History Month celebration right at her bedside. She stroked Dante's hair and said, "You're going to be an artist or something like that, Dante. I can tell." Leandra brought her books and rubbed her back and chest with eucalyptus oil. She made all of Mom's favorite concoctions and fed them to her with a straw, soursop leaf tea, dandelion soup, ginger root and garlic tea. Mom would look at both of us together, putting on a front for her, and tear up. "I just wish you two would work out your problems. Do it for me." And Leandra would excuse herself.

That Friday morning, I awoke in the chair next to her bed. Mom's eyes remained closed, her body still even as I stirred noisily, sending my phone crashing on the tile floor. I stared at her forever, not wanting it to be true. She could have been sleeping. Every moment of our lives together played before my eyes: every time we rode the No. 15 bus together to cash her checks at the Shawmut Bank in Upham's Corner, walking home from her shift at the Purity Supreme in Allston, watching old movies on Sunday afternoons to make me forget I was headed back to Southbury for school, her coming to pick up a crying Dante in the middle of the night while Leandra and I screamed at each other.

The nurse, a terrified look in her blue eyes, literally shook me out of the chair, ordering me to leave while an army of scrubbed and white-coated people swarmed the room.

Leandra arrived breathless. She pulled me into her arms and I felt her athletic body up against mine and desperately wished we could be home alone with each other. She began to sob. "Oh my God, Hector. She's actually gone. I can't believe it. Oh my God."

Things began to happen in a blur. Uncle Track came home. Other people arrived and left. Sent flowers. The long-lost family who lived in Littleton put in an appearance, shocking me with their resemblance to us.

Leandra, not wanting to be alone, let me sleep in our house for a few days. Leandra was the one who took the reins with Uncle Desi and Aunt Bebe to call everyone, plan the funeral, the details. I was immobile and in shock. Leandra drove me to the doctor, who prescribed me sleeping pills and let me sit on his couch for forty-five minutes, crying and unable to utter a word. I don't know what that accomplished but it got me through the funeral.

At the memorial service, I'd planned to say a lot of things. That Mom had always been sick; she'd struggled with COPD her entire life, yet she overflowed with joy and vitality. Few people had even known of her suffering because she was always smiling, always working, and always helping everyone. Mom had warned me. "Don't make those foolish people make a pappyshow out of my funeral. If anybody starts crying and carrying on, just throw them out."

I paced my room the night before the service, rereading the program and the obituary Leandra had written with her at the hospital. "I don't want that stuff about Dominica, about my parents in there." She turned to the wall and closed her eyes.

"Why, Mom?" I'd begged. "It's part of who you are. Don't you think people should know . . ."

"Hector," she held up a hand, clear tubing dangling from it. "Just . . . please."

So we left out all the parts she wanted left out. From reading it, she seems to have been dropped into the United States a blank, clean slate with barely a chalk mark of a past; only in America did her story begin and eventually end.

Despite all the warnings about no one losing control, there was a tidal wave of weeping and, yes, sometimes wailing. Aunt Bebe had to be carried out several times. Uncle Desi and Uncle Track barely kept themselves together. We sat in the front rows, packed tightly together in dark suits and grim expressions. Leandra clasped her hand over mine every time she felt me shift or heard me take a sharp breath. The church was full to overflowing. Paul Maniscalco, my mentor from the bank, nodded at me from across the church.

Everyone waited for me to break, patting my arm, my shoulder, telling me how sorry they were. I was floating on a cloud of drugs and denial and it really didn't feel that bad throughout. I listened intently to every tribute, wanting them to be as detailed and laudatory as possible. That was my main concern, that she came off as perfect as possible. My anxiety only increased as the service wore on that she would hate all of this, that I wasn't doing it right, not the way Mom wanted. Leandra leaned her head on my shoulder and my heart rate slowed a bit when the tributes began.

Uncle Track: I used to watch Hector and walk him to school when he was really small. Most of y'all know I've had my issues with the law and all that. But Jemma, man? Jemma never forget about me all those years I was locked up. And when I got out, she had a room waiting for me in her house with all my clothes and things waiting for me. That's how she was; she take care of all of us from since I can remember. Jemma used to work double shifts so she could move us to bigger, better house. She was so proud of Hector and all he accomplish. She would always say that all of us was like Hector's team. Desi, Bebe, or me would go to all the parents meetings and things if Jemma was working. Jemma say we all one family. Everybody was raising each other's kids. We make sure nobody was on their own, and that's how she wanted it. We were the kind of family that stick together. And that was because of Jemma.

Auntie Bebe: Well, Jemma worked most Sundays because she could make extra money on the weekends. I started taking Hector with me to St. Cyprians since he could walk. When I think of the way Jemma raised Hector, I think it was almost like he had two fathers and two mothers because all of us were his parents, and that was the way she wanted it. She believed in the American Dream, you know? She wanted Hector to be successful, to have everything she couldn't have. She didn't finish all the schooling she wanted because she was taking care of everybody else. But she wanted Hector to be something big in the world. I'm glad she get to see how far he could go. To see Hector as a big executive at that bank downtown. She was so proud of him, and I know she died happy to see how he turned out.

Coach Dan: Jemma was a beautiful, complicated soul, and a wonderful mother. I'll tell you one of my favorite Jemma stories. She was a staunch vegetarian, even though she allowed Hector to eat meat. When Hector came to live with us while he went to high school, she checked in every day with my wife to make sure he was eating enough vegetables. She was the most involved parent I'd ever seen in all the years we've been boarding students. I'd have to run everything by her; if we went fishing, to the movies, to buy comic books, I'd have to let her know in advance. It was a joy to have her in my, our, life. Jemma was . . . Jemma, above everything, was a good mother. She sacrificed everything for Hector. The parents in our community always wondered how she raised such an excellent boy all on her own. Well, that was Jemma. She put her all into everything. It has been said here today but I will say it again, I don't know anybody who has persevered so much in life with so many challenges, yet who was also always full of joy. But that was Jemma.

My wife: I will read this statement that my son and I wrote together. He is too nervous to speak in front of such a large crowd and he is still learning his words, so bear with us. Grandma was my best friend. She bought me toys. She made me guava jam and sorrel juice. She made coconut ice cream for me in the summer. She was with Mommy in the hospital when I was born. She promised to take me to Dominica with her for the summer when I got big. I will miss her so much.

Me: I want to thank everyone who came today. My mother touched so many lives, and you were as blessed as I was to have known her. Everything you see and hear today is true. Some of it is new to me. The stories from her coworkers at the Shattuck Hospital have made me laugh and brought fresh tears. My aunts and uncles have revealed things from her childhood that show me on a deeper level the kind of person she was and the kind of life she lived. I can be nothing but grateful that God gave me such a woman to be my mother. My father is here today. He is in the back, and he did not want to be called out or to say anything. But I'm going to ask him to stand. Thanks, Dad. And thanks to his wife Ms. Karen, who, over the years, became a friend and one of my Mom's most faithful prayer warriors. Sorry, Dad, I know you hate this attention. Some of you may know the whole story or snippets or may have no idea at all that my father was even alive or in the picture. Well, it's a long and complicated story. A story I'm still uncovering myself. But I wanted you to meet my father now and to know that he loved my mother. They met when they were too young to even know what love was, but he loved her, and she loved him. The day before she died, Mom told me she believed in miracles because God sent my father into my life at just the right time. I don't know about all that miracle stuff. But I did want you all to know that my mother was loved by everyone she ever touched, especially my Dad.

Dad sat in the last row, spoke to no one, his faced buried in his hands.

Chapter 40

Dante poked a snot-crusted nose into the screen. "I miss you, Daddy!"

"My little dude!" I called out. "Heard you caught a cold at Grammy's." He giggled and proceeded to run around his room wildly. "I see you haven't lost any of your energy." Leandra came to the phone. Her hair was wrapped in a colorful scarf, and she was wearing a robe I bought her several, several Christmases ago. Her skin was still the perfect maple syrup. I forgot myself and said, "Hey, babe!"

She looked back to where Dante was immersed in a pile of books and toys. "Thanksgiving was really hard," she whispered. "Dante was sick the whole time. My mom had all these people from her school over." She sighed and held her forehead. "Now I think I'm coming down with whatever Dante caught."

In my mind, I was hoping we could have another normal conversation. God, I longed for these conversations when she was tired and needy and I was the only one she could talk to. "I'll be home in a couple weeks."

She didn't answer; her attention was on Dante and I took the opportunity to gaze at the perfect line of her cheekbones, the vein in her smooth neck. "Ms. Karen or Aunt Zoom would take him for a couple days."

She turned back to me. "I think I'll take them up on that. I need a couple days." She peered into the screen. "Where are you now? My goodness, that looks absolutely gorgeous." I gave her a wider view of Cousin Eddie's verandah, Missy's garden, the ocean in the distance.

"Wow! Things are really coming back! Almost like before the hurricane!"

I want to tell her she could come and visit, that we could even move here permanently, away from all the BS in America. But I held back. We were talking. Normally. Anything could shift this delicate balance.

"Most of the island still has a long way to go," I told her. "But Dad and I will be back soon. Tickets are bought."

"Have you buried your mom yet?" she asked gently.

I glanced around me. Dad was pecking away on the laptop, doing what he does with Mr. Sheehan and their business. He told me he was ready, and I could insist, push him more today. But we still had time.

"Dad's getting things together," I told her. "You won't believe me when I tell you about Dad and his family, Leandra." I chuckled.

She laughed. "Can't be any worse than my family."

Dante was still happily with his toys, hearing our conversation on the speaker. I didn't care anymore about her losing it so I went for broke.

"I think we should give things another chance."

She immediately took the phone off speaker and walked out of Dante's room to the hallway. The framed poster of Kamasi Washington filled me with homesickness. "Why would you say that when he's in the room, Hector? He doesn't know yet."

"Leandra," I half-whispered. "There doesn't have to be anything for him to know. I messed up, but we have a family. A real family. Something our parents would have killed for . . ."

Her face was gone and all I could see was the hallway carpet. Tears were spilling from my eyes again. Jeez! That frigging carpet we fought so hard over.

She was back in the frame before I could wipe my eyes. She stared at me, her eyes red and bewildered. "I don't know, Hector. I don't know. I gotta go."

Dad suddenly cleared his throat behind me. I looked back at him and sighed, putting the phone down on the table. It was midmorning, another picture-perfect early December day. He handed me a glass of water.

We sat, not saying anything for a while, watching the calm blue sea sparkle in the distance. "I'll tell you about my life on the sea," he said. "It's a good life but it's a lonely life." He sighed. "Don't forget, we are bringing Dante here next year. Leandra, too." He reached out and patted my arm. "We can take Dante whale watching. I used to see them when I used to work on the tugboat. Big, big creatures! Man! Bigger than a skyscraper. Hector! If you see those things up close, your life will flash before your eyes!"

I didn't interrupt except to bring us more water as he went on about his days on the sea. "I used to think that was the happiest I could ever be in life." He gestured up at the sky. "On the night shift, the stars used to be my company. I even used to talk to them."

He was cheerful, patting my arm and laughing, making plans for our future together. Whatever he had overheard of my conversation with Leandra had certainly given him more hope than it had given me. I had more hopes about our relationship than my own marriage as we began to talk more, staying up late nights on the verandah, mosquito coil casting an orange glow in the darkness.

Dad

Chapter 41

The cacophony crackling through the transistor drowned out Zoom's singing along to Radio Paradise. The heavenward tilt of her voice, the lyrics, the singers' sunny American accents mocked him incessantly. He preferred the feuding voices on DBS hurtling between Creole and English—sharp insults, unhinged theories, *meypuis* throwers—broadcasting their obsession with politics and who would control Dominica—the crown or the people and which of the people.

He refused to go to town, leaving Ma Relene to grieve alone over Augustus with only the neighbors to help her bury him. When she'd made the trip to Bath Estate to see him, she was red-eyed and accusing. "Why you stay in that place with my son? Why you didn't tell him to go back Roseau?" He'd told Ma Relene that Augustus was happy, that he died a true believer, and that she should not cry for him even though he himself still cried at night sometimes. Images of Augustus's hollowed-out pulpy-red face, blown apart, shocked yet lifeless, gripped his dreams. The guilt crushed him, making it hard to swallow his food, close his eyes at night. How did the bullet miss him? The older couple in the cottage next door, lying obscenely spread-eagled on the grass like sleeping drunks. He'd run past them, not wanting to look too closely or too long.

The surviving Rastas from Zion were now in prison for life, yet here he was hiding in plain sight in his sister's house.

He'd learned something about himself the night of his escape—he had accessed an almost magical inner power. That power propelled him to run and run and forget everything else, that power had blotted out the image of the bloody hole in Augustus's head, and it was now scrubbing out every memory of Jemma in his mind, heart, and soul.

Days came and went in his self-imposed quarantine. He began to lose himself in books and daydreams. The Bible, some Enid Blyton that he could finish in a day, the girls' schoolbooks, even a manhandled copy of *Aesop's Fables*. He did some of the math exercises and found he enjoyed them. At night, he talked with the girls about school and their sports. So silly they were with their concerns about hair and clothes and stupid boys. Yet he so envied their carefree existence.

Mr. Edward was away at sea the night Zoom had let him in. She'd asked no questions, fed him, gave him clean clothes and all the privacy he needed. Every day Zoom cheerily relived the previous day. She awoke at five thirty and prayed and read the Bible out loud for a half hour. She then clanged around in the kitchen, got the girls up by six thirty and made them pray and read the Bible for a half hour. They were in knee socks and pressed uniforms, plaited hair shiny with Dax, skittering down the front steps by seven forty-five for the short walk down Bath Road to DGS. How different his life would have been if he could have a predictable, everyday existence like theirs?

In midday naps or in the wee morning hours, vivid episodes continued to shock him out of sleep: sometimes it was Junior, not Augustus, laying on the floor with a bloody face, dreads sprouting from his yellow head. Other times it was Jemma dressed in white, clutching a crying baby to her breast. This one came often. He would lie awake, heart thudding, shaking arms hugging himself.

Zoom grabbed his arm one morning after the girls had gone to school. She looked deep into his puffy, exhausted eyes. "Don't ever think about that evil ever again. You hear me?" She shook him, but he was looking past her into some invisible past or future. "Winston!" she shook him again. "Ask God to give you a new mind, to erase all of those evil things from your mind. Beg him. He will help you forget!" She forced him to meet her wide-open eyes. "That's what I do with Mama." She tightened her grip. "You cannot keep those evil things in your head and expect to live. You have to forget or you will die, too! You hear me?"

He was in the doorway heading outside to the garden, to his favorite papaya tree. He would not fight her. "I will try," he said. "Don't worry about me."

She sighed, groaned, really, and freed him to lose himself in the garden.

He asked God once to make it all go away, but nothing happened. So he tried to work it off. He weeded the garden, cut down bananas, and dug up dasheen. He planted some cabbage. He scrubbed the backyard with Dettol. He fixed the kitchen sink, a leak in the toilet tank. He mended the shelves in the girls' room. He mimicked Zoom's industriousness. Work hard to forget. His days brimmed, ran over, with reading, seeding, weeding. His nights, however, remained a torment, quieted only eventually by sheer exhaustion.

Mr. Edward was returning from his month rotation away at sea. Zoom, fastidious on any given day, wore herself down to the bone cleaning and cooking before that Saturday when the taxi dropped Mr. Edward at the green iron gate.

The girls wore paisley pink Easter dresses; their straightened hair bounced and glistened in the sun. A pleasant, comforting aroma of cinnamon, sorrel, and ginger beer soaked the entire house. Baked chicken, macaroni and cheese, red beans, and salad were covered in the Pyrex on the table, atop a new tablecloth with sky-blue tablemats and coasters to match that Zoom splurged on at Nassief's.

"Daddy! Daddy!" The squeals and laughter of the family reunion reverberated as Winston's bare feet paced the tile in his room, not knowing what to do. Mr. Edward's laughter relaxed him a bit. He'd always liked Mr. Edward, but was the feeling mutual? Would he have to leave Zoom's house? Go back to Roseau? Go back to an inconsolable Ma Relene who he suspected blamed him for Augustus's death?

In the last few weeks, he had gone from feeling like a fugitive to slowly accepting that no one who mattered knew he'd been in Zion with the Rastas for over a year. No one except his family. No one was coming to take him away to prison. Mr. Squires had asked around in the Defense Force and the police department, and the Zion operation was over. Still, he would never feel completely safe.

An insistent knock rattled the door. "Winston, you coming out to eat or what?" Zoom didn't wait for an answer but poked her head in. "Come! Come! Don't stay in there by yourself!"

They sat at the table like a family, a practice Zoom enforced only on Sundays and when Mr. Edward was home. The girls followed Zoom's lead, eating Continental style, delicately raising napkins to wipe the corners of their mouths. Zoom never complained when Winston ate under the papaya tree, balancing a plate on his knees. But she clearly wanted him at the table, to bring to life the *tableau vivant* she'd created in her mind while Mr. Edward was away. She submitted herself fully to the role of servile wife, attending to Mr. Edward's every perceived need in the softest voice Winston had ever heard her use. "Honey, you want more juice? Honey, the food hot enough?"

Mr. Edward, tall, dark, and boyish with an easy laugh, seemed to enjoy the attention, and Winston could see why. How did women perform this trickery of making big, grown men enjoy being treated like children? Or maybe a king? He couldn't tell.

Would Jemma have done the same for him? He recalled her face peering into his, asking if he liked the tea she'd made him. He put down his fork as his head dropped to his chest. Could it be that none of it ever happened? That he'd imagined meeting her that day on the grassy green path? No. He would find her soon or she would find him. But where could he even begin to look?

"Daddy, tell us all the places you went to," chatty Destiny asked.

Winston picked up a chicken drumstick and ate with his hands, despite a dagger look from Zoom.

Mr. Edward beamed at his daughter. "Let me see: Antigua, St. Vincent, the Grenadines, St. Lucia."

The girls' eyes widened as Mr. Edward told stories of the sea, the men who worked for him on the boat, and his American bosses in the big office in Charlotte Amalie, St. Thomas. Winston leaned into the conversation, and Mr. Edward occasionally winked at him when the girls got silly. He wanted Mr. Edward to keep talking and talking about this life at sea that sounded so free, so far away from Dominica.

Mr. Edward also ate breakfast with utensils. Winston was self-conscious, using a fork to eat his stewed saltfish instead of using the bakes as a shovel to pick up the salty codfish, tomatoes, and onions—as he had done his entire life. The girls were off to school, and Zoom was on mission to make the house even more beautiful, fragrant, and perfect.

At first, they ate in silence, listening to the radio. Like him, Mr. Edward could listen all day. Mr. Edward shook his head at the news report on a couple of *bekes* tragically killed in one of the villages.

"I used to know Bongo and his brothers way back. I went to school with him before he go to college in America and those Black radicals fill up his head with all that revolution talk. Yeah," Mr. Edward said. "Bongo come from good people but I think he lost his head a long time ago."

Winston flinched at those words, almost turning his head away. He wanted to forget Bongo and all the man had stood for. He still could not mourn Bongo's death; all he kept remembering was the ever-present glint of anger and wickedness in Bongo's eyes.

Mr. Edward ate slowly, savoring his food. "When my father go Santo Domingo to work, he take Bongo's father with him for a while." He shook his head. "But the work was hard, you know? Cutting cane is not easy work."

Winston recalled the backbreaking work of lashing at cane stalks with a cutlass as heavy as a young child.

"My father stayed long, ten years in Santo Domingo. He was working inside the sugar mill after a while. Still hard work but better than outside.

When he come back here, he had some money in his pocket. That was in the 1930s. Way, way back."

Winston soaked it all in. He could not imagine a Dominica before he was born. "So, why your father go to Santo Domingo and work?" The conversation brought back his long talks with Uncle Thomas on idle Saturdays so long ago they may as well have happened to someone else.

"My father wanted to make money no matter what. He and his brothers were tradesmen. My uncle still making suits up in Goodwill for those bourgeois people. My father now in Guadeloupe with two houses and a shop." Mr. Edward laughed. "My uncles wanted me to go to school so I could be like Patrick John and those partners. Get the paper from the white man." He grinned and chewed his food slowly. "That's the only way you will get those bourgeois off your neck, my uncles say. Get the white man to stamp you as worthy. Otherwise, they will always think they better than you."

Mr. Edward laughed again, but Winston detected no joy or amusement. "No matter how much education you get and how much money you make, those bourgeois still not giving you a break. All the taxes and tariffs. They charge you for every penny you make with your own sweat. I love my country, but boy . . ."

He stared at the sorrel a long time, his long dark fingers clasping the glass tumbler. "If the Americans ask me to go with them, I going. I taking my whole family out. My brother in St. Croix? That's how he did it. He worked for twenty years before he get his green card. But all his children American citizens now. You cannot stay in Dominica and make it, man." He looked out the window to where Zoom was hanging laundry on the clothesline. "It's too hard here. Too hard."

"Or they will kill you," Winston muttered, not even sure where the words came from.

Mr. Edward put down his glass and turned to him. "You fixed a lot of things in this house."

Winston met his eyes, afraid he'd done something wrong.

"At least you are not lazy. So many Dominicans complain, complain every day but they don't want to work."

"Yes, sir."

"You know, your uncle came on the boat for two weeks, but he couldn't stop vomiting so we sent him back with five hundred US dollars. It's good money."

When Uncle Thomas and Cousin Eustace talked about life on the water, it was all they said: the money was good, but the work was lonely and hard.

"How you like the sea so much?" Winston asked.

Mr. Edward shrugged. "I don't know. I used to cut school so I could go down to the port and watch the Geest banana boats come in. Ever since I was a little boy I used to go and watch the ships." His eyes stayed on Zoom pinning clothes to the line. "At first, I'd just watch, then one day a man pay me a dollar to carry bags of rice and flour off the boat. That's how I started out."

These stories went on for the next two weeks, and they began to fill Winston's head with dreams more than any book he'd ever read. He began to hear himself laughing again, even enjoying the gatherings when Ma Relene, Valina, Mr. Squires and little Eddie came to visit on Sunday afternoon to welcome Mr. Edward home, to listen to his fantastic stories of life overseas.

Mr. Edward repainted the house, planted a row of sweet peppers in the garden, and Winston, without being asked, worked alongside him. He enjoyed those radiant, sweaty days ringed by the smell of Zoom's fried fish and Breeze detergent, the sound of the girls' arguing over their after-school chores. They finished a shed in the backyard and built a concrete structure to hold rainwater for washing, and Winston carved his signature: Winston Telemacque, November 1977.

He began to mine Mr. Edward for information: what was Dominica like in the 1950s when people still used pounds and shillings? Why did he have so much respect for Mr. E.O. LeBlanc? Then, did he know anything about banana ladies? How much money did those ladies make? Mr. Edward put down his hammer and wiped his brow with the edge of his white T-shirt. "You asking about your mother?"

Winston shrugged and fumbled in the box of nails. Mr. Edward took a swill of water and sat back on the ground. They were building a table for Zoom's new sewing machine.

"Your mother was a banana lady, yes."

"You know her when she was young?" He wouldn't dare ask Zoom. Mr. Edward was the only person who had a neutral reaction to Mama.

"My mother and my grandmother used to know her. She didn't go to Mass every week like the other ladies, but she sent her children. None of the children's fathers married her even though she was high-colored and pretty." Mr. Edward paused. In those days a woman's high color could make up for the fact that she was just a no-name village girl with some plantation secretary's blood in her veins. Winston's father, Mr. Timothy Masterson, had been Louise's last chance at respectability before he was snapped up by someone else before Winston was even born.

"She was a hardworking lady, but really quiet," Mr. Edward said. "Then all your aunties started to get pregnant or run with men, you know?" He shrugged. "It was hard then, hardly any jobs and not everybody could go to school. Not Zoom though. She go to school and she help your mother. Zoom was always smart, head always in a book." Mr. Edward shook his head. "I wish your mother let Zoom keep going to school. That is the one thing Zoom regret in her life. But Louise make her stay in the house." He chuckled. "Zoom never stop reading her books though."

Winston had peeked at Zoom's Barbara Cartland and Mills & Boon collections with their white-skinned heroines on the cover. They looked like fairy tales to him. He wondered now if these books had sketched the blueprint for the perfect home Zoom worked so hard to achieve.

"They used to quarrel a lot," Winston said as he and Mr. Edward moved on to the backyard water pump.

"That's why I marry her so quick," Mr. Edward said. "After I see how Louise mess up Zoom's face . . ." He sighed. "In the old days, people would do all kinds of things they wouldn't do now." Mr. Edward shook his head, looking down at the dry earth.

Winston flinched as an image of Junior flailing in the ocean passed through his mind.

"Mr. Edward," he blurted without thinking. "I want to leave here. I want to work on the boat with you." A thrill coursed through him as he heard himself asking for what he wanted. He'd always felt pushed along by the currents of his birthright and circumstances. Now he could either stem the tide or at least try to experience the pull of other currents.

Mr. Edward simply nodded. "Okay. I'm leaving in two weeks."

Two weeks.

He sat down that night and wrote Mona a long letter, telling her that he was going out on the sea to work with Mr. Edward. That he still thought of Junior every day, as she must herself. That she should not feel guilty for having given Junior a chance to live his own life. That he believed Junior would choose to leave again given the choice. That he himself was leaving not knowing what would become of him, but that was still better than remaining.

Just one day before he left, and a restlessness hovered like the thick air before a tropical storm. So many things he wanted to do one last time: lie on the big rock in the middle of the Roseau River and look up at the sky. Cook crayfish in a carnation tin on a fire by the river. Buy tamarind balls and ice pops from

Ma Flossie. Play cricket in Windsor Park. Kick a football in the yard at Roseau Boys School. Lie with Jemma near the stream in Zion.

Yet, the next morning before it was even light out, he jumped into the back of a truck with the grip holding all his belongings. They arrived at the port in Fond Cole at 4:00 a.m. where they would board the *Skippy* first to St. Thomas to the big office where he would become an employee of the West Indies Transport Company. As the boat put off, he looked down at the water, still barely perceptible in the darkness. His heart felt light as the horn sounded, announcing that another Dominican son had left home.

Chapter 42

They'd dropped their cargo of several tons of water at San Juan and were shipping out. When the crew burrowed into their bunks after midnight, he took up the watch alongside his favorite companions: a transistor radio, a large box of Ritz crackers, and a jar of Skippy peanut butter. Once the stomach flurries and the *bazoody* head went away over the first month, he began to enjoy the sway and lift of the *Skippy*, the sound of the water slapping against her hips, and the blanket of blue sky and sea surrounding him.

"You have the sea in your blood," Mr. Edward told him in his second week. "You never really know until you go out. But I can see it in you." Mr. Edward wore shorts most of the time like the other men and was often shirtless out in the open water. Mr. Edward's tall, lanky frame seemed omnipresent on board the *Skippy*. The crew respected him, and he made them earn their money. When he changed into a shirt with a collar and long pants, they all knew he was headed to the company office in Charlotte Amalie. His relaxed demeanor would change, and Winston would stay out of his way. Other than that, Winston couldn't think of a better captain, a better boss.

Life seemed light and the possibilities as infinite as the sky. During his post-midnight shifts he could stare at the vast, dark ocean, illuminated by a yellow moon and liquid-diamond stars for hours and hours with not a thought of sleep. What was up there? He thought he remembered a church lesson once that departed souls lived as stars in the sky until they were called to heaven. This suited him just fine. Every night he looked for the brightest star, and that would be Mama. The biggest one would be Uncle Thomas, the twinkling one that mischievously disappeared from view with no warning would be Junior. Augustus would be the small, dim star far off, but always keeping him company.

In the mornings, dolphins pranced, spun, and somersaulted near the *Skippy*. He bought a Polaroid camera in St. Martin and sent pictures of dolphins to Zoom and Mona. A whale as big as Ma Relene's house had breached near the tugboat once, and the crew of seven men stood on the deck, shaking in awe. "Nobody would believe me if I tell them these things," he said, snapping pictures, eager to run to the post office at the next port.

Every day was a new adventure, even the long ones full of nothing but miles and miles of the Atlantic or the Caribbean Sea. The *Skippy* was now his home and his cabin bore those marks of his life. Pictures of the sisters, Mama, Uncle Thomas, a map of Dominica, his red-gold-green headbands, caps, and T-shirts, and the books he had never returned to the Roseau Public Library. Then there was the crew, a complaining, crotchety band of comrades who treated him like a young brother unschooled in the ways of life. Each one had a story, but it was Mr. Edward's he most anticipated.

When Mr. Edward stood behind the wheel of the *Skippy* all his reserve fell away. He talked nonstop about his days playing bass guitar for a calypso band and learning to play steel drum in the steel pan yard. "If I wasn't a seaman, I'd be in a band. Yes, man," Mr. Edward grinned widely at the pink horizon. "But in a way, being a seaman is better. I can't send my children school by playing a guitar and making people dance."

The other crewmembers had less romantic visions of their work. Their conversations stalled and hovered over the high prices of food, school uniforms, rent, doctor bills, medicines, and the greedy girlfriends at the bars in San Juan, St. John, and Castries. Their problems, Winston observed, seem to boil down to their main women, side women, or extra women. Always women.

The final task at San Juan had been to lash down the cargo—boxes of nails, bags of cement, and other construction materials. En route back to the small islands, there was painting to do on the *Skippy* and some light repairs. He enjoyed feeling the rays burn the back of his legs, the breath of the waves as he painted in rhythm, the pace of it all bathing him in a peace he'd experience again only later in life. The memories of those months in Bagatelle, Jemma, the raid began to wash away with each stop in a new port, each new adventure. He began to paint in his mind's eye a new life for himself, one behind the wheel on a boat like the *Skippy*. Mr. Edward walked by, inspecting the paint on the deck. "Good job," he said, and leaned over the deck watching Winston clean paintbrushes. Soon, Winston had gotten him into talking about the old days again.

"On the big ships, man!" Mr. Edward's eyes scraped the blue sky as he recalled his younger days. "You have to call everybody by their title: First Mate, Captain, Officer." He stood up straight to his full six feet, four inches and saluted sharply. "But I do it, swallow my pride. I even clean toilets. I wash grown men shorts! In the meantime, I learned how the ship run and that's why I'm a captain today. Is good work for a young man that want to see places."

Winston had been on the sea about a year now and had gained a respectable understanding of navigation, the shipping lanes of the Windwards and Leeward islands and even a nose for an incoming squall. Standing next to Mr. Edward in the wheel room, the ocean ahead holding so much promise, the past losing its power to destroy.

Mr. Edward's next words did not surprise him. "Zoom don't want me to do this thing forever. She want me to get a job on land and be home, you know?" He grinned. "Go to church every Sunday and collect the offering, lead the congregation in hymns."

Winston bent over in laughter at the idea of Mr. Edward leading the singing at Zoom's church. Mr. Edward lifted his right hand like a band conductor. "When peace like a river attendeth my way," he sang in a surprisingly beautiful tenor.

Once they stopped laughing, Mr. Edward grew serious. "So, you sure you don't want to go back to Dominica with me next week?"

Winston busied his hands with a rope. He had a choice. Give up two weeks of pay and go home or stay on the *Skippy*. He shook his head. "I will stay."

"You don't want to see Ma Relene and them? Your sisters?"

There was only person he wanted to see, and he didn't even know where to begin looking for her. All he knew was that on the sea, there was hardly any hurt. The starry night sky promised peace. With each passing day on the *Skippy*, he could leave Dominica and her losses further and further behind.

Chapter 43

Someone was whistling along to a Credence Clearwater Revival song on the radio. An oversweet smell of rum laced in sweaty humidity hung over the dark bar in the middle of St. John's. Then the radio announcer in an American accent announced that it was hot, hot, hot. "It's the summer of 1979 and, let's just say, we're all melting here." He could hear Bongo's voice chanting, *Babylon, Babylon,* as he tried not to stare at the women wearing halter tops and short shorts slinking by, shiny hair swinging, flirting with their smiles.

Edwin, Mr. Lee, and Mr. Terry ordered rum. He asked for a beer because that's what Mr. Edward said he should do. "Don't let them fellas drink your money away." The beer tasted terrible, but he made a big "ah" after the first swallow.

"Freedom, eh?" Mr. Lee said.

"Watch, okay? Edward going to come in here, have one shot and then go back on the boat or go in the office and talk to the white man. Watch, eh?"

A few minutes later Mr. Edward walked into the dark bar, bowlegged and authoritative in his long-sleeved shirt and belted pants. "What you boys drinking?" He ordered a shot of J&B, which the leathery-tanned bartender sent whooshing down the bar. Mr. Edward knocked it back quickly, then cleared his throat. "Don't stay out too late tonight and take it easy on the young fella. That's my brother-in-law."

Before Mr. Edward had walked out in the sunlit day, Mr. Terry was complaining about having to send home "all de money" to his wife. "Don't go and have no kind of children, you hear me boy?" he warned Winston. "They'll take all your money."

Mr. Lee stood. "Let's go and check a vibes, man."

"Boy, boy . . ." Mr. Terry pulled on Winston's elbow. "When you go in those kind of places, put your money in your shoes, eh? Don't leave your money in your wallet because those girls will thief everything you have. You hear?"

Winston galloped after Mr. Lee and Edwin down the clogged main street, crawling with sunburnt European tourists. How did these people always act so carefree as if nothing in the world bothered them? He stooped, pretending to tie his shoelaces, and placed all his cash inside his black socks. He fell in step behind Mr. Lee, walking straight into his first brothel, hearing Bongo chanting, *Babylon, Babylon!*

ᴄ

They moved on to Santo Domingo and stayed three weeks. The weather was stormy that last week in July 1979, and there was nothing to do but to laze around on the *Skippy* and make short jaunts into town at night. On the streets of Santo Domingo, smooth-haired men in formal suits and white-powdered skin sneered at them or crossed the street, eyeing them suspiciously. "Dem man more white than *beke* themselves," Mr. Lee said derisively after another Spanish man nearly forced him off the sidewalk.

That night they partied hard in a club where a Black Spanish band played music more like the soca Winston was used to. Women flocked to the crew once they laid their US dollars on the bar. He'd learned a thing or two about making himself seen, and it wasn't long before a pair of giggling girls nudged his shoulder. Did he want to dance? Of course, he wanted to try this music they called bachata. It was a slowish song, kinda sweet, and it made him miss Jemma when the soulful, longing vocals came in over the pleading guitar riffs. He grabbed hold of the girl and closed his eyes, inhaling her jasmine perfume mixed with the smoke, alcohol, and sweat of the crowded bar. They danced and danced, his eyes closed the entire time. What was Jemma doing? Where was she? Did she even remember him? Did she find someone else?

The girl whispered something about a guest room as the night wore down and her friends exited with other men, laughing and whispering. But he gave her money and thanked her for the dance in English, apologizing. He walked back to the *Skippy*, his money safely under his feet, watchful for criminals but feeling a strange jubilation that he hadn't gone with that girl. He hardly slept that night, so torturous were his thoughts of Jemma.

A week later when the waters had calmed, they sailed for Charlotte Amalie, where they picked up a new crew member, a boy from Grand Bay named Fadelle. The crew took him out to a bar to welcome him.

Fadelle was short and stocky and talked with his hands, bringing all the news from home they craved. "A lot of demonstrations and things going on in Roseau. All kinds of thing about Patrick John and Ms. Charles." He would talk as long as they bought him beer, so they plied him for hours on end, not tiring of the gossip from Veille Case to Grand Bay.

Winston knew the political news from the radio and the *Chronicle*. But Mr. Edward said you couldn't believe everything they put in the paper or said on the radio. Some say the *Chronicle* was for Freedom Party and DBS was for Labour. Whom could he trust? So he asked Fadelle about the independence celebrations. The crew lit up as Winston described Queen Elizabeth and her husband standing stiffly in Windsor Park. "It was nice. But man, everybody glad to see dem ras clat British go!"

Slowly, the other men had lost interest in Fadelle, so it was just the two of them in their corner of the bar swigging Caribs.

"I go and see the celebrations in Windsor Park. But to tell you the truth, nothing really change in Dominica after that independence business. People still struggling, man. They have the queen up there and all that. But poor man still struggling."

Winston thought back to that first week of November 1978. They had partied on the *Skippy* and in St. John's, looking for other Dominicans who wanted to celebrate independence. He'd danced in bars, spent a hundred dollars on drinks. The song from that night looped endlessly in his head.

Feeling brave, he asked about the crackdown on the Rastas, doing his best to sound as casual as possible.

"Oh, they finish with all that long time now," Fadelle said. "Is all politics now. They had a fella hiding up in the hills. They say he was poisoning the water but that not true. Bourgeois just make that ting up to keep Rastaman down. You hear?"

Winston nodded but his heart was pounding as Fadelle spoke. The image of Augustus's distorted, bloody face sprang up from his memory. He lowered his head over the bar as guilt blanketed his shoulder. Augustus could have been in this bar now; instead, he was here, alive and well.

"To tell you the truth, since that thing with Ras Kabina finish, they don't care about no Dreads no more," Fadelle said, as if wanting to worry him less. "They was just looking for somebody to blame for them *bekes* that died."

He'd read about the Desmond Trotter trial in the newspaper. Trotter was sentenced to death for the death of a white tourist, but his sentence was dropped at the last minute. Trotter was part of the manicou movement, a movement that Winston, quite unknowingly, had joined. It was a tragedy that all Rastafarians were blamed for murders, stealing of farmers' lands, and other crimes. That the government had actually authorized the Defense Force to shoot them all on sight. The trial strengthened his resolve never to return to Dominica. How could your own country value scores of its citizens' lives as meaningless compared to a single tourist looking for a tan and two weeks on the beach. What kind of madness was that? What kind of hold did these *bekes* in America and England have over our leaders, Winston wondered? Did they really have no power, no courage, to stand up and tell them all to take their aid money and go to hell? That we'd die sick and hungry before we let them come into our country and tell us they were better than us? Bongo's vision for a peaceful existence free from government control and colonial influence was not wrong, Winston thought. He'd seen enough now to know that without power or money, such an existence would always face the threat of being put down, silenced and exterminated by the rich. Those with the power to decide whose life mattered and whose life didn't.

He shook his head as Fadelle described how the Rastas were either flushed out of the bush, killed, or driven further into the forest. Living in Zion with the Rastas had begun to heal his inner wounds, the constant pain, hunger, and rejection of his previous life. He had no quarrels with society, with politicians, with the British Crown. He'd just wanted to be in a place where he felt free to live without the constant message that he had to be fighting and striving for something more to be something bigger. In Zion, the struggle was simply to free his mind from the capitalist nightmares that most people called aspirations or dreams. He wondered whether Bongo was right, that there is no peace for the African in Babylon.

Weeks later at a bar in the Turks & Caicos, Winston bought Fadelle a beer and leaned in close to him. "You ever know a girl named Jemma? I think she was with dem Dreads up by Bagatelle. Her father name was Bongo." His heart pounded even as he said her name.

Fadelle thought for a few minutes. "Yeah, man, yeah," he said. "That girl, man. That girl go America, you know? They say once Bongo find out Defense Force looking for him, he send all his children America. He leave the rest of them people to die on a suicide mission." Fadelle shook his head.

"Oh," Winston said, his heart dropping like lead. So it was true. Bongo knew exactly what he was doing when he told the village he was sending Jemma and the children to the doctor. Winston's hand tightened around his beer. But did she know? Did Jemma know she was saying goodbye to him forever when she left that morning? That the Defense Force were coming with guns for them? For him? He couldn't believe that. She had touched his arm. Said he would always be her husband. She couldn't have known what her father had planned. He heaved a sigh into the half-empty bottle.

"Yeah," Fadelle said, a beer on his chest, his legs splayed out in front of him, shoulders leaning on a wall. "My mother and them know her and the whole family. They had family in America so, you know. They run go. But he keep the wife with him. She dead too. Is a good thing the children go to America."

"What you mean?" Winston asked.

"Police go up in that place by Bagatelle and blow up everything. You know?

Nothing, nobody left up there. They make an example for the youth, you know?" Fadelle turned to him. "You didn't hear all that on the news?"

He tried to stand but the stool seemed stuck to the floor. "I never hear about all that," Winston stared down into his Heineken, gripping the bottle.

"Yeah, man. It was rough, man. Real rough times. Some a dem Rastaman that survive that thing still in Stockfarm. They say some a dem man go crazy in prison. They watch their wife, their children, their brothers die. Mess them up for life—more than prison."

He saw faces in his mind of silent spiritual men who lived close to nature and considered themselves sons of the Most High God. How had he survived and they didn't?

"So, they catch all the people they was looking for then?"

Fadelle shrugged. "Police don't care about that no more. Now they trying to overthrow the government."

Winston shook his head, thinking that his life tracked a similar pattern with Dominica's history: for every good thing that happened, a tragedy struck. "Man, even dem Christians was saying 1979 was a year of judgment on Dominica," Fadelle said. "The Defense Force shot a man in broad daylight right under the Ministry Building in front of thousands of people!" Winston winced, echoes of bullets chilling him to the bone. "Independence don't make no kind of difference." Fadelle continued. "Same struggle, same foolishness with them Labourites."

"So, you run out of hope already?" Winston said, still looking down into his beer. "You hopeless about your own country?" He looked up after a few moments. "We are independent now. We can be proud of . . ."

But Fadelle had stopped listening; he was winking at a mini-skirted girl smiling at him from the other end of the bar.

Winston nodded again. And so it goes. A deepening sense of loss enveloped him. So she was gone. Therefore, all was gone. And there was no home to go home to anymore.

Chapter 44

It was August 27, 1979. Mr. Edward sat on the prow of the *Skippy*, a transistor radio to his ear, worry clouding his face. The announcer was grave: a major hurricane was making its way through the Lesser Antilles. The one flight that would have taken the *Skippy*'s crew home before the hurricane landed was cancelled.

"So, you really cannot go home?" Winston asked Mr. Edward. How could that be? They were on a vessel that had taken them anywhere they wanted. Now they were stuck in port because of rain and wind?

"That's what they say." Mr. Edward stood pacing, his T-shirt blowing in the wind. The waves were beginning to kick up, but the skies remained clear, telling no lies yet revealing nothing.

Mr. Edward, his jaw set, went down to the galley, where some of the men had congregated. Their faces erupted in confusion and anger as he told them they could pay for their own lodging or the company would allow them to ride out the storm on the *Skippy*.

"Man, that's nonsense. Every year is the same thing. That hurricane will blow itself out and all that nonsense will be for nothing," said one of the sailors.

"You can hitch a ride home with one of the sailboats . . ." Mr. Edward began to say. But the men weren't listening. Winston had no intention of spending any more of his money. He hoped the more experienced sailors were right. Dominica hadn't seen a major hurricane since before he was born. Why would something like that happen now?

The night of the twenty-eighth, when most of the men had gone to Charlotte Amalie to find boarding, he sat on the deck of the *Skippy* and absorbed Charlotte Amalie's shimmering lights.

"It don't feel like no hurricane coming," he said. Mr. Edward was so worried he had spent the entire day on the pay telephone talking to Zoom and the children.

"I hope your sister and Ma Relene make sure their windows and their roofs secure," Mr. Edward said, staring at the waves.

"You think it will be bad?" Winston asked.

Mr. Edward shrugged. "You can't be too confident when it comes to Mother Nature." He left Winston sitting on the deck and disappeared into the captain's room.

Winston watched the waves swell and turn over. He knew enough to tell when there was bad weather ahead, and except for the light wind, everything looked fine to him. If Roseau was simply getting a little rain and wind now, what was Mr. Edward so worried about?

He went through his routine of eating an entire box of crackers with chunky peanut butter. The urge suddenly came upon him to pray as he looked up at the opaque sky.

"Can you tell Mama something for me? I don't know what. But just tell her something, you know? That I am on the *Skippy* and I like it. I have money saved up. I send money to Ma Relene every two weeks. Valina, too. And Zoom told me not to send her money because she has a husband and I will need to support a wife one day. And can you send me a wife? Somebody like Jemma—pretty and quiet and peaceful.

"Can you tell my sister Mona to answer my letters? I know she is busy with her life, but I feel like she should make a little time to write me back. I just want to know she is not still feeling bad about Junior."

Clouds began to roll in and the winds gained power, tossing his empty cracker box into the ocean. "And Junior. Tell him something for me, too. I don't know what. You know? Like, I feel like he was my true brother in life but maybe he didn't know. You know? And if he . . . if he is still alive . . . that he can come and find me."

He didn't really think of himself as praying. He was mainly talking up to the sky as the storm clouds marshaled forces and trooped in over the Eastern Caribbean.

The next day, he watched Mr. Edward's eyes fill with tears as his fingers frantically fiddled with the radio dial in vain. "Blasted thing!" There was no signal from Dominica.

As the gray, somber morning wore on, the *Skippy* began to rock and roll as the outer edges of Hurricane David sent monster waves their way, washing over the port at Charlotte Amalie. The rain and wind persisted through the day and night, sometimes causing the lights of the city to go dark. They stayed close to the silent radio and did not sleep that night. They did not speak for there were no words for what they imagined was happening in Dominica, in their flimsy houses, their elderly parents' minds and hearts; their children having to face a voracious, howling storm without their fathers' protection.

Mr. Edward would not leave the captain's room even when he knocked repeatedly, so eventually Winston went ashore. He found the rest of the crew sitting on a low wall facing the ocean near Drake's Passage. The men watched with a merry, drunken resignation as the pregnant swells heaved and crashed against the breakers and sandbags. The usual hustle and bustle of Drake's Passage was reduced to a trickle of businesspeople boarding up windows and sandbagging entrances to souvenir shops and restaurants.

After three days of this heavy, somber silence on the *Skippy*, Mr. Lee picked up a signal on his CB radio. The desperate news on the other end coursed through the crew like a bolt of lightning. Dominica had been devastated by the hurricane. Dozens of lives were lost. Most of the houses had been destroyed. Some of the men wept and vowed to never leave their families if God would just let them see their wives and children again.

Winston was numb, almost listless, ready for the worst news. Mr. Edward had heard news that Zoom and the children had ridden out the hurricane with a neighbor. Mr. Lee's head was bowed low over his Heineken every day, and he would not speak to anyone. Unlike the other sailors, Mr. Lee hadn't heard a word about his family. Winston sat with him each day, watching raindrops dance on the gray, troubled waves.

Mr. Edward grew more tense and sulky. "The first chance I get, I am taking my family out of that place," he muttered as the BBC Radio reported the damage and toll from Hurricane David. Over thirty dead, hundreds injured, tens of thousands homeless, the island decimated. "That's it. I finish with that place."

Chapter 45

Winston and the cook stayed on board the *Skippy*, ringing in 1980 with a large pot of red bean soup with beef and dumplings. The rest of the crew was out in Charlotte Amalie spending their money and getting drunk. Cook, as everyone called him, had no more money to spend after sending everything home at Christmas. They slurped the thick, hot soup and chased it down with beer on the deck, watching St. Thomas erupt in fireworks, cheers, and music. It was 1980.

"What your . . . um . . . what they call them things . . . ?" The cook struggled as he downed his fifth beer.

"Resolutions? New Year's Resolutions?"

The cook pointed a spoon at him shakily. "Yeah, man. Dem tings. Resolutions, man."

"Well, I don't know. I will have twenty years. I want to get a visa so I can go and see somewhere else. America, England."

The cook nodded into his soup. "Yeah? America don't have no more money. You hear that? America broker than joke."

Winston shrugged. "I just want to go and see another place. Not to live there."

Two weeks later, on pay day, Mr. Edward called a ship meeting. The tiny captain's room brimmed with crude jokes and jousting among the crew as they gathered. Mr. Edward sat at his desk, a picture of Zoom and the twins in a large, dark wooden frame behind him. When the men wouldn't stop messing around, he raised his voice over the ruckus. "All right, everybody!" His expression was solemn. As his words began to capture the sailors' attention, cursing filled the tiny room. The company was being investigated for immigration fraud, so everybody would have to go home. Tomorrow.

Winston's heart pounded amid the cries of: "What the hell you talking about, Edward?"

"But I get my paper legal, why I have to go home?" Mr. Lee threw his hat on the floor and stomped his feet. Fadelle folded his arms and lowered his chin to his chest. The other men shook their heads in defeat. "What kind of fraud you talking about? I don't commit no fraud!" "Dem damn *bekes . . .*"

Winston tried to meet Mr. Edward's eye. He had nowhere to go. What did this mean for him? Would he have to go back to Dominica? To Ma Relene's house?

Mr. Edward looked straight at each of the six men in front of him. "They will give everybody two weeks' pay and a ticket back home. Plane or boat—whatever you want. That's all I know."

Mr. Edward clasped his hands together as if in prayer. "Is a big thing. They have FBI searching their office and everything. Is better for us to go than to get caught up in that."

"Damn Americans," Mr. Lee spat. "How I going and feed my children now?"

There were no more answers. Anger crackled through the *Skippy* as the crew packed their belongings, cursing angrily or in a glum, heavy silence. The advice to apply to another cargo carrier for work did not quiet them one bit. Winston watched the scene warily, afraid the men would eventually turn on Mr. Edward, who was pacing on the dock, his head down and hands in the pocket of his shorts. Throughout the day, the men bid each other gloomy goodbyes, promising to meet each other again someday, not knowing whether they held enough sway over their own lives to make such bold promises.

By nightfall the *Skippy* had cleared out except for the two of them. Something deep inside—terror, despair—like the cruddy black mess he cleaned from the bilge pump calcified in Winston's chest. The one-way plane ticket felt heavy in his hand. To Melville Hall. To Dominica.

Mr. Edward was at the wheel looking out over the horizon. "Your sister and I been talking for a long time about going to America." Mr. Edward turned to face him. "I couldn't tell you in front of the crew, but I get a work visa from the company and they have a job for me in Boston. It's a land job on the Boston Harbor."

The one-way ticket dropped to the dirty floor of the wheel room. He couldn't meet Mr. Edward's eyes. The betrayal stung. Why would the company do this for Mr. Edward but not for the other crew members? But, of course, why wouldn't they, Winston thought helplessly. Mr. Edward was the captain; they had trusted him with the *Skippy* for years. They wouldn't leave him high and dry.

"It's your choice," Mr. Edward shrugged. "You can come to America with us. I can help you get a visa but it's not going to be easy."

"America?" A brightness exploded around his head. "You mean, I can go with you . . ." Winston's thoughts raced, his mind playing a reel of movie images: Bruce Lee in New York City. Cowboys in saddles aiming their shotguns at Indians. Sidney Poitier in a suit in a white man's house. Ronald and Nancy Reagan on the White House lawn. He recalled Bongo's words. "There is no peace for the African in Babylon." Then Fadelle's words. "Bongo send all his children America." This was a real choice he could make? America?

Mr. Edward was staring at him. "Or you can stay here. I can help you to get something with another carrier. I know how you like the sea . . ."

"I want to go with you," Winston blurted before he'd even had a chance to think.

Mr. Edward nodded satisfactorily. "Nothing good going to happen to you in Dominica, boy. You will have more chances in America to make something big with your life."

Aftermath

Chapter 46

Looking back now, I think I lost my marriage the week after Mom's funeral. If I had gone home with Leandra as she'd asked, maybe we could have saved what was left. Instead, I'd gone to Hawkins Street, thinking there would be some comfort in those old rooms, among Mom's things in the kitchen, her piles of bills, paystubs, fliers from Linens & Things in the drawers. A blanket of darkness enveloped me as I roamed from room to room. It took a while before I realized the lights were out and it was dark outside. 9:00 p.m.

I replayed the day's events in my mind. The interminable service at St. Cyprians. The wrenching repast at the church. The awkward hug from Paul Maniscalco and his wife. "We're rooting for you, Hector. No matter what happens, our door is still open to you and Leandra." Hundreds of people whose faces I could barely recognize. Mom's coworkers from every job she'd ever had, Mr. Paul from the pizza shop in Allston, Mr. Desrosiers and Ms. Patrice sobbing, her friends from Emmanuel College, bus drivers she'd talked to over the years, the lady who did her hair, the ladies from the nail salon in Four Corners, the Barbadian couple from the bakery on Dudley Street. Mom had been a Boston institution with veins of connections stretching across the triple-decker lined streets of Dorchester, Roxbury, and Mattapan from 1978–2016.

I sat in her spot at the window and looked out onto our street, which would normally be buzzing with activity on any summer night. But everyone on Hawkins Street was in mourning. No firecrackers, no loud music piercing the night, not even the kids racing on the sidewalks on their bicycles.

The house could have been a vast, dark, silent desert. Then my phone lit up the night.

A text from the person I described as "Work Adrienne" in my contacts. "Are you okay? I know I'm not supposed to be contacting you, but I just need to know you're okay. You've been on my mind all day."

I put the phone down on the floor. Adrienne was my age; tall, with sensuous dark brown skin, fiercely intelligent, and an intense manner that drew me in the moment we met. She was our outside counsel who I called every time I was in a jam at work on some legal or business issue. The main office had gotten her for me. In a sea of white men and women I could never fully trust, Paul Maniscalco knew I needed a true ally. Adrienne Thomas was with the best law firm in town, had gone to all the right schools, knew her stuff but also knew how to talk hip-hop and sports, hated Donald Trump and every-thing the Republican Party stood for, and, most important of all, she knew the corporate game we were playing inside out. The first real conversation we had, she laid it all out for me at a corner table at Bob the Chef's in the South End. "Listen, I'm not gonna jerk you around. Paul really likes you and he knows a lot of these dudes you work with want you out of the way. So you can trust me, and I'll help you fight them off. Or you can fight me, and you'll be on your own."

Since then we'd become partners; she was my first and last opinion on every deal or decision. Then the conversations became more personal. She sent sympathy cards when Leandra and I lost our first baby. She lived alone in the Back Bay with her dog and emailed me silly pictures of him during the middle of merger hell or financial reporting season. I went there one night to pick up some papers when she was sick with the flu. Yes, I was self-aware enough to know it was right around the time everything was falling apart for Leandra. And, so it goes.

Adrienne and I had tried and failed to do the right thing over the last five years. And we would have kept trying and failing had I not overplayed my hand. A ridiculous fling with a junior banking associate in my division was what brought everything crashing down. The girl meant absolutely nothing. She swept into my office, grinning from ear to ear, tossing her hair into my face, complimenting my every move. The guys in the office wickedly ribbed me over it; her advances were that clear to everyone.

For some stupid reason, I gave in after an office happy hour at her place downtown. I laughed drunkenly at the fact that she still lived with room-mates, that her bed was unmade when we fell into it. I'd never felt so much shame in my life. I stayed away from the office for an entire week, wishing I could unwrite that entire day. I stopped responding to her texts, told my sec-retary to keep her away from my office. I thought it was over with when she finally stopped calling.

Then the reports against major Hollywood figures began to dominate the headlines. Soon, executives from major corporations were either being fired or resigning. Leandra and I were okay at that point. Dante was in his terrible twos phase and I was enjoying being the good cop. We took a family vacation to Fairhaven for a week that summer, and I even considered buying us a beach house near Fort Phoenix State Park.

That Monday morning, I was called into Paul's office. He wanted to warn me, but it was already too late. The brass in New York and Boston had had meetings all weekend—about me. They'd drawn up my severance, and I was out. Paul actually cried in the parking garage. "Hector, I know . . . I just . . . I remember the first day you walked in here when you were still in college. I knew you could run this bank someday. And I still believe that . . ."

I stopped him. "It is what is, Paul. I'll always appreciate what you've done for me."

When the news broke, Adrienne was angry but, in her wisdom, hardly ever mentioned the fling. She was concerned about me. And Leandra, maybe out of guilt. "I feel like I should tell you to call me if you need to talk but maybe that's the last thing you need right now."

There I was, trying to accept the fact that Mom left this world with her one and only son a public disgrace and a private failure.

I didn't respond to Adrienne at first, and something in me felt a resolve to never give in to my weakest impulses anymore. I needed to be alone with myself. I needed to figure things out on my own.

But maybe I needed to just say goodbye to Adrienne for the last time. "Can you come over here?" I texted her.

In twenty minutes, she was at the door. I was not thinking. I did not think that my ex-mistress or whatever role she now played should not have been inhabiting this space, this hallowed ground of my mother and all she represented.

We were in my room when I heard footsteps in the house. She flinched first. I got up to investigate, stumbling in the darkness to the living room.

Leandra turned on the light, a half-smile on her face. "Hey," she said softly. "I just couldn't let you sleep over here by yourself tonight." She placed her hand on my arm, now shaking in terror and shame.

"Leandra . . ." I looked back toward my room. And maybe because she'd known me all these years, could read my every expression, could sense my every emotion, she knew. She pulled her hand back. Her expression fell flat as she followed my eyes to the bedroom. "Say no more," she pronounced in her most professional tone. And with that, she left, shutting the door so decidedly behind her.

The shame of that one night did begin to change me. I moved out of my short-term stay and back into my old room on Hawkins Street. Uncle Track was out now on parole and we lived together like two broken men, eating takeout pizza from Stash's and Chinese food nearly every night. We were both learning—he how to live as a free man after fifteen years of prison, me how to survive without the false shield my corporate identity provided me all these years. I was now simply Hector Peterson of 43 Hawkins Street with a disappointed, angry wife and a confused toddler. How could I possibly live with all that? Well, that was the question for the ages.

I fumbled around to find redemption, trying every stupid thing I remembered from movies I'd watched with Mom. I caught up with Jean and his family, but he was too busy with his medical practice and three kids to play supporting actor in my tragedy, to pep talk me into revival. I helped the neighbors with yard work and small projects. They talked about Mom nonstop. All around me, the TV news featured the carnage of badly behaving men in the world, in Hollywood. Then Donald Trump won the election. Leandra sent divorce papers in the mail shortly thereafter, and I was ready to blame that on Trump, too.

My entire world had burned completely down.

Dad

Dear Mona:

It is two years since I come to Boston. It is so cold here, even in the summer, and I am still not used to it. It makes me miss home a lot. I still live with Mr. Edward and Zoom. Everybody is well. The twins just went to college in a Western Massachusetts where it is even colder than Boston. Zoom is working as a nursing assistant at a nursing home. She is taking classes to become a nurse. Mr. Edward leave his job on the Boston Harbor and is working in shipping and receiving for a company.

I hope the money that I send is helping you out. Thank you for the pictures of you and your family. Your little girl look just like you and your son is becoming a big boy. Ma Relene send me pictures of Mikey's sons and they are big boys too! Ma Relene put a stone on the grave for Augustus with the money I send, and she send me a picture of that too. Valina tell me you come and visit her and bring all kinds of nice things for her. I was so happy to hear that. She say you speak French like a real Guadeloupean now too! Smile.

I don't have a wife and children yet, but I hope to someday. I cannot believe Mikey have children and I don't have none.

I have a job at a place called Delicious Donuts. I go there at four o'clock in the morning to open the store and help the baker. But my main job is to be the manager in charge of the cash register. The owner is a man from Zoom's church who came to Boston from Montserrat in the 1950s. His name is Mr. Bedminster and he is really old, and he have some kind of sickness. Zoom say he will die soon, and I don't know how I will get another job because I don't have papers and my visitor's visa run out a long time ago.

In Zoom's church there are people from Barbados, St. Kitts, St. Lucia, and Montserrat. I don't go every Sunday because is the same long service like they had in Newtown with all the singing, preaching, and carrying on.

I have some friends in Boston though. A Jamaican partner live on our street and we go and shovel snow for people and make some good money. We go all around in the white neighborhood and shovel snow in the winter and cut grass in the summer. Is real good money.

The cook in the donut place, Sheehan, is from Barbados and he drive me all over the state in his car. He drive me to New York on New Year's Eve to see the ball drop. I never see lights like that in my life. And tall buildings close together like matches in a box! And people! So much people! He take me to Cape Cod and Newport Rhode Island. But the water is freezing cold here so is useless to go and swim. That's one of the biggest things I miss—going to the river and the warm sea water.

When I get my papers the first thing I will do is get my driver's license so I can see more places. America is so big, and every little place is different. I wish you could come and see it.

Chapter 47

Mrs. Bedminster was a slight, dark woman with a crisp Montserratian accent clipped at the edges by twenty years of New England winters. From appearances, she seemed always on her way to church, especially when she went to collect the rents. The click of her sensible heels and the heady aroma of Paloma Picasso sent the tenants scurrying before she even knocked on their doors. Behind the counter at Delicious Donuts she made a point to ask after the customers before accepting their money, especially those with children. She patted little arms and offered extra crullers and munchkins to every child who entered the store.

It took her awhile to warm up to Winston, especially when Mr. Bedminster put him on the register. She hovered intently, her eyes squinting, a permed lock falling into her face, when they reconciled the cash drawer at 5:00 p.m. Sheehan the baker would begin to snicker as soon as he saw her exiting the blue Buick on Seaver Street. "Too bad old Bedminster can't do his job no more. That woman is too uptight." After Mrs. Bedminster left, Sheehan would mince around behind the counter, walking with his thighs glued tightly together.

Winston shrugged off Sheehan's mocking and didn't partake. He needed Mrs. Bedminster to like him. For one, she was Zoom's church friend. And, most importantly, she must have known that he was illegal. He couldn't afford to be on her bad side.

At night he stared up at the low ceiling of the basement apartment, listening to Mr. Edward's and Zoom's footsteps upstairs. He dreamed of the unlimited, starry sky and the warm open air on the deck of the *Skippy*. Sometimes he dreamed of himself running, running down dark village roads in the thick of night, the smell of blood in his nostrils and gunshots echoing in his ear. He awoke to snowy mornings, snarled traffic, and white bus drivers avoiding his eyes when he said good morning.

Today, Mrs. Bedminster was light and sunny as she entered the store at closing. "Winston, you want some food to take home for your sister and them?" She dumped dozens of donuts on him in a Star Market shopping bag.

He accepted them knowing he would give them to the kids lingering at the bus stop on Humboldt Avenue. Zoom had diabetes and had lost so much weight in the last year it scared him. There was no way he would bring home those sugary donuts.

He hopped off the 23 bus and pulled the Celtics skull cap further down over his head. He had finally let the barber shave his head all the way down. He was only twenty-eight years old but already balding. One of the twins told him that ladies liked the bald look these days. So far, the look hadn't worked for him on the nights he and Sheehan went to Three C's to watch the girls wine down to reggae and soca music. Still, he looked forward to those nights; the music brought him all the way back to hot, dusty streets of Roseau. Even now, he never rode the bus without a tape in his Walkman blasting the latest Yellowman or Steel Pulse.

The weather remained stubbornly raw and brittle through April 1986. The city was abuzz about the marathon, which made him shake his head. Why would anyone want to do something so stupid in this cold weather? He wrangled his keys in the door, anxious to get inside and away from the gray skies and drizzly dampness. The neighbor waved from next door. "Working hard, my brother?" Winston waved back before escaping into the backdoor.

He hesitated before climbing the stairs to Zoom's floor. He simply wanted to go down to his apartment. Since the twins left for college, Zoom mothered him constantly, buying him sweaters and gloves, asking him what he wanted to eat, and offering to do his laundry. When the girls came home for the weekend, she would quickly forget about him. Zoom had adjusted to life in America by becoming busy. With the children out of the house, she threw herself into her job and church. But Winston noticed that her joy had dimmed. He missed the golden, warm afternoons when she sang gospel songs as she cooked and did laundry. Those days were forever gone. Instead, she sighed heavily as she recounted the double shifts, the stubborn, elderly patients, the minor workplace wars among the Haitians, Jamaicans, and Bajans. Mr. Edward, on the other hand, seemed bored with his day-to-day in a tall concrete building where even the air temperature was controlled by some white man. When he talked to Winston it was always to reminisce about their days at sea.

Their house on Chester Street in Dorchester was large, three separate apartments, with a tenant on the third floor. And they were doing well enough to travel to Dominica every August. But the joy of the Bath Estate house had been siphoned away by America and its demands for upward mobility. The car, the insurance, the mortgage, the snowblower, the leaf blower, the garage door, the 401(k), graduate school for the children, were all things Zoom obsessed about. "Where do you find out about these things?" Winston asked her once, bewildered by her insistence that he start saving for retirement. "Everybody at work have a retirement plan," was the standard answer. For Zoom, it was assimilate or perish. She even told the twins they'd be better off learning to speak like Americans and getting rid of their accents. Mr. Edward would grow stone-faced during these "how to make it in America" discussions, dreaming himself behind the wheel of the *Skippy*, Winston imagined.

They paid $180,000 for the house. A retired Black couple moving back to South Carolina after forty years in Boston sold it to them and included the Antiguan tenant. The house was gray, tall, and welcoming from outside with the porches on each floor that hardly anyone ever used. There were no papaya and banana trees, but there was an oak in the backyard that Zoom and Mr. Edward grew to love. On the second and third floors they occupied, there were few of the flourishes that decorated the sunny home in Bath Estate. For half the year, coats and boots dominated the entrance, and the shiny wood floors were warm from the radiators which also warmed gloves and hats. The living room, however, served as a shrine to the old country with countless photo albums, Dominican maps on the walls, a picture of the Sisserou parrot over the fireplace. He could complain about Zoom all he wanted but on the coldest, snowiest days in Boston, he could come to this house and be warmed inside and out.

That nippy April afternoon Zoom sat him down at the kitchen table before he even had a chance to put down his bag. "Winston, I have something to ask you."

He waited for yet another invitation to church or Bible study.

"You notice Sister Bedminster?" She placed a bowl of pumpkin soup heavy with dumplings and chicken in front of him. Zoom was no longer round, cheery, and red as he'd known her his entire life. Her face was narrower now, her hair cut short in a Jerry-curl style and her body fifty pounds lighter since the diabetes diagnosis. He'd taken to praying at night that God would not also take her away. What would he do then? Go back to Dominica? She was his anchor in America, in life, it seemed.

"You see how she all by herself in that big house since her husband died?" Zoom sat across from him, clearing away an unread *Boston Globe* into a shopping bag for recycling.

"She all right," Winston said quickly. "She come by the donut shop every day to check on things."

Mr. Bedminster's death hadn't shocked anyone who'd seen the withering man in the last five years. What had shocked Winston was how quickly Mrs.

Bedminster pulled herself together. Instead of aging with grief, she bloomed and blossomed with new energy. She managed the donut shop and the rental properties with businesslike vivaciousness, with nary a tear shed, a complaint lodged, or a wrinkle in her modest, tea-length dresses. She smiled more and fussed even more over the children who loitered in the parking lot for free donuts.

Zoom placed her hands on the table close to Winston. He had almost finished the first bowl of soup and was about to ask for seconds.

"Winston," Zoom peered at him. "She's not a bad-looking woman. And she's an American citizen."

He tried to conceal his horror. In Boston's immigrant community, the green card marriage was dreaded as the worst but most necessary of evils. Sheehan joked about this all the time. They never talked openly about the fact that they were both illegal aliens, even though each knew he was hoping to get papers by any and all means. Winston secretly hoped that one of the pretty girls he saw on the bus, walking on the street, buying donut holes, dancing up on him at Three C's, would fall in love with him and that everything would happen naturally.

"Zoom, that woman old enough to be my mother!"

Zoom scoffed loudly. "Alas! Winston, no! She's in her forties . . ."

"That's almost ten-plus years . . ."

"Winston, think about your situation. It will take years before the papers we file for you come through because you are not a direct relative. You want to live like this? Always looking over your shoulder? Can't drive a car, buy a house? Can't even go back and see Ma Relene before she die?"

He didn't want to hear anymore. He left the soup steaming on the table and escaped to his basement sanctuary. He had a large TV he had bought with his own money, and most nights he stayed in, watching basketball or movies on channel 38. He liked the predictability of his days, the working, sleeping, earning and spending on his simple pleasures—TV, shooting the crap with the guys next door or at the donut shop, the occasional beer and loose girl at the darker haunts in Mattapan. So what was Zoom saying? Did she want him to leave? Is that why she was pushing marriage on him? To get rid of him? His mind wandered in all directions. Now that the girls were in college, were she and Mr. Edward considering going back to Dominica? He shook his head as he turned on the TV to *Sanford and Son*. Zoom was wrong. He never looked over his shoulder in America. Even when the news reporters made Mattapan, Roxbury, and Dorchester seem like gang-plagued war zones. He walked the streets alone at midnight and hailed the brothers on the corner. They never bothered him. He was more afraid of the cops who would slowly follow him for a block or so before losing interest. Even that fear was fleeting, however. It was in Dominica he always felt afraid—that lurking in the shadows was something beyond his control that could upend his life. Once he had stepped off that plane on that bright August day at Logan International Airport, the fear dissipated into the humid, American air. He didn't need any better life than the one he had now.

Yet, the next day he allowed his eyes to linger on Mrs. Bedminister. Karen, she told him to call her as Sheehan snickered in the kitchen.

Mrs. Bedminister. Karen. She laughed at his joke about the weather being colder than the river in the morning. "I used to go and bathe in river when I was a girl in Montserrat. Eh! I miss those days!" And this felt good to him, that they could reminisce about going to the river. That night he pictured a young Mrs. Bedminister, Karen, bathing in the river, and it wasn't unpleasant.

He thought about it more and more over the following weeks and months. He wished he could ask Mr. Edward for advice but that seemed unreasonable, too childish. This was one of the things he would have to do on his own as a man.

Chapter 48

Thanksgiving Day in 1987 arrived with three feet of snow. Winston rubbed his back, sore from his third bout of shoveling that day. He kicked off his boots as he entered the warm kitchen where Mr. Edward jabbed at a brown turkey in the oven. "Still coming down hard out there?"

"Yep." Winston sank slowly into a chair. Mr. Edward bobbed his head to the Midnight Groovers cassette playing on the stereo in the hallway. Zoom and the girls were shrieking in the living room over some memory. And Karen was with them, laughing along, in on the joke like she already was part of the family. Zoom had invited her to their Thanksgiving dinner, and he'd felt powerless to say no. Truly, he didn't mind. Why should Karen be alone on Thanksgiving? He himself didn't want to be alone when everyone was with their family. Mr. Edward glanced over at him and grinned. "You all right with that?" Winston shrugged.

"You can't do anything in this country without papers," Mr. Edward said as he basted the turkey carefully. Mr. Edward had never cooked while they were on the *Skippy*. Certainly never while he and Zoom lived in Bath Estate. It still shocked Winston to see him tossing laundry into the dryer or standing over the stove, sticking a fork into potatoes. America had changed the man. Zoom sometimes rolled her eyes behind Mr. Edward's back when he chided her for spending too much money. She would never say it out loud to Mr. Edward, but she she'd whispered to Winston, "I make my own money now."

Zoom and the girls rushed into the kitchen, hovering over Mr. Edward. "Daddy, is it true you used to have ladies fighting over you in Roseau?" They were grown-up now, hardly anything Dominican left in them. They spoke like Americans and they did American things like sitting in a coffee shop for hours and hours just to study or talk to their friends. They came to the donut shop to visit him when they were home from school with a Starbucks coffee cup in their hands.

Mr. Edward laughed. "That's what your mother said?"

The table was pleasantly rowdy, the food a mixture of tropical and American flavors. Zoom made a green banana casserole with chicken and onions covered with melted cheddar, stewed saltfish, fried plantains, sorrel, and black cake. But there was also the turkey, mashed potatoes, sweet potato pie, and a pecan pie Karen brought.

Karen shocked him when she spoke up. "My father used to play in a calypso band, too. He played in church but he used to disguise himself so he could do road marches during carnival season."

Mr. Edward guffawed as Zoom's jaw dropped in surprise.

"I used to go with him," Karen giggled. "My mother never knew. I used to love to dance. I would dance behind the band all day, then at night I'd pray for God to forgive me."

"Well, Karen, I could never see you being that kind . . ." Zoom said, her eyes still wide in amazement.

"You used to come and watch me play sometimes," Mr. Edward said laughing. "Before you met those missionaries, you used to have your wild days."

"Oh, do tell!" one of the twins exclaimed.

Zoom rolled her eyes. "I was taking care of my mother and I had to have to a little fun, every now and then."

Winston laughed along, though he couldn't recall Zoom ever having the slightest bit of fun. The snow piled up outside, along with the merriness, as they ate. The American neighbors stopped by, bringing apple pie and cranberry sauce. It was a joyful exchange as they took plates full of Zoom's West Indian dishes. Winston promised he'd stop by later to watch football with Kenny down the street.

The living room was warm and comforting as they watched a movie after the heavy meal. A feeling of safety and comfort took him back decades to the night before Mama went to Barbados for her final surgery when they—Zoom, Mona, Valina, Junior, Uncle Thomas, Ma Relene—were all together, unsure whether they were celebrating or saying goodbye.

"I'm going outside to shovel," he announced.

"I'll come and help you," Karen offered.

He stared at her, then laughed. "You don't have to help me."

"She'll just keep you company, then," Zoom piped up.

"Good idea!" one of the twins rejoined.

He couldn't have refused even if he wanted to. Karen was a mere five foot five to his six feet; what could she possibly do to help him? She stood on the porch bundled up in a white down coat, the hood covering her head. The snow was still coming down at a good clip, leaving pillowy drifts in the street and on the sidewalks. Kenny's snowblower hummed in the otherwise dusky, quiet, late afternoon. Karen watched while he attacked the snow, and he imagined her dancing, her slim dark body following the carnival band down the narrow stone streets of Montserrat. He asked her what coming to America was like.

"My mother was glad to send me. I was seventeen, and I was getting too hot for her to handle." Karen pulled her hood tighter over her head. She was happy to leave sleepy Montserrat for the excitement of America. But excitement turned to dread when she found out the price of freedom. Mr. Bedminster was a deacon and already owned two houses in Roxbury when she was introduced to him by family at the Holiness Church, the launch pad for many small-island immigrants of that time. He seemed ancient to her although he was only in his early thirties. She thought of running away but had nowhere to go. Those first few years were happy because he sent her to school at Boston State College where she studied childhood education and became a teacher for a while. He went to Northeastern and got a degree in accounting, then got a job at State Street Bank in the audit department. He said he was glad for his accent because it made the white people treat him better than the Black Americans. He never let that get to his head though. He said the best way to make it as a colored in America is to make your money and save it up so they can't buy or sell you any way they want. He still lost the job when the racial situation worsened in the late 1970s. He bought the donut shop from a Jewish man with money he made driving a taxi, doing income taxes for the church members, and by going a *sou* with some other West Indians.

Five years later, Karen accepted that either she or Mr. Bedminster were the cause of their childlessness, and the only thing she looked forward to in life was teaching Sunday school. Mr. Bedminster worked and worked, and when he wasn't working, he was dreaming up more ways to make money. He said he would be richer than the man who fired him from the bank. Karen, meanwhile, was mainly lonely. She didn't fit in with the other young women at the church because she had no babies to complain about or to ferry to the cry room during the service. Her childlessness dug a cavernous breach between her and Mr. Bedminster that grew wider and wider until God finally took him away, leaving her on her own at thirty-eight.

Winston leaned on the shovel and stared at her. The snow fell around her, gathering on the furry hood of her parka, piling up around her boots. She'd been talking and talking, more than he'd ever heard her talk before. Why did he ever think she was old? He saw in her the seventeen-year-old who had come to America unsure of what lay ahead, hoping for the best. Just like him. Now, just like him, she was worn almost completely down with the loneliness of being marooned in a strange land. But doing her best, still trusting in the hope of the American Dream. The snow fell about them like diamonds as the sky darkened above the tall, gray house.

Chapter 49

Some Fridays he would ride the Orange Line to Downtown Crossing to buy incense and liberation color beads from the Jamaican Rasta's cart outside Filene's Basement. That guy sold all the cassettes and CDs Winston wanted— not the Bob Marley and Steel Pulse he could easily get in the bins at Tower Records or Skippy White's—but Eric Donaldson, Toots and the Melodians. On his days off from Delicious Donuts he would plug in his Walkman headphones and ride the bus for hours and hours, taking in all the sights. He rode the 93 to Charlestown, the 57 through Allston and Brighton, the 66 to Harvard Square, the Number 1 up Mass. Avenue through Porter Square. The bus drivers never asked questions when he was the last one off or when he simply waited for the bus to turn around to Boston. He learned to never make eye contact with strangers. People in Boston could be cold and sometimes worse. A man spat at him outside a restaurant near Coolidge Corner one night when he simply wanted to walk in the warm summer air. Another time, a woman screamed and ran when she saw him crossing the street to the ATM she was exiting in Kenmore Square. But those incidents never stopped him from exploring the world around him.

Today, though, he walked with brisk purpose, eyes on the patchworked cobblestone, brick, and concrete sidewalks of Downtown Crossing. The Rasta's eyes burned through him like incense sticks as he passed by, praying the man would not call him out. This was not the time for a casual conversation.

He squeezed Karen's hand, damp with sweat despite the cool spring day. He wanted to tell her not to worry, but he was worried himself. He was not a good speaker, he still stammered when he was nervous, and people struggled to understand his accent. "The lawyer will be there, and everything will be all right," he reassured her. For the remainder of their walk to Government Center, all he heard was the noise of downtown and the tock, tock, tock of Karen's heels on the brick sidewalks.

Winston had taken $2,000 out of his savings for the lawyer and made a cashier's check at Shawmut Bank, which was now in the legal folder he clutched tightly to his side. He was horrified when Karen offered to pay for everything.

The first time he took her on a date, he wouldn't let her drive him. Instead, they took a taxi to the Allston Theatre and watched *Coming to America*. She had never taken a taxi before because Mr. Bedminster had always driven her, she said. They talked about the movie in the taxi and then for weeks afterward during afternoon shifts at Delicious Donuts when she arrived an hour before closing just to chat. He knew he could be her husband because she valued his opinion on things. Important things like the drug dealers in Franklin Field, the gang shootings and what Mayor Flynn and the Ten Point Coalition were doing about it. Sheehan stopped the snickering after a while.

Still, he'd felt that everyone was pushing him to this end as if it were some emergency. He'd been in America less than ten years. He had thirty thousand dollars in a bank account that Zoom had opened for him under her name. His plan was to go back to the islands in a few years, maybe if he could save a hundred thousand dollars. Not Dominica. A bleached-sand-bland, happy place like Tortola, with no memories, no ghosts, no old faces or places. He'd work in a resort or a restaurant as a dishwasher or something. Maybe even find a tugboat to live out his days on the sea.

Then Zoom had this bright idea. As much as he enjoyed seeing Karen fuss with her hair when she thought he wasn't watching and tilting her head up to ask him a question, it all seemed fraudulent to him—to marry a woman he did not love. He patiently accompanied her to church, fending off the pastor's requests to talk about his soul's salvation. He'd begun grocery shopping with her on Saturdays at Farmers Market in Mattapan and Tropical Foods on Dudley Street. Her cooking was merely passable next to Zoom's, but it was never too bad if he doused it with Matouk's pepper sauce.

The house high on Elm Hill in Roxbury remained Mr. Bedminster's house in every way, imposing with its dozen wood-paneled rooms and three fireplaces, none of which worked. Eventually, he began to feel a sense of ownership by mowing the grass and shoveling the snow. He planted dark-eyed susans, hydrangeas, phlox, and even hibiscus in the front yard. Then he began to paint the rooms. Sheehan brought his brother over one Saturday and they repaired the fireplaces and redid the floors downstairs. He had done enough work, he now felt, to arrive at this point.

They slowed as the concrete outline of the Kennedy Building threw a shadow over them. He swallowed the dread, the feeling that this huge concrete building could collapse on his life and squash it to nothing, to a one-way ticket back to Ma Relene's house on Hillsborough Street. He watched as city workers, carefree in their slacks and windbreakers, walked through the plaza, going about their carefree American lives.

It then occurred to him how much he loved America. Like one of those cheerful, laughing girls who always wanted to dance in the bar, America had offered herself to him guilelessly. All he had to do was work hard and he could have a piece of her. And, because he knew how to do that, he willingly accepted his role in their transaction. He wasn't ready to see beyond that transactional relationship, or to investigate other claims to the relationship, not even when the police stopped him for the third time last month on Columbus Avenue and asked to go through his backpack. He'd stayed up late that night, too angry to sleep. But he'd gotten over it. By breakfast, he was telling Karen that they were exiles living in Babylon. Those long-buried words came back so easily to him, so easily dredged up by those piercing eyes on him, blue uniform, hand on gun, pink mouth ordering him to stand back. Babylon. Karen didn't argue with him.

They were a half hour early for the interview. Too nervous to make small talk, they fretted about the lawyer showing up on time. "So much money I give that man . . ." Winston's eyes scanned the wide, concrete plaza, so cold, gray, and governmental. He had rehearsed all the possible questions twice a day for the last month, could maybe do the whole thing in his sleep. But he'd paid for the man to be here, to add to their confidence and security. Karen wouldn't let go of his hand. "He have to come," she said, her voice so soft he barely heard her.

On the night he asked her to marry him, she was overly grateful. It was after Thanksgiving. He didn't want to wait till Christmas; Zoom said the sooner the better. He'd taken her to Legal Seafoods in the Back Bay, then they walked through Copley Place, peering into the fancy shops' implied luxury— only a handbag or just one plain-looking dress in the sparkling glass windows.

He asked her in the large living room with the high, high ceiling and the massive fireplace that he'd repaired last year. Knee-to-knee on the green damask Versailles sofa, they sat with the fire crackling, sending shadows across the room. "I don't want much, just somebody to be in the house with me so I don't feel all by myself," she'd whispered, taking the ring in her palm and closing her hand around it. "You don't even have to come every night. You will have your own room and things on the third floor, right above me." But he'd taken her hand gently and assured her he would be honored to be her husband. He had seen some man do something like that on a TV show and the lady had cried, so he thought this would make Karen happy. But she only smiled at him, beaming, as if he were a little boy who had just said the cutest thing. The wedding day was a blur for him. She wore a simple, lacy cream dress and sensible heels. It was a Holiness Church event and he'd had no input into the short service, the subdued outdoor reception at Venezia. Mr. Edward and Sheehan were his groomsmen. Sometimes he stared at the pictures, not recognizing himself in the tuxedo, bowtie, and blindingly white shirt. The night of their wedding he went to her room. But soon after he respected her wishes and moved to the third floor of the house.

The lawyer, red-faced and breathless, arrived with a large briefcase and a serious blue suit. He led the way through security and Winston was comforted that the man at least was on a speaking basis with the workers in the building.

The waiting room triggered his worst fears; this would never work! Winston tried hard not to betray his shock at the number of white people waiting to be called. The lawyer must have noticed him staring. "There are a lot of Irish immigrants here. And a lot of international students, too." He made small talk about the weather and the fact that spring was early this year and that they should not get too comfortable because Boston has had major snowstorms even in May. Then, the small red overhead display flashed again. It was their turn to go behind the wall. Winston's heart dropped to his stomach and for a moment he forgot everything, including his own name. Karen gasped. "Lord Jesus, help us."

The interviewer was a youngish man with a strong Boston accent, sharp blue eyes, and a suspicious air about him. Winston immediately felt a tsunami of resignation—this man would not give him anything. At least he could go back to Dominica having seen some of the world. Maybe he could go and live with Mona in Guadeloupe.

The interviewer did not smile or ask how they were doing or how their day was going so far. He frowned and paged through their papers slowly—the form I-485, affidavit of support, bills, Winston's entrance visa that clearly showed he had overstayed, Winston's passport with all the stamps from the tiny islands from his sailing days, Karen's passport, the deeds on the Elm Hill house, the rental properties, the tax returns. The man looked up at them several times, as if making sure these papers matched the frightened couple sitting across from him. The lawyer cleared his throat, as if soliciting some acknowledgment from the interviewer.

Finally, he spoke. "How did you meet her?"

Winston stammered. "A-a-at church. Holiness Church."

The interviewer turned to Karen, and Winston felt her shiver. He looked back at Winston.

"Where do you live?"

"Dorchester. Uh, Roxbury."

The interviewer sighed. "Okay." He began to stamp documents, Winston's passport, other papers, with a decisive thump that echoed all the way into Winston's soul. The interviewer performed this miracle act of stamping joylessly while reciting a jumble of words, proclamations and instructions Winston did not understand. But the lawyer bolted up straight, jubilant.

"Congratulations, you two!" He slapped Winston on the back. "Your visa has been approved! You will get your green card soon!"

For the first time since he'd known her, Karen was overcome by emotion. She flung her arms around his neck and pressed her cheek against his. "Oh, thank you, Jesus!" she cried. She pulled back and looked him in the eye and kissed him on the lips, laughing. She shook his shoulders. "We got it, Winston!" Then they were like two laughing teenagers who had just gotten away with a high-school prank. The interviewer watched patiently, bored; he'd seen it before and would see it again before the day was done.

That night, Winston went to Karen's room. This time around it was playful and joyful, and they laughed at their awkwardness. "I was so nervous that day of the wedding," she said afterward to his chest. "I thought you wouldn't show up and I would be left embarrassed in front of all those people in the church."

He was aghast that she would think that way of him. He held her tightly, sure that he would always take care of this woman who was opening up this very big country, this world, her very own heart, to him. No one had ever put him in charge of something so important, had made him feel so responsible for something so precious. Except Jemma. But he was a boy then and now he was a man with a real wife. He could begin to build his own family now. Maybe they could adopt a child from Dominica someday. He held Karen tightly. He would never do anything to hurt her, he vowed.

Chapter 50

The lawyer turned out to be good for more than just immigration. When Dunkin' Donuts approached Karen about buying the Delicious Donuts, she was ready to sell and would have given it away for peanuts had Winston not urged her to call the lawyer first. She had turned forty-three in the last year and complained almost daily about the business, preferring instead to immerse herself in church outings, Girls Brigade volunteering, and hosting various women's groups at the house for meals and gossip.

Winston, more and more, was the one overseeing the five rental houses and managing the donut shop. He had even hired two more people and given Sheehan a big raise and weekends off. It was easy to ignore Karen's complaining since he was so busy and actually enjoyed the work.

In the house's wide oak-floored hallway hung a large framed photo of Mr. Bedminster that Karen felt no need to remove. At first, the sight of Mr. Bedminster on his way out every morning unnerved Winston, but then he stopped minding, and the portrait itself began to serve as an inspiration. Codrington Bedminster had been a poor young boy just like Winston before he came to America. Mr. Bedminster achieved what many couldn't in America, though it eventually killed him. "He loved money too much," Karen lamented. "He would work and work and work. Always counting what he had in the bank. Never wanted to spend anything to go on a vacation, have a little fun. All that work for nothing." She shook her head. Winston suspected Karen brought up these memories as a cautionary tale to him. "Don't work too hard," she warned every morning as he left at 4:30 a.m. to open the store.

Eventually, the negotiations were settled and Dunkin' Donuts bought the building, but with Winston running it as a franchisee. Karen took the cash from the deal and Winston put up forty thousand of his own savings. It was official; he owned his first Dunkin' Donuts franchise. Zoom and Mr. Edward were his first customers, and that weekend the girls came home from college and brought some of their friends for donuts and hot chocolate.

Sheehan took a picture of all of them in front of the store, and Winston mailed the picture to Ma Relene with a thousand US dollars. He did the same for Valina and Mona. He bought Zoom a gift box of Elizabeth Taylor's White Diamonds with the body silk moisturizer, gel body wash, eau de parfum, and silky body powder. She was giddy. "Winston, you are a rich man now!"

∽

One day Mr. Edward came to visit him in the shop. "You ever think of going back to Dominica? You have your papers now. Your house, your wife."

Winston sat in one of the plastic orange chairs that faced Seaver Street sipping sweet, heavily creamed coffee from a Styrofoam cup. The Number 28 bus sped by, then a school bus, followed by car upon car. Two of them circled through the drive through window and he smiled. "Who would watch the store?"

Mr. Edward shook his head. "Man, you see my life now? My children in college with their own lives. Life in America is all about work, bills, work, bills, work, bills. But every year when I go and breathe that island air, then I can remind myself of who I used to be." Mr. Edward had thickened over the years; his hair was completely gray, and wrinkles gathered at the corners of his eyes. At Sunday dinners when they listened to old records, Winston could see traces of the old captain, steering the wheel of the *Skippy* and whistling to a Sparrow song. Mr. Edward, like many immigrants, was caught in a bind. Too afraid to go back to a place they'd fought so hard to escape, in spite of the ever-present feeling of being an alien in America.

"I don't really have nothing or nobody to go back for." Winston observed the flow of traffic with the attentiveness of an actuary. How many cars would stop? How many more customers today? Ma Relene had written him back and sent pictures of the finished house on Hillsborough Street. It was all concrete now with a new roof and two added rooms. She'd painted the whole thing a garish yellow and there were pots of pepper plants on the front porch. She said the neighbors in the yard were so jealous that they wouldn't speak to her anymore.

The money, to him, was mysteriously addictive. Like a dark, lithe young girl walking grassy, tropical paths alone, captivating his dreams. So strange to have it, finally, after all these years of trying and trying. He was finally a big man, an employer of four people who apologized to him when they arrived to work late. He wanted to buy another Dunkin' Donuts franchise. He saw himself owning at least five.

At nights, he took classes at Bunker Hill Community College to learn the language of business and accounting. His main priority was to be a better Mr. Bedminster. He had found a piece of paper tossed in the trash by Karen recently, a statement of Mr. Bedminster's personal and business accounts. The man had three million dollars when he died. That number dug a hole in Winston's head. He would reach it. He would surpass it. He would obliterate it because he was an American now and there was nothing standing in his way.

The painful, humiliating days of his childhood were never far from his mind though. Sometimes, mistreatment at the bank at the hands of disbelieving white tellers would conjure up old images: his father throwing a few bills at him, his shame at St. Mary's Academy, the way poverty had simultaneously deprived him of and fueled his dreams, and how useless those lavish dreams were in a place like Dominica. He determined to shrug off the prejudice as much as he could. To ignore them and move forward. He didn't want to be in their neighborhood, visit their house, he didn't want to be their friend. His slice of America was more than enough for him.

He asked Mr. Edward if he wanted another coffee. "I don't want to go back to Dominica. I'm keeping my eyes forward."

Mr. Edward rapped the table. "Man, don't lose yourself in America. They give you a paper; that is all. You still a Dominican man."

Aftermath

Chapter 51

As if energized by the independence celebrations, nature began to thrust herself forward, clothing the naked trees in fresh green leaves, coaxing an array of flowers out of the barren landscape, even the fruit trees begin to sprout tiny limes, pinky-sized bananas. Cousin Eddie's bus driver friends slapped me on the back. "Boy, when you going at your home in States?" Construction workers nodded at me as I skulked around Kennedy Avenue and Hillsborough Street, Pound, and Bath Estate. I was becoming known, swapping stories and complaints of bad food, leaky roofs, and the slow contractors and the spotty government response to all the woe.

Missy and Cousin Eddie threw a small neighborhood party to celebrate Dominica's thirty-ninth year of independence from the British and its slow return to normalcy. Planes were making limited flights, and I reminded Dad there's nothing stopping us from going back to Boston. But we didn't have to say the words. Neither of us were ready to go back. "We still haven't buried your mother," Dad said quietly.

Missy set up a table on the restored lawn to show off her resurrecting flower garden. There were sandwiches, barbecue, fruit, and lots of booze. Uncle Eddie invited a woman from the neighborhood. I'd seen her before; a single mom who had lived in London for a while but had returned home for good. She was my type: petite and efficient-looking with a quick smile. Dad's eyes were on me, sharp as an arrow, as the introductions were made. Her name was Michelle, and I couldn't help staring at her lovely face as she openly flirted with me. Her accent was sweet, and she laughed when I tried to speak in Creole. Dad's eyes never left me while I showed Michelle pictures of Dante. After Michelle left to put her daughter to bed, I told Cousin Eddie, "Don't do that again. I'm not interested in meeting anyone."

"You going to tell him what happened with your marriage?" Dad asked as we sat on the verandah, listening to the burping frogs, Heinekens on the table. My computer was open on my lap.

I waited for my anger to subside before replying. Why would I bring that up to Cousin Eddie? "No. If he really wants to know, he can look it up online."

I kept a screenshot of the public record of what happened to my marriage stored in my bookmarks just in case I ever forgot.

Local Exec Fired After Inappropriate Relationship with Staffer

The executive vice president of Summit Bank stepped down today after officials revealed he admitted to having an affair with a junior staffer in the Boston office, one of many he admitted to having over the years. Hector Peterson, who had been with the bank for almost two decades, was not available for comment. Bank officials said the relationship was consensual; however, it violated the company's rules. Peterson's wife is a lawyer with a local nonprofit organization that advocates for justice on behalf of lower-income residents and immigrants. The couple have one son. Peterson is a graduate of Northeastern University and the school of business.

The next morning, I received the confirmation email from the airline. It took the temptation of another woman to sober me up. In three weeks, I would go home to face whatever was waiting for me in Boston.

I walked from Canefield to Roseau to clear my head and sweat out my hangover. Kamasi Washington's "Song of the Fallen" piped through my headphones, sending me into deeper blue territory. I switched to the talk radio station. The biggest controversy in the country was whether carnival would be cancelled in February. I took that as a sign that a national healing was underway. Green was sprouting from the trees, and little hibiscus shoots bloomed in front yards. Still, a sea of blue, green, and black tarpaulin over the homes in the distant hills was a stark reminder of the flimsiness of the ongoing recovery. The sun, relentless at nine, forced my head down. Bus drivers slowed down, called out, and I waved them off. I wanted to walk. I wanted to think, never mind the sun beating down on me, the sweating pouring down my back.

Three more weeks to lurk around the streets of Roseau, ride the buses to the villages, take long hikes along the main roads, talk to old men and old women, drink beer in outside rum shops. I would peel back layers of myself long shrouded over with executive privilege I thought I'd keep forever because I'd earned it all on my own.

My father was from a poor place full of people that my board of directors at the bank probably hardly ever considered. That I hardly ever thought of when I was climbing the corporate ladder, craving the approval of those C-suite characters so powerful, like gods, who could finally make me a man above men, way above my lowly beginnings. But in those three weeks before I went home to Boston, I saw all kinds of men in Roseau—poor but dignified men who knew about the world and what it thought of them even though they had never left this 329-square-mile stretch of it. They walked with their heads high, no less secure in their identity as those C-suite men. They seemed to possess something indestructible that the American Dream and the lack of it couldn't touch. I wanted to laugh as easily as they did, cry in public with the neighbor who lost his house and everything in the hurricane, dance in the street when *that* song came on the radio and laugh when the children pointed and laughed at my off-beat dancing.

In three weeks, I would go home. So I climbed the steep steps to the Roseau Cathedral, which was still under construction. I circled the massive structure, which stood high above the city with all the authority of the ages, the faith of the fathers, grandfathers, first peoples, colonizers, slave masters, invaders. The church was a short distance to the cemetery. Aunt Valina told me where to look and I hoped her directions were reliable. It took me close to an hour, but I found their graves, Thomas and Louise, and there were fresh flowers on them.

Chapter 52

A copper sunset turned the Caribbean Sea cognac, and a light breeze stirred gentle waves against the rocky bayfront. I found my favorite bar, a rundown place that looked like it would topple over in the next strong wind. It was early Saturday evening, and Roseau was relatively calm, still no real nightlife to speak of, although a few aid workers and adventurous tourists could be found here and there. The bartender rocked back on forth on a stool, playing with his phone. "Rum for you, chief?"

"Not tonight, Ricky." I asked him for a beer, any beer.

Soon, Mikey joined me, taking the stool next to mine. "You paying, right?" He ordered a scotch. He had introduced me to Ricky, who was about my age but sun-cracked and rheumy-eyed. He normally wanted to talk about NBA basketball, and I think the loss of ESPN sports was his biggest heartbreak in the Maria aftermath. Mikey and I talked about the work on Ma Relene's house and he talked about Dad, Uncle Thomas, and their lives in the 1960s and '70s.

"My father would never tell me those stories," I said.

Mikey shook his head. "Winston was always funny like that." He grinned his stained-tooth smile. "He know I telling you all these things and I think he glad he don't have to do it. Sometimes, things is hard for some people to talk about."

"Yeah," I agreed. So many things, I couldn't talk about. Yet I wanted to know everything about Dad. Aunt Valina told me my grandfather, Dad's father, died during Hurricane David. He died in his dry goods store all by himself. The building collapsed on him. His name was Timothy Masterson and he had thirteen children by seven different women. Dad was his youngest. The bartender knew him and thought he was a good man, a fine businessman, Mr. Masterson.

One night when everyone was asleep, I found Dad on the verandah staring out at the dark ocean. He was burning a mosquito coil even though I'd warned him they're not safe. "You just like doing things the old way." I sank into the chair next to him.

"Those mosquito coils never hurt nobody."

"I'm not too sure about that, Dad. Just use the spray."

He adjusted himself in the chair and I dropped it.

"Dad, can I ask you something?" He didn't answer. "What happened to your father?"

I expected him to walk away or tell me to leave him be. But he exhaled heavily. "You go around and ask about him?" He sucked his teeth. "I don't know why you bothering people about that nonsense."

"I just want to know. You never talked about him."

Sometimes I told myself that my curiosity would benefit Dante; he will know who and what he comes from; he'll have a stronger sense of identity, a deeper sense of self than I had growing up. Other times, I felt that these pieces of the past were putting me back together somehow, some way.

"There wasn't nothing to talk about. That man wasn't my father. My father . . . my father was my uncle. That was my father. You understand?" He turned to me. "It's just like you. Before I meet you in Boston, I wasn't your father." He paused. "Yes. I did something to put you on earth, but I wasn't your father."

"You didn't even know about me, Dad."

He waved dismissively, as if swatting away the past. "I'm your father now. Okay?" The dark hid his expression but I could feel his eyes on my face. "It take a long time for you to realize it, but I'm your father now. And I'm Dante's grandfather." He chuckled. "Sometimes I cannot believe it. After everything in my life, I have a son and a grandson."

"Of course, Dad. Of course. You are my father. I can only hope to be . . ." But he stood before I could finish and left me sitting there alone. Things too hard to talk about. I leaned back in the chair, breathing in the toxic smoke from the mosquito coil.

Dad was right. It took a long time for me to see him as my father, as more than a strange man who materialized out of thin air looking exactly like me. Growing up, I knew I could never be like the boys in my suburban school who complained about their dads getting on them about one thing or the other. Uncle Desi did a lot of the window dressing, but my cousins always got first dibs on his time. I see how I'd trained myself to not show the ever-present hunger, the deficiency I'd overcome with all my success. I recalled Coach Dan's words to me from oh so long ago: *You did it all on your own. Without him.* Not quite true, I realized. It was my longing for him that had pushed me, motivated me, inspired me, broken me up into pieces, and was maybe now even putting me back together. Had he not come along, would I be here now? The moon hung over the ocean, sending beams over the dark water.

∾

We were painting Ma Relene's porch when I tried to get Dad to talk about his mother's funeral. It was so hot, I drank gallons and gallons of water but still felt faint by midafternoon. Dad and the other guys weren't the least bothered as I wilted on a stool, fanning myself with a straw hat I bought at the market. I hated to admit it, but physically Dad was doing much better than I was. He stood straighter now. His dark brown skin was the deepest chocolate, and he had lost his paunch almost completely. Ms. Karen was even threatening to fly down to Dominica to fetch him if he lost any more weight.

He looked at me, paintbrush in hand. "Again with that foolishness. Don't bring me down with your experiments."

"It's not an experiment, Dad. I'm just trying to understand what happened."

"What happened already happened," he said, dipping the brush in the orange paint. "You have to live in the moment, Hector. Enjoy what you have now and forget about the past."

I glanced at his brown face, shiny with sweat and a fleck or two of paint. "So that's what you're doing?"

He nodded. "Yes, sir. I suffered enough in my life. I come back here thirty years later, and I suffer more." He laughed. "Can you imagine that? Thirty years and I come back to a Category Five hurricane." He shook his head. "*Oui, Monsieur.*"

"What do you think that all means?"

He shrugged. "I don't know. Maybe Zoom is right. God is trying to tell me something. Count my blessings."

"And move forward?"

"Yes, sir. Is a good message for you too. You're young. You still have time."

"Time for what?"

"Time for everything," he insisted. "When I leave here . . ." he shook his head. "This is probably the last time I will be together with Ma Relene and Valina. We all old now."

I took a swig of water. "I'm glad we came here, Dad. I really am."

He grinned. "Hector, glad alone cannot describe it."

Then Mikey joined us, handing Dad a bottle of water. "Brother, stay hydrated. That's how you Americans say it, eh?" And we all had a good laugh over that one. Later, I realized the moment was lost. We hadn't talked about Dad's mother, my grandmother Louise.

So I began to try to figure things out. Auntie Valina and Aunt Zoom helped filled in the gaps, sometimes unwittingly. They, too, had their own ghosts. Aunt Zoom, during one long phone call, told me she followed Dad around a lot after Uncle Thomas died because she was afraid of what he would do to himself. "He cried every day after school by the river. I would see him all the time sitting by himself, crying. One day, he cried so much he vomited in the river." She told me she could tell me all the sad stories in the world, but they didn't change the fact that God had always been so good. That was Aunt Zoom's way of dealing with things—she painted over every cloudy day with the sunny goodness of a God I only furtively believed in. Belief seemed to work for her and for Ms. Karen, who dutifully accepted Dad's vague excuses why he wouldn't come home. Someone told me that small islanders tend to romanticize suffering, trading their woes and sorrows like a badge of honor. I won't ever understand that part of them. Or us, for that matter.

I'm accepting that I won't ever know everything that happened with my father's family. I'll never understand my grandmother, Louise, and her motivations. Maria left seven dead in her village, one of the few places still cut off except to those who could hack their way into it. The lack of access struck me as symbolic. What I know is that Louise Charles came to Roseau on foot in the 1920s and never returned to her village. She was a quiet woman who kept to herself, some said. Others said she was ashamed of having so many children by so many different men. Still others said she was angry and resentful of having to work so hard only to suffer with cancer while she was still so young. Everyone I asked said I looked like her. Not Dad though. "You don't look like my mother!" he snapped, glaring hard at me, like I'd punched him or stolen something valuable by even suggesting I had any claim to her.

Dad

Chapter 53

Summer rolled in slowly with lukewarm, humid days that misted the deep green foliage along Columbus and Blue Hill Avenues. In the spring, Winston had begun to outfit the third floor with a large oak desk and a swivel chair and even a Hewlett-Packard computer he bought at Fretter in Watertown. He'd proudly pulled up to the store entrance in his brand-new pearl white Buick LeSabre to have the scowling man load the impressive-looking box into the trunk.

On the wall of his office was the framed paper saying that he had achieved an Associates in Science in Accounting from Bunker Hill Community College. Karen had, for his thirty-sixth birthday, framed the old photos he'd kept in his grip. The raggedy-edged, sepia-toned images—of Zoom standing with Mama in front of Convent High School; Valina and Mona on King George V Street wearing tight bell-bottoms and smiling suggestively; a small version of himself squeezed between Augustus and Mikey with Ma Relene and Uncle Thomas on Hillsborough Street; and Mama in a flowered dress staring shyly into the camera. He allowed those framed photos to distract him while he reconciled accounts, signed checks, reviewed supplies, made important phone calls to suppliers and the franchise office. He performed his new American self under the passive, unmoving eyes in those photographs. He had three stores now and was on his way to his second million dollars. Could they see that? Could they have seen that?

Sheehan married a girl from South Carolina who worked the register in the store on Morrissey Boulevard. They lived in Braintree in a four-bedroom colonial, and Sheehan urged Winston to move out to the suburbs. "Why stay in Roxbury with all the shootings and the gangs? You weren't even born here. Didn't grow up here or nothing."

But Winston stayed because that's where his customers were, and it was where he felt most at home. Zoom and Mr. Edward, too, had no plans to light out for safer pastures as some immigrants who'd made it. This was his home now; he knew and was known. Cops and roughnecks liked chocolate crullers and blueberry cake muffins; they asked for him in the store and called him

Mr. W. These were his people, scoundrels, saints, and in-between. He had no time or desire for the white-washed, false peace offered by suburbia.

"If you had my life you would understand why I consider myself lucky to be among them," he told Sheehan.

He felt no difference between himself and the Black American people. He could share and relate to stories about life in the South with his neighbor Kenny, who came to Boston in the 1950s when this part of Roxbury was still white. Kenny, too, remembered what it was like to spend warm, idle days picking fruit, lazing by a river, but had also acquired the brittle edges of a Northern city dweller. Winston felt privileged to share a history with people like Kenny. They were spit on, hit by rocks, and so much hatred, just so a poor man like him could come to America and make something of himself. He winced when Kenny told him stories of Boston in the late sixties and seventies. He had heard about these troubles when he was growing up, but he hardly knew the reality. Kenny reminded Winston of Uncle Thomas and he told him as much. "If it wasn't for men like you, our people would never survive in this world."

This Roxbury neighborhood now was as home to him as was Hillsborough Street in Roseau. He listened to Pebbles spin R&B on WILD for hours and hours; it was the only radio station he allowed to play in his stores. The high-school kids dancing at the bus stop in their high-top fades, colorful shirts, and patent shoes reminded him of his young self, chasing the steel band during carnival. He was late in coming, late in knowing, but these Black Bostonians were his people. Now when he listened to Toots, Marley, Tosh, the words, the sounds, were fuller and encompassed a wider, deeper universe. Even more now he understood what Bongo was fighting for and could never achieve. Babylon conceded nothing. That fact was plain to him in the skyscrapers catching the morning sun. He watched them from his balcony some mornings, so close yet so far from the soul of the city. Babylon would never give up what the ancestors had torn away from others whether by fraud or conquest. Mr. Bedminster knew and he had forged his own path. Hector was slowly learning how he could have his own little Zion right here on this block of this big, American city.

Kenny would be the one to give him the book, to tell him about the time he ran with Malcolm X and those other cats. "We couldn't stand King and that nonviolence talk;" to show him where the riots began that April in 1968 on Blue Hill Avenue; to lament the fact that he couldn't go see James Brown at the Boston Garden because of the riots. "Man, I'll never get over missing that show," Kenny said as they sat on his porch on Elm Hill drinking coffee one Saturday morning. "Things ain't changed that much in Boston. But we still here. They keep trying to price us out, scare us out, beat us out but we still here." He laughed. "See, white folks moving back to Roxbury now? Never thought I'd see the day. I'll probably still be here when they move on out again."

When he and Kenny spoke about the old days, he tried to force away the thoughts of that bloody night in that cool green village. But those buildings downtown could be a jarring reminder—a symbol of Babylon and its fortresses, the government Defense Force that wiped out Zion and nearly everyone in it. He was too old, too tired to fight the power. But he could stay, like Kenny. Just stay. He still believed that there would be justice. Maybe it would come from the heaven Zoom still clung to; but it had to come. Or this life was not worth living.

The Sunday afternoons he drove out to Braintree to visit Sheehan, the neighbors walking their dogs paused and peered at him pulling into Sheehan's driveway. They squinted at him driving slowly down the wide streets, nervously nodding hello or dropping their eyes when he looked right at them. It was an unwelcome yet familiar feeling—like the queasiness of afternoons in a house in St. Aroment where he could never feel at home. He vowed to himself that he would never live in a place like that. He couldn't understand what Sheehan gained from living around people who denied him his God-given humanity that was staring them right in the face as he shopped right next to them in the grocery store and dropped his children off at school. He'd learned that many of these people were Irish immigrants who not long ago had been rejected and oppressed by the powerful Protestant Boston families. They too had achieved the American Dream and fled South Boston to the suburbs. He realized that whether it was money or skin color, human beings would use every little advantage they could to destroy one another given the opportunity, to protect the insignificant baubles they acquired that anchored their identity. This was the corruption at the heart of humanity that Bongo preached about, that Zoom struggled to explain from her Bible. He began to treasure his place in life, to always seek to be near the people who still had room in their hearts to love.

It was Karen's idea that he go and watch the carnival that summer of 1996. Maybe she noticed the way he moped around every July when festival season arrived, awakening all his ghosts and sending him into a quiet withdrawal from everything he loved—including his three stores.

He would take off for hours from work, driving aimlessly on the highway, thinking, thinking what could have been, what should have been. Had it been that bad? Was he a hero, a villain, a victim? What else could he do about this guilt that came from nowhere and everywhere? He sent thousands of dollars back home, but he never felt it was enough. In fact, no one needed his money anymore. Ma Relene begged him to come home to visit but he could not. Could not. She still mentioned Augustus in her letters. Every year on his birthday she wrote that he would have been thirty-five now, thirty-six, thirty-seven. And Winston would simply drive for hours and hours on those days after reading those letters, drowning out their noise with the parables of Mighty Sparrow, Arrow, the synth and trumpets of Burning Flames, and the Swinging Stars. He'd hit the Canadian border or go west, making it as far as Lenox before turning back to Boston, still feeling that he hadn't reached his destination.

The next-door neighbor, a Barbadian family, had a wide backyard. Beginning in July, they played calypso, soca, kompa, and zouk at full volume on Saturday nights, keeping the entire block awake till 1:00 a.m. The carnival costume designers, seamstresses, and float makers would congregate to sew, glue, and build, the colorful, fanciful creations that would float down Warren Street and Blue Hill Avenue.

He'd rejected all their invitations. "What kind of carnival those Americans can have?" He'd scoffed at anyone—Zoom, Karen, the twins—who would ask him. Mr. Edward never went either. "Those guys are a joke," he said about the bands. Then they would launch into their memories of the real carnival of the old days in the old country like two old men sore over losing a game they'd had no chance of winning.

The twins had begged him. "Come with us! Just to watch. Uncle, you will like it!" But he'd preferred to remain inside watching preseason football, shutting out the pounding beats echoing from the street. He even refused to go to the annual Dominica Independence celebrations at the Montserrat Aspirers Club. One of the twins told him that he had taken the citizenship oath too seriously and was now a "full-on American Capitalist." That hurt, although he knew it wasn't true in the least. What was the point to looking back?

Today, he couldn't explain why, Karen got through to him. He came down for breakfast and she was frying bakes—she'd learned from Zoom. He picked one up from the plate near the stove. "I'm not finished yet," she scolded. "Wait until the codfish is done."

He put it down, half-eaten, as nostalgia and sadness blanketed him, memories of leaky kitchens, outdoor cooking, a constantly hungry belly. He couldn't work those memories away, couldn't sleep them away. Now that he was comfortable and there was so little to fight for anymore, those memories harassed him relentlessly.

Karen elbowed him. "Back to earth. Back to earth, mister."

When he sat heavily at the table, she turned off the stove. "You should go to the carnival today. Don't go off driving on the highway today. Eh? Do something different. You will feel better."

"Did I say I was feeling sick, woman?" he snapped, turning toward her with such a ferocity he knocked over the cup of coffee waiting for him. It clattered to the tile floor and she gasped, jumping back as the hot coffee splattered over her robe and slippers. He froze in the chair, struggling to contain his heartbeat. His forehead and hands were beaded with sweat.

Karen steadied herself and began to clean up silently. He watched helplessly as she swept the broken mug into a dustpan, then wiped the brown coffee stains off the white tile, a lemon scent now overpowering the coffee that had spilled.

Before he could say anything, she stood and put a hand on his shoulder. "You need to do something about yourself, okay? You going to become a madman like Mr. Bedminster, and I will leave you in this house by yourself if that happen, okay?" She sighed and began to put his breakfast before him resolutely. Like a doll. He could never make her angry enough for long. She always gave in and gave up.

It occurred to him that Karen was simply doing what she'd done since she married Mr. Bedminster at eighteen—weathering all of his storms, asking nothing except calm and peace of mind. The mountain of guilt doubled. He could at least give her the very little she asked.

The ninety-degree air on Blue Hill Avenue smelled like jerk chicken, fried dough, and beer. The boom-boom of speakers with half-singing, half-chanting created a wild soundtrack for the kaleidoscope of the oranges, purples, and chartreuses of the feathered costumes on swaying women large and small, bold in the free and open exposure of their bodies. Winston and Sheehan made quite a pair in their khakis and polo shirts following the crowd of colorful revelers.

Winston was transfixed at the sight of an old man with a thin creaky body and balding gray head, dancing in the middle of the street, his eyes closed. The man, his arms out, shook his waist and rolled his head to the music as onlookers cheered from the sidewalk. The man danced as if deaf, blind, completely oblivious. Winston couldn't look away even when the onlookers had moved on to another curiosity. The man swayed by himself in the middle of the street, his face open in a possessed smile, eyes faraway. What world was that man recalling, reveling in? He knew. Winston could imagine it, almost feel hot, dusty paths beneath his feet, breathe the briny air, hear the rough and ragged patois shouted from windows, across the street, market stall to market stall.

The crowd thickened and the heat prompted shirts to be torn off, tied around the head, strung along the back of a sweaty neck. It was louder and rowdier near Franklin Field, and Winston mumbled something to Sheehan about finding somewhere to sit. "It's okay. Relax, man." Sheehan urged him to loosen up several more times.

Cheers and whoops rose up as T-shirts and scarves flew into the air, as the Bajan band approached, loud and boisterous. An old Sparrow song spun the crowd into a frenzy. Ghosts began to nip at his heels, and he took several deep breaths to stifle memories of Junior riding his motorcycle up to Loubiere, of Uncle Thomas jogging to a wicket in Windsor Park, holding his eyepatch. I'm not that boy anymore, he reminded himself. He was indestructible now. That past and the memories could never break him.

So he criticized the musicians, or grudgingly praised their talent, rated how they stood up to the real musicians of the past. Sheehan drank beer after beer and teased every woman who lingered long enough near him. It was embarrassing, their behavior, but Winston let his defenses melt into the beer, retreating back to Hillsborough Street and Kennedy Avenue, running, running through the yard at Pound to get five cents from Valina, through the streets behind the steel pan band, sneaking into Windsor Park to watch the calypso monarch shows.

The Haitian band was the biggest, loudest, and most boisterous. But the smaller islands banded together, and the few Dominican flags scattered throughout filled him with pride.

He was ready to call it a day when he looked straight into a woman who was staring hard at him. There was maybe six feet of space between them so he'd call it a mistake, maybe a ghost conjured up by the beer, the heat, the music and memories. But she was real and wouldn't move. Tall and slender, the same mole on the left nostril, dreadlocks down to her shoulders.

He dropped his keys and the clang of iron against the pavement woke him from what he thought was a dream. Sheehan nudged his side. "You know her?"

The sky seemed to open, and his heart swept upward as she walked toward him, eyes searching for that recognition, mouth half-smiling by default. "Winston?" She said his name slowly as if she too were worried this was all a mirage. "Winston?"

"Yes?" His voice was a quaver, unsure and high-pitched. Had he finally lost his mind?

She stood near now where he could reach out and touch her white T-shirt with the Dominican flag on the front, the capri jeans and white sandals with rhinestones, the red toenail polish. This was no dream.

"Is me. Jemma. You remember me?"

His mouth hung open as he stared at her.

Remember me? Remember me? Remember me? Her voice seemed to echo through decades of daydreams, cool and green like the hills in the early morning, enveloping him like a burbling river bath. Did he even answer her? Who knows? He could stare and stare at her forever and see only that day in the village when he first saw her. When his life seemed to have begun.

Now it began anew—with a T-shirt, simple and white, fitted jeans and plain sandals, and a Dominican flag on her heart and in her hand.

Chapter 54

What he recalled most clearly from that last day in the village was her filling her cloth bag with a few clothes, a couple of books for the few days she would be gone to Roseau. He was slow to move in those days, always in a deliberate fog of ganja smoke. Had he known, he would have been more alert, said or done something to make her return or had gone with her and the children.

But twenty-three years had passed. And that day—like Mama's funeral, like Uncle Thomas's funeral, like the day he found out Junior had disappeared—had fossilized with other good and bad days, all of which now constituted this prematurely balding man looking back at him in a gold leaf-framed mirror. He had gone about his life with only the most rational of expectations, too afraid to ask for the big things even when they flooded into his life: Karen, the business, the money. Now the biggest thing, Jemma, had returned, filling him with a hope for even more than he could ever imagine.

"Somebody tell me a few years ago you were sailing on a boat. I say I'll never see you again." She hadn't fully Americanized. Her voice was the soft brush of a Glory Cedar branch on his arm, like the playful strings backing a Midnight Groovers song. *Ca se mwen.*

"Yes," he said finally. "I here almost twenty years now."

"Where you living?" Her eyes were smiling, but he could see that the years hadn't all been good. Depth and experience had replaced the innocence. She flashed an impish grin just as she would in Zion to cajole him out of his seriousness. He so wanted to know about her scars, the ones he couldn't see.

He pointed toward Elm Hill. Then he remembered Karen in their house on the hill. He rubbed his forehead. "You live . . ."

"On the other side of Columbia Road." She stopped and shifted her weight. "I live with my son. He's going to graduate school next year. Northwestern University."

"That is a good school. He must be smart."

She began to say something but looked down as if searching.

He thought she noticed his wedding ring. "I have a wife . . ."

"An American?" She looked up, a helpless expression.

"She's from Montserrat."

She swallowed. "You look good," she smiled. "A little older, but good."

"I did a lot. I was on the sea before I come here . . ."

She was smiling at him widely now. "You not stammering again?"

He shrugged. "Sometimes, y-y-yes." Like now.

A lady called her name and she looked back and said she was coming. "That's my little sister. We all live close to one another," she grinned. "Remember them?"

Before he could answer she was waving to someone. "I have to work today," she said. "I'm a nurse at the Shattuck Hospital."

"Give me your phone number," he said quickly, losing his usual guardedness. He couldn't afford to lose her again.

She hesitated and a blade of pain began to filet his chest. She shrugged and smiled, pulling out a piece of paper from her purse. And then she disappeared into the crowd.

"You don't have to tell me," Sheehan, who had edged away during the conversation, handed Winston a beer. "That was the one who got away."

Winston took the beer, barely aware of Sheehan at his side.

"Yeah," Sheehan shook his head. "They always come back at the most inconvenient time."

The rest of the day could as well have happened to someone else. Karen was at the church preparing for the Sunday service when he arrived home. He couldn't have faced her without giving himself away. He couldn't have explained to himself what he was feeling, much less someone else.

The humidity persisted through the night, out on the balcony of his study overlooking Roxbury. It was past 4:00 a.m., and his old cadence music played softly from the record player he'd bought. He still preferred to visit Taurus Records in Mattapan, letting his fingers run over the LP jackets and the cassette covers. He leaned back in the chair and closed his eyes and mouthed the words. *"Pour qui ca, Pour qui ca."*

The old music normally brought deep melancholy, but tonight he felt a powerful surge of passion, fueled by memories of dark moments in the village with Jemma. Jemma, who had risen from the ashes of his dreams. He shifted in his chair. Maybe she should remain there. Maybe it was best to let the dead remain buried. He didn't sleep, didn't even come in from outside. He counted hundreds and hundreds of stars way, way above the city lights, until they faded away and the sun began to turn the dark sky blue.

Chapter 55

Nothing had changed, yet everything had changed. For days afterward he kept it all to himself. He did not say a word about it when Karen asked how the carnival went. He told himself he had nothing to hide. She would understand, would even be happy for him. She had to. He fell back into his routines, his back and forth among the stores, kidding around with the employees and the truck drivers, fighting with the franchise office, never letting on the turmoil inside.

But his peace was ebbing and fading, and every day he feared that his life could completely unravel. Feelings, emotions pushed him, bullied him to call her, make a bold statement, sell everything, take her back to Dominica, take her anywhere in the world she wanted to go. He drove the streets late at night, thinking and not thinking, listening to music, ignoring Karen's calls and worried looks.

He sat in Zoom's kitchen one afternoon, his head hung low. She had seen his tears that night he'd escaped from Zion after the raid. She'd said that if it was meant to be, he would find this girl again; that's how true love worked.

"I heard you went to carnival." *As the World Turns* blared on the TV in the kitchen as she bustled around, already dressed for the three-to-eleven shift at Beth Israel. She'd put on some of the weight she'd lost immediately after the diabetes diagnosis, but she would never be as robust as she was in Dominica. He missed that Zoom; he longed for the days when he could run to her and feel safe. But he was a grown man now; he could not look to her to solve his problems.

"It was like walking down memory lane," he said. She placed a plate of stewed chicken, green bananas, sweet potatoes, and red beans. He dove into the food even though he wasn't hungry.

"Did you see any Dominicans?" The house was otherwise quiet, Mr. Edward would not get home from his job at Mass General until after six. He wondered how they were getting along now that their work schedules meant they hardly saw each other.

"Yes," he said. "A girl I used to know."

She turned to him and raised her eyebrows. "Don't go making trouble with Karen already." Then she laughed, not taking him seriously. "A girl you used to know? How long? She can't still be a girl after all these years."

He pretended to focus on the food. Telling her would be a big thing. Zoom would make it a big thing. So he left, full, carrying the burden he'd brought with him.

At home Karen had left him a note to remember to call the exterminator—mouse droppings in the kitchen again.

The house creaked and sighed in the humid afternoon air. The window air conditioners in the upstairs rooms whirred as the August sun retreated from the pregnant clouds. As the clouds began to burst and raindrops began to pelt at the kitchen window, he picked up his new Nokia cell phone. He was at the same table where, two weeks ago, he'd broken the coffee cup in an unexpected rage. He turned the phone over in his hands, thinking. There was no turning back once he went down this road.

Jemma was distant on the phone, even formal when he announced himself. "Did I call at a bad time?" He swallowed as syllables bunched at the back of this throat.

She was just tired, she said. The long pause was so confusing, he couldn't think of a way to fill it. "I want to see you again, Jemma."

"Why?" She sucked her teeth. "The past is the past," she said in a low voice. He recalled that frustrated hiss and their long afternoons together, sniping over stupid village things, making up then fighting again.

He stood and felt for his keys. "I will come wherever you are right now."

She gasped. "No. No. Not now!" She was on the three-to-eleven shift and she was running late already.

"Then I will come to your work."

"Winston, you don't know . . ."

"Well, I want to know," he insisted. "You have to tell me what it is I don't know." The portrait of Mr. Bedminster stared down at him as he strode across the living room to the front door. Karen was at the after-school program where she volunteered. He sighed, hand on the doorknob.

She lived on the first floor of a triple-decker with white trim on a quiet street. The house was surrounded by a hedge with a small flower garden in front. He knew the neighborhood well; one of Mr. Bedminster's houses was on Erie. To think, all the years he had driven on this street to collect the rent, he'd been only minutes from her.

He waited in the car, switching the radio stations back and forth between WBZ and WILD. She emerged in blue scrubs and black patent clogs with bright pink socks, her hair pulled back in a ponytail. She barely smiled at him as she slid into the passenger seat. "Drive up to Franklin Park. We can talk there."

He glanced at her curiously. There was something serious on her mind and it couldn't be that she was late for work. She'd not told him she was married, even though he expected that. He had no idea what he wanted from her at this point anyway. No. He knew what he wanted. But his life was complicated as well. Maybe . . . maybe they could figure something out.

The parking lot at the Franklin Park Golf Course was half-full—a few joggers and golfers sweating on this blazing August afternoon. He parked furthest away from all the cars—in case she was afraid her husband would see them.

She turned to face him, straightened herself and placed her hands in her lap.

He put up a hand. "Whatever you have to say to me, it's all right, Jemma. Life is complicated. We are both adults. I am just glad we found . . . I found you again."

But she closed her eyes and shook her head quickly. "No . . . no. Listen, you have to know. Okay?"

"Yes," he nodded, waiting.

"I have . . . my son, Hector. Okay," she took another deep breath, her eyes still shut. "When I left Zion, I was pregnant."

His thoughts halted and he held back his words, waiting for her to finish, as his palms slid over the steering wheel.

"They sent me to the doctor because . . ." she sighed. "But I was pregnant. And my mother's family in Roseau," she shook her head. "Once they could put their hands on me, they send me away." She opened her eyes but looked past him into the trees. "And Daddy had all the problems with the government, so he wanted us away from that, too. That's how I come up here." She met his eyes defiantly. "That's how I come to America. I had my baby, Hector, here in Boston in 1977 . . ."

"You got pregnant in Zion?" He was confused; she was speaking so quickly.

She nodded erratically then fumbled in her purse and handed him a picture. She looked away from him, out the window and into the massive live oaks framing the walking path.

His hand trembled as he looked at the color photo, it was like looking into a mirror. The boy, a teenage version of himself, the wide nose, big forehead, grim mouth and serious dark eyes.

"Jemma . . ." His tongue seized up on him. "Je-je—"

"Hector is your son, Winston. I didn't know how to find you. I didn't even know if you were alive." She sighed heavily. "Then somebody told me you were sailing in St. Thomas . . ."

"Bu-bu-bu—"

"Hector thinks his father is in Dominica. I can tell him . . . we can make something up if you want to meet him."

"Make something up?" But she wasn't looking at him.

"I don't know," she sighed. "I don't know what to do. He's a sensitive child. I don't know how he'll take it." She sniffed and hugged her arms into her chest. "And I have . . . I have a lot of health issues. It's a lot on him."

"He-he-he is at home now?" Winston's heart was full, his eyes brimming over as they devoured the photograph. He had a son. He had a son who looked exactly like him. He had a son who was thinking of going to graduate school. He had a son who was a sensitive child.

"Yes. But I have to talk to him first. You understand?"

Winston nodded.

"I haven't sleep since I meet you last week," she said, still hugging herself. "We had a nice quiet life. I don't know how he will take this news. He doesn't know nothing about Dominica."

Winston leaned heavily back into the driver's seat. What if the boy wanted nothing to do with him? "I will respect whatever you want to do," he said quietly. But he knew he was lying. He wanted to meet his son. He desperately wanted to meet his son.

Chapter 56

Zoom was suspicious when he agreed to accompany them to church that Sunday. Under the influence of the twins, Zoom and Mr. Edward had left the Holiness Church for a bigger church in Mattapan led by a Black American pastor. To Winston, that church service was more stage performance than anything, none of the spontaneous testifying and Caribbean politics mixed into the sermon. The pastor greeted Zoom and Mr. Edward by name at the end, asking about the twins and how they were doing at college. "You should come here if you're looking for a church home," the pastor grabbed Winston's hand and shook jovially. "You'll find a home and your eternal family here."

At Zoom's table he explained to them about the family he never knew he had. He spoke slowly, watching Zoom's eyes widen as he delivered the news. "I have a son that just graduated from college."

Mr. Edward was pragmatic. "Well, you cannot turn your back on your own offspring. Karen will understand that. She is a godly woman."

Zoom shook her head and busied her hands with a fork and knife. "If you leave Karen, I don't know what she will do." She refused to meet his eyes for the rest of the meal even as she brought him second and third helpings of stewed chicken.

"Nobody talking about leaving nobody," Mr. Edward rejoined. "Winston is a grown man. He will figure out things for himself. There is a way. He will figure it out."

He left Zoom's house that Sunday afternoon feeling heavier than he had that morning, despite all the singing about the Lord being a helper and a burden lifter.

Karen, of course, was livid that he'd gone to church with Zoom instead of with her. She barricaded herself in her room and refused to come out until the next morning.

❧

He waited and waited for Jemma to call. He sat in the store on Morrissey

Boulevard staring past his workers, making them nervous with his not-there presence. Sheehan told him to go home or work out his problems somewhere else. Zoom made things worse by pestering him every day, asking if he'd heard anything, if he'd met the boy. And Karen retreated from him in a haze of fearful suspicion, a relief because he had no capacity for a deep conversation or argument.

Self-pity and guilt crept over him. What could he tell his wife? The woman who, in large part, was responsible for the man he had become in America. He fled to his new car, a Mercedes 500 SL, and took long drives up I-93 and I-95 into Maine and Vermont. He drove hours and hours, thinking and not thinking. Sometimes he listened to music. Sometimes he listened to nothing. He bought a new cell phone and left a message on Jemma's machine with the new number. Still she did not call. He was convinced that the boy did not want to see him, and he'd see neither of them ever again.

August dragged on and the back-to-school rush required him to work harder, hire more help for the stores. He poured himself into managing the stores, anticipating fall and the busyness of winter.

At nights he looked up at the ceiling as Karen slept quietly next to him. Maybe the whole thing had been a dream and he should just get on with his life. Good thing he hadn't told Karen. She would have been upset over nothing. She was such a good, loyal wife, the most constant source of support he'd ever had from a woman who wasn't his family. He stared at her sleeping face, and he felt a deep shame for what he didn't feel.

Then one night as he and Karen sat by side watching the news, the cell phone rang, startling them both. The number on the screen sent a chill through him, and Karen noticed.

"It's nothing," he said and placed the phone on silent.

But he called her back later in the bathroom with the faucet on. Jemma wanted to know: could he come over to their house for dinner?

His heart pounded as he stood on the threshold. The heavy, varnished oak door groaned open and Jemma stood smiling on the other side. "Come in, come in." She was wearing a long, light dress with a madras belt tight at her waist. He could smell brown stewed chicken and red beans. So she ate meat now? The foyer was neat with shoes and umbrellas assembled on one side. He followed her into the living room, which reminded him of Zoom's house with its riches of porcelain and crystal ornaments, the framed Dominican flag, and surprisingly, a portrait of Eugenia Charles next to one of Martin Luther

King Jr. He tried to distract himself by staring at the photos of Jemma's sisters and brothers. They were all adults now, unrecognizable since he last saw them in Zion, with their own children. She was talking—about the weather, the neighborhood, her brothers and sisters who lived upstairs and downstairs, how they came to buy the house together and raise their families together—but he couldn't absorb her words. His shirt was sticking to his back, and his breath came out ragged as if he'd been running.

Just then, a figure, almost his exact height, emerged from the hallway, and Winston snapped to attention. The sense of recognition was instant and primal. He moved toward the boy, who was holding out a large hand to him. "Hello, sir. I'm Hector." The boy didn't smile; instead, he set his lips in a way Winston instantly recognized in himself, in Uncle Thomas, in Mama. A look of wary acknowledgment, guarded mistrust.

No words came. A rush of tears spilled from his eyes, onto the shiny wood floors and onto his shoes. Jemma, standing between them, broke the moment. "Come on, guys. Let's go sit down."

He followed, blinking, to the couch Jemma pointed out to him. Hector sat across from him while Jemma rushed off to the kitchen.

The room fell quiet. "You look just like me," Winston said, disbelief in his voice. In that moment, all the events of his life now made sense. This moment was the why of it all. To see his own flesh and blood sitting across from him. None of it—the hardship, the work, the loss, the fear—mattered anymore. He had received full payment. Looking at Hector filled him with a strength and confidence he couldn't explain. He, Winston, finally knew what it was to be a big man.

The meal flashed by, as if lasting only minutes, though he must have been there several hours. Hector looked up at Winston from his empty plate every few seconds. He felt like he was on display, but he didn't mind. He would sit here all day and be inspected; he would answer all of his questions. He would give him everything he owned in the world.

"My mother told me you guys met in the seventies?" Hector sipped water from a Poland Springs bottle.

Winston nodded. "Yes . . . it was during the 1970s. A lot of youth rebellion was going on . . ."

"So, you cut off your dreads? She told me you both had dreads."

Winston stroked his balding head. "Oh, yeah. A long time ago. I had to when I got my first job on the sea."

Hector leaned back in his chair. "I didn't know about that . . . you worked on the sea?"

Jemma entered and placed salads in front of them. "Winston, you still like soursop juice? Without sugar?"

How did she even remember? "Your mother has a really good memory."

"She didn't tell me that much about the old days. She doesn't like to talk about it," Hector said. Jemma placed both hands on Hector's shoulders possessively.

"That boy asks too many questions! Always curious. I could never keep up with all his questions."

"I hope you will have answers for me." He turned to Winston.

Winston drank the milky soursop juice and it was like the breathy sound of the river, like the soft grass of Bagatelle between his toes, like the voice of Bongo reading Deuteronomy by a crackling outdoor fire.

He stayed until midnight, telling as much as time would allow about his life, about his days working in the kitchen at Delicious Donuts, about Karen, about Zoom.

Winston had never known himself to be a talkative man, but everything he knew about himself spilled out in waves of days, years, decades. Still, the boy wanted more and more. Jemma yawned and said goodnight. Finally, he told him he would come back again.

He wanted an instant connection; he could have spent every day with him. But Hector, like him, was reticent and slow to open up. Still, Winston called the next day, asking Hector if he wanted to get coffee at his store—the first store on Seaver Street, the rock he had landed on. He bought tickets to his first baseball game at Fenway Park on a late September afternoon and proudly sat in the stands with Hector and his girlfriend. One Sunday, he broke the spell of his solitary long drives and took Hector to his favorite beach in Nahant.

And his peace returned, slowly at first. He still hadn't told Karen. But he was happy, and he wanted that to last for just a bit longer, so he put off telling her. He could just pretend that he finally had everything he wanted, that he was living his happily ever after. For now.

Dear Mona:

I hope you and the family are doing all right. I have some big news for you. I have a son. I cannot believe it myself. But I have a son. You remember when I was living in the village with Augustus and those Rastas? Remember I had this girl there that I had loved so much but she leave and go America? It's only God that can make something like that happen, Mona. Only God. She was in Boston all these years with her brothers and sisters. That's where Bongo send them before that thing happen with Defense Force. And she have a son by me all that time. I see him. He look just like me, same eyes, nose, and big head and everything. He is in college in Boston and he is going to get his master's degree in business. He have a nice girlfriend called Leandra, and she is going to school to become a lawyer. I still cannot believe it. He is a good, quiet boy and very smart. I take him to see my stores, and he said he want to be a businessman like me. He said he cannot believe I do so well for myself as an immigrant in America. I wish you could meet him. I am sending you a picture of us together. Write soon.

Aftermath

Chapter 57

One week until we went home, and Dad had begun to disappear in the mornings. I didn't chase him down because I knew where he was; at the cemetery standing over the graves of his mother and uncle or with Ma Relene sitting in the Cathedral. People—bus drivers, street vendors, neighbors—now told me things.

"Man, I'm going to miss you," Cousin Eddie said after we'd watched LeBron score twenty-five points to beat the Atlanta Hawks.

"Yeah. I wanna see my son, man."

"I hear you," Eddie said. It was so unconscious, this friendship we built up over the last few months. Eddie was the one who never asked any questions but instead always brought me a beer and put on the game when I needed just that. We never had any deep conversations, but he put on display all the ways I'd screwed up my marriage. Eddie loved his wife and his kids, and he worked hard to prove it. In all our bus trips, our wild and crazy rides, I'd never seen him flirt with another woman. He was always calling Missy throughout the day, checking on her, tapping her and the girls' photo on his dashboard. It was unspoken between us: he never had to tell me that I'd jacked up my marriage and that I had no one to blame but myself.

We clicked beers to celebrate Cleveland's win. "G.O.A.T.," he announced.

"Man, don't . . . let's not go there. Don't make me have to tell you all what Jordan is that Bron ain't. Don't make me do it." Just then one of his daughters entered the room. She needed his help with her computer. I watched Eddie jump up from the couch, put the beer aside and immediately run to his to kid's room.

I sat watching the post-game interviews, thinking I wanted to be like him.

Dante was a miracle baby. He was our fourth: the one who survived, the one who stayed with us. When he came along that February three years ago, I'd already given up all hope. I was already too far gone to be saved.

That first time I held my tiny son close to my chest, feeling his racing heartbeat, my hands shook, and a train raced around my head. I peered into his eyes and he stared and stared at me. I gave him back to Leandra.

I missed Dante's birth. I hadn't planned to—he came a few days early. I flew in from New York exhausted after having just closed on an acquisition of a small bank. When the taxi dropped me off, I opened my front door to a house full of people, a very tired and emotional Leandra, and a tiny crying son.

Over the years, we'd struggled to heat our cavernous, nineteenth-century house. But it was now hot, claustrophobic, causing my headache to rage at me. Mom was there. Dad was there with Ms. Karen as well as Leandra's mom and sister. Everyone wanted to help. The fridge was full of food and so was the kitchen counter. Ms. Karen and Mom, always icy to each other, were competing for who could be the most helpful. Leandra's mom, never my biggest fan, greeted me first. "Good thing we were here to take her to the hospital."

Leandra had an excruciating eighteen-hour labor, I was told over and over again. Nearly immobilized by the lightning streaking across my forehead, the guilt only made it worse. For two days, I camped out in the guest room with the dark shades drawn, popping migraine meds, while relatives hovered over my wife and son.

One stifling afternoon, I sought refuge outside on the porch. It was twenty-eight degrees and snow crusted the edge of the icy steps leading down to the street. The neighbors still hadn't taken down their Christmas decorations though it was almost Valentine's Day.

Dad came out eventually. I had expected Mom, not him.

"Son, you all right?" He stood with his hand on the doorknob. "It's cold out there. You want me to bring you a jacket?" I told him I just needed some air. Leandra kept the house too warm anyway.

"Dante looks just like me," he chuckled. "That's what Karen and your mother keep saying."

I had noticed that, too. Then it occurred to me that I'd never seen pictures of my father when he was a baby. Maybe there were none. I'd never asked.

"You should come inside. Leandra would . . ." he paused, maybe sensing my drifting thoughts. "You need to give her a break from your mother and Karen with all their advice and things."

"Do you have pictures of yourself when you were a baby?"

His hands fumbled around with the doorknob, then he looked down at his feet as if trying to retrieve a memory from the gray wood floor of the porch. "No. I don't think so. In those days, taking pictures . . . that was a big thing for poor people."

I was shaking now from the cold. He came out and stood next to me. "I understand if you are afraid."

"Me? Afraid of what?"

He grabbed the porch railing. "I don't know what I would do if I suddenly had a fragile little baby in my house." He chuckled. "But I know I would be afraid." His breath crystallized in the freezing air. "It is a blessing," he said quietly. "You and Leandra had some really rough times. This is a very big blessing, Hector."

I looked down at my feet. "I don't deserve it."

He squeezed my shoulder. "Don't say that. Don't say that, son. Let's go inside. Okay?"

I followed him inside to where Leandra sat on the couch snuggling Dante to her breast. She looked up at me and smiled wearily. It was all for show. The text messages between us were almost violent. She'd gone into labor hating me, suspecting the worst as usual. Adrienne worked with our team on closing the merger, but things between us had long cooled off. While Leandra was in labor with Dante, I was in a conference room closing a merger with Adrienne at my side. And Leandra knew.

I was desperately afraid he would never love me. I was terrified that he, too, would be lost to me in an instant by some uncontrollable twist of fate. I hadn't held him for longer than just a few minutes. He would simply whimper, and she would quickly snatch him away. Although I was relieved, I still took her reaction as a slight. How could she hate me yet seem so content, so happy with him? I leaned in the doorway, watching her sitting up in bed holding him, her eyes, large brown pools, drenching him with all her love.

I recalled one late night before Leandra filed for divorce when I was hiding out at Mom's because Leandra and I could barely stand to breathe the same air. I'd spent the evening in my old room, finishing up work. When I went in to say goodnight Mom was lying in bed, her breathing apparatus over her face. She was watching Black Lives Matter protests on TV. I sat next to her shoulder, watching, not saying anything.

"That's still the biggest coincidence I've ever heard of in my life, Mom. The fact that you just met Dad on the street that day."

Mom took off the breathing mask. "I kind of feel like . . . it meant something. That he would just appear at this time in our life."

We sat in silence for several minutes. I reflexively checked my work email on my phone. She grabbed my hand. "Put that thing away when you're with me."

Six months earlier, Leandra had gotten us all out of bed on a cool October morning. "Come on, Hector. We have to go." Mom, Dad, Leandra, and I pushing a year-old Dante in his stroller joined a crowd of thousands in a Black Lives Matter rally on Boston Common. Leandra had wept when the reports broke about Trayvon Martin, Tamir Rice, so many others. I spent days comforting her, telling her I would be fine, Dante would be fine. Everything would be fine. But how did I know? I'd been pulled over so many times—in Scituate visiting my boss, in the Back Bay while driving a client, in my own neighborhood sitting outside my house waiting for Leandra. The anger had calcified into an always-running low-level bitterness. I kept myself too busy to truly care. That first rally we attended spurred Mom into action. She worked Dad into a frenzy as well, taking him along to marches and meetings, ordering him to hire ex-cons at his businesses, to pay his workers a higher wage. "Your mother is going to make me broke," he complained to me, laughter at the edge of his eyes.

That October day at the march, our family stood among thousands of people from all walks of life. My eyes teared up. I'd always thought of Boston as most people did—with hard, cold lines drawn between races, neighborhoods, classes. But here we were all together on the Common. Even us, my broken, messy, complicated family, we stood together for one thing that day. Mom's eyes shone as she listened to the speeches, she nodded her head, pumped her fists and cheered while Leandra and I held hands, watching over a sleeping Dante in his stroller.

Later, Mom wouldn't stop talking about it even letting her guard down. "When I was a little girl, that's the kind of thing my father used to talk about all the time. You know? All the people in the world coming together like that to say no more injustice, no more racism. My father would have been there today," she said, a faraway look in her eyes. "And my mother, too." I listened silently, hoping she'd say more, but she'd gone off to her secret place, and I didn't intrude.

"You forgive me?" Mom would ask before she died. "For all those years?"

But I couldn't answer her. Forgive her for what? Because she knew things she chose not to tell me? I never answered her. I felt powerless—to either forgive her or hold anything against her. She was my mother; what choice did I really have in the matter?

Dad

Chapter 58

Karen was blindsided by the change in him. In just a few months, he had become a new person. One who let the grass in the front yard grow to unsightly heights, who let his treasured hydrangeas and snowball flowers wither and die, who forgot to sign checks, place orders, call the accountant. It was terrifying for Karen, who never fared well when the winds shifted.

She sequestered herself in her room, certain that he would not come at night. In the mornings, she was out of the kitchen before 5:30 a.m., always leaving his breakfast in its normal place.

As the leaves turned colorful then fell off the trees, she operated out of sight, efficiently performing the tasks that kept him to his routine as much as possible. His shirts were always ironed, his meals on time and always delicious. She left notes, dozens of them, lying around for him. "I am with Sister Maureen at the hospital today." "I am taking a trip with the ushers to Sights and Sounds in Lancaster, Pennsylvania. See you on Monday. There is food in the freezer." "I am going to New Jersey to visit my cousin." Her goal was to make it easy, to facilitate an opening, so that whatever was coming next would hurry up and come. But she came back from all those trips and he was there, barely noticing her, distracted, always checking the cell phone.

One crisp November morning he came downstairs to find a letter next to his coffee cup. She had decided to sell the five rental properties Mr. Bedminster had left her. "I think it is better if we begin to lighten some of our responsibilities," the letter said.

He looked out the window, past the lawn which had never looked this neglected in his seven years with Karen. Leaves covered almost every inch of it. He'd been so busy with Hector. And Jemma. Emotionally exhausted from the last five years of the iron weight of guilt every time he placed his key in the front door lock of the Elm Hill house. Guilt for Karen's stooped shoulders, her mute acquiescence. Guilt for Jemma's reproachful goodbyes.

The guilt sent him places he didn't wish to go. He'd develop big ideas. A bigger house for Jemma. They would move back to Dominica and he would build her a house near the sea so she'd no longer breathe that dirty American air. Though she'd laugh. "Winston, you can go back to Dominica if you want. I'm not going back to that place."

They would sit in her dark backyard under the sprawling oak tree, talking late into the night and sometimes before dawn. He'd held Jemma while she wept about the loss of what she thought was her perfect childhood in Zion. How unprepared she was for being thrust into a crude, unwelcoming world at sixteen with three brothers and sisters to care for along with her own son. He cursed the fact that she'd had to work so hard her entire life when he had so much money, when he easily could have helped. He himself had wept, assuring her that she was forgiven. "I don't hold anything against you for what happened up there."

Karen's footsteps woke him from his daydreaming. "Good morning."

He turned to her, surprised. "I wasn't expecting to see you . . . I read your letter."

She leaned against the fridge, arms folded across her chest. "Yes. I'm thinking I want to be more independent . . . free."

He sighed. "Free?" What did she mean? He kept waiting for the right time, which never came. He'd been cowardly, cruelly silent, living inside his head, ignoring her careful footsteps around the house and her valiant efforts to keep the peace.

"You found another woman, right?" Karen's chin lifted. Her hair, gray at the edges, was shorter now in a bob. He couldn't say that she had aged, but she did look different. Sadder, like an inner light had been shut off. "That is why you are always gone out?"

His eyes searched around the room. How to even explain. "It's not like that . . ."

"I followed you one night to the house over there. Somebody tell me is a Dominican woman that live there with her son. A young lady, about your age?"

Winston took in a breath. Of course, Karen would think and do the very worst. "I knew her when I was back home. I hadn't seen her in all those years . . ."

"But you didn't tell me! You going over there every day, and you don't tell me a word!" She was shaking, holding herself tightly around the middle. He wanted her to sit, to relax, to not take this so hard.

"Karen, I wasn't sure what to say." He was in turmoil, feeling her hurt as if it were his own. He'd never seen her this angry, her fists balling up all the rage she'd buried the last decade.

Every morning he heard her pray for the fruits of the spirit, that the Holy Spirit remove all anger, malice, envy, and strife from her. It was impossible then for her to raise her voice or throw a cup across the room. Yet, the smashed coffee cup was at his feet, shards on his Clarks. He'd hardly had time to flinch when he heard the shrill crash. Luckily, she'd aimed at the floor and not him.

"I knew you didn't love me from the beginning!" She wrung her hands, tears streaming from her eyes. "But I'd started to think . . . that something was happening between us." She held her chest and took a deep, sobbing gulp. "I thought you loved me."

"I am so sorry," Winston whispered. "I thought she was . . . dead . . . gone forever."

Karen drew closer, glaring at him, her fists balled. He was afraid to move or to say anything more. When mountains of silence had risen and fallen, he finally said. "I have a son. He is twenty-one years old."

She winced, and her hand fell to her sides. She stood staring at him, dazed by the shock of his words. She then ran from the room. The door to her room shut with an uncertain thud, as if she simply couldn't allow herself to slam it.

Traffic was light along I-90 West for a Saturday morning in February. Winston normally would have been worried about another person driving his beloved Mercedes, but he was too distracted to care that Hector was quite above the speed limit.

Karen hadn't answered her cell phone all day, and he feared the worst. They had maintained a peaceful avoidance of each other over the last several months, but he sensed something simmering underneath her dutiful smile that threatened to boil over every time they met in the hallway, discussed household minutiae, or participated in the strained Sunday dinners at Zoom's house. Would she leave him, ask for a divorce?

"Sir, I'm so glad you're helping us out like this. I mean, the doctors at Sloan Kettering are the best. Mom and I . . ."

"Don't talk about me like that," Winston said, "I am your father and Jemma is my . . . my old friend." He was trying to ignore the fact that Hector had begun to call him "sir." He preferred Dad, but Hector only used that when his guard was down, when they were joking around as if they'd never spent a day without each other.

Hector shook his head quickly. "No. I didn't mean anything bad. It's just so expensive. And with her insurance being so stingy and all."

Winston sighed. "We will talk to the doctors and see what they say. Hopefully, your mother will get into the drug trial."

"I still think those people at Mass Care screwed her," Hector clenched his jaw. "There's no reason why they couldn't let her have that experimental medicine."

Winston shrugged. "They said no. We're trying something else. Okay, son?"

"It's just another reason Boston . . ."

Winston observed the wintry landscape flying past him. Traffic was picking up and the big buses were full of passengers headed to New York for the day. A state trooper blew past them, and his pulse quickened.

"They don't treat Black patients the same," Hector continued. "You don't see it because you're still seeing Boston as an immigrant, Dad. This place is crazy racist."

They fell silent as Winston braced for the familiar disagreement. Hector would begin to tell Winston about one of the several racist incidents from his suburban high school, causing a centipede sting to crawl up Winston's torso. Why hadn't he been there to protect Hector from these things? Sometimes the fury went Jemma's way. Why had she allowed these things to happen? Why hadn't Desi and Hector's other uncles done more to protect him from these racist people who bothered him? Winston vowed to himself that no one would ever treat his son that way again.

"You'll see how racist Boston is, Dad . . . if it weren't for Mom I'd be living in New York or DC, anywhere else."

"As you told me," Winston said, "I have a different life experience so I cannot discount yours. But I don't see how any racism can keep you back. You are a smart, hardworking . . ."

"It's not that," Hector insisted, adjusting his baseball cap. "It's the disrespect and the way some of these folks just can't see you as a human being . . ."

"And this would happen in Boston but not in New York? How do you know?"

Hector shook his head in exasperation. "I have friends who experienced these things, Dad. You can't see it my way. For you, America is the land of opportunity because your island had none. I've lived here my whole life, so I don't have the rose-colored glasses on. You will see in a few years. Even Mom agrees with me."

Winston glanced at the odometer, climbing at eighty-five miles per hour, and shook his head. "She told me you and your friends were pulled over for speeding on the highway."

Hector scoffed. "We weren't going that fast. At least the guy driving hadn't been drinking. Like the rest of us." He turned to Winston and laughed. Winston shook his head.

He was proud of the man Hector was becoming. Hector's complaints reminded him of his teenage years, wanting to flout authority but being so blind and naive to the way the world actually worked. "I understand what you are saying. I wish the world was different for people like us. But we have a lot to be thankful for." Hector was in his second year of business school, practically married to Leandra. His future was solid, Winston thought. Nothing like the kids who worked in his stores and could barely make it in on time, so burdened they were with family responsibilities and the daily setbacks of poverty.

Hector had been harassed by the campus police too in Boston, he was saying now. But those things seemed small to Winston. Even in Dominica the police and the Defense Force were always after young boys because they had nothing else to do. But Zoom had warned him not to push too hard. With children, you had to let them make their own way, have their own ideas, else they would just push you away, Zoom advised him.

"Whatever, Dad," Hector said, shifting to the left lane. "Take it from me . . . you will see."

Winston thought about this. "I agree with you for the most part," he said, remembering multiple slights and insults at franchise conventions, business meetings. He too had been pulled over on the highway for a slight speeding violation. Maybe he was too scarred by life to be angry about such things. Maybe he should have cared more—for the sake of his son and his friends who had no reason to expect life to push them around and make arbitrary demands it made of no one else in this land of the free.

"You have to understand," Winston turned to Hector, "but I was working. I was focused on not being a poor man. I didn't have time to care about white people or their racism." He wished he had something better to tell his son about this racism thing. He had his own ghosts haunting his past, why would he choose to adopt new ones? "Maybe I got so used to bad treatment I didn't see the point in expecting better."

They drove in silence for a while. They were father and son and had only known each other barely two years. There was so much still to discover and so much hanging over their heads. Jemma had just found out about the progressive lung disease that would plague her for the rest of her life. He had vowed to use his last penny to make her better. This is what this trip was about. Even though it meant his wife was home alone, wondering where he had gone. Again, Winston thought, life had thrown him a set of choices that could only end in pain.

That night, at the window of his hotel room in Times Square, hot tears filled Winston's eyes and splashed down to the lapel of his blazer. This was happening a lot lately, the involuntary tears. They were going out for a dressed-up dinner at a fancy restaurant that Hector chose. Everything below these fifty floors were beyond anything he could have ever dreamed of as a boy running through the streets of Roseau dazzled by a few dim lightbulbs in a store window at Christmas. He was struck now, in awe of what was before him. He took a picture of the sea of sparkling Manhattan lights and sent it to Zoom. She texted back immediately. "Winston, all I can say is that God really, really loves you."

Is that what she saw in all of that, in everything that had been going on this past year? He couldn't understand how the twists and turns his life had ended up here. The waiters fawned over them at the restaurant, gawking at the resemblance.

"See," Hector said, "they treat you better here in New York!"

Hector ordered steaks for them. The sullen reserve of when they first met was slowly ebbing away. Now, Winston could envision a young Hector getting into mischief in Roseau the way he did, playing cricket in the park, spending hours in the river.

"What you thinking there, Dad?" Hector asked, surveying the restaurant.

"So, we'll get up early tomorrow and take a taxi to the hospital. You sure we shouldn't get a lawyer or something to help us?" Winston often wondered if exposure to the constant smoke in Zion had somehow damaged Jemma's lungs. "Your mother is a strong woman," he said. "I can't believe she worked all those years with that sickness."

"If Mom didn't work, I don't know what she would do."

Winston knew that; he'd offered to pay off her mortgage, all of her bills, buy her a new house in a warmer climate but she'd refused. "I just wish . . ." Winston stopped himself. He could wish all he wanted but reality was reality.

Hector looked right at him. "Dad, remember that time you took me shoveling with you at your store at 6:00 a.m. last year?"

Hector was off from classes that day and Winston had invited him to come along on his rounds as he made sure the parking lots and drive-throughs were clear before the stores opened. They'd stopped first at the store on Morrissey Boulevard, and Sheehan came out to greet them. "The guys with the ploughs came an hour ago," he announced.

Still, Winston and Hector spent another hour shoveling the walkway to the store and each white-covered spot in the parking lot. "Dad, people don't expect the parking lot to be spotless. It's a snowstorm, for crying out loud!"

"That's right," Winston had said in his soft but insistent voice. "That's why they come here."

"There's a difference between having integrity and being a glutton for punishment." Hector said, leaning on his shovel.

"So why are you here then?" Winston said without missing a shovel stroke. "You must like punishment as much as I do."

Hector stared at his father. "You got me there."

Winston remembered it clear as day. The boy reminded him of himself in so many ways.

"I think I'm starting to understand," Hector said as the waiter brought their food.

"Understand what?" Winston asked, eyeing the moist mashed potatoes.

"Understand you. Understand your reasons."

Winston waited for the server to leave. "Hector, I care for your mother, but I have responsibilities now . . ."

"I see the way you look at her though."

Winston leaned back in his chair.

"But I get it," Hector said, spreading his hands across the table. "I'll never agree with your decision to just leave her on her own like that. But I get it. You made a vow to your wife."

"Don't say it like that," Winston interrupted him. "Someday, when it's your turn, you will see."

Chapter 59

Winston leaned over the edge of the porch of Zoom's house, digging his boots into the snow creeping up the edges. "They will come soon," Karen patted him on the shoulder. "Have patience."

It seemed to take forever, the waiting. He took off his glasses and put them on again for the millionth time.

Then Zoom emerged from inside the house, a ladle in her hand. "They come yet? Edward told me they right around the corner."

"Zoom, you making him even worse," Karen complained. "Just go back inside, eh!"

At the sight of Mr. Edward's cream Toyota Avalon rounding the corner from Erie Street, Winston stood erect, his mouth opened in anticipation. Then his feet sprung forward. He was waiting outside before the car stopped on the snowy street.

"*Mon Dieu! Winston!*" Mona said, one hand on her chest, tear-filled eyes wide as she emerged from the passenger seat. She wore her hair long and flowing, colored jet black, her face was fully made up—red lips, shaped eyebrows, and blush on her cheeks. Gold earrings and gold bracelets gave the look a traditional finish.

"Mona?" He ran toward her. "Girl, you looking like an old woman." He grabbed her shoulders, pulling her near to his face. Laughing, laughing, swallowing his tears.

"Old? Who's old?" She sucked her teeth and hugged him tightly, for a long time. Her rose-pink velvet coat and dark slacks were too thin for the thirty-degree weather, and she was shivering and sobbing at the same time. Then Valina emerged, still a beauty in her old age, her thick gray hair pulled back in a braid. "Look at my little brother!"

Zoom was upon them in seconds, hugging Mona, Valina, Winston, all four of them crying now. Mr. Edward stood aside, smiling. "It is cold. We should go inside."

Winston, collecting himself, disengaged and opened the other passenger door. She had shrunk, maybe to half her size. But Ma Relene's smile was still broad, her eyes still youthful though wrinkles covered her entire face. "Winston! You have to help me get out of this car," she said, frowning and straining at the seat belt. "I don't know how to work these things."

"Okay, Ma Relene," he laughed. Like he was removing a child from a car seat, he unbuckled her seatbelt and offered her his arm to lean on. She had slowed in the two decades; slow to put her feet down on the ground. "Oh, Jesus! This is snow? It is too cold. Too cold!" She held his arm tightly.

Winston held her up. "Ma Relene . . . Ma Relene . . . let me take you inside . . ."

On the other side of the car, Valina, Zoom, and Mona still were hugging each other, crying and laughing. Mr. Edward, unable to speak sense into the siblings, began to unload the bags from the trunk.

∽

The big celebration was finally happening. He had spared no expense, renting out a ballroom at a hotel overlooking the Charles River. Everyone was dressed in their finest; a jazz ensemble played as his sisters and Ma Relene occupied the seats of honor up front.

It was Christmas 1999, and Zoom had passed her nursing boards and was turning fifty. Karen had given him the idea and he had gone full steam ahead. He'd looked deep into her eyes when she'd suggested it, wondering what she truly felt. But she'd smiled at him. "We've been through a lot in the last two years. Let's just say we will start over again."

"Are you sure?" he'd asked her. He'd made her no promises except that he would not leave, and she had, in her quiet way, given him permission.

"I want you to be a father to your son. I think we can work it out together."

And she had done her best, inviting Hector and even Jemma over for dinner. Never letting Winston see the depths of her heart and whether she was suffering or truly at peace as she appeared. Zoom was the one to tell him. "You have a good woman in Karen. If you leave her, you would be a fool."

And he believed that. Karen fit comfortably into the frame of his life, into the line of loyal, strong women who had softened his landings throughout his life. With Jemma, it was a different, pulse-inducing feeling; one that left him unbalanced and afraid. With Karen, he had finally achieved equilibrium.

Ideally, the party was to be a surprise, but there was no way he could have pulled it off with all the visa forms and whatnot. So they'd planned for months, cajoling and convincing Ma Relene that she would not die of cold, and eventually all the tickets were bought and everyone had arrived.

He'd invited everyone they knew—the employees and their families, business associates, church members, neighbors. Everyone who had become part of his big American world numbered about three hundred. That sea of people sparkled in the brightly lit room decorated with colorful, glinting Christmas decorations, a tree as tall as a building reaching up to the high ceilings.

Ma Relene stayed close to him, nervous and needy. "Winston, why you have so much people here? I thought it was a small thing," she complained.

"Ma Relene, you look so beautiful." He patted her arm, partly to assure himself that she really was here, that they were all here in the flesh together. How long had it been, twenty years?

He remembered their last party at the house on Kennedy Avenue, the final goodbye for Mama. He'd been a child then, barely able to tie his own shoes. Look at me now. Look at me now.

Zoom worked the room like a politician, hugging her church friends, the pastors, the work colleagues. Mr. Edward smiled along, bobbing his head along with the music, gazing longingly at the musicians. Winston scanned the crowd as they were about to sit down to dinner. He was about to bow his head in disappointment when he spotted a bearded, younger version of himself entering the ballroom, hand in hand with a lovely, petite woman. Relief washed over him, and he stood and waved.

"Sorry I'm late, Dad," Hector said, looking around the room. "Wow . . . all these people for Aunt Zoom?" He was wearing a blue suit and gray tie, not the tuxedo Karen had ordered everyone to wear. Leandra leaned forward and Winston kissed her on the cheek. She wore a sequined silver top and black skirt, with towering heels that still left her only at Hector's shoulders.

"What a beautiful couple," Karen said, sighing and hugging them. "You two are going to have the most beautiful children."

"I have a surprise . . ." Winston said. "Come over here . . . I have some people for you to meet."

Hector and Leandra followed slowly as they approached the table of older women, dressed formally and fully made up, a regal sight that made him straighten up and put on his best manners.

"Hector, these are my sisters, Mona and Valina. And this is Ma Relene . . . she raised me."

Winston paused. "And this is my son."

The women rose and smiled, inspecting Hector as he drew nearer to them. Ma Relene wiped her eyes with a handkerchief. "He looks just like you, Winston. Just like you when you were young."

The waiters began to make swift rounds around the room, and Winston invited everyone to sit. Hector was polite and stuck close to Leandra through the evening. Dinner was Caribbean themed even though it was barely twenty degrees outside. The ensemble played jazzy interpretations of tropical hits and Christmas carols that reminded the guests of home.

Winston was the only one heartily eating at their table. The aunts stared at Hector, peppering him with questions about himself and his life. He told them his mother was too sick to come tonight and Winston met his eyes and nodded, silently agreeing that this response would suffice. Hector told them he would graduate from business school in a year, that he already had a job lined up with a big bank in Boston.

"Yes! Or maybe you can go and work in your father's business," Mona said.

Hector laughed and shook his head. "I think Dad and Mr. Sheehan have things under control."

As the night wore on and the drinks flowed, the festive mood lit up the room. Couples danced under a disco ball. Zoom blew out the candles on a massive reduced-sugar cake from Kondidor Meister. Hector and Leandra leaned into each other from the sidelines, whispering and giggling at the older folks' attempt to shake a leg.

Winston surveyed the ballroom, the Christmas tree, the band, the guests, the pure joy on Zoom's face surrounded by her family and friends. He felt an indescribable fullness. Here was his family. Here was his wife at his side. Here was his son. Here was his community. Here was his country and his future. Here he was.

They stayed two weeks into year 2000, even with the Y2K scare looming over them like an apocalyptic threat. That New Year's Eve was memorable as they all sat in the house on Elm Hill eating broth with dumplings, pig's feet, fish, and green bananas. Zoom had baked a giant black fruit cake, rummy and heady. And Karen had a pot of black-eyed peas simmering on the stovetop. Their celebrating continued for days and Winston wished it would never end.

When he said goodbye to them at the airport, it was a sweet sorrow. "I don't know when I will see you all again."

"You have to come back home, Winston," Valina said. "You don't have to be afraid of your own country. Nothing going to hurt you down there."

He brushed them off, kissing their cheeks. "We will see each other very soon," he said. But as he watched them disappear through the security checkpoint, he had his doubts. There was still that feeling deep inside of him, that he had nothing waiting for him back there. That everything Dominica had to offer to him had already been lost.

Chapter 60

The following spring, they resumed their early morning walks. Jemma had suffered through the winter with two bouts of bronchial infections and two hospitalizations. But once March rolled around, she was bubbly, eager to step into the sun.

They took the less-traveled walking path in Franklin Park. At first, he was always too afraid to even allow his shoulders to brush against her, but soon they held hands in silence, then the words began pouring forth. Each morning they walked he would tell her his story, and she would tell him hers. What had filled the years between them, what came before and what came after. Did he love her more after these years of finally getting to know the real Jemma and not the idealized one he'd kept wrapped in the finest of memory wrapping paper all these years?

That one morning, she stopped him dead in his tracks. "I have to tell you something, Winston. It's been so heavy on my heart all these years. But I feel like I really need to tell you."

"Why?" he implored her. He didn't want to know. He wanted things to remain the same between them. Their innocence still preserved, the terrible things noncxistent, in these dark, early morning hours in this park.

But she sat him down on a bench and began to speak. One night, long ago in Zion, she'd overheard her parents speaking. "They didn't care. It was like they planned the whole thing." She groaned as if reliving the memory. "It was like they wanted to die; they wanted the government to kill them."

He clenched and unclenched his fists as she spoke, recalling the screams of terror that night in Zion.

"They didn't even give the other people a chance to save their own children. Can you imagine that? All these years, I can't think about my father or my mother without feeling sick." Jemma sobbed.

"When I reach Roseau that day, they told me to go my aunt's house. She and my father went to college in America and they knew all kinds of revolutionary people all over the world. My aunt was married to an American so she adopted us so we could become citizens."

Jemma sniffed then blew her nose. Winston could feel the chill of the spring air seeping through his windbreaker. Birds were chirping and the blue light of day was beginning to pierce the still naked tree branches.

"I was thinking about you the whole time, Winston. I even went by your house on Hillsborough Street to try to send a message for you to get out of Zion. But nobody was there. I knew something bad was going to happen. My father would talk all the time about the man who owned the land. He was a rich man in England, and he was always threatening to get the government to reclaim his land. But I didn't think they would kill all those people. I thought it would be peaceful." She sobbed. "To this day . . . I can't even think about it too much. I have nightmares about all those people. They were like family to me and I betrayed them."

His heart thumped. He blurted the first question that came to mind. "Then why didn't you come back?"

She lifted her eyes to him; they were red, raw, and lost. "I . . . I couldn't. My father brought us to Zion when I was seven years old. It's all I had known. When I went to town and I saw other girls my age laughing and having fun, I was jealous."

A sob caught in her throat. "I wanted their freedom even though I told myself they were in Babylon and slaves to a capitalist system. But I still wanted to see for myself. That's why I didn't go back. I wanted the chance to be free. I let all those people die because I wanted to be free."

She leaned on him as she shuddered and cried, and although he could have stood and walked away at that moment, he let her cry. At one point he gently laid her head on his lap. He smoothed his hands over her dreads and sighed. "It's all in the past, Jemma. Nothing we can do to change the past."

Later that morning, instead of making his rounds at the stores, he went for a drive. This time, he went south. All the way down Route 24 through New Bedford, Fall River, Tiverton, then Newport. Thinking, thinking. So she could have done something. She could have come back for him. But what of it now? That was more than twenty years ago. He could wallow in the pain of it or he could look ahead, look around and count his blessings. She had come back. In her own Jemma way, she did come back.

On this June night of 2000 he sat watching the NBA playoffs while Karen knitted quietly next to him. In the last couple years, she had taken up new interests—yoga especially. She'd also left the Holiness Church and joined Zoom's American church. Now she talked of wanting a job, maybe going back to school for a master's degree. He didn't object. He couldn't believe there was a time when he thought he would walk away from her, from the still predictability of their marriage. Other times, he wondered why he stayed.

But on nights like this he had no questions. He knew Karen, that she would always be here with him no matter what. And Zoom's words, though he still was struggling to believe in her version of Jesus, stuck with him: marriage is sacred, a gift that reflects God himself and his sacrificial love for us. He took a vow, and he would honor it.

That singular ache for Jemma would become less acute over the last years. She was still here, too, looming large in his consciousness, but she was a ghost, a talisman of a past way, way back there somewhere high up on a green mountain. But that's not who he was anymore.

He was a man with responsibilities, father to a son to whom he felt bound to leave a legacy that his own father had not bothered to leave him: himself.

Aftermath

Chapter 61

The few buildings that were not still boarded up or in the middle of repairs tried to paint a happy picture with the simplest of Christmas decorations. No flashing lights, but paper decorations, green and red tinsel and foil, and a blow-up Santa Claus here and there. These sights made my heart ache. I'd always loved Christmas, the colder and snowier the better. My cousins and I became complete maniacs in December, scheming and agonizing about our presents. Even now, we exchanged presents with competitive zeal and I began to look forward to going home for that reason. This year we could finally add Uncle Track back into the mix.

Christmas at Mom's always made up for the fact that Leandra and I felt so utterly alone and forsaken at Christmas, that we had no one to hide presents from, that we could not complain about having to line up at Toys "R" Us or being outbid on eBay for the latest toy. Leandra and I could lose ourselves in the bustle at Mom's house with my cousins, then go home to our empty house, exhausted, and fall straight into bed. Eventually, I began to gin up work projects that took me straight from Mom's house to the office on Christmas Day while Leandra fled to her mom's house, as unhappy as that experience has always been for her. But this was our way of dealing with things. How did we even last this long?

I was sweating when I reached the entrance of the Fort Young Hotel. The driver was leaning on the ancient cannon outside, waiting for me. I'd connected with him at the bar and he'd promised to drive me down South for three hundred dollars. He grinned as he saw me approaching.

"I thought you change your mind, man."

"No. Just running a little behind. The heat still slows me down."

"Yeah, with all the trees gone, the sun can really do some damage now," he said.

I didn't tell Dad or Cousin Eddie where I was going that morning. I overhead them plotting and planning on the verandah. Dad was starting a business in Dominica with Cousin Eddie. They would start with construction projects and eventually branch out into other areas. He was even looking into bringing a coffee shop franchise to Roseau. The excitement in Dad's voice chilled me. "I want to do it for my cousins. Them boys never had a chance. I want to make it right for them," I heard him say in a low voice. "Hector will understand,"

How could he make these plans without including me? What about our plan to bury Mom together? To go back home together?

But I was going home, with or without him. Today, I was going to do what I'd come here to do. Mom was depending on me and I would respect her wishes, even if Dad would not be a part of it. I had promised Dante last night that I would spend Christmas with him, and I had seen the way Leandra's eyes lit up when I reassured him over and over that I would be home. She wanted me home, too. It was time for me to go home, to get my family back together. Dad had lived his story, now it was time for mine to begin.

"The road is not as bad as I thought," the driver said as we passed workers, clearing away debris and patching up craters left by falling boulders. The soldiers were gone now, and the work was done by locals and regional private firms. The roads had progressed enough that local drivers were back to their reckless speeding ways.

We stopped in a town near Grand Bay, outside a dark one-room shop on the side of the main road. The shopkeeper was scrubbing empty shelves and singing along to Christian music on the radio. "We closed," he announced warily from the doorway.

I told him I was just looking for someone to guide me to where the Rasta compound used to be. He looked me up and down slowly. "Why you want to go there for?"

I didn't lie. I told him I had some family members who were involved in the tragedy.

"You come all the way from America to go and see that place?"

I nodded. I was in my "American" outfit: cargo shorts, backpack and T-shirt and hiking boots. He was not impressed.

"Is different now. They have houses up there now long time."

I told him I still wanted to see it.

He offered to take me for two hundred dollars. At the rate I was going, I would need to find a job when I got back to Boston, I joked with myself.

The driver and I followed the shopkeeper under the blazing midday sun. Skeletal trees directly under the sun's glare lined the rutted road. A few people were out and about, and the sounds of a tree cutter buzzed the clear air. The shopkeeper, Jason, mourned the damage done by Maria. "Look at that, eh? All the leaves on the tree gone. Is looking like winter here? Eh?"

He was right. Despite some shoots of green, all around hung a gray sparseness that resembled a February in New England. Tiny, roofless houses lined the road and I tried not to stare at the people making rough repairs, keeping my eyes down to avoid stray branches, rocks, and unexplainable holes in the ground. It still amazed me, the unevenness of the recovery; some areas were so much further along while others still lingered in the immediate aftermath of Maria. As we approached Zion, the ruins of the old plantation house came into view and I snapped dozens of pictures of the eerie, crumbling structure.

Zion was now a small village of about a dozen homes, most badly damaged by Maria. I don't know what I expected but the few people going about their daily business did not wear dreads. Trap music blared from a window somewhere. A teenage girl sat on a verandah railing, dangling one leg and staring off into the distance with a look of such despondence I couldn't look away. She caught me staring and I waved self-consciously. She rolled her eyes at me and disappeared inside the house. Great. I was the stupid, insensitive tourist.

Jason the shopkeeper and the driver remained a few paces behind, talking to each other about Maria as I ambled around the small village, trying but failing to imagine the utopia my father found here forty years ago. I followed the sound of the river and reached a muddy impasse. More downed trees and branches strewn about. I'd have to climb over them to get to the water's edge.

"Don't go too close. It's too slippery," Jason warned. "Sometimes the river get high when the rain come."

I took pictures of the gnarled branches blocking my path.

"I need to go back to Roseau," the driver suddenly said, jangling his keys.

We just got here! "I'm not ready to leave," I said firmly.

I could feel the shopkeeper's impatience, the driver's irritation. But for some reason, I could not move. I turned my back fully to them because I couldn't stop the tears spilling from my eyes.

"Go back then," I said, staring into the gnarly mess of downed trees ahead of me.

"How you will get back to town then?" the driver asked, still jangling his keys.

"I'll figure it out. Go back. I'll be fine. Thank you." I did not turn back to them. They must have gotten the message because they turned away, muttering to themselves about "these damned Americans."

When I could hear their voices no longer, I began to clamber over that massive tree trunk that was blocking the path to the river. It was harder than I expected. The thing was as huge as a Hummer. But I was determined. There were footsteps in the mud, and someone had hacked at the trunk, so it had been done before. Dang it! I wished I had brought gloves. My hands were scratched and bloody after fifteen minutes of my trying to get a hold of the scratchy bark. Eventually, I got a foothold and was able to lift my one-hundred-and-eighty pounds to the top of the trunk. Once on top, I turned away from the ground and slowly scaled down the trunk, using all four limbs. "Geez!" I swore as my hands burned and bled. When I reached the ground, I was covered in sweat and my knees were bleeding. But the river was just ahead of me.

The sun was high, shaded by straggling baby green leaves on waif-like branches. The air was sweet, clean, and damp, the ground soft beneath me. Exhaustion sank me into the ground, and I leaned on a twisted tree trunk for support. I wiped my bloody hands on my dirty shorts and tried to calm my racing pulse, my racing thoughts.

Involuntarily, I sank my head between my knees, trying to quell a rising panic attack. I tried to imagine calming scenes, pleasant memories, but my mind galloped ahead like a mad horse.

Growing up as a fatherless child, I'd learned how to shrug off the absence of a father. My outcomes would be the same as the boys in my elementary school who went camping with their dads on the weekends in New Hampshire, who wrestled with their dads on the floor as I pretended not to notice during playdates. I learned to simply forget about it. It wasn't a glaring lack anyway. My uncles played football with me in our backyard. Uncle Track threatened my first elementary school bully. Uncle Desi taught me how to drive and took me to my first Celtics game. Coach Dan gave me my first pack of condoms and showed me how to tie a necktie for my first internship interview. I grew up telling myself I was fine. Mom had made sure I had everything I needed. I wasn't like basket case boys out there whirling around in a state of chaos and criminality because I never had to make the decision of calling one man Dad, Daddy, Pop, Pa, Papa. And I was okay with that. That's what I told myself.

But to be crouched here now, in this place, where Mom and Dad made me, was disorienting. Clouds veiled the sun and when I looked up, the few standing trees cast shadows over the clear stream that flowed lazily down, gray rocks and silver silt visible under its surface. Purple and yellow wildflowers were beginning to bud on each side of it.

I stood, woozy at first, my feet sinking in the mud, heart still pounding. My mother's face loomed large in front of me, her laughter, her tears, her body contracting as she coughed, her weakening voice, her last smile in her hospital bed. I raised the urn in my shaking hands. Part of me wanted to fling it away so I could be done with her once and for all. Here I could finally admit it. She hadn't been enough. She had lied to me over and over again, and I'd hated her so many times for that. Wanted to leave so many times and never turn back, but it was always something with her: the sickness, her failed relationships, or just her. Mom. The woman I first loved and could never stop loving. Well, here I was at the river where she could finally rest. I held up the urn and closed my eyes.

But I could not do it. I walked closer to the edge of the stream and sat, landed, really, on a large rock to steady my legs, collect my thoughts.

Mom. Dad. I had never seen them together. I had seen them interact like two old friends. But never *together*. I used to joke with Mom that Dad would leave Ms. Karen for her in a heartbeat if she just gave him a signal. She would sigh and tell me to not joke about such things, that Dad was a man of principles who would never do that. "Your father and I were children. We didn't know anything about anything when we had you." But I sensed the violent chemistry between them, the morose longing in my father's eyes when she left a room. They did love each other. Never stopped, apparently. Yes. I had come from love. I was made from love.

Mom told me she never wanted to marry anyone in her life. I wonder if it's because she was waiting for him all these years. It made sense then that she kept all of this buried inside of her, this sinister, emerald-green past. It was her secret and who knows how it sustained her over the years.

Well, I would leave her here in Zion. I believe this is where she wanted to be. I would explain to Dad later. Maybe he would understand.

A shouting and the sound of multiple footsteps broke into my thoughts. I stood shakily.

The voices were louder and nearer now. "Hector! Hector!"

"Who's there?" I looked around and then back to the path. No one was coming over the large trunk.

"Hector! Hector!" The voice was coming from another direction, north of where I was standing. It was Cousin Eddie and Dad. How did they find me?

"I'm over here!" I yelled.

"We coming! Wait!" That was Dad yelling.

It took a couple of minutes, but they emerged from the thicket of downed trees and branches, sweaty and flustered. The driver walked behind them, his forehead creased in anger. Cousin Eddie was livid. "Boy, what you trying to do to your father!"

"What are you talking about?" I asked, confused.

"You leave the house this morning and take your mother ashes with you and you think your father will be all right with that?" Cousin Eddie sucked his teeth. "Come. Let us go back to town before it get dark. I can't believe you have me walking in all this mud, climbing all over tree to come and get you." He pointed to the driver. "I have to pay this thief here hundreds of dollars to tell me where you are and bring me here. You think I have time for that kind of nonsense?"

Dad sighed loudly. "Okay, Eddie. Okay. Go back with the driver to the car. We will come in a while."

I shook my head and sat on the rock again. What just happened? How did they even get here?

"You know, there is another path to the river," Dad said pointing to where they came from. "If you had ask anybody in the village they would have shown it to you."

"Great," I rolled my eyes. My hands and knees were still screaming from my adventurous climb.

"You had me really worried. I didn't know what you was going to do." He glanced at the urn in my hand.

"What did you think I was going to do, Dad? She wanted her ashes spread in Dominica. I thought this was the best place. And you never wanted to come here with me, so I came on my own."

He stood in front of me in his customary Nikes and a sweatsuit. "I don't think this is a good place for you to be, Hector," he said quietly.

"Why not? Isn't it where you and Mom met?"

"It's not that simple," he sank down on the rock next to me. "I will tell you what happened here, and you will understand why I never wanted to see this place again."

Shadows danced across the river as he told me what led him to Zion and what led him out, running for his life. "For years, I had nightmares about this place," he said. "Coming back now . . . the only reason I come here today is for you. I would never come back here for any other reason."

"Not even to bury Mom as she wanted?"

He hung his head; I could barely see his expression. "You will find it hard to believe, but . . ."

"You still can't forgive her," I said, "for just leaving you here all these years ago."

And something broke in me, seeing his shoulders shake and heave, hearing his tortured breathing. A sob broke out of my chest, uncontrollable and painful. I was angry with her, too. For keeping him from me, for keeping this part of her life from me. For keeping Dad and I in the dark, in her own secret world, away from each other, even further away from her.

We sat on the rock for I don't know how long, two broken men crying at the river. Then he stood, wiping his face with his sleeve. "Let us put this to rest once and for all."

I followed him to the edge of the river, the urn in my hand. He looked at me and nodded and placed his arm around my shoulder. I opened the urn and turned it over, letting its contents spill into the clear, flowing water.

We stood in silence for a few more minutes. "It's time to go home, son," he said. "Time to go home to your son and your wife. You hear me?"

I wiped my eyes. He shook my shoulder. "You hear me?"

"Yes, Dad," I finally said. "Yes."

Epilogue

So, as I was saying, my mother told me a lot of lies about my father. Even after I knew him myself there was still so much that remained mysterious. In the end, I had changed my mind. He did come into my life just at the right time.

The West Bridge in Roseau was pretty much deserted, except for our clan. I looked back and there we were: Leandra, holding Dante. Aunt Zoom, Mr. Edward, the twins and their families. Ma Relene and Mikey were here. Even Sheehan was here. Ms. Karen was here, too. Aunt Valina was gone to pave the way ahead for him.

We were standing on this bridge to say goodbye to our father, our brother, our uncle, our friend. Had I known in 2017 that Dad and I had only three years left, I would have done so many things differently.

But there were the good things. He did swim with Dante at the beach in Fond Cole while Leandra and I watched from the hot black sand. He did build his dream house near Cousin Eddie's for he and Ms. Karen to retire to. He did sell his business, his American Dream, to Mr. Sheehan. He was finally ready to come home.

Then America did what it tends to do. The pandemic struck, he was among the first felled by it, his happily ever after rudely interrupted by disaster.

I looked down at the Roseau River, dried up in spots here and there, deep and churning in others. I would leave him here and try to imagine him laying on one of those rocks, dreaming up at the big blue tropical sun, surrounded by water.

Biographical Note

Joanne Skerrett is the author of several novels, including *Abraham's Treasure*, a finalist for the CODE Burt Award for Caribbean Literature in 2011. She has worked as an editor for the *Boston Globe*, *Chicago Tribune*, and *Raleigh News & Observer* and has an MA in writing from Johns Hopkins University. Her recent work has appeared in *Spellbinder* literary magazine, where she won the prize for fiction in 2021, and in Rebel Women Lit. She lives in Washington, DC.